UNEXPECTED

Daphne & Jack

Erin FitzGerald

Foreword

"Instead of saying, 'I'm damaged, I'm broken, I have trust issues' say 'I'm healing, I'm rediscovering myself, I'm starting over.'"

– Horacio Jones

1

Daphne

"In one tenth of a mile, take a right onto Sentinel Way," my GPS system instructed and I frowned at the console. I needed to take a left, not a right, I was pretty sure of that, but I was directionally challenged on a good day, and only marginally better with my GPS, so I flipped on my blinker.

"This does not look right," I muttered to myself as the lanes funneled my big truck toward several guard shacks. "This is gonna be a problem."

I took a deep breath, ready to put on the charm. My mother had always called it "advanced flirting," while I saw it more as a necessary social lubricant.

Rolling down my window and turning down the music, I ran a hand through my messy dark hair and pasted what I hoped was a winningly sweet smile on my face as the muscled, tattooed officer stepped from one of the booths.

"Uh, I'm in the wrong place," I offered stupidly, flashing him my teeth and wishing I'd taken the time that morning to apply just a little makeup, or even just to brush my hair.

"Where are you trying to get to, dear?" he asked with a big smile, his dark aviators obscuring what might have been pretty eyes.

Ugh, I was "dear." Just come out with it and call me a silly old lady already, why don't you?

"I'm trying to get home." I squirmed. "I just dropped my daughter off at her summer job—it's the building over—" I gestured quickly to my right. "I knew I shouldn't have been listening to my GPS. It told me to turn right on Sentinel Way when I should have taken a left out of the parking lot in the first place."

He grinned at me, flashing nice white teeth. He was alarmingly handsome, and even more alarmingly young—maybe twelve, and children were not my type.

"Okay," he said quickly. "So you're not at all familiar with this area yet."

I shook my head. "Nope, but now I know which right turn *not* to take tomorrow morning."

He barked out a laugh and called out a complicated sounding set of commands to the guy in the other guard booth before pointing toward a gate arm up the lane and to my right. "Okay dear, you're going to head over that way ... just follow the path and there will be a sliding gate. You'll go through that and then there's another arm, where you'll wait. Another officer will come talk to you, and he'll show you the way out."

I thanked him profusely, wishing him a lovely day, realizing that traffic was stacking up in all three lanes as everyone else waited for the officers in *all* of the booths to help me get myself together.

Pulling away from the booth and flipping my blinker, I followed instructions carefully, passing under the arm and driving through the gate.

Fifty feet beyond the gate sat another arm, firmly across the road, a flashing red LED strip along the bottom and a sticker that said the gate was magnetic, activated only by a card. Presumably one with the top-secret security clearance I clearly did not have.

Smiling sweetly and flirting with it was obviously not going to do the trick.

Uh ... now what? I sat there, window down, the late June morning sun beating in through my window as I waited for the mysterious officer. Minutes ticked by and I fiddled with the radio, sipping my iced coffee and shielding my face from the glare of the sun coming in through my open window. It was freaking hot already, for eight-thirty in the morning.

A black SUV with blue lettering, *POLICE*, pulled up the drive and parked in front of me, on the other side of the arm. The officer who got out of the vehicle was tall and broad, tattoos snaking up his big arms. He wore a baseball cap and bulletproof vest, his sidearm in a holster on his hip, his mouth set in a flat line that suggested he was displeased—of course he was. Lost old women could hardly be the highlight of his day.

"Took a wrong turn?" he barked, and I sat up a little straighter in my seat.

Mother trucker, I wasn't wearing a bra. I tried to casually cross my arms over my chest.

"Um ... yes, sir. Stupid mistake: Day two of my daughter's summer job and I was in the wrong line when God handed out directional sense."

He didn't even smile. Like not even a freaking crinkle.

Seriously?

"License, ma'am." He held out a hand and I shoved a hand into the cupholder to retrieve the driver's license I'd dropped in earlier. I fished it out, knocking against the huge cup of iced coffee in my nervousness and it went flying, drenching my lap in a sticky spray of caffeinated goodness.

"Dad blast it," I muttered under my breath, stupidly close to tears of humiliation as he made a snorting sound that sounded an awful lot like he was laughing at me.

The rest of the world knew me as a fashion designer, put together and faultless, married to a rising member of the Republican party. Said husband had been elected to Congress the year before and we'd relocated from rural Alabama to the DC beltway for his job, and for heaven's sake, I still didn't know my way around this impossible thing the locals called The DMV.

The very same husband had just announced he was leaving me for his aide, only a few years older than our daughter. I'd been asked to please keep that to myself for the time being, while details were sorted.

It wasn't like he wanted to marry her, he said (though I wasn't so sure she knew that), so for the time I played the role while I sorted through things for myself.

I'd agreed readily, maybe stupidly, not wanting to disrupt our daughter Blair's life any more than it had already been, for something I had always been was agreeable.

My own squeaky image, something my husband had capitalized on for years, was due to a few things: The silence inherited oil money can buy. An expensive PR team. And finally, the all-important fact I hadn't made a single misstep since I was twenty-one years old. I didn't get into trouble or do stupid things, because I was too busy working. And I certainly wasn't playing in the kiddie pool, for the love...

"Preston." The officer looked unimpressed as his eyes bored into the side of my head, trying to reconcile the mess in front of him with the symmetrical face he saw on the license. "Daphne Marie Masters-Preston." He said my name like there was a punctuation mark after each word. He was biting off each one and spitting it out.

"One and the same." I raised my hand, my cheeks burning from the humiliation and I thought I saw his lips quirk into the tiniest smile, just out of the corner of my eye.

"Daphne Preston, as in Congressman Hunter Preston's wife?"

Double flipping fudge.

"Guilty as charged." I sighed, turning my palms upward.

"I figured delicate ladies like you would have a driver." He chuckled and I had the sudden, insane urge to reach out my open window and slap him.

Misogynist pig.

"Delicate ladies like me?" I couldn't keep the snark out of my voice as I gestured toward my outfit, which may or may not have doubled as pajamas. "Because I'm so fancy?"

I really, really wished I'd worn something cute that morning, but my alarm hadn't gone off and Blair couldn't find any clean pants to wear on her second day at work, because she could never be bothered to put away her laundry. So instead of getting myself dressed, I'd taken that fifteen minutes to help her find pants and pack a lunch for her.

Points for trying to Mom, even though it was getting me nowhere right now.

"From what my wife tells me, you're *very* fancy."

I couldn't tell whether he was being sarcastic, but for the first time I noticed with some disappointment that there was a thick black band around his ring finger.

Pity.

"She insisted on buying one of your dresses for our wedding and holy shit, that thing was expensive. I wanted to put a down-payment on a new house; she wanted a designer dress. She won, and I should have known then. She looked like a fucking cream puff in that thing." He ran a hand over his eyes as if he needed to wipe away the memory. "She'd be so mad if she knew I'd met you."

I wasn't even going to try to unpack that one. I was trying too hard not to be mad at him for insulting something I had designed, though the wedding dresses were not my best work. Possibly because they weren't my work at all. For years I hadn't been the one designing them–that was a collaboration with my assistant, hoping to make a name for herself when she struck out on her own.

"If you don't mind, sir," I said, trying to keep a forced tone of politeness even though my teeth were clenched. "I really need to get going. I have a video conference call with my New York office at ten and, as you can see, I am hardly prepared for the occasion."

He grinned at me, a dazzling display of pearly-white teeth, and it occurred to me again that he was heart-stoppingly gorgeous.

Darn smoking-hot mountain of manly goodness.

"I don't know about that," he teased, handing my license back to me and letting his eyes rest just a moment too long on my chest. "This could be an interesting new trend. I suppose it has its merits."

I sighed heavily, tucking my hair behind my ear before gripping the steering wheel with the same hand. Right now I wanted to be *anywhere* but here.

"Right then," he said, suddenly remembering he was a professional with a job to do. "Be careful you don't 'accidentally' turn into this lot again." His emphasis was heavy and pointed, intimating I'd taken a purposeful tour through his paved paradise.

"This is the NSA and getting out of here again would be a much lengthier process." His eyebrows lifted with implied meaning.

I groaned inwardly, wondering if he was promising a strip search in a darkened room. For that I could almost be convinced to show up again tomorrow, even if this guy *was* a huge jerk, since Hunter hadn't been interested in what was under my pajamas in a very, very long time.

The gate lifted suddenly and he nodded at me once, the grumpy expression firmly back in place. I nodded back, putting the truck into gear and waiting as he got back into his SUV, backing into a small access spot in order to clear the way.

My ears burned the whole way home, half an hour of driving in the insane traffic that never seemed to let up, no matter the time of day.

It was my own fault: I'd stupidly let Hunter do the house hunting when it was obvious we'd need to maintain a base closer to D.C. in addition to our home in Alabama. So he'd chosen a quiet, wealthy neighborhood about an hour's drive from the city. It was beautiful and our property was spacious, the house far more than we needed, but since we had family money on both sides there was no issue with getting what we wanted. Or should I say, what *he* wanted, because I was happy with far less.

It drove me insane that I needed a housekeeper for the nearly eleven thousand square foot monstrosity. It could have doubled as an airplane hangar.

Since we had a housekeeper, we also had a yard service, a pool service, a cook, and a dog walker for the enormous Irish wolfhound Hunter had never even tried to keep under control. The one he'd left with me when he moved to Georgetown.

Living an hour from the city was just inconvenient enough that Hunter kept a small carriage house there, closer to work, and while Congress was in session his trips into Maryland happened only occasionally, and only on the weekends at that. Lately they hadn't been happening at all, as all his out-of-office hours had apparently been spoken for by someone who was barely out of diapers.

A glance in the rearview mirror told me I looked just as awful as I felt. My dark hair was in need of a touch up, a few strands of silver starting to peek out at my roots.

I was well past due for a manicure, my gel polish obviously grown out to the point it looked neglected, and my makeup-free face boasted a little hyperpigmentation on my cheeks, lines beginning to settle between my eyebrows and when I did smile, which was often, this weird new crinkling thing was starting to happen around my eyes.

Of all the days to look as old as I feel.

Pulling the car into the driveway, I sighed as I stared up at the beautiful Georgian style home with its cobblestone walkway and cream brick exterior, the shutters painted a Provencal blue—very cutting edge in our Old Money area. It was every inch the fresh young politician's home, at least until you opened the door and Carrick the Wolfhound knocked you flat on your backside.

Carrick was the very reason we didn't have people over. Ever. He was known to bludgeon people into submission with his enthusiasm, frequently interpreted as aggression.

I had half an hour to prepare for the meeting with my New York office, so I gave my hair a quick spritz of dry shampoo, slapped a smear of foundation on my face and applied several coats of mascara to my lashes. Then I fished out the lipstick I used to pull double duty, applying some to my lips while I dabbed the same shade into my cheeks with my ring finger.

The last thing I needed was Emily asking if I felt well, because I appeared ... what was her word?

Oh, right: downtrodden.

Bless her heart.

With eight minutes to spare I dove into a simple white top and black pants, slipping classic diamond studs through my ears just as my computer chirped from the next room.

Friggin' Emily the early bird, probably hoping to catch me with my pants down. I could just envision her sour expression. Emily was polished in ways that I was not, though I frequently put forth actual effort, and just seeing her in the office or on a video call often reminded me of my woeful shortcomings.

I discussed fabrics, orders, staffing details and upcoming shows with my team for the next hour and a half before breaking to slip into the kitchen to grab a cup of coffee.

My initial success was due to the support of my wealthy parents. I'd been talented enough to secure a full scholarship to a prestigious school in Alabama, where my senior project drew the attention of a famous New York-based designer after one of my professors shared some of my looks with her.

But it was my oil baron mother and football royalty adoptive father who financed my foray into fashion, post-internship.

Interning for Candace after graduation had been difficult, and that word was generous.

Blair was only six months old when I left for New York for a six-month internship. She stayed behind with my parents, while I moved into their two-bedroom apartment bordering Central Park and made my way over to the design office on Fifth Avenue every morning.

I spent every day of those six months missing my daughter and questioning every decision I'd ever made, but especially the decisions I'd made the past four years of my life.

While I felt Candace had valuable things to teach me, and I made the necessary contacts, jetting all over the world to attend Fashion Weeks with her, we came from very different worlds. Her family had relocated from Germany decades earlier, when their presence had been unwelcome, and she was born and raised on the Upper East Side.

She was perpetually single—not to say she didn't put herself out there, but that meant she was also childless, and one of the most self-absorbed women I'd ever met. That really was saying something, given the circles in which I'd grown up.

Me? I was a mutt. My mother was second-generation Albanian, but my father was anybody's guess, since she didn't speak of him, and Jonas Masters, of college and professional football fame, had adopted me as his own after marrying my mother when I was six. He was the only father I'd ever known.

They raised me in rural Alabama, with a sprinkling of world travel, often taking me to New York to see the shows; to Greece for summer vacation; to Madrid when I turned eighteen, to have my first drink in a football stadium while watching a Real Madrid game from Jonesy's box.

Daddy's fascination with European football was unusual, given he claimed to be Alabama-born and bred. Maybe even more so now, given that he was the head coach at the University of Alabama, his professional quarterbacking days long over.

As for Hunter ... well, where to even begin?

Hunter and I met at the beginning of my sophomore year of college and I was immediately drawn to him. He was the antithesis of me: tall and blond, outgoing and handsome, whereas I was short and dark-haired, quiet and pretty—just never pretty *enough* by most standards.

It was my own stupid fault I got pregnant with Blair my senior year. I'd come down with a horrible late summer sinus infection and had visited the campus clinic for an exam and some antibiotics. It had never occurred to me the antibiotics might render my birth control completely ineffective, and only six weeks later I was back home.

Hunter cut me loose after learning I was pregnant and I'd rushed home to nurse a broken heart, made even more intense by hormonal fluctuations.

If anyone were to ask my advisor, I was home and attending classes under "special circumstances," due to a medical issue.

The plan was to return to school in the spring once the baby was born, in order to present my senior project. It was the project most of my grades hinged upon and thanks to a couple custom pieces I created for the wife of one of Daddy's famous friends, I'd gotten crazy publicity and a good grade, followed by Candace's offer of an internship in her New York office.

By the time Blair was three, I was a reasonably established figure in fashion design.

Now, my daughter nearing adulthood, I wondered why I'd ever let Hunter lure me back to Alabama. He had all but abandoned us for the second time and I couldn't help but wonder, somewhat bitterly, whether he'd chosen to leave now that he'd attained the pinnacle of his career. It was what he'd always wanted and what his family had always pushed him toward, and he no longer needed me, though he certainly still enjoyed my money.

I hadn't been the best choice for a politician's wife, but my family's deep pockets went a long way toward helping with his campaigns, as his father had spent the last several decades drinking, gambling and whoring his way through the family fortune. That was where the PR firm had initially come into play.

So here I was. After putting up with Hunter's crap for years, he had decided he was done with me.

Again.

"Don't be ridiculous, Daph." Ava's sweet voice laughed in my ear. "My Commanding Officer dragged me in with him for some kind of awards ceremony that I won't pretend I understand, and I want to see my friend. You can't possibly look as bad as all that."

I may or may not have told her I looked like a troll living under a bridge.

"Come on. I'll even come pick you up. I know this great little dive bar just outside of Annapolis Junction. We might get stabbed in the parking lot, but they serve the booziest, wickedest margarita you've ever had in your life. You won't be able to see straight until next Tuesday."

That sounded kind of enticing. Of course, I wasn't about to ask how she knew about a dive bar in a town filled with office parks, but at this point I didn't care. It was a Friday night and I didn't have to drive Blair to work in the morning.

"Fine," I huffed. "Drag your fancy butt over here to pick me up, since you seem to know where you're going. As for me, I accidentally turned into the NSA's parking lot a couple days ago and I am *not* eager to repeat that experience—or most of it."

Ava's laugh sounded in my ear like tinkling bells and I could see why Lincoln was so taken with her sweet, gentle personality. The woman had the patience of a saint, which was a good thing because he was a stubborn jerk who liked to push her buttons.

But when push came to shove, Ava's gentle art of persuasion was insidious, like a rising tide, sweeping away Lincoln's objections.

"I have it on good authority it's the watering hole of choice for some of the sinfully attractive men in the area," she chuckled. "Just don't ask how I know."

"Blair!" I hollered down the hallway. "I'm going out with Auntie Ava tonight. You okay ordering something through GrubHub for dinner? There are probably a ton of leftovers in the fridge, too."

There was a long pause before Blair answered. "Yeah Mom, no problem. Jake's coming over to pick me up anyway, and we're headed out. I'll probably be home late."

Thank God at least she was slightly more responsible than I'd been at eighteen. If she said she'd be home late, she'd be home late—but she'd at least come home.

"Pants on at all times," I called back and I heard the responding "Gah, Moooooom!" as I moved toward my bathroom.

I showered quickly, wrapping up my hair in hot rollers before stepping in and washing carefully, so as not to get my hair wet. If nothing else, I would look good for my best friend, for heaven's sake. It was truly all I had these days.

Pulling a pair of black jeans from my closet, I sighed at the state it was in. I had no excuses for the catastrophe that was happening in my walk-in. I had the money to have a professional organize it, but I'd been too busy to have it done, so most of my clothes still sat in boxes, stacked up in the closet and waiting for me to unwrap them like presents on Christmas morning.

I'd only just begun to unpack my summer things and I snatched a favorite grey t-shirt from the rack. It was soft from many washes and the faded cover of a Queen album graced the front, the V cut just low enough to showcase some of my better attributes, but not so low as to make me look like a desperate groupie.

Did I go a little heavy on the mascara? Perhaps. I'd always been told my deep grey eyes were my best feature. They confused people and invited them in for a closer look and, screw it, Hunter didn't want to look at them any longer, so an extra coat of Diorshow it was, for whoever *did* want to look at them.

And Ava would approve.

Applying a light spritz of perfume to my neck, I hurried down the stairs with a pair of strappy green heels in hand. I was short—short enough to wear heels every day so that people wouldn't call me a midget—and I was hopping on one foot to put them on as I answered the door.

"Shit, Daph!" Ava looked genuinely shocked as she surveyed me. "How is it possible your boobs look better every time I see you?" She wagged a finger in my face. "Spill the details, woman. Fat injections? Hyaluronic acid? Come on. Give it."

I couldn't stop the grin that spread across my face. Forty was coming for me, hard and fast, and being told something was still giving gravity some sass made me feel a little better about myself. After all, it was no secret my self-esteem had taken a beating lately.

Pulling my equally pint-sized friend into my arms, we squeezed until it hurt, rocking back and forth in the entryway. It had been a while since I'd last seen her, but no matter how much time had passed our greetings were always the same: joyful, effusive, and genuine.

Personal research led me to believe the friendships you ended up keeping were the ones you never expected to make in the first place.

"Blair!" Ava hollered up the stairs, an impressive set of pipes in a tiny body.

Blair appeared at the top of the stairs and smiled down at her honorary aunt. "Auntie Ava! Mama didn't tell me you were coming."

I just did.

She stumbled down the stairs on her colt-like legs, her long honeyed hair flying behind her. When she reached Ava she folded her willowy body in half to hug her tightly and Ava looked up as Blair released her, running her fingers through my daughter's long hair.

"Look at you." She shook her head. "I can't believe you're all grown up already. And clearly you did not get this..." she gestured toward my daughter's tall, lithe body, "from your mother."

She turned to me then with a smile. "I'm taking your mother out for the night," she announced, shooting a look and a conspiratorial wink at Blair. "I wouldn't expect her back until quite late, so don't call the cops if you hear some fumbling around down here. I plan to get her good and hammered."

Blair giggled. "Mama never gets hammered. Don't be silly."

"A lady doesn't," I said, casting a warning glance in her direction. My southern roots ran deep and despite being of Balkan origin, my mother had wholeheartedly embraced the manners expected of a lady living in the deep south. She'd instilled them in me like a devout sister drilling Catechism into a group of bored four year olds.

Good girls don't curse.

Good girls don't drink.

Good girls don't sleep around.

Good girls are modest and sweet and tasteful.

"Tonight you are not a lady," Ava said with an evil grin, and I smacked her playfully.

"You were a southern girl for a minute," I reminded her, and the grin stretched wider.

"I was there too short a time to absorb the necessary nuances," she reminded me and I remembered my joy at the age of eleven, when Ava's military family had moved in across the street. "Besides, I barely lived there a year. It was enough time to appreciate some of the local color, but these days I'm a California girl through and through. Of course, your mama still thinks I'm a heathen." She tossed her expertly highlighted hair, in enviable shades of caramel and warm sunlight. She was definitely a California girl: flawless.

Blair pushed us out the door and told us to have fun and before I knew what had happened, Ava had easily driven the twenty minutes while I went into a heated diatribe over Hunter and his exploits.

She listened patiently as she parked the car on the street, pointing toward a rundown little bar I'd never noticed before. Probably because I'd never before driven into this part of town.

"How do you know these things?" I asked, inclining my head toward the building as I crawled out of the low, expensive car.

Lincoln was a collector and he made sure Ava had a fun collection of her own. His favorite thing seemed to be spoiling the woman who rocked his world–the one he'd nearly lost when he went through an intensive asshole phase. A real doozy, even for him.

"Ah, you forget, my darling. My beautiful husband is a powerful man with many connections. There is nothing I cannot find out."

There was that evil grin again.

She grabbed my hand and hauled me across the street, and I narrowly missed being run over by an old pickup truck filled with landscaping workers. All of the men hollered something at us that I was fairly sure wasn't complimentary, and rather than give them the finger, I stuck out my tongue—not that they could see it anyway.

The smell of stale beer and cigarettes just about knocked me over when Ava yanked at the door and a small bell mounted at the top slapped against the lacquered face, the noise lost in the din.

"Yuck," I said as I surveyed our somewhat dingy surroundings. "This is why I drink at home."

"Keep that up and you'll become an alcoholic," she commented, and I was pretty sure she was only half teasing. "I know from experience, that is a slippery slope."

Boy, did she.

Ava rarely drank anymore and her husband avoided it completely after nearly losing her after a drunken rage. To be a little fair to him, he'd been under enormous stress at the time, but he'd quickly compounded the matter when she packed a bag and left him.

Ava caught the attention of the bartender and I admired how she owned the room so easily. She was confident and beautiful. She could easily knock years off her age and people believed her. Men still flocked to her like cold water on a hot day.

It was hot outside and the humidity was trying to seep into the room, several small wall units struggling to keep up. And when it was this hot, there was only one thing for it: margaritas.

The drinks were so cold and slushy and good, and everything in the room was starting to slow down a little as I ranted on and on about Hunter and his toddler aide to Ava, who listened quietly, nodding at the appropriate moments. She was so focused, I knew, because the bar was loud and she was practically reading my lips.

"So, I was going to interrupt you earlier," she finally *did* interrupt, "but you were really on a roll there." She was looking over my shoulder. "But there are a couple guys back there...and from what I can see, they are *really* hot ... and one of them has been staring at you for like the last ten minutes."

I turned slowly, my courage high and my inhibitions low—thanks, tequila!

"Point," I instructed, feeling a little wobbly, and she lifted a finger to point diagonally across the room, where a group of four muscular guys in jeans and tight t-shirts stood near a pool table, each with a bottle of beer in hand. They were looking at us like deer caught in headlights as they watched Ava point them out.

"That one," she said, pointing to the tallest one. He was wearing a grey t-shirt that nearly matched my own, ink crawling up his arms.

Slamming back a huge mouthful of my frosty margarita–ow–I marched over to the group of men, ready to give them a piece of my mind for the sake of women everywhere.

As I drew nearer, the shortest one stepped forward. "Can we help you with something, ma'am?"

Oh. Oh, crap. He sounded like a cop. But no, I was not going to let this stop me—not even my healthy fear/respect for men involved in law enforcement. After all, I'd grown up in Alabama, where one does not mess with the boys in blue. Not unless one wishes to spend an evening in jail on forthcoming-yet-nebulous charges.

"I need to talk to that one about the scorch marks on my backside." I hiccuped, pointing a finger at the man in the grey t-shirt, and I was already standing so close I nearly stabbed him in the chest with my finger.

When I drank, my feistiness came out.

"I thought I recognized you," the man said, and there wasn't even a trace of a smile on his face. "I've been trying to figure it out for the last ten minutes, but now that you're so close, I'm certain. I didn't recognize you at first, without coffee all over your pajamas."

My eyes went wide and I almost sloshed the rest of my margarita on him.

This can't be happening.

The hot cop.

I was ready.

"I should have known it was you, by that miserable scowl on your face. You really would have better luck with the ladies if you looked a little friendlier, you miserable grump."

His face lit up with a huge grin and, have mercy, it was like staring directly into the sun, blinding in all its glory. Those teeth, that hair, those eyes, that face—it was all unfair.

"Being friendly is a liability in my line of work," he responded, the smile still on his face, and I had to lean one hand against the pool table to steady myself.

"It's okay," he said, noticing my lean, "I do that to the ladies sometimes. You wouldn't be the first to go weak in the knees."

You arrogant little...

I swallowed hard and splashed the rest of my drink in his face. It ran down his nose and plopped in slushy little globs on his chest.

He looked amused rather than shocked and my hand itched to slap him, but I was still holding my empty glass. The other hand was employed keeping me upright.

"Does yer wife know yer out trolling fer easy ladies?" I almost slurred, a hiccup punctuating the end of my question, and his face fell. In fact, I could see the faces of the other three out of my peripheral vision, which was suddenly, weirdly razor-sharp. All three of them looked shocked, like I'd just said something I was going to regret, and I turned as quickly as the spinning room would allow me. "What?"

The smallest guy shook his head at me quickly, his eyes flicking to the guy who was towering over me.

"Boys." Grumpy's voice was like ice, cold and unyielding. "I'd like you to meet Miss Daphne. She just happens to be Congressman Preston's wife."

Oh, no. No, no, no. I was that for now, but he wasn't supposed to out me like that. I jabbed an index finger into his firm, unyielding chest.

"Nuh-uh," I warned. "That wasn't fair."

"You just called him a man whore," one of the guys said, shaking his head disapprovingly and I recognized the handsome, friendly officer from the guard shack. "That wasn't fair either, so technically you started it."

Okay, he was kind of right.

I didn't like him anymore.

"I'm. Not. A cheater." The big guy was right in my face, and I'll be darned if he wasn't even bigger than he'd been just ten seconds ago. He held up his left hand so his wedding band was right in my eyeball, and I had to work to focus on it. There was some kind of pattern etched into it, but I couldn't make it out.

"Neither am I." I held up my left hand, shoving my wedding set toward his right eyeball. "But he left me anyway."

There was a tug on my arm and I turned to see Ava, her face exaggeratedly apologetic. "I'm sooo sorry, gentlemen. When we planned on a night out, I'd thought it might last longer than twenty minutes. I'm afraid my friend here, and myself, are horrible lightweights. As you can imagine, we don't get out often."

The short one cracked a smile. "Not a problem, ladies. Jack was just talking about heading out." He elbowed the big guy, and my face flamed when I realized my hand had made its way back to the tall man's chest. It was possible I was actively feeling him up, his shirt soft but the muscles of his chest hard beneath my wandering fingertips. "I'm sure he can get you home safely."

There were a number of things I'd like to see whether this large man could conduct safely, but ... ugh, of all the luck ... my own personal police escort. Chances were good there would be no stop-and-frisk.

Jack shot an evil glare at Guard Shack, who smirked back at him.

"I rode here with Marston," the smaller man announced, pointing to one of the other men. "I'll follow you in your truck and then you can take me home."

Clearly he was speaking to my tormentor.

"If you'll give me a moment," Jack was looking at Ava with an apologetic expression, "it would seem I need to clean up a bit. If you ladies would be so kind as to wait..."

He didn't finish the sentence, but as he moved toward what I assumed were the restrooms, I hurried over to the bar and ordered another margarita. If I had to be humiliated I was going to make sure I was good and smashed so I didn't have to remember it in the morning.

"You are insane." The voice was low in my ear and I turned quickly, accidentally sloshing more of my arctic drink on his muscular chest. He winced and rolled his eyes, taking a small step back. "Don't you think you've had enough?"

"Not even close," I said, tipping it back and wincing as the cold shot daggers straight into my brain. "I still remember too much."

He sighed, shaking his head as he grabbed a cocktail napkin off the bar and dabbed at yet more stickiness on his shirt. "You really are something else."

Was that a good thing? I couldn't decide. With the way he was looking at me, chances seemed good it was not.

Ava handed over the keys to her car and led the way to the parking lot. Jack followed, dragging me along by the arm, careful to temper his long steps so he didn't drag me, since I seemed to have forgotten how to walk in a straight line.

"You're kidding me, lady." His jaw dropped as he stared at the Alfa Romeo Ava had parked on the street. "A fucking Spider?"

Ava smiled sweetly at him. She had always been full of surprises, and his jaw dropped when she responded, "Yup, not my favorite, but still a good one. The modified Corvette is still one of my favorites for AutoCross."

"You do not." He was standing in the middle of the street, staring at her like she'd grown another head. "No way."

My friend had another admirer. I felt a bolt of jealousy zing all the way down to my toes, because I had never been the exciting one.

The one full of surprises.

The one who made men fall at her feet, begging.

"Davis," he hollered back across the street, and Officer Guard Shack turned.

"You hear that? This little thing does AutoCross." He pointed at Ava, and Guard Shack's jaw dropped too.

"You two are full of surprises," he chuckled, stopping short of the car.

"Hey, wait ... one of you is going to have to ride in my truck with Officer Davis—this thing only fits two."

Ava's eyebrow arched and a tiny, wicked smile curved her full lips. "Silly me." She sighed. "Daph, you're up; I'll ride with Officer Davis." And before I could protest, she skipped back across the street, looking far more sober than she had just moments ago. I was pretty sure I was being set up.

"You're *both* trouble," Jack muttered as he held open the passenger door for me, and I dropped into the seat with far less grace than I'd have liked.

"I haven't been trouble a day in my life." I hiccuped and giggled at the same time. I truly had *never* been a troublemaker, but lately I'd considered getting into a little more of it. At this point I had nothing to lose, but he didn't look like he believed me.

Jack started up the car and tapped at the dash a few times, a frown creasing his handsome face. I hoped he didn't notice, but I was totally staring at him out of what I hoped was the corner of my eye.

"Stop looking at me like that," he barked, flipping the blinker and pulling into traffic. Somehow he'd located my home address on the GPS and he handled the car easily as we headed in the direction of the two-lane highway that would take us most of the way to my home.

I snapped my eyes to the road, which seemed blurry and indistinct. *How* had I been looking at him? I had definitely *not* been imagining running my fingers up and down what I knew were tight washboard abs and a delightfully defined chest. I shook my head to clear the visual, disgustingly aware of how pathetic I felt. It had been a long time, though I hadn't thought I was upset about that. Hunter had never been anything other than a two-minute man and in his opinion, foreplay was something one read about in romance novels and was completely unnecessary in real life.

That, judging by his practices, was what lube was for.

Suffice to say, I had a purely physical and completely unfulfilling relationship with several pieces of plastic Hunter didn't know about, but he wouldn't have cared anyway.

The highway was surprisingly empty and Jack drove with one hand resting easily on the top of the steering wheel, his eyes intently focused on the road ahead. I chose to say nothing, so as not to distract him, and from the passenger side mirror I could see headlights following us at a respectable distance. Surely it was Officer Davis and Ava, undoubtedly engaged in a very lively conversation. Ava was so bubbly and engaging and freaking adorable, she could get rocks to talk.

The GPS directed us to turn left and Jack pulled carefully into the long, winding drive that led to the house. His eyes widened as it came into view, the impressive facade lit by flood lights recessed in the lawn. "This is what a government salary will get you, huh?" He looked impressed.

"This is what family money and a successful design career will get you," I said bitterly and immediately he clamped his lips shut. "Not that I was the one who wanted it," I said, weirdly incapable of getting myself to shut up. "I'd be happy with a cottage and a cat. Instead, I got an empty castle with a dog no one can control."

As if on cue, Carrick set up a terrible howling inside the house and Jack's eyes widened in alarm.

"Don't worry," I said. "The electric fence is set so that he can't even get out the front door. The back yard is his kingdom, much to the relief of the local delivery drivers."

A lesson learned the hard way, when Carrick cornered a delivery woman on the front steps. I'd found her clinging to the front of the house as if she could climb the brick. She'd had no idea he'd rather lick her to death than harm her. All he wanted was a scratch behind the ears and she wasn't giving it.

She'd been dropping my packages at the end of the driveway ever since.

Headlights swept up the drive behind us and Jack threw open his door, rolling up the window and rounding the car quickly to open my door. It irritated me that I was such a lightweight, I'd somehow managed to get tangled up in my own seatbelt during the course of the short drive, and he pulled my hands away from the belt as he leaned over me, reaching over to undo the clasp. Something winked in the light as he leaned and I reached up without thinking, hooking a finger beneath the thin gold chain and pulling it from beneath the neck of his soft t-shirt. A small charm hung from the necklace and I focused on it hard, my vision still blurrier than I'd have liked. He'd gone still over me, heat radiating from his huge body as I drunkenly tried to study the design pinched between my thumb and forefinger.

"First Brigade," I whispered with a hiccup and his hand moved up to pull the small emblem from my fingers.

"I'm impressed," he said, backing out of the small space and holding out a hand to me to help me from the car. "You've heard of it."

"Long story," I said, groaning as I tried to stand up straight. "I dated a First Brigade man for a minute after Blair was born. You guys are a mess." His eyebrows went up almost imperceptibly, but I saw it. "He was a fucking disaster; there was no way it would have worked."

I clapped a hand over my mouth. *Good girls did not say fuck.* "Pardon my French. I shouldn't have said that."

"Shouldn't have said what?" His eyes danced with amusement. "That some douchebag you dated twenty years ago was a fucking disaster?" He laughed and his features relaxed, his lips pulling back from even white teeth in a genuine smile and I swear my pants burst into flame.

"Good girls don't swear," I said, a little miffed, like I expected him to know my own secret inner code. "It's not ladylike."

"Mrs. Congressman Preston." He chuckled, his voice lilting and it sounded like he was teasing me. I made a face. "You really are a trip."

"Daphne." I frowned at him and turned, tripping up the front steps to my house.

"Daphne the Disaster," I muttered under my breath as I fished in my small bag for my keys and tried to fit the key to the lock. I was having trouble with my aim.

"Thank you, Officer Thompson." It was Ava behind me, her hand closing over mine to take the keys from me. Oh right, because I had a keyless entry. There was a series of confusing little beeps and the lock disengaged, so I stepped inside and turned slightly, expecting Jack to follow me inside for some insane reason.

Carrick sat just inside, now weirdly silent, though his butt wiggled across the floor as he waited for me to give him the command that allowed him to assault me with fur and slobber and exuberance. It was the only command he knew, as it had taken me so long to teach him just that one that I'd given up after.

"You're welcome, ladies." Jack offered a lazy salute, seemingly unperturbed by the giant beast of a dog looming just behind me, his eyes meeting mine just before he turned and headed down the few steps.

Guard Shack had pulled the huge Silverado in behind Ava's car and had already moved to the passenger seat. I could see the glint of white teeth and knew he was grinning at one of us, or maybe all of us.

"Ms. Daphne," Jack said lazily, and my eyes snapped to him. "A pleasure once again. You're even lovelier when you're not wearing coffee." I expected a smile but he looked stern again, even though he was definitely still making fun of me. I wanted him to take me seriously and I didn't feel like that had happened yet, no thanks to my current state.

Ava hustled me into the house and shut the door behind her, fanning herself dramatically as Carrick wiggled and whimpered, irritated that I hadn't released him from his sitting position.

"Well," she drawled, a huge smile on her face, her eyes dancing and it made me groan. Ava had been *dying* to see me with someone other than Hunter for years, harping on and on about how he wasn't good enough for me and was too arrogant to accept it.

"That was an interesting turn of events," she said, putting a hand to the small of my back to propel me toward the sitting room I never used. I let myself be pushed, my heels clacking noisily across the marble and I held up a hand to slow her, reaching down to yank off both shoes, tossing them haphazardly aside.

She shoved the heavy pocket doors aside, just as the dog trotted into the room on my heels, tired of waiting for me to give him his favorite command. He ambled over to one of the leather sofas and threw himself on it, sighing heavily as he rested his head on his paws and watched me with alternately wiggling eyebrows.

"That dog adores you," Ava remarked offhandedly as she moved toward the large lacquered cabinet at the back of the room.

Thank God someone does.

She poured a seltzer water for me, pulling the stopper out of Hunter's favorite bottle of scotch and pouring several fingers into a glass. She sniffed it carefully, then moved toward me with a glass in each hand, indicating we should sit.

We each sank into a creaky buttoned leather chair and I brought the seltzer to my lips as Ava brought the scotch to hers. She wrinkled her nose after a small sip. "He has appalling taste," she sputtered. "And not just when it comes to extramarital affairs."

I snorted. We were back to my favorite subject of late.

Setting her glass on the low side table, Ava tucked one leg under her petite frame and gazed at me seriously. "That man couldn't take his eyes off you," she said, not a hint of teasing in her voice.

"Yeah, whatever." I sighed. "Jack is married and Guard Shack isn't an option, because I don't date children."

"Guard Shack?" She laughed, covering her mouth with one hand. "You mean Officer Davis? You have to admit, he's pretty cute. But Jack..." She fanned herself. "That is one tasty man mountain."

"I'm not interested. I have enough going on without adding any of that drama." I gulped down another swallow of my drink and coughed a little when the bubbles fizzed in the back of my throat.

"You're not interested in that delicious wall of hot, brooding man? Nuh-uh. I saw you feeling him up at the bar. Nice try. Your fingers were telling a very different story, my friend."

I rolled my eyes at her, holding up my left hand and waggling my fingers until my engagement ring and wedding band clanged against one another. I'd never had them fused. "We're both *married*," I reminded her, a little irritated. My friend was not a slow study and I couldn't begin to comprehend how this was evading her notice.

"You are unhappily married, and if your husband's actions have any weight here, biblically not at all," she said evenly, crossing her legs and leaning back in her chair. "I think we both remember that Hunter maintains a residence completely separate from your own." She gestured around the room. "For all we know, Cassandra is living *with* him in Georgetown."

I made a face. I really hated that name—had always, but now with double vehemence.

"How many times has this happened, Daph? You've been on your own for a long time."

My face crumpled and my shoulders sagged. I set the glass of seltzer on the side table and collapsed into the back of the chair, defeated. Ava had a point. This wasn't the first time Hunter had messed around on me. In fact, I knew of three affairs during the course of our marriage and I was fairly sure there were others. Why I'd put up with them, I wasn't so sure any longer.

"I'm tired," I said, and from the look on her face, I knew she understood that I meant I was tired in my soul.

"I was too," she said quietly, braving another sip of her drink. "It was why I left. Scariest and best thing I've ever done; I can't imagine my life without Lincoln, but I'd have lost him if I stayed."

She was probably right about that. Her leaving meant Lincoln took getting his shit together pretty seriously.

She sat quietly with me, letting me chew on my lip and sigh as I took a tipsy moment to consider the reality of my situation. I'd been letting this go on for years and had no one to blame but myself.

"I'm pretty sure Hunter married me to avoid child support," I said quietly, but Ava didn't look surprised. She'd seen worse. "Daddy's lawyers were closing in. And since he didn't have any reliable family money to fall back on, he charmed my mama to get back to me, knowing he could also count on my family to provide campaign contributions for the long slog to Capitol Hill. We've always protected our own." I said it bitterly, not bothering with the air quotes.

Ava nodded. She was familiar with my kindhearted, giving mother and her philanthropic ways.

"You are a beautiful woman, Daphne," Ava said softly, and I swallowed hard. I wasn't used to compliments. Besides, I hadn't felt beautiful in a very, very long time.

"If the way Jack was looking at you tonight is any indication, and I know it is, you've still got it. Hunter is not *it* for you. You're still young and gorgeous. You have life experience and you're successful and accomplished.

"You can't hold your liquor for shit." She grinned. "But you have a heart of gold and a great sense of humor. Stop wasting yourself on Congressman Asshat."

I snorted, spraying my sinuses with seltzer and coughing into the back of my hand.

Ava stood, abandoning the rest of her subpar scotch. "I'll call you tomorrow," she said finally. "Lincoln is busy all day and I can only amuse myself for so long. I could use some company at the spa." She looked pointedly at my nails. "And you need to spend some time on yourself for once."

Hugging her goodbye, I locked the door behind her and debated setting the alarm, deciding against it since I wasn't sure Blair was home yet. We lived in what was probably one of the last completely safe neighborhoods left in America. There was zero crime in our wealthy community and we could have gone on vacation and left the door unlocked, returning to find everything in perfect order.

If anyone broke into the house, they'd probably clean it.

Carrick was at my side, pressing his huge head into my thigh to get my attention. His aggressive leaning was his not-so-subtle hint he wanted his dinner and my feet made soft slapping sounds on the marble, Carrick's claws clacking alongside as I led him toward the back of the house to the laundry room and his food dish.

Climbing the stairs to the second floor, Carrick hot on my heels, I paused at the landing to remember the moment I'd fished Jack's necklace out of his shirt. Even three margaritas deep, I'd known what it meant when my fingers brushed the warm skin of his neck and he'd stilled over me. I'd felt the tension in the air, thick and unforgiving, and I'd heard him swallow hard–I knew I had, I couldn't have imagined it—and I knew it wasn't a normal reaction.

I sighed, shaking my head and grasping the banister to haul myself up to my room. I was being completely ridiculous, wasn't I?

I would never see the man again.

2

Jack

Davis would not stop. Not only had he managed to fall completely in love with the little blonde firecracker, Ava, during the twenty-minute drive from the bar to Daphne's house, but he wasn't about to stop teasing me about the woman I'd been staring at since she'd walked into the bar. It didn't matter that I'd been trying to place her familiar face, because most of the time I'd been staring at her ass.

"Yeah man, real fucking funny." I scowled at Davis. He thought it was *hilarious* Daphne was the woman we'd rescued from herself only days earlier. He was going on and on about fate, since the idiot was an eternal optimist, and Mr. Glass-Half-Full wasn't about to let this one go.

I suspected part of the reason was that he loved the contradictions: the polar opposite of my calm, tall, blonde, bohemian wife Natasha, Daphne was short and curvy, her dark hair almost black, a fire burning in her that I could tell she didn't let blaze out of control—ever, but I was sure she gave as good as she got. I knew exactly what that was like: I could read her because I *was* her.

"Come on, Thompson. You gotta admit she's cute, and it's not like Tash ever did anything to put a smile on your face."

My temper flared at the mention of my soon-to-be ex, but mostly because he was right. Natasha had stopped trying to make me smile a very long time ago.

Thank God the trip to his place was short, and when I pulled into the parking lot of his condo he unclipped his seat belt. *He* was going home to someone, I thought jealously. He'd been with his girlfriend since high school, and even at his twenty-six to my forty-two, he was way ahead of me when it came to holding onto what he wanted. They would be starting a family any day now. Generis was so swollen with his baby that anyone trying to get near her looked like they were in her orbit.

I'd held onto Natasha for exactly four years. It had only taken her that long to figure out that I was damaged goods, ruined by what I'd seen on two tours and working a steady but boring job, because I'd already had enough excitement in my life.

Natasha, she was twelve years younger than me, beautiful and ambitious, convinced she was meant to *go somewhere* and *be someone*, and nothing I did seemed to be furthering her dreams. I was her biggest mistake, she told me before she left. Her one regret. Those words settled like a rock in the pit of my stomach, rising again to the surface when I woke each morning, like bile burning my throat.

You were a mistake.

She'd had me served with divorce paperwork five months ago and I'd filed a response—one she hadn't liked. She'd left me almost two years earlier, and I knew she'd been waiting for me to file the paperwork to begin divorce proceedings. She'd been gone long enough to establish legal separation and I knew she waited longer because she didn't have a lot of extra money—not yet, anyway, since the aggrandized social media version of van life had been less profitable than usual while South America locked down over a respiratory virus.

She'd picked up a new boyfriend and was extolling the virtues of her nomadic existence on social media, though honestly she was probably a little old for it already. At her age she should have been settled into a career. Instead, her grid was filled with snapshots of beautiful sunsets and tiny bikinis, her smooth, long-limbed body bronzed by the sun, her wavy blonde hair whiter than I remembered.

She was still so beautiful, it hurt to look at her.

Yeah, I was the fool who had contested the divorce. I'd thought, when I responded, that I didn't want a divorce. I was the idiot who was still in love with my wife, although I was beginning to wonder if she'd ever loved me. It was clear she'd moved on and perhaps it was because she'd been in love with a fantasy: a person I could never become, or even hope to be.

Tyler threw open the door and flashed me a blinding grin as he unclipped his seatbelt. "All I'm saying, man, is you could stand some action. You've been a miserable shit the last couple years."

I blew out a puff of air that came out as "Pffft," and leveled him with a glare. "How do you know I'm not getting any action?"

He jumped off the running board, effectively removing himself from my reach even if I lunged. "Your hand don't count, bro." Then he slammed the door, running across the parking lot, his laughter drifting back to me.

I shook my head in disgust, mostly because he was right. Anything approaching sexual activities lately had been a sadly lacking, empty experience that barely scratched a physical itch and did nothing to calm the beast raging inside. The one that needed human connection: sweet smelling skin and the soft noises a woman made when you stretched your body out over hers.

Pulling into my driveway, I parked the truck inches from the garage door. I couldn't park in the stall itself, as I'd converted it years earlier into a studio for Natasha. She was a painter, an artistic soul, and she'd complained that the house was too small to set up a proper space for her art supplies. So over several months of weekends I'd finished the garage for my wife: obtained permits, wired, insulated, drywalled, tiled and painted. I'd installed expensive light fixtures and wide, double-paned windows, along with a mini-split with surprising blast capacity to keep her warm in the miserable winters and cool in the monkey-ass-hot summers that Maryland liked to bestow.

Installing a small, three-piece bathroom guaranteed Natasha had the ability to spend more and more time outside of the house as she chose to let our relationship deteriorate. Many nights she slept on the small sofa—I suspected in order to avoid me—and I often found the external door locked when I went out to carry her upstairs to our bed.

After a while, I stopped knocking or hoping she'd let me in, and I'd slink back into the house, defeated.

The small house was dark. There were no pets here to welcome me home, and I fitted my key to the lock, letting myself in through the front porch that was enclosed with leaded glass windows. They leaked heat like a sieve during the winter months and kept in the heat during the summer, rendering the space completely unusable. It had always been on my list to insulate the space and replace the windows, but I hadn't exactly gotten there yet. Malaise and depression sometimes swallowed my weekends whole.

For a while after Natasha left, I tried playing by her rule book. I'd done exactly what she had accused me of, and in order to justify her leaving I'd gone out looking for a good time. It wasn't hard, not when the women were half drunk, and I was in good shape–enviable, some of them said. Most of them were so intent on getting my clothes off, they couldn't have identified me in a lineup unless I'd been naked.

I drew the line at sloppy drunk. Those were the women I put into a cab headed home, their fares paid in advance. I wasn't so desperate that I wanted to bone a chick who couldn't remember which name she'd been screaming the next morning.

The few successful hookups I'd experienced had been successful only technically speaking: We'd gotten naked, I'd wrapped up, she screamed and clawed my back and I rolled away, waiting for her to leave my bed and my house. I'd never wanted any of them to stay. It felt too sordid and dirty, which was pretty accurate.

After a while I stopped trying to bring women home at all. It worried me that I couldn't wait to get them back out the door once I'd gotten them off, and more often than not they couldn't have given two shits about whether or not I'd gotten off as well.

I cut that out pretty quickly, after I ran into one of the women again. I recognized her immediately, but she spent the next hour staring at me and whispering with her friend before approaching me with "I think I know you from somewhere."

You sure do, sweetheart: my bed.

I think my response was something like "Yeah, you were under me a couple months ago." It got me slapped and I'd have deserved it if I was being flippant, but I was dead-serious. She'd been in no shape to discern whether I was being an ass or just blunt, but to her credit it was sometimes hard to tell the difference.

"Blunt" was one of the nicer words often used to describe me.

If I'd been trying to fill the hole Natasha had left, I wasn't successful. It went back a lot farther than I wanted to admit, the chasm in my chest opening up while we were still married. Something that felt awfully needy. She'd chipped at the cracks for a long time before they crumbled into a full-fledged hole.

You're such a typical, boring man. You come home from work and sit on the sofa with your beer. Maybe after my day I want to just veg with a glass of wine and you can do all the housework and make me dinner.

So I'd learned how to cook. Not great, but passable, which still exceeded any of her efforts, like her only job was to be beautiful. I'd come home after my shift to make dinner while she sat on the sofa with an enormous glass of wine and watched me cook. Any praise offered was still highly critical and she had no freaking filter. Like the words "I do" had just flipped the switch to Off.

Stop it, Jack. I don't want you touching me; you just do the same thing all the time and it's so fucking obvious. Where's your imagination? I should have married a man who was more exciting in bed.

So I stopped initiating physical intimacy.

My friend Kara's husband is so sweet. He surprised her last week with a necklace she really wanted, and it wasn't even their anniversary. He told her it was "just because." I can't believe there are any men left who can be so thoughtful.

So I bought her jewelry that she never wore, pronouncing it too cheap, too tacky, too gold when she wanted platinum. She never let me return any of the pieces, but she didn't wear them either, and when she left me I realized she'd pawned them all to finance her new nomadic lifestyle.

Not everything about Natasha had been bad, though most of it had been a lie. I saw what she wanted me to see, and then it was too late. She was a great actress and a masterful manipulator, something I didn't really peg until my supervisor called me into his office one day, months after Natasha had left and told me if I didn't get my shit together I was going to lose what was, by most standards, a very easy job. He was tired of me mooning over the worthless woman who'd left me and it had turned me into a zombie at work. He didn't know that part, of course. I'd never talked to him about it and never missed a day of work, my solid black wedding band still in place on my hand. But he was right: I could barely focus, and in no uncertain terms he told me to fix it.

Seeing a therapist went against everything I believed in, but I didn't have the mental bandwidth to conduct a new job search. I knew I'd fail any psychological evaluations and while I could afford to be without a job for a while, thanks to careful saving and investing, my precarious mental health wouldn't survive staying at home and staring at the walls all day. So I tapped into the coverage permitted by my health plan and saw a head doc a few times, for whatever that was worth. It helped me keep my job, but it did very little to help me sort the shit that still whirled around in my head. Probably just gave me enough distance to survive.

I lived each day in fear of process servers. Each morning I had to psych myself up to get out of bed, telling myself "Today can't be the day. It *won't* be the day." But eventually, it *was* the day. By then I'd lived in fear for so long, being served with the paperwork was actually kind of a relief. The sword had finally fallen and my head was still on my shoulders. The same couldn't be said for my heart, but most people weren't looking that deep when they saw me. As long as I was shaving, showering and eating somewhat regular meals I could present myself to the world as a largely normal human.

That night, like so many nights before it, I kicked off my boots just inside the front door and stood in the entryway listening to the soothing hum of the refrigerator, like the heartbeat of my house. I'd stopped hoping long ago to find a light burning in the house, Tash sitting in one of the chairs waiting for me, a smile on her beautiful face. She would apologize, she would confess she'd screwed up, she would plead for forgiveness and I would grant it.

Without bothering to turn on a light, I walked into the kitchen and drew a glass of water from the faucet. The moon was out, pale rays shining through the old casement windows, narrow beams of light on the old vinyl floor—another project I hadn't quite gotten to yet.

As was my habit, I'd only had two beers while out with the guys. That was my hard cut-off, since I refused to compromise myself in a public place or drive home drunk. Instead, on the nights I went out with the guys I came home and grabbed another beer, maybe two if I was really feeling the need to escape the vicious thoughts in my head. Usually they wouldn't shut up and I just learned to put up with them, like a bad roommate who insisted on blasting shitty music at all hours of the night.

Tonight I needed something stronger, and I grabbed the bottle of scotch from the top of the fridge, tipping a generous portion into the only real glass I had left. It was one of the stupid Mason jars Tash had insisted were "on trend" as drinking glasses. It was the only survivor, all the others subjected to a splintered, ignominious end a few weeks after she left. I'd gotten good and shitfaced and hurled them, one at a time, at the side of the garage. The neighbors, if they heard anything—and they must have—hadn't called the cops.

The liquid burned as I swallowed, and I leaned back against the counter in front of the sink. The moon cast my elongated shadow over the floor and I stood there looking at it for a long time, watching the movement when I brought my arm up for another sip.

It was rare I got into the scotch, but screw it. I didn't have to work tomorrow. Maybe for once I would be able to sleep past 5:30. And if I was really lucky, I wouldn't have any nightmares and wake all twisted in the sheets.

I poured a few more fingers, reminding myself of the hangover I would surely have the next morning. Then I bumped my way through the house, clinging to the wall for balance and direction, past the tiny breakfast nook and the cozy living room.

Up the steep stairs with the exposed brick wall on one side.

Into the small master bedroom that was right above the kitchen, the same moonlight that spilled across the kitchen's linoleum floor bathing my bed with its cold blue-white glow.

The bed was made with sharp, precise military corners, as it always was and, as always, I heaved a sigh of disappointment that it was empty. There was no warm, fragrant woman tucked under the light blanket, her arm tucked under my pillow. No one I could crawl in behind, to bury my face in her hair and tuck my body up tight behind hers.

I missed that more than anything: the physical closeness to another. There had always been something so inherently comforting about coming home to find my wife already in our bed, the sheets warmed by her body, and most nights I was content to just pull her close and fall asleep in the cloud of golden hair.

Tash hadn't been much of a cuddler, though she had me fooled at first. Eventually she started complaining I made her too hot and would quickly push me away, throwing off the weight of my arm and disengaging her legs from our tangle of limbs.

I sat on the edge of the bed, leaning my elbows on my knees as I stared out the large window. So many nights I'd sat here, just like this, watching the street and begging every deity I'd ever heard of to bring my wife back home. I promised to try harder; to be better; to make her happy this time. And then, after a while, I stopped begging. The only thing that remained was the watching, almost unconsciously, sitting on the edge of the bed sometimes for hours at night just staring out the window.

The flash of memory came unbidden, of the flustered woman spilling iced coffee all over herself several days earlier, and I chuckled to myself as I remembered the look on her face when she spun around at the bar to find me staring at her. She had recognized me instantly—I saw it on her face—though it had taken me a long time to place her, which was why I'd been staring at her.

I sighed, pulling my shirt up over my head and pushing off the bed to brush my teeth in the dark bathroom. Then, bedtime ritual complete, I dropped my pants to the floor at the foot of the bed and crawled up until I'd buried my face in the pillows.

Daphne, was it? The drinks were still dancing around in my head, messing with my thoughts and making things fuzzy.

Daphne was a real knockout. Her deep ebony hair was thick and long, hanging in loose waves to the middle of her back. And what a back it was, sloping down into the beautiful curves of an ass that was enough to make a man weep. She wasn't tall, but she wasn't exactly a little person either, at least in the shoes she'd been wearing.

But it was her eyes that had really knocked me sideways. I specifically remembered she'd been wearing sunglasses when I'd first approached her in that ridiculous truck, and she'd shoved them back into her hair because she was flustered. I hadn't gotten a good look at her eyes then, what with the sun in her face, but I'd gotten a good look tonight, when she'd poked a finger into my chest and stared up into my face. They were a color I'd never seen before, a color most people probably would have called navy blue because they didn't know better, but hers were definitely a deeper shade, closer to grey, something like cold, hard rainwater, or maybe slate. And they were sad eyes, like they had seen too much.

I pondered Davis's bald insinuation, that I had been an ass for years because I wasn't getting laid, and my thoughts drifted again to the Preston woman. She'd been wearing a real leg-lifter of a wedding set, the one she'd almost permanently blinded me with when she shoved her hand in my eye. Someone had marked his territory and marked it good, so that no inferior males would come sniffing around. But she'd plainly said she'd been left for ... what was it? Some sort of government aid. Congressional—that had to be it, since her husband was a congressman. Maybe that meant she was suffering a dry spell similar to my own.

Rolling over, I buried my head under a pillow to turn off the thoughts. Daphne Preston would have no more interest in being a fuck buddy than she would in driving out to the backwoods of Maryland to go mudding in her ridiculously huge truck.

That weekend I forced myself to be productive. It took a while to get into the swing of things on Saturday morning, since my head was a little foggy from taking things too far the night before. But after a few cups of coffee and a quick breakfast, I felt inspired to change something.

The house had been sitting exactly as Tash left it, and something nagged in my brain that in order to move past, as I knew I had no choice but to do, I needed to make tangible changes and perhaps the mental changes would follow. By cleaning and renovating and changing up my house, maybe I could clean my wife right out of my thought processes.

Taping off the living room trim, I grabbed a can of paint from the shelf along the basement steps. I'd picked it up a long time ago, a rich color like the deep navy blue waters found in lakes to the far north.

By lunch I had the first coat up and I was pleased to find that I liked the color in that space. It covered that disgusting mid-tone grey Natasha had insisted was *the color* for our entire house. It had always made the rooms look cold and sterile, and I didn't think it worked in *any* of them. But she was the artist, so she'd been the one to make the decisions when it came to decorating because, for the most part, I couldn't have cared less so long as it made her happy.

But I really fucking hated that paint color. It was like living in a doctor's waiting room.

By the time I pulled the tape off and moved a couple things around the room, it was solidly into the afternoon. My work here was done, especially since I'd promised Davis I would come over and help him assemble some furniture for the nursery his girlfriend wanted help putting together.

Lord love him, but the kid didn't have a handy bone in his body. He was an expert marksman, the best one in our tight little group, but when it came to other things, like putting together furniture or fixing things, he was hopeless. I'd been over to his condo more times than I could count, to help out with things like "The garbage disposal doesn't work," or "The toilet in the upstairs bathroom is leaking all over the floor."

He was a disaster.

Tyler was on me about Daphne all afternoon, so much so that I finally snapped at him that *he* should ask her out, and he'd grinned at me. "Yeah, maybe I will."

"The hell you will," his girlfriend yelled from the bottom of the stairs. Pregnancy had already given her supersonic hearing and she could be heard muttering something fierce under her breath in Spanish.

Tyler laughed. "Not for me, baby," he called out the door, his voice drifting down the staircase. "For our uptight friend."

She muttered something from the living room and Tyler snorted just a little, clamping his lips together to keep it in, and suddenly he couldn't look me in the eye.

"Yeah?" I prompted.

"Generis picked something up for you last week." He looked like he couldn't decide whether to laugh or run. Christmas was solidly five months away. "Right up your alley too, because it won't give you any attitude. Real quiet and accommodating."

My eyes narrowed and he pushed himself up from the floor, disappearing into the hallway and I heard a cabinet open and close. Then he was back in the room, a brown paper-wrapped package in his hands, like he'd sent away to Hustler for a subscription.

"It's a joke, man." His expression softened and it seemed like he was having second thoughts, because he wasn't laughing anymore as he handed me the package. I set it beside me, my eyebrows drawn uncomfortably tight on my forehead. I didn't need to open the package to know his girlfriend had gotten me a life-size blow-up doll. At the time they'd probably thought it was funny, but I couldn't have laughed right now if I tried. It took everything I had to keep down the stupid feelings that wanted to come out, emotions uglier and messier than anger.

Hurt, probably.

We worked in silence for a long time, uncomfortably, and after completing the crib I turned to see Tyler had put together the glider. He was surrounded by leftover pieces and I shook my head at him, not saying a thing, quickly affixing the bottom to the chair so it wouldn't kill either of them when they sat in it to rock the baby.

Generis fed us pizza, bringing several steaming hot pies, fresh in their delivery boxes, right up into the nursery. She piled them on the floor in front of us and eased her baby hippo-like girth down next to Tyler. I watched him jealously as he absently placed a hand on her swollen stomach, his other arm going around her hips to pull her closer.

Some guys really did have all the luck.

She was the one to catch the look on my face and she hung her head for a second before speaking. "I'm sorry, Jack. It seemed really funny when I was in the store." I raised an eyebrow at her. "I don't know what I was thinking. Can I blame the pregnancy hormones?"

I tried to shrug nonchalantly. I didn't want to know what had driven Generis into that particular type of store in the first place. But I put so little effort into it that only one shoulder would cooperate. "It's fine," I said, snagging a piece of pizza from the box and cramming the slice into my mouth. I hoped all the hot, melty cheese would stop up the angry words that wanted to pour out like vomit, because if I let out even a few there was no way I'd be able to turn off that faucet. The words wouldn't be very nice, and already I didn't have many friends.

Watching the two of them, I couldn't help but feel envious. Their relationship was so easy and silly, thoughtful and sweet. Tyler couldn't keep his hands off his woman and for her part, she snuggled into his side and basked in his affection. It was pretty damn disgusting and watching them made something ache inside, reminding me I didn't have that.

When I pushed to my feet and made excuses about getting home to play catch-up with the laundry, Tyler pulled Generis to her feet and she gave me a careful hug. "You've saved me yet again," she said with a grin and I looked behind her to see Tyler shaking his head.

I left the two of them in the nursery after slapping Tyler's shoulder, and I let myself out of the condo and walked across the parking lot to my truck, tossing the package into the back seat. There were a couple things I wanted to get done at home before calling it a night and for once, I thought, maybe I'd sit and watch some mindless TV for a minute. I needed to erase the jealous thoughts that were trying to fester in my brain, because I was genuinely happy for my friend.

The thought was startling in its clarity: I didn't want what he had, exactly, but I wanted the *promise* of what he had. It was what I'd thought would be mine when I married Natasha, hoping to come home to her beautiful, smiling face each day. And with time, perhaps I'd imagined coming home to a few squealing rug rats, too.

I grunted at myself in disgust as I jammed the keys into the ignition. The picture was too pretty and ridiculous. That would never be my reality.

3

Daphne

My face was hot and my fingers shook as the blue and red lights swirled behind me. I flipped on a blinker, taking an awkward right turn into a parking lot and the SUV followed me, the smaller vehicle boxing my big truck into a tight parking spot.

Digging through the center console, I fished out my registration before pulling my driver's license out of the cup holder. I knew I'd been doing a few miles an hour above the speed limit when I sailed past the vehicle parked in the median, the lights on the car lit up as a reminder folks should watch their speed. But never, in the several weeks I'd been bringing Blair to work, had I seen anyone pulled over.

Thank the gods at least this morning I was wearing some tinted moisturizer and a bra. This area seemed to be where they kept the hot cops, and I wasn't eager to make another disheveled impression on one of them.

There was a tap on my window and, flustered, I hit the button to quickly slide it all the way down with an electronic whir.

"You know why I pulled you over, ma'am?" The voice was familiar and I turned my head to see a pair of blacked out aviators and a wide grin.

"Guard Shack!" I couldn't stop the exclamation, my words a little shaky as adrenaline continued to course through my body. I was not pulled over—not ever.

"Guard Shack?" His grin widened. "It's Officer Davis, Mrs. Preston, but I like the way you think: descriptive naming conventions. Good one."

I paused, shoving my own sunglasses back into my hair and he returned the favor, pulling his shiny aviators from his face to hook through the neck of his uniform.

"I was going too fast," I said, my face flushing a little. I felt like I'd been caught out, called to the front of class for cheating on a test.

"Not something I'm particularly worried about," he drawled, and my eyes narrowed. "I'm not usually on duty out here—guard shack and all," and he shook his head with a laugh. "But today I get to sit out here and remind people to slow it down. Maintain an orderly presence. You know."

I sat quietly, waiting for him to tell me why he'd pulled me over. Suddenly a niggling suspicion was grinding in my gut. "Then why did you pull me over? Was I being disorderly?"

His eyes widened, like he hadn't considered the ramifications of his actions. "Shit, Ms. Daphne, I didn't mean to scare you." He gestured broadly in the direction of the huge parking lot I'd found myself in weeks earlier.

I crossed my arms over my chest and leveled him with my best glare. He shifted uncomfortably in his boots before heaving a heavy sigh. "Okay, I suppose you deserve the truth. I've been watching for this beast." He patted the side of the truck almost affectionately. "My friend is never going to admit to anything, Ms. Daphne, but he had a good time the night you spilled your drinks on him. I actually saw him *smile,* and trust me when I say that man does not smile, or have a good time—not ever."

"I threw it at him once, but the second time was an accident," I reminded him and he laughed with me.

"Yeah, he complained the whole way home about sticky girly drinks, but there's no way he was mad about it. Secretly, I think he enjoyed the attention."

The seatbelt had grown hot in the sun and the polyester threads were burning my arms where I'd crossed them over my chest.

Officer Davis looked down at his feet for a moment before fishing around for something in his pocket. Wordlessly, he handed a scrap of paper to me and I unfolded it quickly to find an address and a cell number with the name Tyler next to it.

"That's where the guys will be tonight," he said, his cheeks coloring quickly. "Maybe you and your friend could accidentally show up again? Six-thirty? Charitable purposes, of course."

My eyes narrowed and I pursed my lips as I thought. "Why would we do that, officer?" I asked finally, and he cleared his throat, a sure sign of discomfort. "Are you trying to win over my very happily married friend? She's a little old for you, and I'd be very afraid of her husband."

He laughed uncomfortably and his handsome, boyish face went a mottled red. "Oh no, Ms. Daphne. She was something else, that one, but my girl would kill me if I so much as *thought* about another lady like that." He laughed a little more but the sound was strained. "No, uh ... you seemed to get on pretty well with my buddy—gave him hell. He doesn't take to new people real often. He's closed off and quiet and he could use a little excitement in his life."

Well, wasn't that just my middle name? *Excitement.*

Clearly Tyler had been talking to the wrong people.

"I'm sorry, Tyler," I said finally, shaking my head and his eyes widened when I used his first name. "I'm afraid I'm not all that exciting, nor am I in the mood for any excitement myself. If you're insinuating what I think you are, I think Jack's wife should be offended."

Tyler took a step closer and leaned his arm on the open window frame of the truck. "Mrs. Thompson has filed for divorce and is living in a van in Argentina as we speak, having replaced my friend with some twenty-year-old kid who's a surfer and a bum." He looked completely disgusted, which seemed quite out of character for someone who was such a perpetual ray of sunshine.

"It would seem that Jack and I have a few things in common," I said slowly, my mind lingering over an image of Cassandra on her knees. It had been burned into my memory.

Bless her foolish little heart.

That wasn't a compliment or an endearment, let me tell you that much. It was as vicious a curse known to man in some parts of the south.

Tyler nodded at me with an understanding look in his eyes, and I was pretty sure that Jack had filled him in on a few of the sparse details I'd let slip. Certainly enough for him to draw his own conclusions as to the state of my marriage.

"Okay," I said slowly, rubbing the paper between my fingers. "But don't say anything. I don't want any ... expectations. This is already weird enough."

Tyler grinned at me, turning slowly to head back toward his cruiser. "I wouldn't dream of it—you either, because we're just gonna chalk this up to coincidence," he threw over his shoulder, saluting me before snapping the door open and dropping into the darkened interior.

What in the world had I just gotten myself into? I drove home pondering whether the butterflies in my belly meant I was being unfaithful to the man who'd tossed me aside. The one who had no compunction about being unfaithful to me.

I took the exit and sat at the light in the long lineup of cars, waiting to turn. Snippets of memories bounced around my head while I stared at the solidly red light: Hunter crawling back to me when Blair was three, claiming he wanted nothing more than to be a family. He was sorry for his indiscretions and his stupidity and that it had taken him so long to grow up.

Blair's innocent discovery when she was seven: A woman's earring, hooked into the waistband of my husband's pants.

The faint pink lip gloss smear on the collar of a white dress shirt and the undershirt that smelled like he'd spent an afternoon riding someone hard.

I was an expert when it came to the smells I associated with Hunter and they were tea tree shampoo, pine deodorant and cologne that came from a blue bottle with a horse on it. He was a creature of habit—at least until it came to women, at which point all bets were off.

I was the only habit he couldn't seem to keep.

Anger bubbled up my trachea as I sat waiting. It was a foreign feeling, hot and violent and acidic, and I slammed a palm furiously into the steering wheel. *Done.* I had done nothing to deserve what he'd put me through. I had always pulled my weight. I'd kept my figure and while I sometimes needed reminders to get my hair done or book a pedicure, I was very aware of the admiring glances his colleagues shot in my direction. Maybe I wasn't the typical trophy wife, but I knew I was still appealing.

The light turned green and I surged forward, one finger on a button on the steering wheel. The truck dinged at me and I commanded it, "Call Hunter."

"Calling Hunter," announced the soothing female voice and the ringtone chirped three times before someone picked up.

"Congressman Preston's office, this is Heidi."

"Heidi!" My voice was warm and friendly. I liked this one: possibly one of the only aids who hadn't let Hunter get his hands—or any of his other parts—up her skirt. "It's Daphne. I know the schedule's probably just as nuts as it always is..." I let it trail off and she quickly filled the space for me.

"It's not a problem at all, Mrs. Preston. If you'll give me just a moment to alert him, I can put you right through."

The truck filled with the weird silence of dead air as I waited on hold and I mashed my teeth together to keep from chewing my lip bloody. It was time to end this farce.

"Congressman Preston." Hunter's rich baritone bounced around the car and I wanted to punch the digital display on my dashboard. Pompous ass—he knew who was calling, since Heidi had alerted him. He just liked the sound of his own voice saying those very self-important words.

"It's me," I said flatly and when he didn't respond I forged ahead. "I just thought I'd let you know that since you've decided to move forward without me, I'm doing the same. I won't file for divorce until the May recess, so that should give you plenty of time to get things in order and alert the firm so they can get ahead of any firestorms. I can be discreet in the interim."

"Daph!" he sputtered, finally coming to life. "You can't do that. You know this will ruin me. I ran on family values. Come on, sweetheart ... we can talk through this." He was using his placatory politician voice, like I didn't know exactly what he was doing. I'd been there, watching while he perfected his craft.

I snorted, flipping the blinker and pulling into the long driveway. *Family values, my hiney.* He feared the loss of his position, not the demise of his marriage. "*Sweetheart*, that's something you should have considered before shacking up with someone barely older than your daughter. It's disgusting." I gagged. "And really, that's the hill you want to die on? Your *political* platform? You've thrown away fifteen years of marriage, Hunter. I think the cat's out of the bag when it comes to your true moral standing." I gagged again at the thought of all that time wasted. "Not that you've ever held our vows sacred; I guess giving me up was no sacrifice at all."

That made me the fool.

More dead air from the other end and I hit the button on the garage door opener, waiting for it before pulling in and closing it behind me on quiet tracks. I killed the ignition switch and held the phone up to my ear, unstrapping my seatbelt but making no move to get out of the vehicle. I didn't want to carry the conversation into the house, to be overheard by Catalina.

There was a rustling sound. "Have you met someone?" His voice was low and accusatory and while it should have made me feel triumphant, instead it made me sad. He was worried about optics, not about losing me. I lowered my head to the steering wheel, sighing quietly.

"No, Hunter," I said softly. "But I'm considering giving it a try. I think it's my turn to have my needs met."

More silence.

"You have never been faithful to me," I continued, tapping out each word on the steering wheel. "I would say that I don't know why you bothered to stay married to me, but I'm finally admitting to myself that I was financially and politically expedient." That stung to say out loud. "I'd rather have nothing at all rather than what we have."

He sucked in a sharp breath. "No Daph, this is a mistake. Hear me out."

I cut him off quickly. "You've had twenty years to convince me to stay and you haven't tried until *just now.* It's too little, too late, husband." I threw that last bit in there as a jab. It was mean, but I wanted to hurt him a little. I'd certainly earned the right.

There was labored breathing.

"You're done then?" He sounded angry.

"Are you done dating the infant?"

More labored breathing. That was my answer.

"The prenup laid the groundwork," I said, lifting my head in order to tap a nail against the wheel again. "Unless you feel like enduring the publicity of a long, drawn out divorce, I think we can agree to the equitable division of any marital assets. We're adults."

Equitable division, or any division, would still leave him in perilous finances, as a divorce meant each of us left the marriage with exactly what we'd brought to it. The prenup existed for that very reason: His was his and mine was mine, and mine had always been a lot more than his. Anything we had purchased on our own was not subject to division and anything we'd acquired jointly since, which was precious little, would be split evenly.

He had been the one to insist I sign the document my daddy's lawyers drafted and, for the first time, I let myself smile smugly at how badly he'd played himself when he'd tried to lock me down. No doubt he'd meant to find a loophole over time, though it seemed his loophole was just staying married to me. God knew it had done nothing to keep him faithful.

He'd purchased the small home in Georgetown and was making regular payments on it, whereas I'd paid for the enormous house out in the middle of nowhere.

Our modest home in Alabama was also in my name, as I'd been the one to purchase it when my business began to take off.

And the New York apartment? I'd been the one to buy it from my parents.

He mumbled something that sounded like the mixture of a curse and something uncomplimentary and I leaned back into the seat, sad again that this was what it had come to. I had given twenty good years to a man who'd remained a stranger.

Without another word, the line went dead and I sat there staring at the face of my phone: three minutes, fifteen seconds. That was how long it had taken to end my marriage.

It was only six-thirty in California, but Ava was an early riser. I knew that when I called her to relay my news, she would pick up. And not only would she pick up, but she would be perky and well-caffeinated. She was a natural early bird. It was obnoxious.

Incapable of focusing even after our talk, I sent a quick note to my office staff that I would be out of the office for the remainder of the day due to personal reasons. It was something I never did and I was quick to reassure them that I was fine, but I needed to deal with some matters that had arisen in my personal life. It was already more than I wanted to say: I needed to blow off responsibilities for once and spend some quiet time thinking through the decision I'd made this morning.

Restless and incapable of sitting still, I walked out some of my frustrations on the small treadmill I kept in my office. Then I booked a salon appointment and showered, driving myself into the small town to have my hair and nails done. Because screw it, I felt like crap but I didn't have to look like it—especially in front of Jack, because I was sure as hell going out tonight.

When I picked Blair up from work, she noticed immediately, reaching over to thread her fingers through my shiny, blown-out hair. "Oooh," she teased. "Is Auntie Ava back in town?"

It was the perfect time to tell my daughter what she already knew, but I didn't have the energy for the conversation. Instead, I shook my head shortly. "No, but I am going out to meet some friends tonight. I doubt I'll be out all that long."

"Friends," she said haltingly, snapping her seatbelt. I'd made it too easy on the child; she was *never* going to get her driver's license. "You don't have friends."

Thanks a lot, kid.

"I mean ... you have Auntie Ava, and sometimes you do happy hour with What's-Her-Name, the neighbor. But otherwise you're always working." She looked at me suspiciously. "Did you run out of things to binge watch on Netflix and you're ...

branching out?" She paused, her eyes landing on my nails. She gasped. "Mom, you *didn't*!"

I looked at her in alarm. "Didn't what?"

"You joined a dating app." She was looking at me like there was a bad taste in her mouth.

"Why would I do that to myself?" I asked her, throwing a weak smile in her direction as I backed the truck out of the space. After the steadfast loyalty I'd shown Hunter all these years, I was shocked my daughter would turn against me so quickly.

"You should definitely do that," she said firmly, and I had to step on the brake to look at her.

What?

"Come on, Mom." She rolled her eyes and I slowly released the brake, letting the truck roll closer to the stop sign. I flipped the blinker and looked both ways, waiting for oncoming traffic to clear enough to shoot across the lanes. "I know about Daddy and Cassandra, and it's not fair that he gets to do that to you," she said quietly. "He's not as discreet as he thinks he is. It's your turn to have some ... *man* friends."

Boy, didn't I know it.

"Discreet or not," I said, taking my opportunity and shooting out into traffic, knuckles white on the wheel as I banked a hard left, "I'm not planning on dating—not really. Just broadening my horizons a little, and if I happen to meet someone, it won't hurt my feelings."

It seemed we were going to have that conversation after all.

"I told your father that I'll be filing for divorce in May, during his recess."

My daughter swallowed hard and I waited for tears, but instead she reached across the console to squeeze my shoulder and I was surprised to find it was my eyes that filled.

"I'm sorry, Mama," she said softly. "You deserve to be happy and I can't remember you being happy for a really long time."

Those words were sobering. What kind of example had I been setting for my child, not only in my marriage, but in life?

"I'm sorry you saw it," I said, swiping with one hand at my cheek. "I guess I thought I was doing a better job of hiding it."

We rode the rest of the way in silence and I drove with my left hand, not bothering with blinkers, since Blair was holding my right hand.

She followed me up to my room when we got home, Carrick close behind. There she threw herself down onto my bed and looked pointedly at my closet, waiting for me to change and model my outfit choices for her. It was something we'd done when she was younger, whenever I had to attend a big event.

"That one," she said finally, pointing to the silky dark green top I'd put on. "It makes your eyes this crazy color and it's perfect with your hair." Apparently it went without saying that I was dressing to impress, even if that someone was just myself.

Blair picked out my earrings and my lipstick, then tucked a few pieces into a small clutch and handed it to me with a grin. She hugged me quickly. "Jake's coming over to watch movies tonight and Catalina said she'd make homemade pizzas, so if you get home early ... uh..." She trailed off a little uncomfortably.

"I won't look in, so long as you can tell me clothes will still be on," I said. She'd gotten enough lectures to last her a lifetime about how having a baby at this age would change her life.

She blushed a little and nodded and I counted back in my head as to how long she'd been seeing Jake. It seemed I was fighting against the inevitable, but I wasn't particularly fond of the kid.

Crawling up into the truck, I punched the address Tyler had given me into the GPS system and waited for it to pull up. It was just outside of Baltimore and I didn't recognize it, but as it was a short drive from the house I pulled up a favorite playlist and hit I-95 to creep toward my exit.

It occurred to me as I turned onto the wooded drive and noticed a proliferation of pickup trucks in the parking lot, that perhaps I was not properly dressed for the occasion. I kept a pair of flats in the truck at all times, but from the plaid button-down shirts, camouflage tank tops and trucker's hats I saw on the few men I passed as I navigated toward a parking spot, I was going to stick out like a sore thumb in my black dress pants, black heels and silky green top.

I should have asked Tyler for more information.

Throwing the truck into park and reaching behind me for the flats, I kicked off my heels and shoved my feet into the velvet slippers. I freaking hated being small sometimes, and the ballet shoes brought me right back down to my full height of 5'2".

Okay, barely. I was more like 5' 1", and only if I took a really deep breath.

Good things come in small packages, said my mother's voice inside my head.

I tucked the clutch into the console, shoving the key fob into the small pocket in my pants and throwing open the door to climb down. I held my phone in my hand as I hopped off the running board and pushed the button on the door handle to lock the truck. I turned to find two men leaning against the tailgate of their vehicle, openly admiring either my truck or my ass.

Probably both.

"Don't get many *ladies* in here," one of them remarked somewhat offhand and his eyes were on me, though he seemed to be talking to his friend. "'specially the fancy ones."

I rolled my eyes and hurried past them as quickly as my short legs would carry me, hoping to find Tyler in one of the booths I could see across the lot. The man had invited me to a dang outdoor gun range, I thought with irritation, with no warning. I could have at least been prepared.

A shot cracked sharply through the air and the cicadas stilled for a moment. It was early evening but it was quite warm, the sun still bright in the sky. There was a whoop from the direction of the shot and I started counting the number of bodies clustered around that particular booth: one, two, three ... four. The fourth one was built like a mountain range, broad and rugged, and I swallowed hard. *Jack.* My knees wobbled a little, the traitors. Apparently they found him attractive, too.

I let myself inside quickly to check in, signed the necessary paperwork and went through a quick briefing with one of the instructors. When I let him know which group I would be joining he laughed, trying to hide it behind his hand. "Never mind then," he said, gesturing toward the door. "If you're with them, you know what you're doing."

I moved up quietly behind them and Tyler sensed me before any of the others, the other two intently watching as Marston took careful aim, the butt-stock of a long barrel shotgun pressed up tight against his shoulder.

Tyler turned, raising an eyebrow and moving slowly back toward me so as not to disturb the others and he leaned in quickly to kiss my cheek. "Glad you could make it," he whispered, his eyes running the short length of my overdressed body before gesturing toward Marston. "Probably should have warned you, huh?"

The air was split by a loud crack and Marston barked out, "Ha!" as he obliterated his target. "Bet you fuckers can't do that."

He turned and his eyes fell on me, his face sobering instantly. "Beg pardon, ma'am."

Jack turned sharply and a look of displeasure flashed across his face. He hid it almost as quickly, trying to replace it with anything but a forced smile. He looked stern instead.

Ouch.

I caught Tyler's glare out of the corner of my eye, leveled at Jack, who didn't appear even remotely contrite. It was obvious that as far as Jack was concerned, my presence was not welcome. That was a feeling I was quite used to.

While the four of them rotated through rounds, swapping out one gun for another, I stood patiently and watched. I could tell I made them nervous, especially judging by the tight set of Jack's shoulders, and each time he stepped up to take his shot I watched his back rise and fall with several deep breaths before he squeezed the trigger. He was patient, precise, focused and had a damn good aim.

"You up for a try?" Tyler finally asked, setting down his weapon and turning toward me. It made me grin, because what Tyler didn't know was that I'd been born and raised in the deep south: God, guns, and love of country. Daddy joked I'd been issued a rifle at birth, and as I stepped toward Tyler, he shrugged off his light flannel, handing it over to me so I could cover up any exposed skin to avoid sparks or brass burns.

The tattoos snaking down his arms and running into the armholes of his tank top were far more impressive than what I'd seen partially obscured by the short sleeves of his uniform.

"After the day I've had?" I asked him with a raised eyebrow and a grin. "This might be a bad idea."

"Not scared of these, are you?" He stepped carefully up behind me, reaching for the small handgun on the table and I stopped him with a look.

"Nuh-uh." I grinned at him, pointing at the shotgun. "That one. The big daddy."

"That one's not for beginners, little lady."

Little lady? Oh, no he didn't.

I acted like I hadn't heard him for a second, but I pursed my lips and shook my head tightly. Someone must have trained him well when it came to reading Irritated Woman, because he held up his hands and stepped back without saying anything more.

Slipping my arms through the sleeves of his shirt, I made quick work of the buttons, slipping on the ear and eye protection he handed over. I buttoned the loose cuffs and grabbed the shotgun, loading it carefully and keeping it pointed downrange.

All four of them were staring at me as I moved confidently through the process and positioned myself with the butt-stock tight against my shoulder. Widening my stance just a little, I looked down the bead site, lining it up with the target and exhaling slowly before I squeezed the trigger and the gun kicked like a mule into my shoulder. I absorbed the substantial shock into my body, the sharp bite of pain in my shoulder, and I shook out my arm.

"You gotta be shittin' me," someone whispered behind me and I knew I'd slugged my target dead-on, just as I always did.

I flicked the safety, popped the breech lock, tossed the shell and looked down the barrel before setting the gun on the bench containing three other guns, all pointed downrange.

There were four unhinged jaws when I turned around and I unbuttoned the shirt quickly, handing it to Tyler before smoothing out my hair.

"No way." Tyler handed the shirt back to me. "Bet you can't do that again." He pointed to a different gun, the one he'd tried to pawn off on me moments before, a small pistol I recognized as a Glock 44. I smirked at it, deciding not to tell them that I'd been raised on a gun range. Daddy had taken me at least once a month from the age of six until ... well, the last time I'd gone down to visit Mama. We'd opted for heavier equipment that last time, since he was going through an AR phase.

"All ten?" I asked, grabbing a handful of bullets and feeding them into a magazine before clapping it into the gun. I heard another muttered exclamation behind me as I racked the slide, chambering the first bullet, and taking a confident stance before squeezing one eye shut and unloading ten rapid-fire shots.

There was utter silence and I made sure the chamber was clear, setting the empty magazine on the table and following it with the disabled gun. I didn't need to look at the target to know I'd put all ten bullets in the same place, dead-center.

If I'd been born man, Daddy always laughed, the Army would have recruited me at the age of nine as a sniper.

"I'll be damned." It was Tyler, shaking his head as I unbuttoned the shirt and handed it back to him. He looked dazed. "You'll keep the big guy on his toes."

There was a low growl behind me and even without turning to see it, I knew Jack had bared his teeth at Tyler. He was standing about as far away from me as he could without actually leaving the shared space.

I watched the four of them take turns, each of them casting nervous glances over their shoulders at me before they stepped up to take their shots. It was all I could do to keep from laughing, having gone from rookie status to *she's better than us* in the space of just a few moments.

The sun dropped lower on the horizon and each of them stepped forward to claim one of the guns, going through a safety check before tucking it into its protective case.

Not surprisingly, the shotgun was Jack's and I tried to suppress a grin, because I'd known it the instant I saw it.

"Whadaya say, boys?" Tyler called to the others and I understood quickly that he was the glue that held the group together:

open, welcoming and friendly. “Renninger’s for drinks? I’m not ready to head home just yet. G is doing this crazy nesting shit—that’s what she calls it—she’ll make me paint something or hang up another damn picture and I just I can’t. I’m done. This baby needed to come three weeks ago already.”

Jack was standing just behind me and to my right, and something in my body hummed at his nearness. My every nerve ending was as aware of him as if he were a live current and I was the wire, ready to conduct. I felt his reaction to Tyler’s innocent statement; felt him tense and draw in a deep, painful breath and hold it.

Interesting.

“You too fancy for beer?” Tyler asked, lifting his chin in my direction and I blew out a “Pffft” at him.

“Go fetch my target and you can tell me who’s fancy.” I grinned, feeling awfully victorious for the first time in a long time. These were things I knew how to do, and I could do them well. Things I couldn’t do—a self I couldn’t be—with most people. Because yes, most of the time I *did* have to pretend to be fancy. Most of my clients and the very few people I called friends would have been shocked to find gasoline ran through my veins, barbecue and banana pudding were my favorite food groups, and I could hydrate like a beast with Dr. Pepper and pickle juice, though never at the same time.

I also secretly loved college football, and learning to bow hunt was on my bucket list.

The four of them had parked in a row, all right next to one another, and I smirked at the four big trucks. “Looks like we have ourselves quite the convoy,” I announced, pointing across the row to my monster.

In an ode to Game of Thrones, and because I named *every* vehicle I owned, this sleek, jacked-up black beauty was The Big Woman.

Marston had a strange look on his face, while Agnello looked from the truck and back to me several times before his eyes flitted to Jack. It was odd that he should look to him, I thought, like he was asking permission for something.

"You car in the shop?" Marston asked, and it was clear that was the best he could do. In his mind there was no other way to explain why I had custom ordered a vehicle so grossly disproportionate to my tiny self.

Hitting the lock button twice and pressing down on the autostart, a slow smile slid across my face when the truck roared to a start, and Agnello's eyes widened. "Nope," I said, finding it harder and harder to contain my glee. "I like my ladies big and loud."

Tyler snorted, and out of the corner of my eye I saw him punch Jack in the shoulder. Jack didn't even look at him, turning quickly to march away from us to climb into his own older truck. It was one I could tell had been through many things with him already, if the fading paint color was any indication.

I didn't follow them. I let the four of them pull out and I waved them on, taking a moment to sit and collect myself. It had been one of the stranger days I'd experienced lately, and though the heavy sadness of the morning's conversation with my husband tried to hang around my shoulders, I chose to feel lighter. I took a deep breath, trying to let it go, then put the truck into gear and followed my GPS in the direction my four new friends had gone.

4

Jack

"I can't fucking believe you."

Tyler didn't look at all surprised. In fact, the asshole grinned at me. "I don't know what the hell you're talking about, big guy, but I *do* know that a certain little thing put your aim to shame tonight and maybe that's why you're so mad: Pint Size showed your ass up."

Daphne hadn't even set foot through the door and I'd already pounded my first beer. I stared at the glass in confusion, unsure how that had just happened. I was fully aware I'd need to be on my toes or I'd go over my self-imposed limit without even noticing.

What was Daphne doing showing up at the range anyway? It had to be Tyler's fault, always playing the Italian grandmother, shoving food down our throats and trying to match us up with women. His attempts hadn't been successful with Marston or Agnello, and now he'd turned his attention to me.

There was an appreciative sound over my shoulder and I turned to see Daphne, all dark eyes and long, glossy hair moving toward us. Did she always walk like that? There was a sway to her hips that had me unwillingly mesmerized and I had to work hard not to stare.

"Mrs. Preston." Agnello lifted his drink in salute before handing her the beer Tyler had ordered for her, condensation beginning to run down the sides.

She made a face. "Mrs. Preston is my mother-in-law. The woman has never thought I was good enough for her son, so I'm giving him back." She held up a finger to her lips and raised her bottle to clink the neck against Agnello's, a small smile on her face.

"You joining my friend here in the wasteland of single life?" Tyler grinned, hooking a thumb in my direction and Daphne nodded, taking a deep pull from her bottle. "Having *no* husband is better than having a fake one."

"Hell of a lot less to argue about," I grumped, and she snorted a little, swallowing hard to avoid spitting her beer in my face. She nodded then, lifting her bottle upward in a sign of agreement.

For all I knew, she'd never had a disagreement with her husband, but given the undercurrent of feistiness, I could tell she would give as good as she got. She was the sort who'd have to be pushed, provoked into a reaction, but it would be glorious when it happened.

She kept her distance from me for the next several hours and I'll admit I was just a little disappointed. Despite my need to keep myself at some physical distance from her, I wanted her to try to stand close enough that I could smell her hair or really take in the color of her eyes again.

It meant nothing, I told myself. It meant that I was starved for female companionship, which was entirely true. But something about this little spitfire was intriguing, and I hadn't felt that for a long time. After besting all of us on the range, I wondered what other secrets she hid.

Marston was just shy of sloppy by the time Daphne slapped an open palm down on the small hightop. "I should call it, boys. Until Blair completes her driving hours and takes her test, I'm her Uber to work in the morning."

I looked at her with a little more appreciation, her curves soft but everything firm and tight and where it belonged. That she had a daughter who was nearly an adult was baffling.

"You sure you're capable of handling that big ol' monster in the parking lot, Ms. Daphne?" Agnello teased, and the smile fell right off her face.

"I've been driving pickup trucks since the day I got my license," she told him flatly and he smirked, not ready to let it go.

"Forgive me, Ms. Daphne, but I'm having a hard time with this. The range aside, all other signs would point to you being a BMW lady. Or Mercedes. Or Audi. Or maybe even Maserati—something fancy."

"I used to love the look of a sleek little black car—still do sometimes," she said gamely, setting her empty bottle on the table and stepping off her stool. It was very nearly as tall as her. "Until an eighteen-wheeler ran Mama and me off the road in a Z8.

"Now, in a truck I might have stood a chance, but flip a tiny open-top car a couple times down a steep embankment and see what's left over. They had to *cut* me out of that car." She dug through her small bag for keys. "I was in the hospital for months." She slapped her right leg. "Pins and rods everywhere, my friend, and months of rehab. I can tell you it's going to rain six weeks before any meteorologist."

Agnello paled.

"I was twelve when it happened, and it screwed up my growth plates something wicked." She looked a bit rueful and her shoulders lifted in a small shrug. "I've been this size ever since, though I probably should have grown another eight inches if my mother's height is any indication. So..." Her face brightened. "Big, nasty trucks it is. Besides—" she dropped her voice conspiratorially, "a gun rack on a BMW would be completely ridiculous."

Both men snorted at the visual and, leaning over the table, she shook Agnello's hand and then Marston's. She leaned to her right and pressed a kiss to Tyler's cheek while the other two hooted and hollered about how much trouble he would be in with Generis.

I got a nod from her. A tightening of her face. "Jack." She was already putting distance between us. "Lovely to see you again. I hope you weren't offended that I decided not to wear the coffee this time."

Fuck me, was that snark?

Then she was gone, and I heard the bark of her truck starting up when someone else walked through the door.

"Fuck off," I said preemptively, without even looking in Tyler's direction. I could feel his big, fat Cheshire grin, and I didn't like it. He just couldn't leave me alone.

I excused myself not long after. I didn't like leaving guns in my truck, locked or not, even though security at the little bar was surprisingly good and the parking lot had cameras at every conceivable angle. It was probably due to the fact an ex-cop owned the joint.

Once a cop, always a cop.

I'd feel better once I got home and put everything away, I told myself.

But I didn't.

It wasn't all that late, so I cleaned and oiled everything and put the pieces away in their designated cabinet. Then I sat on the sofa in the living room with a single lamp on, a glass of water in my hand while I tried to decide why I felt so ... something. Out of sorts. Like things were all jumbled up inside and I couldn't quite get them straightened out.

The answers didn't present themselves and since I knew sleep was a long way off, I set the glass on the kitchen counter and went down to the basement to spend some time with my weight bench. When nothing else worked, physical exertion, exhaustion, sweating—those were the things that helped to clear my head.

I'd been clearing my head a lot the last couple years, choosing exercise over the more destructive habits that would have been easier and more enjoyable to pick up. It would have been too easy to fall straight to the bottom of a liquor bottle and since my dad was a demonstrated alcoholic, that was not an option. It was an area of resolve I wasn't eager to test, feeling I already walked a fine line in that regard anyway.

After forty exhausting minutes, I racked the weights and hit the floor, the rubber mat cushioning hips and elbows, knees and palms as I moved from sit-ups to push-ups. And though I was sweating profusely and my muscles were screaming at me to take a break, I was nowhere near ready to close my eyes and drift into the land halfway between sleep and waking. Tash was waiting for me there, ready to tease and taunt, always moving just beyond my reach.

It was nearly midnight by the time I cleaned up the space, tossing a towel around my shoulders and climbing the stairs back into the main part of the house. It was cooler in the basement and heat bloomed to the surface of my skin as I walked into the much warmer kitchen to pull glass after glass of water from the faucet.

It was properly late and I should have been tired, especially after a full day of work and the evening's activities with that exhausting woman. She ate up all my energy. It took everything I had to just keep her at an arm's length, and doing that was mentally exhausting.

I hated that she had shown up with no warning, giving me no time to prepare or to brace myself for her covert glances, or the fact she acted as if I had a polarizing force field around me. At all times she gave me plenty of distance, which made me feel a little like a leper, because *I* was the one who was supposed to be keeping her at a distance.

She was supposed to know that.

Then she'd kissed Tyler on the cheek and I'd been furious with myself for the flare of anger that stabbed me in the gut, because she didn't want Tyler. Did she? He and Generis were having a baby any minute now and he had nothing but eyes for his woman, so he couldn't be a threat. But my physical reaction to that kiss told me that my subconscious had something else to say about that assessment: I was fucking jealous.

Irritated, I stomped up the main stairs and tossed the sweat-soaked towel down the laundry chute. My body was tired but my brain rushed ahead, the endorphin rush from working out manifesting itself in uncomfortable thoughts and desires I didn't have the luxury of entertaining.

Showering did nothing to calm me down and in an angry huff I tore the bedroom apart, tossing clean laundry into the closet and into dresser drawers before pushing all the furniture to the center of the room.

Grabbing my painting supplies from the basement ledge, I poured the same dark paint I'd used in the living room into the tray and dipped in a roller.

There was something about physical labor that soothed me and allowed me to turn off my brain. I needed that escape, which was what all of my renovation or repair attempts on my home had ever been. It was why I so often found myself at Tyler's place, looking for something to repair, just to keep my hands busy and my brain engaged in something other than unproductive, self-destructive thoughts.

The only thing that kept me from putting on loud, angry music was that it was after one in the morning and I was fairly sure my house wasn't soundproof. The neighbors weren't all that close, but sound carried in our quiet little neighborhood, the only late-night sounds usually the barking of a dog or the hooting of an owl.

Metallica would probably have been a lot less welcome.

Since the room wasn't all that big, I had the entire thing done in an hour and, still wired and unable to sleep, I went downstairs to do a small load of laundry. It was a blessing and a curse that I kept the house pretty neat most of the time, so there wasn't a lot to distract myself with even when I really needed it.

Finally, nearing four in the morning, my room was freshly painted and I passed out on the too-small living room sofa. I slept for two hours, half an hour longer than I was supposed to, finally pulling myself from the cushions to make coffee and toss a bagel down my throat before suiting up for work. I should have been exhausted, but I felt weirdly energized and though no one would accuse me of being Mary Sunshine, I was to work on time with a travel cup of coffee in hand.

"Thompson." My radio crackled and I perked up at the sound of Tyler's voice. "Time to run another catch-and-release."

I grinned. Inevitably someone mistakenly turned into our parking lot at least twice a day, and went through the process of a stern warning from both the guard shack officers and myself before being released. It was probably telling that we had a designated loop designed specifically to shunt wrong turns back out and on their way.

After talking with the frazzled woman, checking her license and giving her my standard warning, I released the gate and backed my SUV into the small access drive to allow her to pass.

I couldn't help but remember Daphne sitting there in the hot morning sun and I had to wipe the stupid smile off my face as I thought of her tangled hair and red cheeks as she sat, soaked in iced coffee in that big, ridiculous truck of hers.

What was it about her?

By the end of the workday I was no closer to an answer than I'd been that morning, and I drove home to start dinner and mow the lawn. My life was dull and routine, the same old patterns between home and work. Though there was a certain familiarity to it, there was a growing discomfort lodged somewhere in the back of my mind: *This is your whole life, and this is how you'll spend the rest of it.*

I made an angry noise, shoving the thought into a box in the back of my mind and hurrying out to the back shed to start the lawn mower.

The weekend came around again and, predictably, I was awake by 5:30 Saturday morning, with no idea how I was going to fill the day. It was a scourge, this thing other people called free time: empty hours I had to fill up with things like work and errands, working out or watching Sports Center.

More than once I'd considered getting a dog, since I didn't have kids to fill my evenings with arguments and bath time, bedtime stories and endless glasses of water or milk.

After a workout and breakfast, I completed my typical Saturday tasks: vacuum the house, clean the kitchen, change the bedsheets and swap out the towels, tossing everything in the washing machine.

By noon I was ready to climb the freshly painted walls, and I grabbed my keys. Grocery shopping would fill another hour or two and I'd do a little cooking for the coming week, just enough to keep something prepared on hand.

By four I was ready to go out of my mind. The house was clean, my belly was full, and the fridge was stocked for the next week.

There was nothing on but tennis, and I fucking hated tennis, so I grabbed my keys again and drove into Baltimore, turning down one familiar street after another until a faded sign came into view. I pulled into the small lot and parked.

The brick building sat at the corner of two streets, neon lights in each of the small, high windows. The smell of cigarette smoke seeped through the brick and I shuddered a little when I remembered walking the block as a kid. Mom had always sent me to fetch Pop from the corner bar. More often than not it was a fool's errand, and usually I returned home unsuccessful.

As I got older, Mom stopped sending me and I made the trip less and less. Her face grew sadder and harder and when she left, I stopped trying to fetch Pop at all. He'd come home when he was good and ready, and most mornings I tiptoed around the house as I got ready for school while he snored like a buzzsaw on the sofa in the front room.

Throwing the door open, I peered inside with some trepidation. Yup, the old crew was still here. It was a miracle the drink hadn't already taken more of them, their numbers reduced by a few since my childhood. These men and two rough old women were the hardened alcoholics, the ones who'd cheated death only because they'd been drinking in such excess, and for so long, that they'd probably pickled all of their internal organs.

Pop looked like shit.

Let me rephrase that: He looked shittier than usual, which was really saying something, since he clearly could no longer be bothered to engage in normal human activities like regularly showering, shaving, or getting a decent haircut.

When I was younger Pop had been a big man, and that wasn't just a matter of perspective. Mom always said I took after him, which I'd never taken as a compliment, but it was plain that I'd taken after him physically: the same wide shoulders, the same height, the same dark hair.

Over the years, Pop had begun to shrink. If I really had to pinpoint when it began to happen, I think it was after Mom left.

He'd hardly seen fit to come home when she *was* there, and once she left he had no more reason. There was nothing left to hold him.

Since then, his shoulders had folded inward. He'd developed a stoop, his thinning hair reaching nearly to his shoulders, his thick beard doing little to distract from the gauntness of his face. He'd been a dead man walking for the last thirty years, doomed to suffering the physical ravages of the drink he prized above relationships with actual people. He was only sixty-five now, but the hunch of his shoulders and gaunt frame made him look solidly twenty years older.

"Been a while since the little woman sent you to fetch me home," he barked, a sound something like an awful laugh, no humor or joy in it. But he was right about one thing: I hadn't been out to see him in a very, very long time.

"Hi, Pop." I didn't answer the question hanging in the air, and one of his compatriots quietly vacated the barstool next to him so that I could slide in. They all knew me around here, and had since I was ten, when we'd moved to this neighborhood.

Truthfully, I didn't know what it was that had pulled me here this afternoon. Possibly the need to feel close to another human being for a moment; to feel like I had something in the way of family. Pop was my only family, Mom long since having disappeared from both our lives without a trace, and no sisters or brothers to help keep me anchored to "home," a place with very few happy memories.

Pop wasn't a big conversationalist, but he seesawed between asking about my work and Tash, to asking how my mother was doing and whether I'd done well on my big chemistry test. He'd been conducting conversations like this for a while and I'd always chalked it up to the fact he was never anything but blitzed. But something clicked when he asked me for the third time when Tash and I planned to pump out a couple rugrats.

"Natasha left, Pop," I reminded him gently, and his eyes clouded over briefly. He took another long swig from his warming glass of beer before nodding. "That's right, you told me that. Sometimes I forget these things."

All the time. Lately you forget these things all the time.

“What’s wrong with you—big, strong guy—that makes a woman walk away?” He eyed me squarely and I felt something shrivel inside. He should know a few things about that, and I’d been asking myself that same question for a long time, though I wasn’t sure I wanted to know the answer. If I had an answer, it was something I would have to fix. And from the outside, that would make me no better than him.

“Don’t know, just exactly,” I admitted, palming the glass of beer the bartender slid in front of me with a sympathetic look. “Guess I was too boring.”

“Hmph.” Pop made a humming noise in the back of his throat. “Must be shit in bed.”

The bartender snorted and I shook my head. There was no sense in setting him straight on that one, even though I was pretty sure he was wrong. Just a little room for doubt.

“Yup. A problem, that one. Told you not to marry her.” He had a finger in my face. “Knew she was no good—too young and too good-looking for you. Too wild, and you’re not. You’re settled, like you always been.”

Was I, though? He said it like it was a bad thing.

If he’d told me not to marry her, he’d been using his inside voice. He was so committed to his drink that he hadn't even bothered to attend the wedding. If memory served, he’d managed to drop by a couple weeks after we returned from the honeymoon, a box in his hands. It was filled with mismatched dishes, like he’d gone through his kitchen cupboards and piled in whatever he could find.

Natasha hadn’t bothered with politeness. Meeting him for the second time, accepting the ramshackle box from his shaky hands, she’d barely hidden her disdain for the man or the gift. When he left she’d walked it out to the garage to shove into a corner, instructing me to “get rid of it” whenever I got the chance. She hadn’t even bothered to look through it.

“Runner,” he said, seemingly to no one, and the bartender raised an eyebrow at me. “Just like your mother.”

It took a lot of restraint not to respond with something to the effect that he’d pushed Mom away. And while he may not have remembered the details all that clearly, I sure did. I remembered coming home from school to rake leaves and mow the lawn, take out the trash and do the dishes, since Pop couldn't be bothered to be the man of our house.

I well remembered the paper route I'd maintained long after most of my friends had given it up, just to help keep some groceries on the table.

I'd kept myself so busy that I hadn't had time to wonder why she'd left me behind, too.

Even before graduating high school, I'd enlisted. It was just Pop and me by then, and I couldn't wait to be free of him. I was ready to get out, to leave, to live my life free of the responsibilities brought about caring for one's irresponsible, grown parent.

We sat quietly for a while, each sipping on our respective drinks and when I hit the bottom of my glass, I drew a finger across my neck when the bartender lifted an eyebrow. I had never liked the cheap beers they kept on tap in this particular establishment, and I asked instead for a glass of water.

Pop scoffed. "You chickening out, son?"

I opted not to tell him about the inordinate amount of drinking I'd done, with friends and without, the past couple of weeks. It would have been like admitting defeat and it was something he'd always watched me for, waiting to see when I'd follow in his footsteps. It was like a badge of pride with him, just waiting to see if his genetics were strong enough; if I'd one day tip over the edge and never resurface.

With time I had come to understand it was because he was not well. He didn't have a normal set of expectations for me, because he didn't know how to be a father.

"She's finally filed for divorce," I said, kind of to no one, and I could see Pop's craggy brow rise in my peripheral vision.

"'Bout time she let you get on with your life, I s'pose."

"Not sure I know how to do that," I admitted, a flash of honesty breaking through and irritating me. I was not here for a heart-to-heart.

"Eh." He grabbed for the bowl of peanuts the bartender had put out on the counter. "You'll figure it out. You always were a smart kid, and you got your head on straight. You got a good job and a nice place—that's all a man needs. Can't depend on women."

I didn't want to appear disagreeable, so I didn't say anything, but I was pretty sure my life as it was wasn't exactly as fulfilling as the picture he had in his head. As far as he was concerned, I was regimented and orderly, and because of that I had my life together. What more could a man want than a steady nine-to-five and his own porch to sit on and drink beer?

By late afternoon I convinced him to let me take him home, which was saying something, since he usually closed down the bar. But he climbed unsteadily into my truck and we drove the few blocks back to the house I'd grown up in: the one I hadn't gone back to since I'd left at eighteen. The few times we'd seen one another, we'd almost always met up at the bar.

The sight of the little brick building was almost enough to break my heart, the fascia rotting and falling away from the house, the brick dirty. The living room window had a hole in it, stuffed with plastic bags and I braced myself for what the inside must look like as I pulled into the narrow drive and followed him in through the side door.

It was worse than I could have expected: Dirty dishes filled the sink, stagnant water sitting in those at the bottom, the counters stacked high with mail and newspapers.

There were parts all over the kitchen floor, various pieces from old engines, a couple disassembled clocks, a few bicycle gears and some gardening equipment. It was a junkyard, stacked high and random, so that there was just a small path through the kitchen and into the living room.

"No wonder you don't want to spend time here," I said, the words out before I could stop them. I was still trying to reconcile what I was seeing with the clean, orderly home my mother had kept when I was a kid. It would have killed her to see the place this way.

"No reason to be here much." He shrugged, shuffling through the mound of stuff and into the living room where the dusty curtains obscured most of the daylight. But more than that—light, and the very air—was obscured by stacks and stacks of books, records and random piles of paper that threatened to spill over at the slightest breeze.

"Where'd you get all this shit, Pop?" I tried to keep my voice natural but the panic was clawing its way up my windpipe and threatening to choke me. I'd had a bad experience in a foxhole in Syria and ever since I'd called my discomfort in tight spaces claustrophobia.

The truth of the matter was far more complicated than claustrophobia, but calling it a reaction based in PTSD would be admitting there was a problem I needed to fix. I much preferred the head games I played with myself: semantics and shit.

Pop shrugged, shuffling his way to the recliner I knew was in the corner, but it was completely hidden by a towering wall of books.

Holy shit, he's going to die in here.

I ran a hand over my mouth as I surveyed the disaster, completely unwilling to investigate further. I had a feeling if I stepped around one of the piles and into the narrow hallway leading to the two bedrooms, I'd find the hallway filled with crap and the bedrooms overrun.

"You hungry?" I asked him finally, and a grunt came from behind the stack of books. "I'll go see if I can fix something," I said, hardly eager to walk back into the kitchen but needing to distract myself with something—anything.

I heard a TV flick on, though I couldn't imagine where he'd hidden it in the piles of stuff, and I picked my way back into the kitchen and surveyed the space with what I knew was a horrified expression on my face.

Starting with the sink, I ran the hottest water I could stand, washing one dish and drying it with a dish towel, putting it away in a cabinet and then starting with the next dish. I didn't have the luxury of a drain basket or the counter space to stack them up or to air dry them.

Before I could get to the refrigerator I needed to clear some floor space, so I walked piece after piece out to the small shed in the back and tried to put things into some kind of order out there. That was easier said than done, as he'd obviously started hoarding in the shed itself.

It was dark by the time I had the last piece cleared from the floor and I swept quickly, shaking my head at what must have been years of accumulated dirt and grease.

The paper stacks were next. I filled his recycling bin and box after box with newspapers and old, useless mail, but after an hour and a half of straight clearing, the sink was empty, the floor was a floor again, and there was actual counter space in the kitchen.

Opening the refrigerator door, I was not prepared for the sight or smell that greeted me. While the fridge appeared to be largely functional, the food that resided within was no longer identifiable. There were various dishes of half-eaten meals shoved into the shelves, covered by impressive mats of mold. The food had been in there so long, even the stick of butter in the tiny door compartment of the fridge had a fuzzy blue rug over it.

Swinging the door closed, I snapped my eyes shut and swallowed down the urge to vomit. If the food in here was this bad, what was he actually eating?

The pantry offered little more help, filled to overflowing with expired cans and boxes, spiderwebs and rat shit. And the rat shit did it–it was what broke through my disbelief and made me bend over to brace myself on my knees, breathing in through my nose and out through my mouth as I tried not to let disbelief turn into raging f-bombs. This was far more than a man just giving up. Something here was truly, genuinely wrong.

"You okay in there, Pop?" I called finally, half convinced the stack of books had swallowed him up while I'd been working in the kitchen.

"What's taking so long in there?" he grumbled.

"I'm just going to run down to the corner and grab a couple things for dinner," I called back. "I couldn't find much here."

"Yeah, yeah. Pick up some beer while you're there." He sounded tired and irritated, which was the way he always sounded.

The summer evening air was dense and heavy, like a wet blanket that slapped you in the face the instant you opened the door. Maryland had decided to grace us with yet another swampy summer, the cicadas clacking busily in the trees while the neighborhood's older women sat on their front stoops fanning themselves, their husbands wearing thin tank tops and chugging icy beers as quickly as they could get them down.

Living on the outskirts of Little Italy had its perks, one of them being the innumerable and insufferable old Italian housewives who knew everyone's business and who belonged to which house. They'd operated as the Neighborhood Watch system for as long as I could remember, and while people didn't exactly leave their doors unlocked at night, most people were on a first-name basis with their neighbors and felt some kind of kinship with them.

A few of the older gentlemen grumbled begrudging greetings as I strolled down the sidewalk. I raised a hand to each, aware that it was unlikely many of them would recognize me as Jackie Thompson, the ten-year-old who'd ridden these streets on my bicycle and stuffed firecrackers into their trash bins. At the time my full name seemed to be "Jackie, quel piccolo dolore nel culo." But lucky for them, or maybe lucky for me, I outgrew my pain-in-the-ass phase quickly, because I had to grow up almost overnight when Pop finally let his bad habits swallow him whole. Otherwise, I'd have joined most of their sons in various business pursuits, some savory and others not.

I rolled into Sal's bodega to collect pasta and sauce, a loaf of bread, and whatever fruit could be salvaged. Since Pop's fridge warranted a full clean-out, I grabbed a carton of milk and some coffee, a loaf of sliced bread, hot dogs and buns, a tub of coleslaw, a jug of orange juice and a couple boxes of cereal. It took me two trips to get it all up to the counter, because I was the stubborn asshole who wouldn't use a basket.

As an afterthought, I grabbed a bottle of strong, pine-scented floor cleaner that I knew could cut the grease on an engine block.

"Jackie." Sal smiled. "You got old."

Like he could talk. He was no longer the wiry, hairy little Sicilian I remembered from my younger days. Now he was operating with a pot belly and his hair had migrated south, the curly, thinning hair on his head shot through with thick strands of silver. There was an ungodly amount of black and silver chest hair poking out of the top of his polyester button-down, the ever-present St. Agatha hanging from a thick gold chain on his neck.

If there were things about the neighborhood that were a permanent fixture, Sal and his saint were one of them.

"You back home?" He lifted one hairy eyebrow, a loaded question in just three words. He was masterful that way, able to condense heavy meanings into tiny bites.

"Just looking in on Pop," I answered, piling the last of the items in my arms onto the small counter space and he punched in numbers almost without looking at what I'd dumped there.

"Better bring a case," he suggested, and I rolled my eyes. The last thing I wanted to do was toss fuel on Pop's problem, but he was probably right. If I wanted to get anything else done in that horrifying house, I'd need to placate Pop with the one thing he'd requested, or I'd hear about it until I drove away. The man had Olympic-level nagging abilities.

"Fine." I sighed, trudging the short distance to the back of the store and grabbing a case of the cheap stuff. Sal nodded when I turned, which told me I'd made the right selection, and I added it to the pile.

Reaching behind the counter to grab two heavy reusable bags, Sal loaded them up while I fished in my pocket for my wallet.

"Wife?" he asked, not meeting my eyes as he loaded things, and I took in the thin gold band on his left hand as his eyes took in the black one on my thick ring finger.

"Wrong one, but not for much longer," I answered somewhat ruefully and he pursed his lips, nodding thoughtfully before swiping my card and handing me a pack of the cigarettes I'd always bought from him before leaving for the Army. I couldn't believe he still remembered.

"On me," he said with a small smile before I could tell him I'd stopped smoking years earlier. "I do my best thinking at night, out in the back yard at my little table with a glass of wine and a smoke. You make sure the rest of the house is asleep first so they don't interrupt you—more relaxing that way." He gestured with fingers and thumb pressed together, rolling his hand toward me in circular motions from his chest. The gesture took the place of the things he didn't know how to put into words: feelings no man would ever be caught dead talking about, because we didn't discuss that shit. It had to do with families and women and hopes and dreams, things language couldn't hope to contain or express.

Despite myself, a rare grin spread across my face. "Thanks, Sal." I held a hand over the counter to shake his and he grabbed it with one meaty paw, reaching over the space to pull me into a half-hug, slapping my back heartily. "Don't you wait another twenty years, Jackie; I'll be dead. You come check on your Pop more often so I can keep an eye on you." He winked. "Maybe introduce you to my baby girl—back home with her Ma and me these days." He lapsed into his mother tongue and whatever vicious Sicilian curse came out of his mouth was delivered with passion, venom spewed in the direction of what was probably a no-good son-in-law.

I did my best to hide a shudder. I remembered Chiara all too well, and the kindest word that came to mind was swarthy. It didn't matter that she had a heart of gold, because she looked like her father, and I sure as hell wasn't interested in cuddling up to that.

The bell over the door made a strangled gurgle as I swung it open, hoisting the two bags up onto my shoulder and carrying the case of piss water in my other hand. I wouldn't be caught dead drinking the stuff, but I supposed for Pop it was more about habit than it was about taste, or he might have been more discerning.

Nodding toward the same porches as I made my way back up the street, I relived the hundreds of times I'd made this short trip as a boy. The same men sitting out on their front stoops, drinking beer and swatting at bugs with a rolled up newspaper. TV noise drifting out into the evening, the noise hardly filtered by screen doors. Kids playing and hollering somewhere, though it was fully dark and the street lights were on. It made me feel something that wasn't quite nostalgia. It was a desire to go back, yes, but only to rewind just far enough to unmake a few of the choices that had changed my life forever in very hard ways.

"Took you so long?" Pop hollered from his hiding place in the living room when he heard the screen door thwack against the frame.

"Got to talking with Sal," I explained loudly, so that my voice would carry through all the *stuff* blocking the path. I dropped the case of beer down on the counter and cracked one open, finding a few dusty beer glasses in one of the cabinets and rinsing one out before filling it with the weak liquid.

"Good man," Pop said affirmatively as I wound through the maze of crap in the living room to hand him the glass and he grunted appreciatively as he took it from my hands. "Comes around sometimes just to make sure I ain't quit breathin'. Always brings me something."

"He's a good guy," I agreed, turning carefully so as not to knock over any of the stacks and moving back toward the kitchen. "Hot dogs?" I called back, figuring it was one of the fastest options, and Pop made a noise that I took for a yes.

Slicing open the package and dumping the dogs into a skillet, I set the burner on low and got to work clearing the contents of the fridge into four separate trash bags. It was odious work, smelly and dirty, and more than once I had to bite back the urge to dry heave. But finally, the fridge cleared and the bags out in bins, I washed my hands and assembled the hot dogs on a plate, adding a large dollop of coleslaw before carrying it out to him. I'd have suggested eating at the table, but the alcove between the kitchen and living room, where the dining table used to sit in a bank of windows, appeared to have been swallowed whole by a pile of boxes. Someone's attempt at organization, perhaps.

I forced down a single hot dog, mostly because I needed the energy to finish cleaning up, but my appetite had been killed by the cleaning process.

Then I was back to it, a bowl of hot, soapy water and a sponge in hand, doing my best to clean out a refrigerator that probably hadn't been wiped down since Ma left. It was going to take more than one box of baking soda to freshen up this monster.

By the time I finished cleaning out the disgusting fridge and I'd loaded in the things I'd hauled up the street from Sal's, I was ready for one of those weak beers myself. So I cracked the top open, only to hear Pop snort from the other room. I knew that meant he was ready for a refill and I took another can to him, standing in the tiny walkway amongst the piles of crap while he poured it into his glass.

"What happened here, Pop?" I tried to keep my voice light so that it didn't sound like I was leveling any accusations. Pop was a champion at avoidance, and when he felt criticized he locked up tighter than a sub ready to dive.

Looking around, I watched a weird recognition flit through Pop's eyes, like he'd lived with the mess for so long that he'd forgotten how to see it. It had become such a part of him and his every day that it no longer bothered him, if it ever had.

"Dunno," he said finally, pushing thin, dirty hair over his ear and dropping his eyes to his beer as he took a chug. And then, "Suppose I let things get a bit worse after you left."

My hackles raised a little, in case that was a dig, like it had been my job to stay and look after someone who'd been an adult for longer than I'd been alive. "A bit?" I couldn't keep the words in as I looked around at the leaning towers. This was giving me anxiety. "Pop ... seriously. You can't live like this."

"Don't bother me none." He leaned over to set his plate on yet another precarious stack of books. "I'm not here that much anyway."

"I don't think it matters that you're not here that much, Pop. This isn't safe, the way it is. You shouldn't be in this at all. If anyone else knew about this, I don't think you'd be allowed to stay here."

He didn't say anything and he didn't meet my eyes.

I sighed, leaning over to grab the plate from the top of a stack of books. The air was stifling, incapable of moving around the incredible mass of stuff.

"Where are you sleeping?" I asked finally, fearful of the answer. I hadn't had the balls to venture down the narrow hallway to investigate the state of the bedrooms firsthand. The simple answer was that I feared what I might find.

There was an answering creak from the chair as he leaned back, engaging a hand lever to pop out a footrest.

Oh hell, no.

"Pop." My voice was hoarse. "I'm ... no. You can't. This isn't at all suitable."

He shrugged slightly, obviously not bothered by the situation. "Nothing I can do about it, really."

"Do you *want* anything done about it?"

"Eh." He shrugged again. "Wouldn't hurt my feelings if the place was cleaned up, but I don't know how to do it." His hand shook as he wiped it across his mouth.

The wheels in my brain spun as I tried desperately to formulate a plan. I knew there was no way I could handle the whole house on my own and I wasn't sure that I trusted him to keep things that way once it had been put in order.

"Well, we'll figure it out." Guilt, heavy and stifling, was crowding my windpipe. I should have been checking in on him regularly. I should have been bringing him groceries and hauling him out of the bar, helping to add more structure to his life—something he clearly needed.

"You can't stay here, Pop. Grab what you need, because you're coming home with me."

He groused a little, muttering under his breath about disrespectful children and being an adult, and I fixed him with the hairy eyeball I'd inherited from my mother, which seemed fairly effective. He collapsed the chair and carefully pushed himself out of it, following me back through the trail of stuff to move down the hallway and I could hear shuffling and rustling in one of the rooms.

I heaved a deep breath, suddenly very aware of the cigarettes Sal had given to me, shoved into my back pocket. I wondered if they'd help me to quell the anxiety, or if they'd just set the house on fire. Given the current state, I wasn't sure that would be a bad thing.

That night I set up Pop in my guest room. He'd been inside my house before, but never upstairs, and his expression was appreciative as he took in the simple room, the large bed and fresh linens.

"Bathroom in the hallway." I gestured behind us. "Towels in the linen closet behind the door, and you can use whatever you need."

Nodding, he set down his small bag and sank down onto the bed. He was still shaky and I couldn't decide whether it was the drinking or if there was a larger neurological problem in play. It was something I hadn't noticed as much while he was sitting.

The house felt different that night, like a living, breathing creature and I was aware of every creak and groan.

I hadn't slept under the same roof as my father for over twenty years and it was strange to feel I'd gone back in time, forced into adulthood during my childhood, making sure Pop had clean laundry and there was food in the fridge.

When I finally fell asleep, the dreams that came for me were disjointed and disturbing, and even as I slept I ached for peace as my subconscious churned through past and present and the things I feared were yet to come.

5

Daphne

I texted Tyler to thank him for inviting me to the boys' night out and when he responded, well over a week later, it was with a photo of an infant wrapped in a pink blanket. His daughter had finally made her way into the world and it explained the lengthy silence from a man who seemed otherwise incapable of shutting his mouth for more than two minutes at a time.

It was August by the time I took a moment to breathe. Bridal collections were a very small part of my business and my little office hummed with activity as everyone prepared for New York's Fashion Week. It required me to be in Manhattan for several weeks and I set up a recurring rideshare for Blair, so she could still get to and from work while she finished her summer job.

I'd missed the energy of NYC, a place that had always felt just as much like home as did the beaches and small fishing boats of my tiny hometown. But here I was largely anonymous, free to blend in with the crowd as I crossed streets at a brisk pace or rushed to hail a taxi.

The place I now owned along the park was my little oasis, and though I spent long days in the office, the few hours I had to myself each night were spent with takeout, a good glass or two of wine, sitting in a chair at the bank of windows overlooking one of my favorite parks in the world. During those hours I contemplated what life would have been like without Hunter. I contemplated what it would have been to raise Blair entirely on my own, which was very nearly how things had gone anyway. And I wondered if I'd just been patient, if I'd have met someone better.

Kind.

Faithful.

One thing was for sure, I thought as I swirled the wine around my glass that Wednesday evening and admired the deep garnet color in the low light of the single lamp burning: I was done and finished with marriage. The institution had provided me with nothing but heartache and now, surely, hefty legal bills. Hunter would not be the sort to go quietly, nor would he ever accept his responsibility in the demise of our marriage, even as he kept the extraneous live-in girlfriend.

I wondered briefly how long this one would survive his wandering eye. Perky boobs notwithstanding, the expiration date had been stamped on her forehead the instant she got on her knees, since Hunter's attention span was terribly short.

My phone buzzed with an incoming text and I held it up to read the preview, internally cursing the fool who would dare interrupt my quiet moments of reflection.

If I survive all these nighttime feedings, G might let me out for a night at some point in the near future. You ready for an evening with the guys? Jack won't admit it, but he likes it when you show up.

My lip curled derisively. What was Tyler's deal with trying to force me on Jack? It was plain to me that the man had less than zero interest in me and honestly, though it spurred me to keep the necessary grooming appointments, I had no interest in dipping my toes into those waters since I refused to be a charity case.

Tyler could just focus his matchmaking intentions elsewhere.

"Mom, why aren't you home yet?" Blair was irritated and considering she *knew* I was in New York again, and she knew why, I couldn't understand why she sounded so upset.

"Baby, you know I have shows this week. I'll be home next week and we can log some more practice driving hours."

Wait. What was she doing at home?

"It's okay, Dad's been putting in long stretches with me this weekend and I should be done after tomorrow. He's already signed me up with a driving school, so now I just need to log the instructor hours over breaks and I can go take my test."

I heard a record scratch somewhere, probably in my brain, but possibly somewhere in the outside world. "I'm sorry, babe ... what?"

"Yeah." She giggled. "Cassandra's been driving him a little crazy lately, so he's been home the last few weekends. We've had some fun together. Like movies and stuff."

"You've been coming home the last few weekends?"

I had driven her to MIT myself and settled her into her dorm only weeks earlier.

"Yeah, Mom. I told you that—remember?"

I did not.

"Dad has been flying me home so I could practice driving, since you were busy in New York. And while I've been here I've gotten to spend some time with Jake."

Jake was a sweet kid, but I couldn't begin to understand what Blair saw in him. I blamed her father for that. Due to missing a solid male role model in her life, she had no idea what to look for in men.

Then again, I'd had a solid male role model in my life and look what I'd chosen.

Something flared inside that felt like anger, because now that I'd told Hunter we were over, he was tired of Cassandra.

Now he wanted to come home on the weekends.

Now he wanted to spend time with the daughter he'd interacted with only intermittently for years. Thank God she didn't remember that, but to her he was still the fun parent.

"Huh," I said, since it was the nicest thing I could say.

What I didn't say was that he'd better be gone by the time I got home, and I was ready for him to *stay* gone. Now that I'd made a decision, after twenty-something years of waffling and wavering, I was done with a capital D.

Ava sat through a two hour conversation with me that night, listening to me whine about how there was nothing waiting for me on the other side of divorce and it was still more enticing than remaining married to a chronic philanderer.

I was one hundred percent jealous of Ava. I wanted a man to look at me the way Lincoln looked at his wife: like she was a goddess.

Like she was edible.

Like he couldn't believe his good fortune.

Because I knew without a doubt that Hunter had never looked at me that way.

Ava made a weird comment, something that clued me in that Tyler had exchanged numbers with her since her reference had something to do with his sweet little baby girl.

"Does Lincoln know other men text you?" I asked, not exactly teasing.

"Drives him wild with jealousy. He's such a caveman." She laughed her low, husky laugh. "But darling, I am too old and settled in my ways and deep down he knows that: His heart is safe with me. I don't want to leave him for a little boy because I don't have the time, the patience, or the energy to train another man." She giggled. "Besides, I know how to use his jealousy against him. Poking the bear has some advantages."

I shivered a little, a reaction I couldn't decide was jealousy or revulsion. I didn't want to think about my friend's fulfilling sex life, though God knew she deserved one.

Instead, I wanted to bask in my jealousy for a moment.

I did know that not many people were truly happy. A very small percentage of married couples were violently in love with one another, but I'd always held onto hope.

I'd loved Hunter and I'd had my heart broken by him, but as the years dragged on I'd discovered that I could breathe just fine on my own. I didn't truly need him for much of anything and I blamed it on the way he'd broken things the first time: I had never loved or trusted him the same way again.

Loving someone with a violent passion and being loved that way in return was something I'd never experienced, and now I wanted a taste. Just one. Maybe I couldn't hold onto it forever but for once, before I was too old to do anything about it, I wanted to be an absolute fool over someone and I wanted him to be just as gone over me.

The phone rang again and I sighed, mentally bracing myself for another round.

"Mom." Blair's voice was sharp with irritation and I sighed. Her father was rubbing off on her in all the negative ways.

"I'm listening, honey."

"Dad wants to know when you're coming home."

"Put your father on, Blair."

There was a brief rustling, leading me to believe Hunter was sitting there, already listening in.

"Uh..." Hunter cleared his throat nervously. This was new for him. "Hi, Daph."

"Take me off speaker." I waited for a beat. Then, "You are no longer dictating the terms of our relationship." I started right in. I'd spent my marriage being the meek, accommodating wife and I'd had quite enough. I knew it would knock Hunter back a bit. "I'll be home next Tuesday and I expect you'll be gone. You're back in session, I believe?"

I knew very well that he was, since he'd gone back at the end of August–an entire month he'd spent with Cassandra in Europe, thank you Instagram and public accounts.

She was the idiot who hadn't made her accounts private.

"We can talk about it when you get home," he said, his voice smoother than I'd expected, even though I knew it took a lot to ruffle him.

"Nope." I popped the p. "We *have* talked about it and I've laid out the timeline for you. You've already made your decision and after three affairs that *I know about*, I've made mine. Blair is now legally an adult, meaning I don't need to stand up for you any longer, to her. I can clearly fend for myself, and now I'm going to."

There was a deep sigh on the other end of the line, the sound Hunter made when he thought I was being unreasonable. He held a doctorate in gaslighting.

Pulling the phone away from my ear, I hit the button to end the call and threw it down on the chair beside me. I'd come back to the office after the day's shows, to go over a few things and respond to requests for comments and interviews from the press, and suddenly the small space felt stifling.

It was late by the time I left, the sun having long since set. I knew I should get something to eat, as I was unlikely to cook once I got home, and I ducked into a restaurant. I'd been in a few times recently and the hostess recognized me, so she seated me quickly and I ordered a small salad, a piece of fish, and a good glass of wine. That was something I loved about New York, and something I missed when in Alabama or Maryland: the ability to step outside my door and have my choice of good restaurants only steps away.

My phone lit up with a message as I sipped at the wine, observing my fellow diners with a casual eye. That people rarely recognized me was a blessing, and New Yorkers were skilled in the art of allowing public figures respectful space.

The boys are getting together this weekend to help Jack for the day. Sounds like his dad's house is pretty bad; we're gonna help haul and clean and paint. Wanna come? G said she'll bring the baby and you can finally meet my girls.

Oh, Tyler. I shook my head. He was like the puppy who wouldn't stop humping your leg. He was a persistent friend, I had to give him that, and I wondered if he remained Jack's friend simply because Jack couldn't figure out how to shake him.

I tapped out a quick message relaying my regrets: I would be in New York until Tuesday morning, and I was surprised when he didn't immediately respond to ask me why. Tyler was nosier than any woman I'd ever known.

K, then maybe you can make it next weekend? The other two can't make it, but Generis's Ma is coming over, so I'm gonna go back to help more. Jack's pretty worried about his pop. Has him living at his place right now and he won't talk about it much, but I think the old man's going a little batty.

I responded quickly that I would show up the next weekend, if he'd text me the address. Then I put the phone face-down on the table and finished my meal.

I took my small staff out to dinner on Thursday night, after the conclusion of our show. Everyone, from my assistant to my PR director, the four seamstresses on staff and the guy who handled the books, the ordering, and generally kept the office tidy. He, I'd learned in the past few years, was just as essential to the office's operations as was Emily, my irritating but incredibly capable assistant.

Emily drove me bananas, but in a good way. Where I was flighty and disorganized, she was my label-maker-bearing counterpart, organized to a fault and nit-picky as hell. It was a good trait for a designer, though sometimes I had to talk her down, back into the bigger picture. Encourage her to breathe. Remind her there were some things she could let slide and the world would continue to spin.

It was tonight that I would announce my unofficial retirement to the staff, and I expected the very reaction I ended up with: gasps and heart clutching from the seamstresses.

A raised eyebrow from my PR director, who knew I'd been considering this for the past couple years, since Hunter had begun toying with politics. Balancing his career with my own had been exhausting and she knew I'd been going through a slow burnout.

Emily had been with me since the beginning, for fifteen years now, and was only slightly younger than me. We had agreed she would maintain the house name and would continue the day-to-day operations. She would be named the new head designer and I would collaborate with her from time to time, on special projects.

I was planning to phase out over the next six months, slowly, available to answer questions and give guidance, but I was stepping back. Emily had proven her skill time and time again, and over the last several years her designs had featured prominently in my shows. So over time, with her continued success, she would buy me out.

The week's show had been a great success, as it usually was, and I made sure to praise each and every person for their contribution to that success. I knew I couldn't have done it without each and every one of them, all of whom were devoted, loyal employees, and I did my best to address and soothe their concerns.

All of them would maintain their jobs and in the same capacity. The only difference was that they would see less of me—much less of me—and while I'd pop in time and again, the house would be mine in name only.

The truth of the matter was that I was having as close to a midlife crisis as anyone I knew. While I'd accomplished great things professionally, and in what was probably a very short period of time, my personal life was a disaster reminiscent of another famous designer who suffered a perpetual remarrying sickness. Last I'd checked, she was on Husband #3 and he'd been implicated in a bribery scheme. Didn't look like that one was going all that well either, so maybe I needed to count my blessings.

I needed to take some time to iron things out, away from the prying eyes of the press, and to figure out what I wanted from the rest of it. Because really, the only thing I'd done right in my personal life was to raise my daughter. I had nothing else to show for the last twenty years. Other than Blair, what I did have felt empty.

Clearly I was not hurting for money, and thanks to a great team of financial advisors, it was likely there was enough to make it through several more generations. So fortunately for me, I had the option to quit working and go find myself, whatever that might involve.

Hopefully it involved some travel.

Blair was going to be upset with me, I was sure, as I hadn't yet announced the full extent of my plans to her. She would feel like I was unmooring her; leaving her behind, when I'd be doing anything but.

The weekend was for me. I spent Saturday at my favorite spa, getting the works: facial, hair, nails, exfoliation, wax and self-tanner. It was just what I needed, a boost to my self-esteem and a great improvement in my appearance, and I floated home on a happy little cloud and ordered in, watching old black and white movies and sighing wistfully over strong male leads while I emptied a bottle of wine. Then I went to bed, where I may or may not have had a sweaty sex dream about a certain tall, dark, broody man who seemed determined to hate me.

Sunday morning I woke early, refreshed and excited. I had already planned to spend the day in several of my favorite museums and I ended it with a leisurely stroll through the park, the air already crisp with the promise of fall.

That night I ordered in again, curling up in front of a gas fire in soft pajamas, a book in my hand. For several moments I considered staying indefinitely.

I had a comfortable rhythm in the city.

I knew my way around and had my favorite places.

I had the means to live there very comfortably and I already owned real estate.

There was nothing to tie me to Maryland but some property, a dog, and the whims of my daughter.

My phone rang as I contemplated my options and I answered it quickly, without looking to see who was calling.

"Officer Guard Shack calling for a Ms. Daphne Marie Masters-Preston. See, Daph? I remembered the whole thing, you fancy lady!" He cleared his throat, slipping back into his mock-formal tone. "Is she available to accept the call?"

I rolled my eyes. "Tyler, you are certifiable." I could hear cooing in the background and my heart melted just a little at the thought of the sweet, muscle-bound man holding his tiny baby girl.

Inked men holding babies made my ovaries do funny things.

"Generis thinks it's hilarious you call me Guard Shack, by the way." He chuckled, and I remembered why it was so effortless to slip into conversation with him. "She says you'll keep all the boys in line. She's grateful to you for that, since it's been a big job for her."

There was a sharp exclamation in the background in strongly accented Spanish and I grinned. This Generis person must have been a strong woman if she wasn't intimidated by the woman Tyler kept trying to wedge into his group of friends.

"It's bad, Daph." Tyler launched right in, all humor gone from his voice. "Me and the boys helped the whole weekend when we went over to help Jack clean his dad's place. I've never seen a house in such a state. Jack had to rent trucks to get all the shit hauled away because it was too much to just put out on the curb."

I had a vague, fuzzy recollection that they were planning a work bee at Jack's childhood home the last time we'd talked.

"We had to send the old man down to the bar for the afternoon, just to get him out of our hair. He was hovering over us, upset we were throwing things away, and finally Jack just kicked him out. Told him we were doing this for his own good and we were gonna fix it up real nice so the state didn't take it away from him."

"Okay," I said slowly, folding the dust cover over my spot in the book and setting it down on the sofa. "So I enjoy our conversations, Tyler, you know I do ... but what is it you need me to contribute?"

"Well, I guess I'm calling to ask for help. I figure you've got all sorts of connections and people who know stuff. Jack's just starting to figure out his pop's gonna need a whole lot more help than any of us can give him and I was hoping you might have some ideas, and maybe some names to pass on."

I waited patiently, hoping Tyler would explain what kind of help he was looking for.

"So, Jack's pop ... he's been a heavy drinker his whole life. So that's a problem ... but now there's another one. Agnello was literally shoveling stuff out of the bathroom today and he found a couple pill bottles he took to Jack. So, uh ... I looked them up. And all three of them were ... hold on." There was a fumbling noise, making me think he had it written down somewhere. "A cholinesterase inhibitor." He stumbled over the clumsy syllables. "None of them were empty, the newest one refilled last year. It doesn't look like the old man's been keeping up with his meds."

"Uh-huh," I said, putting my phone on speaker and pulling up a browser window to read about the medication. "So..." I scrolled quickly through a description. “Often prescribed for mild-to-moderate Alzheimers or for dementia associated with Parkinson’s.”

Oh, that was bad.

“Yeah.” Another squeal in the background. “I’ve never seen Jack lose his shit before, Daph. But he lost his shit after his pop admitted he’s been on the drugs for a couple years now. It *is* Parkinson's.”

I wasn’t sure I wanted a full description of how Jack had broken down, and I didn’t want to imagine it for myself, either.

“He’s close to his dad?” I asked, my eyes squeezing shut as I tried to imagine what I’d do if I found a similar bottle in my parents’ house. Because I remembered what it looked like: the rows of bottles laid out on a high-top dresser while my Daddy’s father wasted away in the bed across the room.

“Don’t think so, and I think that’s why he took it so hard. His pop’s all he’s got left and he’s gotta be overwhelmed. Feels guilty, I suppose. He’s moved the old man in with him and he’s been taking care of him.” He went quiet for a moment. Then, “He’s exhausted, Daph.”

An unwelcome vision of the big man’s stricken face crowded into my roiling brain. I could imagine it clearly, painfully, irritated with myself that it made me feel something very uncomfortable for the man. Something I didn’t want to feel.

“He said his pop’s had tremors for a while now and he just figured it was the alcohol.”

“So, what do you need my help with?” I asked quietly. “Are you looking for a rehab facility? Some kind of in-patient care facility? A therapist or counselor?”

“Well...” Tyler cleared his throat uncomfortably. “I’m a real big Tide fan.” My ears perked up. “I did a little reading on you the day you showed up at the guard shack. You looked just a little familiar, and since I didn’t grab your plate or license, I asked Jack, because he’s the stickler. I knew he’d remember your name, since he always checks the licenses.

“Took me a bit to find an old picture of you at a game with your old man, and then I knew why you looked so familiar: I probably saw your face on TV for years, when you went to games with him."

Unless Tyler had been watching college football since he was a toddler, it seemed unlikely he'd seen me at many games.

"So you know about my dad," I said.

It wasn't *quite* public knowledge that Daddy had spiraled into terrible depression after a career-ending injury. He was thirty-eight at the time, already geriatric by football standards. But you know how men are, and he was no exception. He had anticipated several more years of professional football and hadn't planned for anything else, when just one vicious sack took it all away from him.

Mama nearly lost him to the bottle, and it had taken every ounce of her strength–and walking away for a time–to force him into rehab.

She'd thrown an awful lot of money at keeping things quiet.

"Yeah, a little ... I figure you got some powerful connections and know where to start looking, especially since he has a foundation that helps out folks with substance abuse."

"You're a smart man, Officer Davis. I had you pegged wrong, all goofy friendliness and jokes—jokes for days."

"You'll never meet a better man, Daph." Somehow I knew we were talking about Jack again. "Most loyal guy I've ever known. He'll give you the shirt right off his back. He saved me, you know ... and now I need to help save him. This is the best I can do."

That sounded like a story for another time, and I sighed heavily. "I'll make some calls, my friend. I don't know how much help I can be, and there's not much I can do if the man refuses help. But I can probably get some wheels rolling."

I spent some time that night on the phone with my parents, which wasn't unusual. I tried to call them once a week and they always acted like it was the highlight of their year. I'd learned early on to tell Daddy to put me on speaker so he and Mama could talk to me at the same time, or I'd just have the conversation all over again with her when he finally signed off.

Mama was a powerhouse: ruthlessly organized, obscenely well connected, and truly as subtle as a government operative when it was called for. When I explained the situation to her I knew I didn't have to ask for help, because she was already on it.

I didn't even have to say the word for Mama to know what I was talking about, because when I was young, Daddy's father had lived with us for a few years before passing away. I remembered the shakes, the confusion, the delusions and hallucinations with remarkable clarity for someone who had been just a child at the time.

Through it all, Mama had been stoic. She'd been the one to find caregivers, to take him to his appointments, and toward the end, she physically held my father up as he mourned the loss of his remaining parent. On the heels of his own recovery, it had wrecked him all over again, because Daddy had been extremely close to his father.

The next morning I went into the office to tie up a few loose ends, telling Emily we'd keep our regularly scheduled video meeting on Wednesday. But after that I was free, since my flight didn't leave until the next morning. So I headed back to my place to conduct research and, not surprisingly, Mama called me just after lunch with a list of names, numbers and referrals. She had always worked fast and I knew she'd blown things up at the foundation office to get things done quickly.

"So, baby girl," she drawled slowly and I closed my eyes for a second to fall into the richness of her southern accent. It was so at odds with her dark, Balkan beauty. "Tell me about this man."

That was Mama: quick as melting ice cream on a hot summer day.

"Nothin' to tell, Mama." I felt myself slipping back into the thick, honeyed accent I'd worked so hard to shed the first summer I'd come to New York. It was a tidal pull. "He's the father of a friend and he needs some help, end of story."

I knew that wasn't the man she meant. Not at all.

"Mmm." Mama was not convinced, and I heard ice cubes clink on the other end, undoubtedly her fifth glass of sweet iced tea today. "Not even the beginnin' of the story, sugar. I know that much. You know that wasn't the man I was askin' about, but you'll talk about him when you're ready."

There was a deep rumble in the background and I looked quickly at my watch. "Shouldn't Daddy be at practice right now?" I asked, surprised that he was still home, since it was the middle of the day on a Monday, and the house was several hours' drive from Tuscaloosa and his job.

"He took a couple days." More clinking cubes. "He hurt his back in the boudoir, if you know what I mean." Mama's voice was smug and I choked on a swallow. *Gross. My mother was having more sex than I was.*

"Mama!" I couldn't help it. There were things I did *not* need to know about my parents, and Daddy's sex-induced muscle pull was one of them.

She giggled, and I had to remember she'd only been nineteen when she had me. She wasn't even sixty yet and she'd kept herself in such great shape, she could pass as my much taller, only slightly older sister. So if I was going to start throwing rocks when it came to age-appropriate activities, I'd have to dodge a few of them myself.

"Sweetheart, you need to live a little." She had me there. "When's the last time you and Hunter got away to do something special, just the two of you?"

Oh, heaven help me.

The whole sordid tale poured right out of my mouth, and for once my mother was rendered completely silent. Utterly speechless. It was a real feat.

"So," I concluded neatly, "I've told him that I'll file during his break in the spring, which gives him time to deal with the public relations aspect and to handle whatever he has going on with the toddler he's been living with."

"Oh, darling." My mother's voice was full of sorrow. "I knew he was no good, but I had no idea it was all this bad. Oh, baby. Come home. Come spend some time with your father and me while you get all this sorted out. We'll fatten you up a little and you can spend some time on the beach ... and bring our girl, Ava. We can spend some time just doing girl things. After all, Blair isn't home again until Thanksgiving, right?"

I told her about Hunter flying Blair back home the last few weekends, and about my plans to sell the palace in Maryland. I'd decided that very recently.

Both tidbits were met with as much quiet as my mother could manage, especially once I assured her I needed absolutely no "fattening up."

She was wisely biting her tongue.

It took everything in me not to talk about what was pulling at my heart since talking with Tyler, because I kept hearing "He's overwhelmed," in my head. It was something I well understood, and with each passing minute I was dedicating myself more and more to the rehabilitation of a man I didn't know in order to save the man I wanted to know.

I needed a project, and this was a good one. It was a charitable endeavor that would save the life of one man with some luck, and maybe even the sanity of his really stupid-gorgeous son.

I *certainly* didn't think about the way he'd looked at me that night at the gun range, or the way he'd watched me when we went for drinks, even though he'd looked grumpy every time he caught me looking at him. He'd been wary and guarded with me—fearful, even. And I had no idea what to do with that. I had no idea what it meant. Maybe just that I was a pariah, untouchable and leprous, because God knew I'd been that for the last twenty years.

6

Jack

I took a few days off from work to get Pop in to see the doctor, the one listed on all his prescriptions. And though it shouldn't have surprised me, Pop had missed his last three appointments and the doctor was ... well, the guy was pissed. So apparently he cared, which was some small level of comfort. Someone was looking out for him, even when I'd failed.

Pop was mad, too. I mean, like a level I'd never seen, but right now I didn't care.

He was mad we'd cleaned the house without his input.

He was mad I'd moved him into my place and wouldn't let him leave.

He was especially mad that I was making him take his medicine every day, and I was watching his beer consumption like a hawk.

I didn't know what it was that made me suddenly latch onto him, and I really wasn't about to let it bother me. All I knew was that I felt responsible for this person, maybe because it gave me purpose, and I was going to do right by him even if it killed me.

I sent Pop out to the waiting room while I discussed the alcohol problem with the doc, and though I knew the doc wouldn't be surprised, I was disappointed by his reaction.

"I'm aware," was all he said. "There's typically more than one complication and if it's not emotional stress, the substance abuse is a definite stressor.

"Does he have somewhere safe to stay at present?"

I told him Pop was staying with me, at my house, and he nodded solemnly. “Good,” he said, making a quick notation on his tablet. “See to it he gets nutritious, regular meals. Chances are he’s starved of essential fatty acids and this will only lead to faster deterioration.”

I made a quick note to self to do some internet searches once I got home and got Pop tucked safely into bed for the night. Hopefully tonight he wouldn’t wake at three and start wandering.

I am so tired.

I briefly, seriously considered putting a padlock on the guest room door. It would keep him safe and it just might guarantee me a full night’s sleep.

The scariest part for me, lately, had been leaving for work each morning. Pop was out of his element at my place and I had no desire to drive him back into Baltimore each day to languish at his house or to sit at the bar. So most nights I came home to find him collapsed on the front porch after hours of wandering the neighborhood, oftentimes returned to the stoop by a kindly, well meaning neighbor who recognized his last name. He had a key that he couldn't seem to figure out how to use.

Most afternoons that meant I came home to find he’d killed the remainder of the beer in the fridge, and some days I thought that made the shakes a little better. It meant I was buying more each day, on my way home, only to placate him while I tried to figure out how to deal with it, finally deciding I needed to look into finding someone to babysit him while I was at work because having removed him from his familiar environment, now I could see how quickly he was spiraling.

I insisted he take his pills each morning, leaving them with a note for him and some kind of breakfast on the counter before I left. Sure I had a standard 9-5, but I also had personal fitness and sanity standards to maintain, so the days were long.

While I was out of the house before eight, I was also home before six, often with something in hand, because I didn’t know whether Pop was capable of feeding himself lunch. More often than not, I feared, he had filled up on beer all day and was famished by the time I got home.

It was exhausting. I'd started getting up earlier, to work out in the mornings since I couldn't count on free time at night.

Pop, it seemed, was a serious night owl. He didn't seem to sleep more than five hours a night at most, and while I could usually get out of the house before he was awake, he dogged me from the moment I got home until the moment I shut his door at night and wished him a good night's sleep. Because yeah, I'd established a rigid bedtime for my grown-ass father, just like he was a little kid. I had to, or I was going to lose my shit.

I asked myself that night, as I crawled into bed, if I'd have driven to the bar on a whim that afternoon, had I known what was waiting for me.

Yes. The answer was always a heavy, guilty yes. Despite the fact I had few childhood ties to the man who couldn't be bothered to raise me, caring for him was my duty as his son.

Yes, despite the fact he'd driven my mother away. I was his only family.

Yes, despite the fact I'd never been so tired in my life.

I still hoped for some kind of relationship breakthrough with him, probably because I needed something good I could associate with him. I'd needed a relationship with him my whole life, minus that lengthy middle part where I just gave up, and I worried that perhaps my time had already passed. Maybe I'd had my chance, and somehow I'd fucked it up, so this was all I had left: my last shot at something meaningful since I'd ruined everything else.

Tyler had texted me a couple times in the last few weeks but I'd been so busy with Pop, I hadn't really had time to respond, and that the whole crew had shown up to help out at Pop's house had meant everything to me. But I wasn't great with words or emotions or demonstration and I'd clapped each of them on the shoulder before they left both days that weekend. They'd helped tremendously and though we'd discovered some terrible things that day, I felt like I had a tribe of people I could depend upon for the first time in years. I hadn't felt that in a long time–not since my days in the military.

When I woke the next morning, it was long before the sun came up. I didn't hear any noises from Pop's room yet, much to my relief, and I hurried to the basement, shutting the door while I worked out. It was my only stress release of the day, and if I didn't get in some lifting and some cardio I would be a miserable beast all day long.

After a shower I jumped into my uniform and put together a quick breakfast, wrapping a plate for Pop and setting his medication out beside it with a glass of water and orange juice, leaving hot coffee on the warming plate.

It felt like it had been just the two of us for a long time now. I couldn't even remember when I'd dropped into the bar and my life had changed forever. It must have been months ago. Months that I'd spent working on his house over the weekends, Tyler always by my side, making slow and steady progress.

One truckload at a time.

One gallon of paint at a time.

I would never admit to the man, in words, that he was a saint.

The discovery of Pop's medication and the fact he finally admitted to being less than well meant I couldn't very well leave him alone in that house, cleaned and fixed up or not.

Now, months after finding the house stacked full of so much shit that I couldn't breathe inside of it, it was cleared out. It was completely cleaned, freshly painted, broken glass panes replaced and most of the flooring replaced. It had taken time and dedication, money and man hours, and I had been able to count on my brothers and their calm, steady resolve.

Even Daphne had shown up, much to my surprise, wearing work clothes and wielding gloves and a box of trash bags.

Pop, whom I'd had to bring with me so I could keep an eye on him, took to her right away.

I hadn't talked to her, because I was busy trying to stay away from her. I hadn't thanked her, nor had I asked what she was doing there, because I had no idea. I hadn't invited her and I didn't know who had, but I could guess.

Whatever the case, she'd shown up, her glossy dark hair piled up on top of her head, firm resolve in her eyes as she cast a pointed look in my direction.

I knew from what I'd observed that she'd been patient and gentle with Pop. She'd answered his repeated questions with grace and kindness.

She made sure he got something to eat and frequently reminded him he needed to get a drink of water or needed to rest for a few moments.

She was gentle with him in the way a man needs care from a woman, something I knew he'd been starved for, and her tenderness toward him nagged at me. Made me angry that it made me jealous.

The guys saw it, too. It was Marston who commented on it before he left that evening, clapping my shoulder soundly while he leaned in and said in a low voice, "You could use some of that, man."

A few days later, an addictions counselor showed up on my doorstep, only moments after I got home from work. And at first I was pissed. I thought for sure the guy had gotten wind of the situation from the state somehow, and they were going to swoop in to proclaim him unfit and take what they could.

But I was wrong. The guy said he was privately paid, so I let him in after making sure I wasn't the one privately paying him. I was too tired to ask about who or why or what.

Four visits later, Pop told me he'd signed papers that would put him in in-patient rehab for a full ninety days. The cost, he said, as stymied as I was, was covered and the therapist was totally close-lipped, saying all I needed to concern myself with was that the bill was already satisfied and Pop would receive excellent care. So we packed him up and I made the hell of a drive up to a facility in Long Island, then back by myself.

Two days later Tyler convinced me, despite it being the middle of the week, that I should meet with the guys for dinner. Since I didn't have to rush home to make sure Pop hadn't set the house on fire, I took a deep breath and accepted. My evening had been empty anyway, not that I'd admit to that out loud.

I would say that it was just the four of us, meeting at a small Italian restaurant near Tyler's condo, but that would have been a lie, because Daphne was there too.

Damn it, but the woman was everywhere. Where had she come from this time, and why did she keep showing up? Who kept inviting her and what the hell did she want?

It didn't escape my notice that she looked great, even though it might have helped me if she'd been a mess. Something closer to the day we met. But nope, my eyes kept sneaking back to her when I knew she wasn't looking and I clamped my lips firmly together to keep from paying her a compliment. Because I couldn't say nice things to people. I was the asshole who would say something stupid and probably offensive and dumb shit would just keep coming out. So I kept my mouth closed and just appreciated the view in secret. In fact, I shifted a little farther over in my seat, away from Agnello, who sat between us, just to be safe.

I had been the one to insist he sit there; I wasn't a complete fool.

There was a flatscreen TV over the bar and quietly, Daphne leaned over to the waiter and asked him if he'd turn up the volume just a little, so she could watch Alabama vs. Tennessee, something I overheard in just the smallest whisper. It made my right eyebrow hitch a little and I swear to God Tyler smirked.

She paid rapt attention to the game while we talked about baby Violet, about my plans for Pop's house, and about the motorcycle Agnello was restoring in his spare time.

Daphne winced suddenly, folding into herself quickly in a motion that looked physically painful, before pounding a fist into the table. It snapped all four sets of eyes to her just before she had what must have been an out-of-body experience.

"Come on, Johnson—you had ONE job! Protect your quarterback, you idiot!" she bellowed, whipping her phone out of an invisible pocket and texting with a fury I thought might break her fingers.

Agnello's face flattened out with surprise as he watched her fingers fly across the keypad and it was Tyler who finally smirked, asking her bravely, "Daph, who you texting?"

I felt like he was looking at me as he said it.

"Daddy." Her response was clipped. "His defensive line sucks and I'm telling him so."

"Uh..." Agnello gave Daphne side eye, looking as if he actually meant to school the woman.

"Dickson's a leftie," she explained, gesturing toward the screen where Alabama's quarterback lay on the field, looking dazed. Her voice was clipped as she focused on tapping at her screen and four sets of eyebrows, including my own, shot into our hairlines.

"Because of Dickson's blind side, Johnson's *only* priority is to protect him," she explained, her voice gentler, looking up and directly at me. "Johnson is the right tackle, for you ladies who didn't know."

I hoped to God there was a hidden meaning in the way she'd looked directly at me, because Daphne talking sports was hot.

Agnello, for his part, looked duly chastised.

"How the fuck you know these things, Preston?" It was Marston, his bottle of Peroni held to his lips. Points to the restaurant for authenticity.

"Wait..." It was Agnello again. "You're texting your *dad*?" He glanced up at the screen, where Jonesy Masters was conferring with an underling on the sidelines, a delighted grin stretching across his craggy face. "What the hell, Preston?"

Daphne grinned at him, her lovely face lighting up in a way I hadn't seen before. It made me realize she didn't smile very often, either.

"Masters, if you don't mind," she admonished him with a raise of her own bottle of beer. "I'm taking back my maiden name once I divorce the cheating asshole."

Marston choked, spitting beer all over his lasagna.

Davis grinned at Daphne and I got the feeling he had an inside scoop none of us had. "I do believe, Ms. Daphne, that you just might be football royalty."

She slapped playfully at his face with an open hand and he swatted her away. I felt my lips tighten at their easy banter as he shook his head at her. It made something inside my chest tight when she touched him.

"I might be." Daphne grinned at us, holding up her bottle in the direction of the waiter and holding up her other hand, five fingers spread wide. "But only due to the generosity of one sweet man who decided to take on a very lost little girl when her real daddy couldn't be bothered. Jonas saved my mama and me by loving us." Her eyes filled quickly with tears and something twisted in my gut at her emotion. It scared me, because I knew she'd just given up a truth that was dear and precious, and to four total cavemen.

"Davis," I barked, hardly anxious to actually see her in tears. "Leave her alone."

He shot me a glare that was nothing short of triumphant and I wondered briefly what his game was. The man had little time for anything beyond a diaper change, yet he seemed to be masterminding some sort of scheme.

"You need to sit over here by me, Thompson?" It was Tyler, patting the seat next to him, next to where Daphne sat. He was almost purring at me, a completely disgusting grin stretching slowly across his face, and I shot him a glare that no one could misinterpret.

"No." My lips moved, but my voice was almost silent as I responded to his non-question. He'd been pushing me in Daphne's direction for months and it made me angry, since I'd worked damned hard to avoid her. She was sweet and wicked-cute, we all knew that. She was kind to Pop and she was a hell of a shot, but I couldn't handle any more complications right now and my guess was that she couldn't either. It was awfully presumptuous of Tyler to try throwing us together every chance he got, just because he found us both distressingly single.

I was simple. I had simple expectations and a simple background. I didn't want any help changing that and Tyler just kept stirring the damn pot.

"Fuck off," I mouthed at him just before he picked up the bill and motioned Marston and Agnello toward the bar at the other end of the room. And that left me completely alone with someone I couldn't even pretend to communicate with, she scared me so damn much.

"Is he doing okay?" Daphne asked softly, and shit, my heart fell out of the booth and bottomed out at my feet. Her question meant she knew details, and there was only one reason she knew: Tyler.

I eyed her warily. There didn't seem to be any sense in playing dumb.

"I think so," I said, feeling intensely uncomfortable. "I drove him there and checked him in over the weekend. The staff said not to expect frequent contact. It sounds like he'll be pretty isolated from the outside world for a while, while they work with him—a pretty intensive head trip."

I hadn't given much thought to how hard it would be for Pop to dry out, and I realized I didn't actually know who he would be when he was stone-cold sober. I wondered if the person returned to me at the end of three months would be a total stranger—more so than he already was.

The facility he'd checked into was prepared to deal with his medical needs and the doctors on staff were well aware of his medications and could tweak them as necessary. It was some small level of comfort, though I'd had the weirdest feeling I was leaving my kid at sleep-away summer camp when I'd started up the truck to drive away. It was terrifying, the level of responsibility I suddenly felt for the man who'd never embraced his responsibility for me.

Any therapist probably would have told me that I'd designated Pop my lifeline. I'd found something to cling to, maybe just to give myself purpose, since I had nothing else. It gave me an anchor when clearly I'd been drifting around unmoored for a very long time.

"Are you close to him?" Daphne's face reflected her genuine curiosity and I was surprised by it.

"Not really," I responded slowly, finishing the last bit of water in my glass. Being alone with her in any capacity made me wildly uncomfortable, because if she'd known what was going on in my head when I looked at her, I was pretty sure she'd have slapped me.

"I guess Pop and me have kind of been shoved together by circumstances and we're sort of getting to know each other now." It was a weird thing to admit to someone who was still a virtual stranger. There was no way she could understand what that was like.

"I suppose that's kind of what it would feel like if I ever met my real father," she mused quietly and though I felt an eyebrow hitch, I didn't say anything. I was still processing that she was the adopted daughter of an ex-NFL player.

She wasn't looking at me anymore, fiddling with the paper from her straw, winding and unwinding it around her index finger.

"I think the dynamic of getting to know someone as an adult, someone that should have been there during your childhood but wasn't, would be very different," she said finally. "Maybe ... in some ways it would be easier, because the expectations would be clearer."

I wasn't so sure about that, but I didn't contradict her.

"What have I done to make you dislike me so much, Jack?" Her question hung in the air while I swallowed hard, blindsided by how she'd just barged right into it.

The waiter came by again and refilled our water glasses, removing the other three almost noiselessly, and for the first time I realized the other guys were gone. Like really and truly gone: they'd gotten up and left us even without saying goodbye. Tyler had engineered this yet again. It seemed fairly certain he didn't even know he was meddling, this shit was so second nature to him.

I shook my head at her. "I wouldn't call it that," I said, casting around desperately for a distraction. "So ... Masters raised you?" Dumb question with an obvious answer, but it was all I could think of at the moment because I needed to be on safer ground.

"Like I was his own." She let me distract her, her smile small and her eyes far away. "I think he always wanted a boy, but he and my mama couldn't have kids, so I sort of made it my mission in life to be the son he didn't have. I was just so thankful I had somebody who cared and didn't treat me like I was an annoying little girl, I'd have done anything he asked.

"He taught me about football and took me to all the games; taught me how to drive a car and a boat. He took me with him to the range, and every September he'd put one of his assistant coaches in charge for a couple days and we'd take a long weekend to go hunting in Georgia."

In my mind's eye I could picture Daphne in camouflage, sitting completely still in a tree stand. Only, I couldn't picture her as a kid. I could only picture her now, adult Daphne in a tree stand, her big eyes wide as she scanned the woods for deer.

"What?" Her eyes widened as she said it, and I felt like I'd been struck stupid. Her eyes were the most incredible color, that deep grey that I'd never seen anywhere else. I didn't like their magnetic pull, or the fact that I couldn't stop staring at them.

"When's the last time you went?"

Oh, thank God. Words. Good save.

Her face scrunched up as she thought and she ran an absentminded hand over her hair. "When Blair was little, I guess. Hunter wasn't ... um ... around during the pregnancy, and we didn't get married until Blair was a toddler. So I suppose the last time I went hunting with Daddy was probably about fifteen years ago."

I decided not to tell her about my little hunting cabin in Pennsylvania, for fear she would misconstrue the information as an invitation. Agnello had gone with me last year and he'd bitched about the cold the entire time, like a little girl. I would not be inviting him again—or anyone else. Ever. My solitude was sacred.

"We haven't missed the season here yet, you know."

Son of a bitch. It was out there like someone else had said it.

"Deer season starts at the end of November in Pennsylvania."

Shut up, you idiot!

"Hmm." She held the bottle to her lips and drained the last sip. I tracked the movement of her smooth throat without meaning to or wanting to. It was something instinctive that I couldn't ignore and it was stoking that angry, hungry feeling in my gut. She was a complication I didn't need, thanks to stupid freaking Tyler, and it was becoming pretty damn clear I couldn't help myself around her no matter how much I tried to rein it in.

"This one." Her hand was suddenly on my forearm, her fingers trailing up the coordinates I'd inked into my skin. Little jolts of lightning raced up my arm at the soft brush of her fingertips and

I looked down at my wrist in alarm. I was going to need to cut that thing off now. *Traitor.* "I know it's not domestic, but that's about it. Where is it?"

It had been years and still I wasn't ready to talk about it. So I stared down at her fingers, transfixed, while they traced the numbers on my arm. The coordinates to the place where I'd nearly lost my life in an ambush, a constant reminder of hope and despair. It was the place where I'd decided that if I ever made it out alive, I would settle down and start a family. I would find a woman who loved me with the same ferocity I loved her with, and I would make something with her that mattered.

Yeah, clearly that had gone exactly as I'd planned.

Her fingers stilled but remained on my arm, curled gently against my skin. I needed her to stop touching me so I could think straight, so I leaned back, bringing my arms with me to fold across my chest. "Aleppo."

Understanding dawned in her eyes without me saying a word and she nodded slowly. "Your sacrifice made a difference," she said softly. "Your presence there saved lives."

"Not enough of them."

It was the memories of the children that haunted me most, kids ripped apart by the mortars launched by their own people. Little bodies, broken and bleeding, still and lifeless.

The sounds of women wailing in my dreams still woke me in the middle of the night.

"And that one?" She pointed, clearly not done with me, and I folded my chin toward my chest, unable to see the script that started on the side of my neck and trailed down toward my heart.

"From the Bhagavad Gita," I said slowly. I didn't want to tell her when or where or why I'd gotten it, not long after Tash had left. It was a stupid decision, but pain had always helped me let the anger out.

She waited patiently, her eyes all sparkly and shit and when she looked at me like that I was ready to give her my social security number, date of birth and mother's maiden name.

"It's a rough translation of the original," I said, and she nodded. It made me sigh heavily, because she wasn't going to let me off the hook. "Alone, re-centered, no yearnings, no trinkets. The Gita said now I'd be happy..." I had to swallow hard.

"So why's the ache still there?" She finished for me, shuddering. "I don't like that one," she whispered, having completely forgotten about her football game as she kept her focus on my face, like she was looking for the one emotion I didn't want her to see. The one that would prove to her I was human; that she could reach me.

Before she could touch me again or ask any more questions, I made a movement to slide out of the large booth, thinking twice about holding out a hand to help her out. If she touched me again I wasn't sure what I'd do—burst into very unmanly tears, maybe, or lean down to find out what her lips tasted like, and that wouldn't do at all.

"Those assholes left us behind," I offered, throwing down a couple bills on the table and waiting for her to collect her phone and small bag. It made her look around for a second, peering around my shoulder and through the window as her eyes searched for their vehicles. She blew out a big breath.

"I'm not sure why Tyler keeps doing this," she said quietly and I raised an eyebrow. So she'd noticed too, and for just a second it made me uncomfortable to consider that maybe she didn't like it any more than I did. That changed things just a little; made me view things differently, like maybe she didn't want to be left alone with me either, but not because she couldn't control herself.

I held the door for her, letting her out into the parking lot first, and I couldn't control the snort that slipped out when I caught sight of her huge truck. It was still so entirely ludicrous, to see her haul herself up into the monster. But after she'd explained her reasoning, I wasn't going to purposely make fun of her for what made her feel safe.

"I know what he's trying to do," she said without looking over at me as I walked her toward her truck. "I'm sorry for that, especially because I know you don't enjoy being around me. I've kind of crashed your boys' club." She shrugged a little apologetically, finally turning her head to smile at me. "You won't have to worry about that much longer, since I'm selling the house. Once I figure out what I'm going to do, I'll be out of your hair."

That pulled me up short and I stopped walking, frozen in place. "You're not staying here, then?" I asked stupidly, confused as to why my brain suddenly refused to work. I wasn't processing thoughts in a rational, logical manner any longer.

I was an idiot. Of course she wouldn't stay. What was here for her? Her job wasn't based here, her daughter was in Massachusetts, and her cheating husband had another house and a new girlfriend.

"Starting over is tough," I admitted. "You'll do a better job of it than I did. You'll actually get out and do things and meet people and..." Something stole my words, kicking hard inside my chest, and it hurt like hell.

She would find someone quickly. Easily. She was beautiful and kind and warm and if the guys and me were any indication, men were drawn to her. I tried to imagine her with Marston or Agnello and irritation rippled across my skin like a heatwave. The brief visual made me violently angry and I swallowed against the hot feeling clawing at my throat.

She sighed, clicking the fob and the lights on her truck flashed as the locks disengaged. "I'm too old to start over, Jack." Her voice was weary. "I'm tired. I've known how to be alone for a very long time and I just see it stretching out in front of me, endlessly." She swallowed hard. "Fifteen years ago I thought I had everything I wanted." Her smile was rueful. "It seems I've been very good at lying to myself for a very long time, and by now it might be too late for me."

Hoisting herself up and into the truck, she rolled down the window and leaned out. It was a familiar pose, putting our faces almost level. "I suppose that's why Tyler tries so hard." She grinned. "We're the two most pathetic souls he knows and he's crap at it, but he likes to try to fix things."

She was probably right about that.

"Thank you for what you did for Pop," I said quietly, my eyes on the running board. "Of all the things he can't seem to remember these days, you aren't one of them. He talked about you the whole way up to Long Island."

I looked up in time to see her big, grey eyes widen. “I didn’t do anything,” she said softly. “Everyone needs to be treated with a little care every now and then, and I could tell that he was lonely.”

I gave her a small smile, shoving my hands into my pockets.

Wanted to tell her I was lonely, too.

“Your dad has had a tough go of it and I think you have too. All of us deserve a little grace and, in this case, helping him in some way is to help you. I just figured ... well, when I showed up to help with the house I could tell that you had the weight of the world on your shoulders. You don’t have to carry it all by yourself, you know.”

Well, that was fucking cryptic.

“You are a good man, Jack.” Her voice was gentle but her eyes were like lasers, boring right into my soul. “There’s a huge heart hiding out in there. No one would think less of you if you’d let them see it.” She tapped my chest with an index finger.

I barked out a short, bitter laugh. The few people who had seen it had hurt me. That was when I’d tried to stop caring, when it seemed like life had nothing left to give me. Nothing but years of drudgery and physical pain management for the injuries I’d sustained in Syria.

There would be no wife and no children, and probably no pets. I was fairly certain if I got a dog it would run away, because that’s how my life went: Everyone left me.

Daphne reached out quickly, catching me by surprise when her hand cupped my cheek and she leaned through the open window to press soft lips against my cheek.

When she leaned back I was shocked, breathless, and she had a mischievous smile on her face. “If you’d just open up a little ... someone’s out there who will make you very happy, my friend. Stop fighting it so hard.” She let go of my cheek to pinch her fingers together in indication of measurement.

I didn’t have a response and I was pretty sure my expression relayed just how shocked I was by what she’d done. But she didn’t stick around to witness it, firing up the noisy vehicle and tearing out of the parking lot like the hounds of hell were at her small heels.

Like he was freaking psychic, Tyler was sitting on my front steps when I got home, with a giant shit-eating grin on his face.

"Can't go home, man," he hollered as I parked the truck and walked the short distance between the driveway and the front steps. "G's ma showed up this afternoon, and my woman—she didn't even warn me! Almost got me." He dropped his head into his hands, but the smile on his face was still huge. "Pulled into the parking lot ... saw her car ... kept on fucking driving. So you're stuck with me until I'm ready to deal with *two* of them in my house."

"Fresh sheets on the guest bed, but you have to cook breakfast," I deadpanned, shoving past him to open the door, and I heard him snort.

The two of us settled easily into the living room, and Tyler rooted around in my fridge until he found a few bottles of decent beer. I had cautiously restocked with better stuff after dropping off Pop.

"Good talk with our girl?" he teased, giving each top a quick twist and handing one to me where I sat in one of the big, squishy chairs.

I shook my head at him, trying to decide what I was going to say.

The truth was that my conversation with Daphne had been uncomfortable, but weirdly, I'd enjoyed talking to her, as much as I could considering the weight of the conversation.

It may have had something to do with the distressing fact that I liked it when she touched me. Maybe I was just *that* starved for a woman's attention I thought ruefully, taking a deep drink from my bottle.

It was uncharacteristic for Tyler, but he sat quietly in the chair across from me and watched me as he sipped from his own bottle. It was almost disconcerting, like he was waiting for me to get so uncomfortable with the silence that I'd just start barfing out words and personal information. Thing was, he knew me better than that. It would never happen; I'd sooner have a tooth pulled without anesthesia.

"She's real cute," Tyler finally observed casually, leaning back into his seat.

She was absolutely beautiful, I wanted to correct him, but that opened me up to even more uncomfortable things, so I simply nodded. "Yup. Short, though."

"Fun, too." Tyler's lips quirked. "Probably better at being one of the guys than you are."

I nodded again. Tash sure as hell had never tried to fit in with the men I thought of as brothers. She'd never gone to a gun range or out for dinner and drinks with them. She didn't like the company I kept, and probably because they saw right through her. They'd hidden their feelings better than she did, as she'd made no secret of her distaste for them, but the only reason the guys were sorry to see her go was because of what it did to me. Otherwise, I think they'd have helped her pack.

"I like her," Tyler led yet again and my head bobbed some more. He muttered something under his breath that I didn't hear.

"Mmmhmm."

Tyler had finished his bottle and he pushed himself up slowly, carrying it into the kitchen with him and I heard it clink into the recycling bin before he fished through the refrigerator again. The bottles in the door rattled when he swung it shut.

"I saw you in the parking lot." His voice drifted back over the short distance and I sat waiting, not wanting to respond without his clarification. "I was sitting in my truck, texting G to ask if we needed more diapers ... and I saw Daph lean out and lay one right on you. Pow, my man. Looked like a sniper got you."

"Did not." I snorted, slamming back the rest of my beer. Something uncomfortable and hot was happening in my chest. I was trying to remember the last time I had been kissed by a woman—*really,* properly kissed, the way a woman kisses a man she wants. I pondered briefly, expanding the definition to include the few times I'd been mauled by one of the women I'd brought home.

Still nothing.

"You lit up like a fucking Christmas tree, bro." Tyler's grin was so huge, it looked like there were extra teeth in his mouth.

"Nope."

Tired of my caveman answers, Tyler reached for the remote and I breathed a sigh of sweet relief when he flicked on Sports Center. Here was safe, common ground. Here the toughest question was, "You think they'll start Love in the first game?" And because he could read my mind, Tyler said, "Kinda starting to think Rodgers might not stick with Green Bay much longer."

I kept my mouth shut as Tyler started up a running commentary, afraid he'd find a way to bring Daphne back into the conversation.

Over the remainder of the afternoon I learned that Generis had invited Daphne over for dinner weeks earlier, and Daphne arrived bearing gifts for baby Violet. Tyler whipped out his phone to show me pictures he'd snapped of her holding his daughter. In the first, Violet was suspended in the air, obviously giggling as Daphne grinned up at her. But it was the second picture that made me suck in a quick breath, hoping Tyler didn't notice. Violet was nestled comfortably in Daphne's arms and Daphne was looking down at her with such a sweet, tender expression that it made something ache.

Heartburn, maybe. Shouldn't have had the spicy meatballs.

"Said she couldn't have more kids after her daughter and she always wanted a house full of 'em," Tyler said carefully and I could feel him watching my face with interest. He knew that I'd wanted the same, something I'd foolishly confessed to him in an unguarded moment when he told me Generis was pregnant and I'd congratulated him.

How Daphne had insinuated herself into my group of people, I wasn't entirely certain. It was true that she was charming. She lit up a room just by walking into it, though she wasn't loud or boisterous or obnoxious. It was something that shone from inside her, some kind of sweet, irrepressible light that she couldn't help but just beam out into the world.

I fucking hated it, because I was starting to understand that *I* lit up every time I saw her, and I didn't want that.

She was making me weak.

Tyler got tired of the one-sided conversation, which was really saying something considering the word count that guy could generate in a day. He was entirely capable of holding up *both* sides of a conversation.

Eventually he handed me the remote and checked his watch, sighing heavily. "Gonna head out," he said, stretching his arms out over his head once he pushed out of the chair. "One good thing about G's ma coming to visit is that at least she'll cram the fridge full of food. Maybe I got lucky and she made some arepas and that incredible beef stew." He rubbed his belly, a bottomless pit I always teased him about, considering I didn't know where he was putting all of it.

I put in a shorter workout than usual that night, finally back to more of my normal schedule since I wasn't looking after Pop. I felt weirdly tired after a day that hadn't required a great deal of exertion. Something about the things that had been running around in my head had tired me out and as I twisted the dial for the shower, my phone dinged with an incoming text.

I showered and brushed my teeth, pulling a fresh t-shirt over my head before I read the text. It was from an unfamiliar number and I knew immediately it was from Daphne.

I'm sorry if I made you uncomfortable today. I don't know what came over me.

I couldn't respond to that because I didn't know how. The woman that I needed to stay far, far away from me was extending an olive branch of sorts after I had been the one to treat her rudely. She was finding ways to wriggle under my skin and I didn't like it. I didn't want to think about her in the way I was starting to think about her, because it meant she was getting in.

Though the text bothered me for the next few days, I was firm in my resolve: I would not respond and risk opening a very dangerous door, one that would be all too easy to step through. She absolutely did make me uncomfortable, and what scared me most was that I was starting to like it, that little zing that raced just beneath my skin every time I saw her.

Or thought about her.

Or any of the guys so much as mentioned her.

On Friday morning I got another catch-and-release call from Tyler. I rolled my eyes, since it was the second one of the morning and it wasn't even nine. So I jumped into the cruiser, doing a quick pat down to make sure everything was accounted for and in place, and without any particular hurry in my game, made my way to the gated drive. I liked to make 'em wait, because it made them nervous. That guaranteed no repeat offenses.

A familiar truck sat in the paved drive between the gate and the arm, the engine off, and I sat in my cruiser for a moment, hands on the wheel, staring across the magnetic arm at Daphne. She returned my glare, not looking away or backing down as I got out of the SUV and walked up to her truck.

"You're avoiding me, Thompson," she said as I neared her window and she turned briefly to set a coffee cup in the holder with an excessive amount of caution.

"Second offense, Masters," I barked, irritated that my heart sped up and it had nothing to do with walking the short distance from my cruiser.

"Oh blah, blah, blah." She flapped her fingers at me like a chattering bird beak. "You're not really all that scary, you giant beast. I bet you're a big, snuggly kitten when a girl gets you all tucked in." She rolled her eyes at me and I had to bite my lip to keep from smiling. I liked her attitude, but even more I liked the idea of her tucking me in.

"What are you going to do, Jack? Spirit me away to some undisclosed and suspiciously darkened room in the basement and tie me to a chair?" She lifted her eyebrows. "I might like it. What would you think about that?"

A wave of heat rushed up to my face and she burst into laughter when she watched my mouth drop open. What had gotten into this woman? Flirty Daphne was an entirely different person.

"Are you flirting with me, Masters?" My voice was still rough and her grin stretched even wider.

"Oh no, Officer Thompson, I wouldn't dream of it." She sucked in her left cheek to hold between her teeth as she thought about something. It looked like she was trying not to laugh. "But I have it on good authority from ... ah..." She cleared her throat.

"A good authority, if you will ... that you have been purposely distancing yourself because I make you uncomfortable." She leaned on the open frame, fixing me with such a stare that I couldn't look away. "And I make you uncomfortable for a very silly reason." Her grin was enormous and triumphant and yeah, she was really damn cute.

"Fucking Tyler," I hissed under my breath, completely unable to break eye contact, and she burst out laughing. "I don't know what he told you, but he's a nosy-ass yenta."

She was adorable when she laughed, especially because I knew she wasn't actually laughing *at me*, which was a relief. She was wiping her eyes and chuckling, making little sniffling noises as she gestured behind her, toward the guard shack. "It *was* his idea."

She'd sold him out in a heartbeat.

"I complained to him that you were avoiding me, so he told me to come give you hell."

I sighed heavily. I would deal with Tyler later and retribution would be sweet. "So you drove all the way out here to give me a hard time?" The idea didn't actually make me angry.

"I had to pick up a few things from Blair's old work place that she forgot." She gestured toward the next building with a small smile. "I figured I could spare a couple minutes for a good friend."

Tyler. Right. I cleared my throat hard, hoping the disappointment didn't show on my face, a little jealous that it was just so damn easy for him.

"Hey." Daphne's voice was still warm, but there wasn't a trace of humor left in it. "I didn't mean to upset you. Have I?" She looked worried now.

"Did he really tell you that you make me uncomfortable?"

Her head tipped just a little to the side and her eyes narrowed. "Do I, Jack? Is the proximity of my person to yours so distressing that you have to hide your distaste?" Uh-oh, she was starting to look mad. "When I touched your arm the other night, did you rush home to scrub off the cooties so you didn't get leprosy? Maybe you washed the filth of my lips off your cheek? Or did you spend the night tossing and turning?" There was fire in her eyes, a drastic shift from her gentle laughter only a moment earlier and she said something under her breath that I didn't quite catch. I could have *sworn* it was "Like I did."

My radio crackled briefly and Daphne's eyes drifted shut for a brief second, her chest rising and falling quickly with violent breaths. "Let me out then."

"Huh?" I'd almost forgotten where we were. My heart was hammering so hard, I couldn't hear well.

"If you can't stand to be near me, let me out. I'll stay away from you; Tyler and Generis are the only ones who seem like they want to be my friends anyway, so you can have your boys club back."

She jammed a foot down on the brake and pressed the ignition, the truck roaring to life and I sighed, turning to head back toward my vehicle and backing it into the access spot.

When she thundered past I could see Tyler standing outside the guard shack, inked arms crossed over his chest, shaking his head at me.

7

Daphne

I had several meetings with Emily that week and I decided to drive back to New York to attend the ones at the end of the week in person, spending the weekend at my apartment.

Honestly, I think I went so I could eat my feelings. I was angry and hurt by Jack's reaction to what was as forward as I'd ever been with him, even though there was *absolutely no reason* I should be upset with him. Jack was an asshole and I knew that, but I'd overstepped my boundaries.

I'd warned Tyler that poking the bear was a bad idea but he'd begged and wheedled and cajoled and then he'd given me what he swore was "Just the right ammo to really light a good fire," telling me that Jack avoided me not because he hated me, but because he was almost magnetically drawn to me.

I liked that, but who wouldn't?

And because I was still having a hard time reading Jack, and it was starting to irritate me more and more that he made me feel all fluttery, I decided to go along with Tyler and push Jack outside of his comfort zone. Hard. And clearly that had backfired in spectacular fashion. I'd lit a fire alright, and I'd burned down the whole stupid forest.

It would be Thanksgiving soon and solitary walks through Central Park weren't quite as enjoyable as they'd been a month earlier, the air sharp with cold, and I ducked into a coffee shop on my way back to the apartment, just to warm my hands around a cup of something hot.

I glanced down at my phone for the 693rd time since leaving the parking lot on Sentinel Way. Not a peep from Jack and, what had me just as riled, not a word from Tyler.

On Saturday afternoon I talked to Blair, who was too busy studying to talk for long, and when I hung up the late afternoon sun reminded me I'd skipped lunch. I wasn't hungry, really, just weirdly sad, and while I sat on the sofa and looked out the windows at the spectacular view, the ache of loneliness stabbed so deep and so hard that I thought when I looked down there might actually be blood.

As if she could read my thoughts, my phone lit up with Ava's number and I answered it gratefully. I was absolutely fine with any distraction I could get, because my next distraction was living in the wine fridge.

Since Ava was on her way to some kind of event with her husband, we weren't able to talk long and I sat quietly after we hung up, letting the sun go down without turning on the lights. I sat there for a long time, the ambient city light providing enough of a glow that I could still see most of the space around me and it was like being in a comfortable little cocoon.

I could stay here, I thought again. I could sell the big house and the one in Alabama and just live here, a place where I'd always been comfortable and anonymous. It provided me with entertainment, fabulous food and shows, good exercise, and if I was going to meet anyone, this was probably one of the easier places to do it.

The next morning I packed up rather early, eager to get back so I could start packing up the house. The most tedious part would be selling the furniture, but it felt like a burden had been lifted. Getting rid of all the unnecessary stuff would be a weight off my shoulders.

I wouldn't be paying property taxes in three states.

I could travel at a moment's notice.

And just maybe I could figure out what I was going to do with myself now that I was cutting the strings to things that I'd chosen to tie myself to for twenty years.

Pulling out of the parking garage under my building, the truck just barely clearing the bar that indicated passable height, I pointed the nose toward I-95 and pulled up a favorite play list.

Traffic was light, which was weird, and even though I stopped to fill up once, I roared up the pristine driveway just before four. The gravel crunched satisfyingly beneath the tires and I lowered the volume before hitting the garage door opener, noticing in my rearview mirror as I pulled in that there was a truck parked at the far corner of the wide driveway. I'd driven right past it without noticing.

Grabbing my few bags, I let myself into the house, a strange smell meeting me. "Catalina?" I called, surprised I hadn't seen her car. She was the housekeeper who sometimes came by on weekends and cooked for me, just because she said I needed some fattening up, bless her and her poor eyesight. She was an older Colombian lady, all her children grown and out of the house, and I suspected she took care of me purely because she was bored. I was her employer, but I may as well have been an honorary daughter.

A voice rumbled in the kitchen, and unless Catalina had been mainlining testosterone for the past week, there was no way it was her. I set my bags down cautiously, kicking off my shoes and walking quietly through the house, toward the large kitchen that opened up in the back, the tremendous windows overlooking a large expanse of lawn.

"Ah, there she is!" Hunter's face lit up just as mine crumpled and I took in a tall, wide, familiar form sitting on one of the barstools, a beer in front of him. His shoulders were tight and when he turned to face me, Jack's eyes were hard and glittering. They saw everything.

"How's my girl?" Hunter moved quickly to scoop an arm around my waist, his lips landing on my temple and Jack watched my face closely as my lips thinned and nostrils flared.

I pushed back at him, walking quickly toward the fridge. If he wanted to have a public fight, I was going to need wine.

"I was wondering the same," I said brightly as I pulled a crisp white from the small wine fridge and uncorked it with shaking hands. It made me look nervous and uncoordinated, I thought as I tossed the corkscrew back into the drawer and poured a huge glass.

The way Jack was watching me, I knew he could read my jerky, uncoordinated actions: I had been on edge for days.

Weeks.

Months.

My last interaction with Jack had pushed me past some sort of boiling point I hadn't known existed, a place where anger commingled with hormones. I was furious and hot and spoiling for a fight, so I turned to Hunter. "How *is* Cassandra?"

The smile fell from Hunter's handsome face, his blond hair beginning to show just a few silvering streaks at the temples. His lips tightened ever so slightly and Jack's eyes flicked to the hand Hunter clenched into a tight fist on the counter.

"Mr. Thompson came by to make a personal apology to my wife." Hunter's tone was light again, but I could read the accusation. His voice hinted at something unpleasant. "He says he was unkind to you."

Hunter's expression was what was unkind.

"So we've been getting to know one another. And as you can imagine, I was surprised to find a man that I'd never met, or even heard of, at the door asking for my wife."

If that was meant to wound Jack, Hunter's words missed their mark. Jack just smirked at him, lifting the bottle slowly to his lips and I wondered what my husband had said to convince him he should come in, let alone sit and have a beer and a conversation.

Maybe it was Jack who had done the convincing.

"I'm so sorry," I said softly, setting my glass on the counter with a clink. "This should only take a moment. Would you excuse us?"

Jack nodded, the smirk still on his face as his eyes swept again over Hunter like he had sized up his prey and found it lacking.

"You." I snapped my fingers at my husband, pointing toward the sunroom just off the dining room with an outstretched arm. "We need to discuss something that doesn't require an audience."

It was almost laughable, the panic that flashed across Hunter's face as he followed me toward the sunroom. He was a big guy and it had to look like a Great Dane following a Chihuahua. He was tall and broad and blond, a sun-kissed god thanks to genetics and a good tanning package. It was something I had always admired about him, the way he looked so strong and capable, and his sharp nose and bright blue eyes had always made my heart flutter.

Now, seeing him just made my heart sink.

Shutting the French door behind me in order to muffle the sound, I turned toward Hunter where he stood looking out the wall of windows toward the frozen lawn.

"Why are you in my house?" I asked flatly, with no preamble, very much out of character with the woman he'd known the last twenty years.

"I thought I could stay here a while," he answered without turning around. I was surprised he didn't immediately launch into an argument. "You know, see if we could work things out."

"I have no interest in working things out," I responded and he finally turned to look at me, his face sagging with defeat.

"So you don't want me anymore, Daph? Is that it? You want that guy?" He jabbed an accusatory finger over my shoulder. "Some steroided, uneducated, tattooed ex-soldier who's probably more comfortable living in a cave than a house? Or is this just you being rebellious, finding someone who is my total opposite so you can shove it in my face? How long have you been sleeping with him?" His lips curled derisively.

Oh, Hunter ... I breathed in a deep, calming breath. He had never been able to take responsibility for his actions and the politician in him had always been able to twist truths so that you felt yourself in the wrong even when facts were on your side.

"When I told you I was pregnant with our daughter, you told me you wanted nothing to do with us," I reminded him slowly, my voice much gentler than I felt. The rejection was just as fresh, burning my tongue as I released the words. "So I raised her on my own, broken-hearted, convinced at that time that I'd lost the love of my life." I swallowed hard and he mirrored my action. I'd never told him he was the love of my life, and now I knew without a doubt that he wasn't.

Mama had begged me not to take Hunter back. Daddy had done the same, not in so many words, but he'd made his mistrust of Hunter very clear. He'd warned me I would be hurt and used. He'd promised he and Mama would always be there for me, in my corner, ready to help me fight if I asked. And as he'd made me that promise, he'd swiped angrily at one eye, doing his best not to let out that single manly tear.

I had known about the Prestons' financially precarious state before marrying Hunter, since Daddy had hired a private investigator. He had the prenup drafted and he'd wanted to be sure I knew exactly what I was getting myself into, trying to convince me as gently as he could that there was a slight, tiny, baby possibility that Hunter was being pushed to marry me for money.

The trust Mama had set up for me when I was born contained more zeros than I could ever spend in my lifetime and I came into half of it on my twenty-fifth birthday, which took place mere weeks after Hunter and I were married. It was mine and mine alone, ironclad in my legal ownership, but Hunter benefitted from it greatly as I allowed him to pursue positions in local politics, often positions with a very small stipend, as he worked his way up the political ladder.

Even I could admit he was a master in his arena. He was engaging and warm when necessary, and shrewd and calculating when the situation called for it.

The problem was that he couldn't turn it off and be a real person at home, because the life of a politician was all he knew. It made him manipulative and aloof, capable of forming very quick surface relationships but few with any roots or real meaning.

Every person Hunter met was only as good as their next favor.

"It would serve you right if I was sleeping with him," I said softly, "but only if you actually cared for me. You don't care about what I'm doing until you fear I might make you look bad."

Hunter blew out a huge breath and sank down into one of the large overstuffed chairs in the room, throwing up his hands in a sign of defeat. Jack was watching as he did it, I could feel it, and it took every ounce of willpower not to flick my eyes up to meet his, because I wasn't sure what I'd see there, and right now I needed to concentrate all my energy on Hunter.

"I gave you everything you needed to pursue your dreams," I continued. "I gave you the picture of a beautiful, perfect family. I poured tremendous amounts of money into your campaigns, then took time out of my schedule to attend fundraisers, breakfasts, and meet-and-greets. Then I packed up a house and moved across the country for your career, at your request. I'd have been perfectly happy to stay in Alabama and fly up to New York every couple weeks. But now I live here, in a house I didn't want and with no reason to be here, because I live here without the husband who has never wanted *me*."

I expected to feel the sting of tears, the hurt and rejection pouring out through my words, but my eyes remained dry and my face tight.

Then I saw it in his face, the defeat and fear, and I *knew*: "Oh Hunter, you are a fool."

He was running scared.

He shoved his hands through his hair and dragged them down his face. "I can't do it again, Daph."

"Wow." I collapsed into another of the chairs and fixed him with a gorgon stare that should have melted the flesh from his bones. "So yet again, you're going to leave a young girl to fend for herself."

I was shocked by the wave of sympathy I felt for Cassandra, especially as she'd been so enterprising. She'd earned the heck out of her situation.

"That really would make for an interesting story," I mused, and the lower half of his face pinched. "She could make a pretty tidy sum selling it. Maybe not enough to last more than a couple years, but if she was careful and invested wisely ... kids are expensive, you know," I trailed off, realization suddenly washing over me. "Oh. Right. But she thinks she's in love with you."

Hunter sighed heavily, shaking his head. "I have only two ways out of this. One is the obvious, which would be instantaneous political death, and the other ... well, I don't have the funds to pay her off."

Of course he didn't. Despite his congressional salary, Hunter hardly lived within his means. Making a blackmail payment, or even regular child support, was well beyond his abilities with his current lifestyle. His mortgage alone undoubtedly gobbled up a huge portion of his salary.

I shook my head in disbelief, pushing to my feet and standing for a moment to look out across the lawn while I tried to gather my thoughts. It took a moment to organize them, all jumbled and competing for attention, and when I finally spoke Hunter didn't raise his head to look at me.

"We won't be working things out, because you don't love me. You don't love anyone, Hunter, and I'm finally starting to realize that it's because you can't love anyone more than yourself.

"You'll have to go to your parents this time, and for once maybe your father can step up and do right by you, instead of pushing you to marry your way out of a tough financial spot." I scoffed as I said the words, trying to feel sympathy but only feeling the burn of anger and disgust in my gut for how blind I'd been.

"Should you choose the first option, I am perfectly willing to sign the papers, based upon the stipulations of our prenup, just as quickly as you can have them drawn up. Otherwise, my first offer still stands, and it's all you'll get from me: I'll file in May. What you do with the pregnant girlfriend is up to you."

His shoulders sagged in defeat. He'd never known this side of me before: resolute and opinionated, firmly standing up to him rather than acquiescing to whatever it was he wanted. It was the only thing standing in my favor, I thought, that he'd never had a chance to practice his seductive political skills on the person who'd always put up the least amount of fight.

But old Daphne? That docile, passive idiot was dead.

Dumb Daphne didn't live here anymore.

"Pack whatever you need, and whatever you can't handle now I'll send to you or consult with you prior to selling it," I said, surprised by the coldness in my voice. "It took me half my life, but I've finally learned a very important lesson: I'm not willing to settle for crumbs any longer."

I slipped off my rings and held them out to him in the palm of my hand. "That's all you'll get out of me. Pawn them if you have to. I've done my time in this marriage."

He shook his head at me. "Keep them." Then he pushed out of the chair and brushed past me, stalking quickly through the living area and the kitchen, and I could hear the steady ring of his footsteps as he climbed the stairs.

To my surprise, Carrick didn't chase after him but remained where he'd lodged himself between Jack's knees, his expression smiling as much as a dog could as Jack rubbed his ear.

People said animals were good judges of character, and now I wondered if I should have been paying attention to Carrick's behavior years earlier. He was Hunter's dog, but had never been his devoted companion.

Jack raised an eyebrow at me and when he raised his beer bottle again, I realized he'd only taken a few sips.

Maybe he hadn't been here as long as I'd first thought.

I took a few deep breaths—I was shaking a little—and nodded toward Carrick, lifting my own eyebrows as a wide grin split Jack's handsome face. It struck me breathless again, which I hated. It was already hard enough for me to catch my breath around grumpy Jack, but smiling Jack was fallen-angel-level beautiful.

Hunter's footsteps clomped down the staircase again and when he slammed the garage door, at some distance from the kitchen, glass rattled in the cabinets.

It seemed to add to Jack's amusement.

It took Hunter another forty minutes to finally leave the house, each time blustering his way up and down the staircase and slamming the door as he loaded things into his car. I knew he was making a show of it in hopes of making Jack uncomfortable.

"He's jealous," Jack said quietly, and I set my empty wine glass in the sink with a shrug.

Of nothing, I thought.

"Jealousy isn't the same as broken-hearted." I couldn't even look at him as I said it, so I made a show of rinsing the glass.

When he didn't respond, I still kept my head down because I could feel the intensity of his gaze burning through the top of my head. There was something he wanted to say that couldn't be let out, that much I knew, and for once I wanted to see what happened when he had to push himself.

Shrugging out of the long sweater I'd used in place of a coat and winding up my hair, stabbing a chopstick through it to anchor it to my head, I surveyed the kitchen while Jack watched me silently.

"So, what made you drive all the way here?" I asked finally, turning to pull open the fridge, and the wide boatneck I wore slipped down one shoulder. I should have shrugged it back into place; smoothed it back with a quick flick of my fingers. But I heard a slow, deep intake of breath from behind me and hesitated for just a moment.

The stool squealed when Jack stood and he moved on quiet feet to stand behind me.

I was immobilized, pretending to stare into the fridge, more focused on his body heat behind me than I was on anything in front of me. I hated that he could do this to me and that he seemed completely unaware.

"Tell me about this." His voice was gravelly as he swept a finger over the outlines of four small black doves that swept up toward my shoulder. I took a deep breath, unsure of where to start, when his finger hooked into the back of the soft shirt to pull it away from my skin. I knew it gave him enough room to read the delicate script that scrolled up over my spine.

Me jep forcen.

I closed the doors with a slow movement, which pushed me back, closer to him, and I knew without looking that I was standing under his chin.

"It's Albanian," I whispered finally and I struggled hard with a swallow. This was a very sensitive subject for me and I never talked about it without tears. "It means 'Give me the strength.'"

His fingers traced over the small birds again and a hot breath gusted over the skin where my neck met my shoulder. "You need the strength to forgive?" he asked softly, inviting my explanation, and I ducked my head.

"To forget." I shook my head, but my head stayed down, my eyes predictably full and one scalding tear fell from my eye to splash on the floor. He couldn't have seen it, but his other hand came up to my other shoulder, pulling me gently that last inch back into him. He was a hot, solid wall of muscle and it shouldn't have been welcoming or comforting, but it was.

I leaned willingly and he turned his head to rest his cheek on the top of my head as he wrapped one arm around my shoulders and the other around my waist, holding me tightly to him, completely unaware that I had completely stopped breathing. I was crying and wanting and angry all at the same time.

There was nothing more I could say and he didn't ask any questions, just held me gently as I choked down the tears and tried to remember to pull deep breaths in through my nose.

It was disconcerting, to be breathing in the smell of his laundry soap and his skin, and I couldn't ask him where this tenderness had come from, or why, scared as I was to break the moment. It was as close as I'd been to another human being in longer than I could remember, and while the physical closeness could have filled my stomach with butterflies and made my heart hammer, it mellowed into something soothing and deeply comforting. It felt right.

We stood there for a long time, and slowly I brought my own hands up to his shoulders, pressing his arms harder into me. I wanted to break down and ugly cry for all the things I'd been holding in for so long, but all that came out was a strangled laugh and it was finally what made him release me. He did so with a sigh that I hoped was reluctant.

"I'm sorry," he said finally from behind me, and I wasn't yet brave enough to turn around and face him. "I'm sorry for what you've been through and what you'll still have to go through. I'm sorry he's been so clueless that he can't see what's right in front of him. And I'm sorry that I was so unkind to you. I won't pretend I'm that important, but I'm sorry anyway."

Finally I turned, and there was deep sorrow in his eyes.

What had changed?

I launched myself at him, throwing my arms around his chest and squeezing so hard that it pushed a heavy breath from his lungs. He wasn't a hugger, I could tell by the way his whole body stiffened in response—well, that and I'd literally knocked the breath out of him.

The look on his face told me he desperately wanted to be that important to someone, but I wasn't so sure it was me, so very slowly I dropped my arms and stepped back. "Ugh, now I'm sorry. I did it again."

His lip curled up just a little and his eyes warmed.

Jiminy Cricket, he was beautiful, I thought, almost craning my neck to look up at him. He had well over a foot on me, which wasn't tough for most people, and I briefly entertained the delightful fantasy of scaling him like a mountain.

I took a step back, bracing my back against the fridge as I brought a hand up over my eyes and heaved a huge breath, pressing the back of my hand against each cheek as I did.

He stood there still, immobilized, watching me intently. He'd tucked his hands into the back pockets of his jeans and I admired the way it stretched the thermal henley over his wide chest. I wondered briefly what other tattoos I might find if I lifted the shirt up or pushed at his sleeves.

"You don't exactly make me uncomfortable," he said finally, his voice so quiet that I thought I imagined it. It made me look up at him, my hands tucked behind my butt as I leaned against the fridge.

"I do," he said firmly. "I let things make me uncomfortable because I fear change and an outcome I can't control."

"That's pretty normal." I laughed softly and Carrick whined, sitting beside Jack and leaning into his leg for attention. Jack reached one hand down to the dog's head and patted absently as Carrick's tail began to thump against the floor.

Rounding the island, Jack picked up his bottle and brought it over to the sink, tipping it in and rinsing it. "Truth be told, I didn't come here to have a drink with your husband." He made a face. "I wasn't expecting him at all, but once he opened the door..." He held out his hands helplessly.

"So you were kind of hoping I'd be home?" I couldn't stop the big grin that spread across my face, but I was only teasing a little bit. I wanted to get him to admit something I could hold close.

"Actually, I was kind of hoping no one would be home so I could tell myself that I'd tried but it hadn't gone according to plan."

"Oh." My eyes dropped to my feet. Well, at least he was honest, and that was more than Hunter had ever been.

Jack was grabbing a jacket I hadn't seen before, slipping those tree trunks he called arms into it, and my stomach dropped in disappointment at the thought of spending another evening alone in the cavernous house.

Carrick followed us to the door, where he sat and watched as I followed Jack out to his truck.

I wrapped my arms around myself, having left the heavier sweater in the house. A nasty breeze had picked up, tearing the last few leaves off the trees and tossing them across the pavement with a scraping noise.

"Did you come to apologize because Tyler yelled at you?" I asked as he unlocked his truck, the realization that it was a distinct possibility making my gut feel sour.

I wanted it to be Jack's idea.

I wanted to know that I occupied some corner of his thoughts, no matter how small.

Jack unlocked his truck before turning to face me with a small smile on his face. "I was afraid that if I didn't, the next time Tyler summoned you for a guys' night out, you might run me over with your jacked-up monster." He pivoted back, swinging the door open easily and I waited while he clipped his seatbelt and slid the window down. "After seeing your aim at the range, I trust you are a woman of many talents. We both already know you're full of surprises."

I don't know what came over me, I really don't, but there was something I had to know for sure and there was only one way to find out. I hopped up on the running board and leaned right through the window, curling cold fingers under his warm jaw for the split second it took my face to follow. "You have no idea, Jack," I whispered right up against his mouth before closing the tiny distance to press my lips to his.

This time I didn't give him a quick peck and dash away.

This time I waited out his reaction, feeling him tense, hearing the leather on the steering wheel creak when his fingers tightened around it. Then slowly he softened, the muscles of his face relaxing and he brought up one hand to slide into my hair, his lips moving beneath mine though he didn't allow me to deepen the kiss. It was as close to a white flag as I was going to get from him, I thought, feeling simultaneously victorious and disappointed.

He was the one to break the seal of our mouths, leaning back ever so slightly, his eyes still on my mouth, his thumb pressed to my bottom lip. "Enough," he said sternly, but he couldn't hide that his chest heaved with a deep intake of breath.

I didn't say anything back; just held his gaze for a long moment before kissing the pad of the thumb that rested against my mouth and watched his eyes flash. Then I leaned back and jumped off the running board, watching him scrub both hands over his face to run through his hair before he shook his head slightly and threw the truck into gear.

I watched as he drove down the long driveway, never looking back, my arms wrapped around my middle.

I knew he was wrong about being unimportant to me, because I would never get enough of him.

8

Jack

I couldn't sleep that night. No amount of tossing and turning, cold showers or weight lifting seemed to do the trick.

The ten seconds Daphne had stolen from me when she leaned in and kissed me played in my mind on an endless loop. With my eyes on my bedroom ceiling, I could remember the softness of her lips and the silk of her hair, the smell of her skin and the way her small fingers clutched at my face.

What had happened? I asked myself over and over. I'd been doing so well keeping her at a distance, throwing her off with cold shoulders and physical distance and keeping my hands to myself.

Stupid move, hugging her in the kitchen, but she'd been so broken...

Make no mistake about it, she was all I could think about since the day she'd traced the tattoo on my arm with her fingertips, and I hated that. It had been so easy for her to slip past the defenses I'd been building up bit by bit. I'd been constructing the walls since Natasha left, getting quieter and more withdrawn, my reactions to people more serious and stern; finding less to laugh about. Because if I didn't seek out happiness, I reasoned, I couldn't be disappointed.

If I expected nothing, the smallest moments of joy or contentment would be rewarding enough.

It was totally unlike me to call out, even when I was sick, but I was so tired and out of sorts that next morning, there was no way I'd get through a shift, so I called out. I must have sounded like death too, because my supervisor told me I should take as many days as I needed to feel better.

Everyone knew I had plenty of vacation time, sick days and personal days banked. I hadn't even taken time off when Tash left me, which should have been my first clue I was a mess.

Tyler showed up Tuesday evening after work, with a brown paper bag in one hand and a six-pack in the other. I answered the door in the clothes I'd been wearing for the last two days and he wrinkled his nose at me.

"Shower broken?" he asked, shoving past me to set the bag on the coffee table and turn up the volume on Sports Center. Rodgers had announced he was willing to bury the hatchet with his GM, and Tyler watched the interview with rapt attention.

I didn't answer him, dropping down next to him on the sofa as he grimaced, handing me a large container of chicken noodle soup and a huge chunk of bread.

"I'm doing you a favor," he announced around a mouthful of his sandwich. "If I tell G's mom that you're all mopey and shit—over a chick—she'll start sending over casseroles every damn day. I can't deal with that, you understand? She'll want *updates.* Updates on her 'big, strong Jackie.'" He adopted a falsetto voice, batted his eyelashes at me and then rolled his eyes, making a gagging noise.

Slurping some of the soup, I grinned at him. Generis's mother loved me, and that she'd already been to visit them four times since the birth of her granddaughter and I hadn't seen her once was pretty surprising. Whenever she was around, I had a standing invitation to dinner at Tyler and Generis's place, and she hovered over me the entire time, admonishing me to eat. "Big, strong man like you," preceded everything she shoved toward me.

"I'm not moping," I said and he fixed me with a stink eye that would have made my mother proud.

"Whatever, dumbass. You think I can't do simple math? I tell you to go apologize to her and then you don't show up at work for days. What happened, you finally made a move and that little minx shot you down? 'Cuz that seems unlikely."

Sinking into the sofa a little more, I busied myself with the soup, slurping it straight from the container so I wouldn't have to answer Tyler.

"You ass." Tyler's voice held a little anger in a sudden, kind of terrifying shift. "What did you say to her?"

It took a while to separate the container from my face and he waited while I did, arms crossed over his chest.

I contemplated asking him if he'd been born a woman, because his emotional radar was damn near uncanny.

I told him about Hunter being home when I arrived to apologize.

Then I told him about the tattoo I saw peeking out of Daphne's sweater and how it had rendered me completely stupid—it was the only explanation I had for her meltdown and the reason I'd broken every rule I had when I pulled her into my arms, because I felt like she needed comfort.

I didn't tell him that I wanted to be the only one who gave it to her.

By the time I got to the part where Daphne followed me out of the house, Tyler was bouncing like a little kid. It was fucking annoying. "I knew it," he was singing under his breath. "I knew it, I knew it, I knew it."

"What?" I finally blew up, stopping so that he could finish the story himself since, clearly, he *knew* it.

"You finally caved, my man!"

My lips turned down at the edges as I conceded his point. Technically I had, indeed, caved.

"And? And? And?" Tyler was so damn excited, he'd developed a stutter.

"And nothing." I shoved more bread into my mouth so I physically could not speak, not that remaining silent was a difficulty for me, and he knew it. He could wait me out like a Roman troop laying siege.

His lips flattened out into a thin line that I could see in my peripheral vision because yes, I was being a toddler and refusing to look at him.

"I can call Catalina right now," he whispered, and I exploded.

"Fuck off, Davis."

He held his hands up immediately in a gesture of surrender. "Just sayin', dude. Sounds like you're gonna need some casseroles."

Tyler cleaned up while I sat there, doing nothing more than pouting on the sofa, but in a super-manly way. With my arms crossed over my chest and a scowl on my face that would have made small children cry.

When he finally left I managed a grumbled "Thanks," and he slapped my shoulder a few times before I locked the door behind him and walked my ass up the stairs to take a shower.

Whatever this funk was, I didn't like it. It wasn't quite depression and it wasn't quite an illness brought on by lack of sleep. It was some sort of inertia that was trying to kill me one day at a time.

I fished out an old pain prescription I'd hidden so Pop wouldn't find it. Then I brushed my teeth, killed all the lights and flopped into bed, hoping like hell I could fall asleep because, come hell or high water, tomorrow I was going back to work before this thinking shit killed me.

A full week went by and my phone remained silent.

Daphne didn't text or call, and Tyler had remained weirdly silent on what I'd come to suspect was his favorite subject, despite the fact I saw him almost every day.

For a man who practically shit glitter every time her name was mentioned, it was a little distressing, because as usual it meant he was up to something. I was half tempted to ask him if he had any other hobbies—you know, besides meddling.

The worst part was that now Generis was on the case too, and if G put her mind to something ... well, she was backed up by her mother. And though Catalina hadn't started blowing up my phone or showing up at my door with foil pans filled with sympathy food, I knew it wouldn't be long.

Tyler was sneaky and Generis was determined, but they had nothing on Catalina.

And that, my friends, was how I walked right into the trap they set for me: with my eyes wide open.

Generis invited me over for dinner that next weekend, telling me how adorable my honorary niece was. She could sit up without help already, which clearly meant her daughter was a genius.

Wisely, I kept my mouth shut, having been tempted to tell her that she'd obviously canceled out Davis's Missing Link genes.

I knew the instant Generis answered the door that I was in trouble, and it was my nose that alerted me to the fact: empanadas, those little meat orgasms wrapped in delicious, flaky pockets of dough. Catalina's empanadas had been known to make grown men weep and I will neither confirm nor deny that the grown man was me. So you can understand that as Generis stepped aside to let me in without her customary bone-crushing hug, the jig was up.

This was a damn ambush.

"My Jackie!" Catalina bustled from the kitchen, all four and a half feet of her. The tiny woman folded herself around my middle in a fierce hug, and there was a twinkle in her eye when she looked up at me and took my face in her hand. "No." She shook her head. "This is no good, mi hijo. Come, you are too thin." Then she latched onto my hand with an iron grip, dragging me with the force of ten horses toward the dining room.

I held the baby so Generis could eat, which slowed my progress considerably. But since Tyler claimed Violet was smitten with me, and babies were my freaking kryptonite, I held her close with one arm while I ate carefully.

Violet did her best to distract me by blowing bubbles and flailing, trying to grab my face, my shirt—anything she could get her tiny hands on. I'd be lying if I said it didn't turn me into a big pile of mush, but I had a man card to maintain, so I kept it together when all I wanted to do was blow raspberries on her little belly and talk stupid-squishy baby talk to her.

Catalina was much quieter than usual, leaving Generis to grill me like she was a CIA operative, because the girl didn't miss a trick.

And throughout Generis's hard glares and pointed questions about my love life, Catalina watched me with small, knowing smiles that made me very uncomfortable.

Generis was elbow-deep in soapy water by the time I carried a sleepy Violet into the kitchen and Catalina warmed a bottle.

I was surprised to find that while Catalina clucked and cooed at Violet, she didn't try to take her from me.

As Catalina tested the temperature of the milk there was a horrible gurgling sound and the baby's face turned a violent red. I looked down in alarm, ready to perform CPR. Then her expression relaxed, she gave me a bright-eyed, pink-gummed smile, and I choked on the most ungodly smell.

"You got this, Jack?" Generis hadn't pulled her hands out of the sink and she was grinning wickedly. She knew damn well that I adored her daughter, but I didn't have the first clue what to do when it came to the care of small children. "She's very agreeable when you change her. You'll find everything you need in her station upstairs."

I climbed the stairs with a stinky, squirming baby in my arms, muttering to Violet that I refused to believe the outcome of my forthcoming attempts could be blamed solely upon my own ineptitude. Clearly her parents were being negligent.

She churned her little body in my arms, releasing fresh bursts of the smell I was sure could be patented as a biological weapon, and I flicked on the light to her bedroom before settling her on the small changing table.

It took me a while to get the hang of things, mostly because I was out of practice and didn't have a gas mask. The fumes had activated some kind of leaky tear duct situation I couldn't get under control, like someone had strapped a raw onion to my face.

Eventually I figured out how to handle Baby Krakatoa: lift her from the diaper by her tiny ankles, wipe from the backs of her knees, where the shit started, all the way up to the middle of her back.

Repeat with clean wipes.

Eventually, though it took a solid handful of wipes and a few adjustments to the diaper tabs, she was fresh and smiling again.

Looking over my shoulder to make sure no one was watching, I leaned over her changing table and blew a raspberry on her little tummy. She squealed with laughter, so I did it again, because it made both of us smile.

Then again.

And finally, when she no longer found it humorous, I grabbed the clean onesie lying at the end of the table and dressed her like I was handling a porcelain doll.

Settling into the chair near her crib, I pulled a book from the basket and tucked her into the crook of one arm, spreading the book open on my knee and reading to her quietly while I held her bottle with the other hand.

It took almost no time for her little eyes to begin drooping and I nudged her several times to finish her bottle before she drifted off into LaLa Land. Then I set down the bottle, patted her back until she rewarded me with a loud burp, and closed the book, moving her carefully to her crib.

Generis was grinning at me from the doorway when I looked up. "That was amazing, Jack," she whispered. "She never nods off like that for me. Clearly you have the magic touch."

"Nah." It was in my nature to be self-deprecating. "She's not used to me being part of her bedtime routine, so flirting with me wore her out. She's just like her mother." I grinned at Generis, who dropped her head to level me with a bemused glare.

Tyler appeared behind his girlfriend, smiling over her shoulder. "She *was* flirting with you awful hard at dinner. I was almost worried, since she's always such a daddy's girl. Think we're gonna have a problem."

The three of us tiptoed down the stairs and sat in the small living room and Catalina brought in glasses of Aguardiente, which would have been dangerous to begin with, but this stuff was her own home recipe. Calling that stuff fire water didn't come close to describing the feeling of the Devil tap dancing in my gut as I swallowed. The anise flavor somehow intensified the burn, and it didn't matter how many times Catalina swore it was "medicinal," I was pretty sure I'd end up checking into the hospital to treat a bleeding ulcer. So I sipped slowly, just to avoid the "big, strong man" comments Catalina liked to lob my way just before she forced more on me. The last thing I needed was a refill, or to walk home because I couldn't see straight.

It wasn't until I was driving home that I realized Daphne's name hadn't actually come up the entire evening. Immediately that made me suspicious, since she'd been Tyler's Numero Uno topic of conversation pretty much since the day she showed up at the range. And now that Generis was Team Daphne, I hadn't gotten a moment's rest around those two. Maybe that was one of the reasons I'd dug in my heels so hard: I hated being pushed toward something that hadn't originally been my idea.

I'd inherited a stubborn streak from both parents: Pop blamed it on the Irish, while Mom had always blamed it on Pop.

Speaking of Pop, he'd completed the first half of his stay. When I'd talked to him on the phone the night before, he'd been in good spirits, pretty lucid when he told me his therapist recommended he finish out the full ninety days. Since that meant he'd be gone past Christmas, there was a small window of opportunity. I was allowed to visit him on Sunday, for a maximum of two hours. It meant almost no sleep that night, as I was up by three.

The center was a pricey one, more like a resort to the untrained eye than anything else. That it was all the way out in Long Island meant over seven hours in the truck, and I preferred to spend that time with as few of my fellow drivers as possible, so after brewing about a gallon of coffee, I was out the door and on I-95, heading north.

The drive gave me a lot of time to think and I pondered whether Daphne's appearance in my life had been linked in any way to building something tentative with Pop. I didn't think so, but this woman worked in mysterious ways. She had me discombobulated and unsettled, and I had to admit to myself that without her pushing me, I probably wouldn't have made a point of driving out to visit Pop, anxious and restless for something I didn't yet understand.

I spent the full two hours with Pop. He looked good, which filled me with relief. He'd had a haircut and a shave and they'd managed to fatten him up a bit, filling out the hollows in his face. His eyes had been bright, the tremors slight, and when I'd given him the small gift I brought, since I wouldn't see him again until after Christmas, he choked right up.

Driving home that evening, I felt the most at peace I had in a very, very long time. Pop was through the hardest part of it, though I knew the battle was far from over. Every day would be a struggle, but I knew it had to be worth it. With any luck this would help slow the progression of the disease; it would give us time to get to know one another, something I hadn't realized I wanted so desperately until lately.

It was after nine by the time I pulled into the driveway and I knew when I closed my eyes in my bed, the lines dividing the lanes would continue to flash through my brain.

I'd listened to all my playlists and four podcasts during the long drive and I was filled to overflowing with lyrics and information. I'd done it to try to drown out the incessant nagging inside my own head. You know, the voice that sounded an awful lot like Tyler, reminding me that I was being a thick-headed, numb-skulled Neanderthal. I was pretty sure he'd said that word for word recently, and it sounded like something that had come running right out of Generis's mouth.

There was a light on in my house. I noticed it as I got out of the truck, into the cold snap of the December air. There were no other cars in my driveway or parked along the street, and it wasn't impossible I'd forgotten to turn it off before leaving the house.

I kicked off my boots on the front porch before unlocking the door, stepping into a scene that made my jaw drop. Daphne was standing on a step stool in front of an honest-to-goodness real Christmas tree, hanging the ornaments I remembered packing away in my garage several years earlier.

There was a cheerful fire burning in the fireplace and Dean Martin's voice drifted through the house, telling me he'd be home for Christmas, thanks to the pretty damn decent sound system I'd installed not long after Natasha left.

I shut the door slowly, drawing in a deep breath of something that made my stomach roar and Daphne turned quickly, nearly falling off the stool. "Oh!" She looked positively alarmed. "Poop! Tyler told me you weren't supposed to be home until tomorrow—I wasn't going to be here!"

She looked so damn cute, tinsel stuck in her hair, her sweater falling off one shoulder and I shifted uncomfortably, angry at myself when my dick jumped in my pants.

Looking around, I realized this did indeed have Tyler written all over it. The man left glitter and good cheer in his wake like a freaking fairy, and he most certainly knew where I'd stashed all of the Christmas shit Natasha had insisted upon buying. It was stuff I didn't want to see, because it hurt, so for the past few Christmases I had been the embodiment of the Grinch: no decorations inside or outside of the house, and no Christmas carols. Nothing special at all, other than trying to sleep in on Christmas day and buying a pre-made turkey at the grocery store.

Another voice drifted from the kitchen and it drew me up short. "Mi carino, everything is prepared and cleaned; I will leave now."

Daphne stepped carefully off the stool, moving quickly through the doorway and toward the kitchen.

I heard an exclamation of surprise and quick movements and there was Catalina, wiping her hands on a towel and grinning up at me as she hurried into the living room. "Jackie." She leaned quickly into me and I brought up an arm around her shoulders to give her a squeeze, certain the look of confusion hadn't left my face.

"Catalina and I discovered we have people in common." Daphne's voice was gentle, from where she stood leaning into the doorframe, watching the two of us. "When Tyler and Generis had me over for dinner a few nights ago, I found out the precious woman who keeps my house spotless and my fridge filled with tamales was your friend, too. It was an easy sell, to get her to help me."

I didn't know what to say to any of it. Catalina was still grinning up at me, her hand pinching my cheek. She looked like the cat who'd eaten the canary and I wasn't entirely sure why.

There was a short honk from the driveway and Catalina stepped back quickly, grabbing her coat off the back of the sofa and shrugging her small shoulders into it. "Merry Christmas, my Jackie," she said with a sweet smile, dragging my face down to hers to kiss my cheek, and before I could form any words she slipped around me and out the door, leaving me staring at Daphne.

In my house.

In leggings and the softest pink cloud of a sweater I'd ever seen.

And in that moment, confusion turned to absolute horror. Because this was my every fantasy of late: coming home to find her in my house, the house warm and welcoming thanks to her touches, delightful smells coming from the kitchen.

Daphne, smiling, warm and welcoming—welcoming *me.*

I knew what made a house a home—I wasn't a complete idiot—and I knew it couldn't be the woman who stood in front of me, because I couldn't have her.

Daphne said nothing, looking far less repentant than she had just moments earlier. She moved smoothly toward the sofa, tucking several boxes back together and stacking them into a large bin. The tree glowed behind her, the twinkly white lights setting off tiny reflections in the small glass ornaments.

"Catalina knew you would be hungry after such a long drive," she said, her voice still soft, and I wondered if she was speaking quietly to keep from spooking me.

How did she know where I'd been?

"She's been cooking all day while I worked on decorating. I hope..." She looked down at her feet, her cheeks flushing a deep pink. "I hope I didn't overstep, Jack, and I'm aware this could be really offensive. We just wanted to do something nice."

"Something nice?" It was the first thing I'd been able to say, more a fragmented thought than a complete sentence, and it came out all rough and gravelly sounding, since I hadn't spoken in hours. "So you broke into my house to decorate for a holiday I don't celebrate."

"Everyone loves Christmas." Her smile was nervous now, uncertain, but I'd started down the asshole trajectory and saw no cause to stop now.

I hadn't invited her here.

I hadn't invited Catalina either, and despite the food, despite the cheery decorations and the warm, comforting way the house felt, something hot and sharp had splintered inside my chest and it was something that hurt. It was like lancing a boil: there was relief, but the recent memory of the pressure, the intense pain, made me irritable.

"My wife left me at Christmas," I spat angrily, feeling my hands curl into fists when I said it.

At the time I thought it was my fault, too. I'd remained convinced of that for months, until a therapist helped me to understand Tash had never really intended to stay. I was an oasis; a stopover; her starter marriage. She took what she wanted, whatever she could get from me, and when she felt I'd outlived my usefulness, she was gone.

Daphne's face fell and I felt instantaneously guilty, like I'd just kicked a puppy.

Of course. This was her first Christmas truly without her husband.

"I can understand that," she said, turning to fold up the step stool and leaning it against the wall. "Blair and I have spent eight Christmases alone." She looked down at her feet. "That's not counting the three she and I spent alone before I married Hunter."

Quick math told me that meant Blair had celebrated very few Christmases with her father. That seemed unkind, even to me and my tiny little Grinch heart.

"I stopped asking a long time ago, what was more important than his family at what was supposed to be the happiest time of year."

Would she just quit talking, already? It was making my head hurt.

"It didn't take Blair and me long to decide that we would make the best of it. We would bring happiness to others. So each year, we've tried to find something to do to bring a smile to someone else's face. This year I wanted it to be you, because you deserve to be happy, Jack. And this is none of my business, but I feel like you've *chosen* to be miserable."

I looked up, swallowing hard, because her eyes were all shiny and hopeful.

This woman didn't owe me shit, and here she was sprinkling her damn fairy dust all over my house, doing what she had probably done for years, making things beautiful, warm, and welcoming.

"Well," I said finally, easing out of my coat. "I guess I should say thanks. And since it looks like you're done, I suppose I should offer you a ride home."

"Oh..." She pulled her fingers into the long sleeves of her sweater, wrapping her arms tightly around her middle. "Well, no, Blair should be here soon to pick me up. I just ... had a few things to finish up."

I held an arm out in a gesture that indicated she should proceed and she eyed me warily as she carried the bin toward the kitchen. I heard the soft click of the door, making me think she was returning it to the garage.

When she came back I was sitting on the sofa, my elbow leaning on the arm rest, a hand over my eyes.

I knew I should thank her with more feeling, but it made me uncomfortable to think of her in my house.

Touching my things.

Seeing the things I showed to no one.

It made me uncomfortable, because I wasn't ready to share those things with her or anyone else—it was a miracle I let Tyler into the house, and I'd known him for years.

It didn't surprise many folks to find I was intensely private.

"Okay, well..." There was a rustling noise that I knew meant Daphne was getting into her coat. "I know you've had a long day, so I'll let you be."

Did I want her to leave?

Yes, I needed her to leave.

Do you really want her to leave?

No, no, no. Please don't leave me here by myself; I'll just be miserable and angry and sad and I'll drink way too much.

"Jack." Her voice was sweet, her hand sweeping gently across my shoulders in what I supposed was some kind of consolation, and it made my heart jump. I couldn't look up at her, something uncomfortable making my throat close up. What I should say and what I wanted to say were similar things, but I couldn't get the words past my own lips. Instead, I stood and dipped my head at her in a nod just as lights swept across the wall.

That would be her daughter.

"Merry Christmas, you big grump." She pushed up on tiptoes and dropped a soft kiss on my cheek, making my heart hammer in my ears.

Then, with a small smile over her shoulder, she was gone.

I sat back down on the sofa for a moment, trying to save up the energy to haul myself to the kitchen. The smells permeating the house warranted further investigation, especially since I hadn't eaten anything since the early afternoon.

Eventually my stomach won, dragging me forcibly into the kitchen, where I found the refrigerator stuffed full of Catalina's incredible cooking. And God bless her, but there it was: a pre-filled plate loaded with all of my favorites, the plastic wrap covered in condensation since everything was still warm.

I unwrapped the plate and took it back out to the living room, sitting on the sofa again to look at the tree while I ate. I wouldn't have made this kind of effort for myself, so I tried to appreciate it since Daphne had done it for me. She obviously thought I needed joy and cheer in my life, although the last thing I was about to do was admit it to her or anyone else.

Especially fucking Tyler.

The mantel had been decorated and one stocking hung there, my name scrolling up the front in a font I recognized as Natasha's handwriting, permanently stitched into the fabric. It was lumpy too, like something or some things had been shoved into it.

The room smelled of pine, a smell I actually really liked, from the fresh Christmas tree and the fresh garland she'd tied down along the banister of the stairs. It too had twinkling lights wrapped into it.

I sat back, my empty plate beside me. The room was warm and cozy, every sitting area in the room covered with soft, warm blankets and holiday throw pillows. I mean, really, a craft store had thrown up in my living room and the most surprising thing was that I wasn't actually irritated over it, because usually I hated this girly crap.

Thinking back to when Natasha and I had first married, I chuckled at the memory of her shock when she found I had exactly one Christmas decoration: three strings of colored lights I hung around the house, on the hooks I'd installed under the eaves. It was my only recognition of the holiday, trying to come across as something other than the Grinch himself, and it was only since everyone else in my neighborhood seemed to be smoking the Christmas crack each year, their houses lit up with alarmingly bright lights, figurines on their lawns and huge trees visible in their front windows.

Tash had dragged me from one store to the next for several successive weekends, collecting lights, ornaments, figurines—an incredible amount of shit that I had no idea how we would store, because I sure as hell wasn't filling up my workout area with plastic storage tubs.

We had exactly two good Christmases. The two immediately after we were married, before she stopped trying altogether.

Oh, she had still decorated all right, but the shine was off the penny. She was done trying with me. I hadn't lived up to her expectations, but she'd never told me what they were. I didn't even get the chance to try, because God knew I would have tried. I had loved her too much, and she hadn't loved me enough.

Words weren't exactly my strength, but I could do things: If she needed something, I got it for her.

If something was broken, I fixed it.

If she wanted something changed: paint color, new sofa, renovated bathroom, I did it for her.

And maybe I complained a little, but I really tried not to.

The day she left, I called Tyler and even though it was Christmas, he came over and helped me take down all the decorations for a holiday I never wanted to celebrate ever again. Then he helped me pack everything into boxes and tubs and haul it out into the garage, where I stacked it up and left it to rot.

I hadn't taken any of it out since.

My capacity for anger was impressive, according to Tyler, my own little Mary Fucking Sunshine. He said I'd always been an angry son of a bitch, but when Natasha left I took things to a whole new level.

I was mad at everything and everyone.

I could always find a way and a reason, and for the first time in a long time, I couldn't find it. Instead, I felt hollow. There was a gaping, needy hole in my chest that I couldn't fill and I had the terrible, sneaking suspicion that what could fill it was a very specific something or someone: about five feet tall and wearing a pink sweater.

I didn't like this feeling. I preferred being angry to this thing that was an irritating, empty howling inside that I suspected just might be loneliness. That was the fucker I'd been keeping out so long by filling myself up with anger, because it was insidious and relentless.

The music had become less jovial and mind-numbingly nostalgic, and as Andy Williams's rendition of *Ave Maria* began to play over the speakers, I leaned forward onto my knees and finally, officially, lost my shit. It was something I hadn't allowed myself to do since Natasha had left, afraid that once I let out some of the poison it would just never stop flowing. Instead, it had festered and boiled just under the surface for years, and finally letting it out burned and stung.

Setting my plate on the floor, I curled up on the sofa and wrapped my arms around myself. It was a poor substitute for what I needed, that much I knew, and I'd known for a long time that what I needed wasn't Natasha. She'd run away from me, whereas I was running away from Daphne.

The woman kept running toward me, her heart so big and open. I knew there was room for me in there and damn it, I wanted my own space in there.

There, I said it.

I pushed myself to a sitting position, struggling with my thoughts. I was tired from the long day of driving, the emotional toll of spending time with Pop, and coming home to find something completely unexpected.

Daphne's kindness was a kindness that hurt.

Banking the fire quickly, I walked my plate into the kitchen and hurried back to the living room to shove my feet into my boots.

I pulled on my coat and grabbed the keys to the truck.

I was done with this lonely shit.

I was done with being angry and miserable and sad, all at the same time.

There was a woman only a few miles away who seemed to care for me, and it was about time I figured out just how much.

9

Daphne

Blair drove us home quietly, a real feat considering I knew there were a million questions she wanted to ask.

I hadn't told her much about Jack, or about any of my new and unusual group of friends, for that matter.

She'd only just met Tyler and his family a few nights earlier, when we'd gone over for dinner and discovered our odd link to Catalina.

Catalina had gone on and on about "her Jackie," to the point Generis was rolling her eyes and Tyler confided in me later that Jack could do no wrong in Catalina's eyes.

I saw it as something else. There was pride in Catalina's voice when she spoke of Jack. He was always helping Tyler and Generis, and didn't hesitate to show up when Catalina needed something: a dead car battery, a faulty outlet—he was there. And I began to suspect that my sweet little housekeeper loved Jack like the son she'd never had. She was a Spanish mama, after all, and God knew their boys could do no wrong.

Blair parked her car in the garage, a little Volkswagen that Hunter had purchased for her, the size of which gave me agida every time I thought of her out on a major highway in the little rattletrap.

"Daddy wants to spend Christmas here," she said softly as she pushed the ignition switch to turn off the car and I sank back into my seat, listening to the quiet rattle of the garage door closing behind us.

I wasn't so cruel as to keep Hunter from his daughter, but I knew better than to think he wanted to spend Christmas with me. I suspected that just perhaps he had nowhere else to spend it, other than with his pregnant girlfriend, or perhaps alone in his small Georgetown home if she decided to return to her parents' place.

His relationship with his parents had always been somewhat strained, so that had really never been an option. In fact, I couldn't recall us spending a single Christmas with them in the last twenty years.

"Nana and Papa will be here," I reminded her, a little thrill of happiness zinging through my brain when I thought of my parents, due to arrive the following afternoon. "Just remind him of that, because he may decide he doesn't want to stay long. He and Papa don't exactly see eye to eye on a number of things."

Blair snorted, turning to roll her eyes at me in exaggerated fashion. "Like you, Mom. You can just come out and say it: Papa's known the whole time that Dad had his hand in the cookie jar, and this time no one's looking the other way. He deserves it, I know. You put up with him and his crap for a long time. But even if you're finally gonna go off and be happy, he's still my dad. I still want him to have a place in my life, even if he doesn't really deserve it."

I hated it when she made sense.

I would never do something to keep her from her father, but it hurt a little to realize he'd done nothing to earn her love—had pushed her away by most accounts—and she still maintained room in her heart for him.

Carrick snuffled both of us noisily when we let ourselves into the house, and he followed me into the living room, where I flicked the switch on the gas fireplace and moved immediately to a small cabinet to mix something to settle my roiling stomach.

I needed something strong.

Jack's reaction had been largely what I'd expected, but something was in the air. It was something that bothered me, and I couldn't put my finger on it. For once it had absolutely nothing to do with Hunter or his escapades.

"Geez Mom, alcoholic much?" Blair teased as she watched me pour and I startled, sloshing a little on the small table. "I guess you've got no one home now to keep an eye on you." She grinned, but it was a little wary.

I swirled the glass, filled with the basic ingredients for a lemon drop, heavy on the vodka. "I'll have you know that I haven't had a drink in weeks." I lifted the glass in the air. "I just ... I don't know, I feel unsettled tonight."

"That's what you're calling it? Unsettled?" Blair snorted, making huge air quotes before settling onto the sofa herself. "Are you that out of touch, Mom? It's called lust. I mean, duh. Your lady bits are on fire after spending some time with that smokin'-hot manly-man." Her grin was wicked.

My cheeks flamed instantaneously. "What? No. I wasn't talking about that."

"Yeah, whatever, Mom. Generis showed me the video of Mr. Tall, Dark and Handsome rocking Violet to sleep. *My* ovaries practically exploded, and I have *zero* interest in old dudes or babies. He's all yours." She snorted a little, fanning herself before running a hand through her long hair.

That's the problem: he's not mine at all.

Oh, but that video. To torture me, maybe, Tyler had sent it to me and I'd watched it no fewer than seven hundred times in the last few days: Jack exclaiming over the mess, then carefully wiping the baby, gently adjusting her diaper and tenderly dressing her.

Blowing on her tummy until she squealed, his beautiful face in profile as he smiled down at her, one of his big hands cradling her head.

Holding her in his arms to feed her a bottle while reading a bedtime story ... *swoon.*

Saying it made my ovaries explode wasn't *remotely* adequate when it described what that sweet, four-minute video did to my insides.

I settled onto the sofa beside her and watched the flames roll and billow in the fireplace, my thoughts equally volatile. I was still all kinds of worked up just from kissing his cheek before I left, and it seemed highly unlikely the situation would be resolving itself anytime soon.

Clearly, I was going to have to take matters into my own hands, something I did only when completely desperate.

The quiet was pierced by a ringtone on Blair's phone, and her face lit up. "It's Tristan, Mom. I'm gonna go take this upstairs."

I nodded at her, making a note to self to ask her about this Tristan person in the morning.

As long as he took the place of No-Motivation Jake, I could potentially be convinced to get on that train.

Slowly finishing my drink, I pushed myself up off the sofa and flipped the fireplace switch again. I sighed, leaving my empty glass on the mantle, just above the stockings that hung from heavy iron pinecones.

The room was beautiful, the enormous Christmas tree in the corner covered with the multi-colored lights Blair had insisted upon since she was a child. It was bedecked in tinsel garland and strewn with the mishmash of ornaments we'd collected over the years. It wasn't magazine-worthy or even pretty, as far as most people were concerned, but to me it was perfect in its imperfection.

That should have been obvious, right? I snorted. Daphne Masters: collector of oddities and broken things.

I liked quirky.

A little disorder in the sea of perfection.

I stood for a while, looking at the small pile of presents I'd been sneaking under the tree, one gift at a time, for the past month.

Crap, I'd forgotten to take Jack's gifts to his house. It would be Christmas in a few days and I would spend it with the people who meant everything in the world to me.

Except for Jack.

I looked around the room angrily, sure someone had whispered that into my ear.

Stupid, stupid vodka, making me all crazy.

I mean, whatever. It wasn't like Jack wanted to spend *any* of his days with me. Obviously. He could hardly handle being in the same room as me, and for heaven's sake, I was tired of being obvious.

I was tired of trying.

I was tired of trying to get close to someone so prickly and incapable of letting anyone else in.

Clearly, when he'd held me in my kitchen it had been an anomaly. He'd felt guilty or something, and he paid his debt by trying to offer me comfort.

Carrick followed me up the stairs, nudging his cold nose into my hand as we went and absently I patted his head. I could feel him smiling his sweet, dopey doggy smile.

Brushing my teeth and washing my face, I slipped into some warm flannel pajamas and flipped the switch to the bedroom fireplace, setting the timer, because it was hard to keep such a big house warm. Burning stacks of cash might have been more effective, and I shut the bedroom door to keep the heat in, the dog settling happily into his bed in the corner.

I'd just begun to drift when there was a sound at the door.

"Mom?" Blair's voice came from the other side and I sat up in bed, pushing the covers back, alarmed.

"What is it, babe?" I pulled the door open, shivering when a cold blast swept up the stairs.

"Um, so ... not to be weird about this or anything..." her eyes were bouncing between me and something in the stairwell. "But, uh ... you sorta have company." She coughed something into her fist, something that sounded an awful lot like "Booty call."

I pulled the door open wider and peered over the railing to see Jack standing at the bottom, barely into the entryway, his jaw set so hard that he looked angry. It made my stomach flip. Was he here to apologize, or was he here to take out some frustrations?

"I'll be in my room if you need me," she whispered, pointing down the long hallway. "But you'll have to knock *very* loudly if you do." She tapped at an earbud in one ear, smirking at me.

"Blair!" I hissed, blood rushing to my cheeks as I stared at my daughter in mortification. Seriously. What did she think was going to happen?

Then I looked down at Jack again.

Oh, yeah ... that. That was definitely going to happen.

He didn't say a word. He waited until Blair disappeared down the hallway before he climbed the steps, taking long, purposeful strides down the hallway toward where I stood.

I couldn't interpret the look on his face, something flat and hard that might have been anger, or it might have been desire. In my flannel pajamas and bare face, I very much doubted it was the latter.

I moved as he stalked closer, backing into the room and he followed, shutting the door firmly behind me. The latching noise was loud in the big room and Carrick lifted his head from the dog bed, but he didn't get up, settling again with a sigh.

Some guard dog he was.

"You were in my bedroom." His voice was hard and I swallowed, figuring it was silly to argue the obvious.

Yes, I'd been in his bedroom. I'd draped a festive garland over his headboard, having woven tiny fairy lights through it for effect. Then I'd set up a sweet little nativity scene on his dresser and swapped his bedsheets for some warm flannel sheets with a snowflake print, pulling a heavy duvet from his linen closet and covering it with a green flannel cover. When I left the room, it looked like a giant hug.

Overstep? Totally.

The garage held a wealth of seasonal decorations and I'd dug happily through each bin when Tyler showed me where he'd helped stash the holiday stuff. I'd found bath towels and rugs, throw pillows, garlands, battery-operated candles and cute figurines—you name it. Clearly not things he'd have purchased for himself.

"What were you trying to do in there, Daphne?" His voice was quieter now, but there was still an edge to it. "Are you trying to ... tame me, or something? Show me what a capable little wife you would be?"

My eyes widened in shock and horror. Had that been what I was doing? Certainly that was the way it had been perceived, and this made him angry.

"I wanted to do something that made you smile," I answered weakly, completely offended. "Something that made you feel like your home was welcoming and cozy, so you could enjoy the holidays."

"Without anyone in my life to enjoy it with?" The expression on his face was as bitter as his voice.

"What do you want me to say, Jack?" I whispered it, sinking down onto the bed and pulling my knees up, wrapping my arms around them. "Do you want me to say that while I was putting soft sheets on your bed, I was imagining myself in that room with you? Maybe you want me to tell you that I wanted you to spend your holidays—your nights—with me?"

If I didn't push him, this wasn't going to go anywhere.

He swallowed hard.

"Fine, I'll admit it. I did. I imagined what it would be like to have you come home to me at the end of the day and curl up behind me in that warm little cocoon. I want to be the little spoon, okay? I'm being stupid, I know." I let out a helpless laugh, because there it was: no misinterpreting that confession, and I waited silently for his expression to change.

For him to respond.

For him to move.

Turn.

Walk away.

Anything.

He stood there for a long time, his eyes closed, pulling deep breaths in through his nose and I waited, unable to breathe.

When he opened his eyes he held out a hand to me and I pushed up from the bed with blood pounding in my ears. I took his hand, looking up at him nervously.

If I were Ava, I'd throw him down and have my way with him.

Seduce him.

Strip off my clothes and climb him like a tree.

Drive him so crazy that he couldn't see straight.

But who was I kidding? Me and my soft plaid jammies weren't exactly libido boosters.

He pulled me closer, each of his big hands coming up to rest on either side of my face and I swallowed, confused, as he dropped his forehead the considerable distance to mine and stood there, thoughts obviously boiling behind his closed eyes.

For the first time, it felt like he'd stopped fighting or pushing or trying to maintain a distance. I couldn't recall a time he'd ever touched me purposely beyond the time he'd hugged me in my kitchen.

Something nagged in my brain, telling me that my words wouldn't be enough, because this man spoke through actions. I knew only the barest of details, thanks to Tyler and Generis—things Jack would never have told me about himself. And with those few glimpses into the life he'd had, I wondered if he suffered a similar lack of confidence.

Jack needed what I needed: to feel wanted and loved, desired and cherished. Important to someone, just *one* someone. The one that mattered.

Reaching between us, my fingers shook as I tugged at the heavy zipper on his thick, rough coat and I swallowed so hard, my throat made a funny noise. Just one corner of his mouth quirked up in the tiniest, sweetest smile. It was glorious, softening the hard, unforgiving planes of his handsome face.

His hands dropped slowly to my neck, his thumbs brushing just beneath my jaw, his eyes hot and searching, and when I finally tugged the zipper free, he let me pull the heavy winter coat off of him. Yet he brought his hands immediately back to my neck, propping his thumbs under my jaw like he wanted to hold my face in a certain place.

Letting my eyes drop to his full, soft lips, I sucked in a breath at the bolt of lightning that speared my middle. The intensity of *want* I felt for him was almost enough to fold me in half; bring me to my knees. He must have felt it too, his hips pressing into my own and I felt the hard ridge of him, hot and solid up against my stomach. It made me shiver deliciously, a thrill running down each limb to fizz in my fingers and toes with a shot of pure adrenaline.

He pushed me gently and I took a step back, my knees giving way as I sank onto the bed while he knelt in front of me. It put his face just slightly lower than mine, his face tilted up, his eyes on my mouth.

"I'm not imagining this, am I?" My voice was weak and breathy and he smiled at me, top teeth sinking into his lower lip. It made him look like a little boy and my heart stumbled over itself.

"You've imagined this? With ... me?"

"Every single stupid second that I'm breathing," I sighed, and his eyes flicked up to mine, sparkling with happiness.

"Good," he said softly, running a thumb slowly back and forth across my lower lip. "I like knowing I wasn't the only one struggling."

"Pffft, hardly." I snorted. "You ignored me like it was an Olympic sport. Gold for you, by the way."

He didn't laugh or smile at that. "I couldn't ignore you, Daphne, and I've *hated* that."

"Well..." My voice felt like it had dropped an octave, all victorious with his admission. "Let me remind you why you shouldn't."

With that I leaned forward the few inches that separated us and sank my fingers into his short, dark hair, bringing my legs up to wrap around his hips, my lips hovering just a breath from his.

He made a sound in the back of his throat, a growl or a groan, while he waited for me, the tension in his body making him vibrate like a live wire.

Kissing him was an explosion. He pushed forward on his knees when our mouths met, meeting my lips for the first time with purpose rather than frozen shock, and it was like he wanted to eat me alive after denying himself for so long. His teeth grazed my lips, his hands wound through and clenched my hair in great big fistfuls, and the sound I heard in the room might have been me whimpering.

Or maybe it was him?

For the love of all things holy, the man could kiss. I could feel every stroke of his tongue all the way down to my toes, hot and tingly and oh, so delicious. It made me grip him tighter with my thighs, and when he pushed up onto his feet it shoved me backward onto the bed, sliding me across as he stretched out over me.

"You persistent, frustrating, beautiful, annoying, wonderful woman. Why couldn't you just let me be?" he growled into my neck, breaking away from my mouth to kiss his way down my neck and across my clavicle.

His big hand wrenched several buttons loose, his tongue dragging across my overheated skin, followed by tiny nips with his teeth. It was freaking incendiary. My stupid flannel pajamas were suddenly so dang hot, I thought I might overheat.

Burst into flame.

Be reduced to a pile of ash right then and there.

Wouldn't that be a shame, because then I'd miss the really good stuff.

Finally, he pushed himself up on his elbows to drag in some air and I unwound my legs from his waist, my thighs numb and weak. I panted along with him, pushing up on my hands and forcing him back so that I was in a sitting position. Then I bunched my hands into the fabric of his shirt and pulled him back to me, my legs draped over his thighs while he tried to figure out how to keep getting closer.

Sneaking my fingers beneath the hem of his shirt, I slid them up, fingers wide across the hot, smooth expanse of his back. The muscles that shifted under my touch made me wish there was more light in the room, because I wanted to strip him naked and follow the line of every tattoo I knew I'd find with the tip of my tongue.

Until he was shaking and begging and desperate.

I wanted to watch this man break and know I was the one holding the pieces.

"I was fine until you showed up in that stupid monster truck," he groaned helplessly. "I was doing just fine." Like he was trying to convince himself.

I begged to differ.

He let me pull his shirt up after unbuttoning the two simple buttons at the top. And spank me cross-eyed, but the view was just fiiiine. It was far better than I could have anticipated, tattoos covering most of his arms and an impressive portion of his chest.

I leaned in, kissing one pattern after another, stealing delighted peeks at him as he sat there with his eyes closed. He looked ... rapturous ... and the sigh that came from his lips was a sound of relief.

"So you like a little ink," he finally whispered, and I bit his shoulder lightly, which made him smile.

Sitting back then, a little irritated he'd been so patient with my shirt, I unfastened the remaining few buttons and let it slip from my shoulders.

He had seen four of the little birds on my shoulder before, but what he didn't know was that three more flew from the bottom of the script, toward the side of my ribcage, the last one rounding my ribcage.

Catching his breath, he lifted his hands to cup me reverently, holding me like I was the most precious thing he'd ever been given.

This Jack was different.

This man was tender and sweet.

This was the man who cuddled tiny babies and read them bedtime stories.

This was a man I wanted to trust with my heart and my body, and I must have let out a huge breath, because it made him smile at me. "You're so beautiful that it hurts," he whispered, releasing me to smooth his hands down my sides, his index finger landing on the last little bird.

"Show me." He twisted a finger in the air, indicating I should spin. I had to pull my legs back to do so and I turned carefully, sitting on my feet while his fingers brushed my hair over my shoulder, then traced over the delicate script and counted the birds.

"Oh, Daphne. No..." His voice was full of sorrow and I turned quickly.

"Seven?" His expression was incredulous.

I nodded slowly.

If anyone knew a bird was a symbol of loss, it was him. I had counted five little sparrows on his shoulder blade, and without asking I knew it meant he'd lost friends.

Brothers.

But mine?

Mine were lost children, and he knew that.

Most women would have stopped trying after two or three, but I was not most women. I was either the most pigheaded woman alive or the biggest glutton for punishment, because I'd tried again and again and again. Each time I'd told myself that giving Blair a sibling would finally be the glue that would bind Hunter to our little family, and with each loss I told myself he slipped further away.

Somehow I knew Jack understood, since Tyler had let it slip that Jack ached to have a family of his own, something he never put into so many words, but something I could plainly see in the video with baby Violet.

He kissed each little bird softly, turning me slowly and bending low to kiss the last one that wound up my ribcage, and when he raised his head his expression was very different. It was proprietary and protective and he leaned, pulling the blankets back before he stood, scooping me up and crawling in after me.

The fireplace timer clicked, killing the flames, and Carrick grunted in the corner, heaving out a discontented sound at the loss of the extra heat.

Jack's body wrapped around mine and in the dark his fingers found my chin, lifting my face so he could place a sweet kiss on my lips, not letting me deepen it as he smoothed my hair, pulling me close so that my skin was pressed against his.

"Is this what you imagined?" His voice was low in my hair and I shivered a little, causing him to wrap me up tighter.

"And other things," I said quietly against his chest, and I could feel his lips curve into a smile in my hair.

It wasn't hard to interpret the disappointment in my voice.

"I'm not any good for you," he admitted quietly, and I knew my eyelashes tickled him as I blinked against his chest, waiting for him to finish the thought. "There are things in my life that aren't finished. A lot of unknowns. My divorce isn't final and it looks like my pop will be living with me for ... well, the foreseeable future. That pretty much means I don't have anything to give. I don't want to complicate things, even though the *only* thing I want to do is complicate things."

Jack was giving me an out.

"I'm filing in May," I said quietly. "It's a courtesy to Hunter—one he doesn't deserve, since he's been cheating on me for years—but he wants to get out ahead of the news, for political purposes, I guess.

"And as for your dad, I'd like to help, if you'll let me."

He drew a deep breath, and I could feel him considering.

"You'd do that?"

"Yeah," I whispered. "I would."

Something I hadn't told anyone yet was that I'd decided what to do going forward. Once I'd completely transitioned my company to Emily, I would join Daddy in managing his foundation. He'd had a number of employees over the years, typically only two or three at a time, but it took the whole lot of them to do the job of one dedicated, devoted person. It was something I planned to discuss with him the next day, once he and Mama arrived.

Jack didn't say anything more, but I felt him draw deep, contented breaths from my hair and I pressed my lips to his chest where I could feel the strong, steady beat of his heart. Given our activities of only a few moments earlier, it shouldn't have been soothing, but it was.

I closed my eyes against his chest, grateful for the comfort of his strong arms, his body wrapped protectively around mine, and I didn't even care if sleep came for me. I would simply revel in the moments spent in his arms.

Something woke me with a start and when I realized there was a body behind mine in the bed, I had a split-second panic attack. I was used to taking up as much of the bed as I wanted, being able to starfish if I so desired—which I never did—and most mornings I simply got out of the barely-rumpled bed and folded the covers back: One chore already completed and I'd only been up for five seconds.

Go, me. Such an overachiever.

When I realized it was Jack, something warm and happy flooded my heart and I smoothed my fingers over his, where they were tucked around my middle. From the way he drew sharp, shallow breaths, I knew he wasn't sleeping, and now he knew I wasn't either. And suddenly I didn't care about what was finished and what wasn't. He was here now, after pushing me away again and again.

Turning to him in the darkness, my hand found his cheek and I ran a thumb slowly across those full, deliciously soft lips. Back and forth, back and forth, until I couldn't handle it any longer.

"Daphne." His voice was dark, almost angry. "You don't know what you're asking for."

Oh, I had some idea: He was big and I was small.

He was huge and grumpy, rough around the edges, whereas I was petite and optimistic, always the good girl, sweet and chaste and proper.

He would corrupt me.

Break me.

"I appreciate you trying to warn me, Officer Thompson," I teased softly, feeling the heat from his body as he pushed himself up on one arm to loom over me. "But I'm here for Jack. Could you send him out, please?"

I leaned up, squeezing his jaw in my hand as I sucked his lower lip into my mouth and pressed down with my teeth. Harder, harder, pulling him with me as I sank back into the pillows and I could feel the tension in his big body as he followed me back down: anger, desire, violence, restraint, all of it wound up in a taut energy that coursed through him.

"Jack is a lot to take," he responded as he pulled his lip from the grip of my teeth, and I giggled at him referring to himself in the third person.

"Are we discussing intensity, or just size?" I asked demurely, wishing I could see his face.

He rolled away from me, the blankets pulling up and letting in the cold air.

Scooting to the edge of the bed, I reached for the lamp on the nightstand and a low, filtered light cut through the darkness. It revealed him sitting on the edge of the bed with his elbows on his knees, head hanging down between his shoulders.

This man didn't want to be seduced, or he'd have let me do it hours earlier. But yet he'd been the one to come to me...

I couldn't help it. Something about those wide shoulders and all that smooth skin and the thick muscles.

In the end, I would blame it on the tattoos. Especially the one that wrapped around his bicep and climbed his shoulder. It dipped down the backside as well, covering his shoulder blade, and I moved carefully up behind him, pressing my front to his back, looping my arms around him and resting my cheek against his warm skin.

"*She* told you that you were too much?" I asked quietly, wondering if his wife had done this thing to break him.

He remained quiet, drawing deep, slow breaths.

And then, just the tiniest nod of his head. I could feel the motion.

Well, now I was curious. I didn't know what "too much" meant, as I'd never experienced it for myself.

Nothing Hunter had done in bed had ever been *too much*, typically erring on the far safer side of *not nearly enough*.

I wanted some of that "too much" for myself, just to see what it was like, hoping it was wild and loud, passionate and crazy, after the underwhelmingly quiet, perfunctory, nearly clinical experiences with Hunter, the man I'd thought myself in love with for half my life. Mostly because I hadn't known any better.

When he didn't move, I slid around him, slipping out of my pants and standing in front of him in the thin lace cheekies I'd slipped into earlier that evening.

It was cold in the room and my nipples pebbled immediately, goosebumps threatening even as heat pooled in my belly.

For once I'm not going to be the good, sweet girl.

He lifted his eyes, taking me in hungrily in a slow, purposeful look, up and down, and he swallowed hard. His hands gripped the edge of the bed harder, like he wanted to form fists and I moved closer, forcing him to lean back until I could step between his knees.

Moving my hands slowly up his shoulders, I curled one hand into his hair, bringing his cheek to rest against my breasts.

There was no way I was going to let this man resist me, because I was done being ignored.

I held him for long moments before finally tipping his chin up with slight pressure from my fingers, and I waited until his eyes opened. The way he looked at me was so darkly sensual, so ferocious, I knew I should have been scared. Instead, I took the plunge, leaning down to take his mouth with slow, deep licks that grew quickly harder, deeper, more desperate when he opened to me quickly, hauling sharp breaths in through his nose as his hands moved up the backs of my thighs to dig harshly into my butt.

There would be bruises tomorrow; marks of his possession.

With a deep growl he jerked at my hips and I fell forward as his hands swept quickly beneath my knees to pull me up, over his lap, straddling him.

His hands went immediately to my backside, pulling me tight against the granite slab I could feel hidden away in his pants and I shivered deliciously, my knees braced on the bed, my hips beginning to rock against him as I pressed and pushed, whimpering into his waiting mouth.

Without warning he fell back, snaking an arm around me to bring me with him and I must have moaned when it brought our bodies into better contact, because he answered with a desperate sound of his own before slipping a hand between us, his fingers seeking, probing, testing.

I couldn't take it any longer. The soft sweeps of his thick fingers were driving me beyond sanity, and he hadn't even gotten *into* my underwear yet.

Breaking the kiss, I pushed myself up quickly and his eyes went wide with alarm as I climbed off him. He was breathing hard, like an angry bull, every muscle in his arms and chest popping and straining as he pushed up quickly, like he feared I would run and he needed to give chase.

Standing again, I shoved my underwear down my thighs and his expression relaxed with relieved understanding, the fear melting from his expression.

I asked silent permission with my eyes before leaning closer and undoing the button of his pants.

He stood then, to let me unzip them carefully, and I pulled them away from his body as I did to keep from hurting him, dropping them to the floor and waiting as he stepped out.

"Officer Thompson." My voice was low and raspy, something I knew he could understand was due to my desire for him, something he needed to know. "This is why they keep you locked away in a quiet little spot..." My eyes traveled down the muscular length of his body, his tight abs, the impressive V dipping into black cotton boxer briefs which did nothing to hide the magnificent beast he was.

Stepping closer again, I licked across the muscular left pectoral to tease and suck his flat nipple, closing my hand over the hot length between his legs.

His whole body shuddered when I did it and after a few experimental strokes over the fabric, I slipped my fingers inside the band to wrap around his velvety flesh. It made his breath shudder out of him with a low groan, the sweetest, most incredibly carnal sound I thought I'd ever heard, and it made goosebumps sweep across my back.

In a heartbeat I was whirled through the air, finding myself on my back on the bed before I knew what had happened. I looked up in confusion to see him towering over me, his face hard with an expression that would have terrified me in any other situation.

Then he crawled over me, covering me with that huge, glorious body, linking his fingers through mine to push up over my head as he kissed me slow and deep. His intent, his rhythm, very clear, and my back arched toward him, lifting my body to his.

He broke the kiss reluctantly, moving down quickly to worship my breasts with his mouth and hands, trailing wet, open mouthed kisses all the way down my stomach, then back up the inside of my thigh, sucking the skin there until I thought I might die if he didn't move on.

When his mouth closed over me the sound I made was almost a sob, my hands flying down to sink into his short hair. He whispered something softly against my skin, his tongue parting me to push deeper, to taste, to draw slow circles that drove me mad.

If this was *too much*, I'd been missing out, and some other unappreciative woman had been getting all of this.

He fumbled for a moment and I watched in a daze as his huge shoulders rippled while he situated himself, one large finger slipping slowly into me and I gasped at the sensation. But when he added another, twisting and curling and tugging, I came unglued.

He worked me furiously with his tongue and the sweet suction of his mouth, my hips pistoning against his fingers as I threw myself over that blissful edge, his name tumbling from my lips over and over until I regained some sort of consciousness and realized there were tears streaming down my cheeks.

"I hurt you?" he asked, terror in his eyes as he quickly crawled up my body to pull me into his arms, his hard body shaking with his own need.

I pressed my face into his neck, shaking my head quickly, wrapping arms and legs around him like a monkey and hanging on for dear life.

"Talk to me, baby."

My heart thrilled at the endearment and I pulled back to look up into his concerned face.

He was so beautiful. What kind of fool had given this up?

He held me until I relaxed my grip, letting my legs fall back onto the bed and moving my hands into his hair, lightly scratching his scalp with my nails, trailing them as far as I could reach down his back.

"I want to do the same for you," I finally whispered into his skin and the way he sighed sounded like he was ... relieved? Disappointed? I couldn't tell.

I pulled back to look at him.

His expression was guarded again.

"What do *you* want, Jack?" I asked gently, reaching up to smooth one dark eyebrow before cupping his cheek, and he leaned into my touch like a puppy. It hurt my heart when he did it, seeing a man who ached for tenderness and affection, maybe even forgiveness.

"What I want is too much," he said thickly, unwilling to meet my eyes, ashamed.

I swallowed hard, not knowing what I was getting myself into, but I wanted to know how he defined this thing. This measurement someone else had performed on his desires, branding them as taboo.

He was going to make me work for this.

"Then take it," I whispered, and he saw the nervous bob of my throat when I swallowed hard.

He shook his head.

I nodded mine.

He shook his again.

Jumping up, I crossed the room to slip into the closet, returning with several silk scarves, the vibrator I kept hidden in a shoe box and the huge blue dildo, spiked handcuffs and bottle of lube Ava had gotten me as what she claimed was a gag gift.

I wasn't so sure; it made me nervous just to look at that giant blue piece of silicone.

I dumped the pile onto the bed and his right eyebrow arched just a little. It wasn't an extensive collection, but I knew he was surprised.

"You can't shock me," I whispered, crawling back up toward the pillows on my knees. I pushed a pillow under my stomach and spread my arms out to my sides, waiting for him to make his decision, because somehow I knew what he needed involved penitence on my part.

Submission.

Punishment for a crime I hadn't committed.

The room was silent for a long moment and my heart thundered in my ears, because maybe calling him on his bluff was a bad idea.

I reached a hand toward him, where he sat with his feet propped under his thighs and slid that hand along the inside of his thigh, until my fingers trailed over him and he kicked under my touch. He sucked in a breath then, moving fast, and I felt the soft slip of silk sliding over one wrist, then the other as he hurried to bind the ends to the bed frame.

There was the sound of a bottle cap clicking open and warm, wet fingers slipped through my flesh, then pulled at my hips so that I pushed up on my knees.

"Daphne." His voice was low and silky, his lips hovering over my lower back. "I don't have anything with me. I'm not asking you to give yourself to me like this."

I was ready for this. "I'm clean, Jack. I'm tested often and I couldn't tell you the last time..."

It was permission, and he breathed out a heavy sigh.

I could feel the warmth of his body as he covered me, his teeth sinking into the flesh of my backside, and I pushed my face into the pillow to smother the yelp.

He trailed kisses up my spine, then back down, dragging his tongue from the little dimples of my butt all the way up to the back of my neck, and I shivered at the sensation. Just before I felt him settle into place behind me, line himself up carefully, and drive forward so hard, my knees went out from under me and my head cracked against the headboard.

Holy shit.

I couldn't even be angry that I'd cursed in my head.

I saw stars as I struggled to push back up on my knees, feeling like I'd been split in two, my head aching as he pulled back and slammed into me again, one hand on my hip to hold me in place this time, but again I slammed into the headboard.

Ow.

I wasn't going to be able to take much more of him or I'd be in a coma, I thought, the sharp sting of tears in my eyes.

This isn't exactly going the way I thought it would.

After half half a dozen more brutal thrusts he paused, stretching over me and releasing the simple knot on each scarf, probably because he realized he was battering my brains out.

My arms dropped to the bed, tingling with the rush of blood, and I pushed up on my elbows, thankful I could better brace myself.

He dropped down then, nuzzling my neck, his hips working at a slower, gentler pace and when I pushed back to meet him he groaned into my hair, his hand reaching around my body.

He was gentle then, stroking and soothing, murmuring into my hair, words I couldn't understand over the rush of blood in my ears, and his fingers worked in time with his body.

I began to make soft sounds as the burning, aching sensation faded, pushing my hips back into his as his fingers moved in their slow rhythm.

"Please, baby," he begged, his words hot on my cheek.

As he gentled, I relaxed, my body accepting him easily, his fingers working to open more of me to him, and I grunted softly each time his hips snapped back against me.

"Tell me what to do," he begged, and I stopped moving, straightening my arms to push up, moving carefully to separate our bodies.

He looked frantic, sitting back on his haunches when I turned to face him.

Too much, his face said. *I knew it was too much.*

I didn't say anything. I rubbed the top of my head, lowering my eyebrows and pursing my lips before giving him a small smile. Then I crooked a finger at him and he moved slowly toward me, uncertain again, as I gestured he should sit with his back to the headboard.

I arranged his legs to form a seat and climbed into his lap, kissing him slowly, deeply, before reaching between us to guide him and sinking slowly down.

I had only a hunch to go on, and that hunch was that he was still angry and hurt. It was nothing that his vicious pounding was going to fix, but maybe he didn't know that. He needed a little kink and a lot of tenderness, both things I could give him, and as I moved against him I knew he watched the expressions on my face.

He drank in what he saw there, and the moans that fell from my lips as I clenched my deepest muscles around him, pulling upward, waiting for the moment he surrendered himself.

"Come with me, baby," he begged through gritted teeth and I increased the pace, gasping for breath, groaning as my nerve endings began to fire with that intense sizzle of pleasure.

I threw back my head, a choked cry leaving my lips as my muscles trembled in release.

He watched me greedily, then gripped my hips, holding me to him as his breath caught, and I felt him begin to throb inside of me. He jerked hard, his breath leaving him with an angry, violent roar.

Pressing his face into my neck, I felt something hot and wet against my skin as he struggled to regain his breath, and for that split second I wondered if it had been too much for *him*.

He stayed pressed into my neck for a long time, kissing the skin of my throat, making an occasional noise I thought might be a sniffle, and when he finally sat back he gestured toward the wetness on my own lashes and smiled at me bashfully.

It nearly split my heart wide open.

"Too much?" he asked softly, worry creasing his forehead, and I grinned at him, leaning closer to take his face in my hands and to very slowly shake my head.

I kissed him then, softly, and against his lips I said, "Poor, poor Cassandra."

I fell asleep in his arms, the sound of his delighted laughter ringing again and again through my mind.

10

Jack

I woke several times during the remaining hours of the night just to make sure she was real. Something in the back of my mind kept kicking me to wake again, to make sure the woman in my arms wasn't a figment of my imagination—or Natasha.

There was a dark sense of foreboding hanging over my head, something that crept into the room while we slept and wrapped its icy fingers around my heart. Something that told me I still wasn't good enough; that I didn't deserve the happiness or the pleasure I could find with this woman, and I'd damn near screwed it up when I'd battered her brains out.

The drive to Daphne's house wasn't something I'd programmed myself to do on autopilot, as I'd only been there twice. So it was a very conscious decision to go to her, and I'd done so without hesitation.

It felt final: I was making a choice, deciding between the errant wife who'd been gone for several years, and the woman who'd shown me kindness when she wasn't busy calling me on my shit.

And boy, did she see right through me.

When Daphne told me she wanted me and wrapped herself around me, I could breathe again. She was soft and delicious, my brain completely incapacitated by the warm, sugared smell of her skin and the way she took my terms and flipped them on me. Surprising me.

It was Carrick who woke me in the morning, his cold nose pressed up against my lower back as he snuffled me with big, deep inhalations.

I chuckled, reaching behind myself to pull the blanket back down over my skin and dropped a blind pat on the top of the dog's head.

Daphne had hardly moved during the night, only rolling and scooting her back into my front, her fingers wound through mine and my arms banded tightly around her.

It was comforting, to wake with the woman in my arms who'd been driving me to madness in my dreams for so long. This time she was warm and sweet and real, and I pressed a kiss to the back of her head, which elicited a happy little hum from her and she pushed herself back even tighter against me, like she could fuse our bodies with the pressure.

"I was just having the loveliest dream," she yawned quietly, and I inhaled the sweetness of her hair. "And then I woke up ... and it was real."

She turned slowly, her beautiful grey eyes crinkling with a contented smile, just before she burrowed back into my chest and dropped tiny, feathery kisses over my thudding heart.

This woman was going to be my undoing, something I'd been fighting against since the moment she'd thrown her drink at me.

It was quite early, but there was a noise somewhere in the house and Daphne hummed low in her throat. "The last thing I want to do is get out of bed, but I don't think I can convince the coffee to walk itself up here. This house isn't quite *that* haunted."

I smiled into her hair and watched as she slipped out of the bed, her nipples tightening in the cold air. She hissed a little, wrapping her arms around herself as she hurried to the closet and I jumped up after her, following her in and pressing my front to her back, bringing my hands up to cover her breasts as she reached for a heavy sweatshirt. "I'll bring up the coffee," I said into the top of her head as I scooped my hands under her arms. "It would be a shame to put these away so soon." I squeezed gently, which made her giggle.

She crawled back into the big bed, the sweatshirt thrown into a chair, and I slipped into my pants and pulled my shirt back over my head before opening the door, patting my leg so Carrick would follow me.

Letting the dog into the backyard from a side door, I rounded the corner into the kitchen and just about had a coronary when I saw an older, much taller version of Daphne sitting at the island. Next to her sat a teenage girl with long, golden hair and my face flamed. I'd forgotten all about Daphne's daughter, and I sent up a frantic prayer that the girl slept like the dead.

For the older woman's part, she didn't look at all surprised to see me. Her lips curved up slowly as she lowered the coffee mug from her face and I stood frozen, my mouth hanging open.

"Well now," she drawled in the thickest southern accent I'd heard in a very long time. "My sweet daughter did not see fit to mention she'd be entertaining additional company this holiday season. I am going to make the very large assumption that you are the junior Thompson."

I finally remembered how to work my feet and I moved to the island, across from her, holding out my hand. "You would be correct," I managed to answer just as an enormous man rounded the corner, his eyes narrowing as I shook the woman's hand. I had the good sense to drop it quickly, as Jonas Masters's reputation preceded him: He didn't much like other men touching his gorgeous wife, no matter the capacity, and he was of a size to do something about it.

"Where *is* my sweet daughter?" the woman asked me with a lilt in her voice, the smile on her lips and the glint in her eye telling me she knew damn well where Daphne was, and I felt my cheeks instantaneously flame.

"Uh ... I was just gonna take some coffee up for her."

The girl snorted and tried to cover a smirk with her hand. I felt like a teenage boy getting caught in his girlfriend's bedroom, and Jonas was still looking at me like he'd enjoy nothing more than to separate my limbs from my body.

One in particular that I was quite fond of.

I didn't exactly feel it was wise to turn my back on him, but I threw a look at the coffee pot over my shoulder and moved carefully in that direction.

"Sweetheart, this is Mr. Thompson's son."

"Thompson?" Jonas barked, still fixing me with a withering glare. "Why do I know that name?"

Mrs. Masters nudged him gently and he looked down at her, recognition suddenly dawning on his face. "Thompson. Right. How's your old man doing?"

It took me a little aback, but I fixed two huge mugs of coffee while I relayed the little I knew about Pop's progress, thankful that I had a few good things to report. Then I excused myself to walk the coffee up the stairs, sucking in a deep breath of relief as I escaped the kitchen and the steely blue eyes boring into my back.

Daphne was still snuggled up in the bed, her dark hair streaming across the pillow and I pulled the blanket back a few inches to drop a kiss on her bare shoulder, stealing a very satisfactory peek of what waited for me under those blankets.

"So," I whispered, setting the mugs on the bedside table and pressing one warm palm against her back. She made a contented noise and burrowed into me, where I sat on the side of the bed. "Were you expecting your parents to be here ... ah ... quite this early?"

Daphne's eyes flew open. "They're supposed to get in this afternoon."

"They moved something up," I said with a small smile, "because they're sitting in your kitchen as we speak. With your daughter."

"Oooh ... no, no, no." Daphne threw the covers back and sat up, squeaking again at the cold air in the room. "Oh, that's bad. I'm so sorry, Jack. I should have known they would pull something–and you went down there looking all ... well, like you spent the night in my bed." Her voice went all throaty and she bit her lip, but the smile that tugged at her mouth won and she reached up to run her fingers through my short hair. "Did he threaten you yet?"

I chuckled, reaching for my coffee and taking a sip. "Not exactly, but your mother seemed to know exactly who I am. Why is that?"

"Um..." It was a stall tactic as Daphne's brain obviously whirled to come up with an excuse. "I may have talked to her about you ... a little bit."

She leaned across my lap to grab the other coffee mug, watching me over the lip as she drank deeply.

And suddenly, something occurred to me. It was something Tyler had mentioned in the course of casual conversation as we sat in my living room watching college football highlights on Sports Center. Something about a foundation an NFL player had recently set up, ostensibly to benefit inner city kids who didn't have access to great sports programs even though they were gifted.

It had turned out that the foundation was more of a piggy bank for his "glam influencer" wife than it was used to support any actual kids, and Tyler made an off-handed comment about how Jonesy Masters seemed to be the only guy doing any good, honest work with his foundation these days.

"You pulled some strings." It was all starting to fall into place. "Jonas's foundation, whatever it is that he does with it. *You* were the one to arrange everything for Pop." It came out a whole lot like an accusation, because suddenly I felt like a fool. It had been right in front of me the whole time, and she'd kept quiet about the enormous amount of charity and expense, because she'd known I'd be too proud to accept help, especially from someone I was trying awfully hard to detest.

It made her so *good.*

She could have held it over my head.

She could have tried to barter for my affections.

I knew a lesser woman who'd have done just that.

"We were charity." The words were bitter. "I'm not fucking charity, Daphne."

She was quiet, the mug still held up to her face, her eyes wide with shock over the top. And when I heard her swallow I took the mug from her hands, setting it on the stand and waiting for her explanation.

"Your father wouldn't just blindly help some down-on-his-luck old man from Baltimore out of the blue. No one would. Someone had to vouch for him—and probably for me." I was trying to decide whether I was angry or hurt, but the words were coming out in a rush, hot and loud. I felt like she hadn't been honest with me, even if I didn't understand why it upset me.

That Daphne was sweet and generous went without saying, but a fear nagged at me that I had been a project. She was fixing up my life little by little, adding beauty here and stability there, and maybe once she had me back on my own two feet, she'd cut me loose: A success story for daddy's foundation and a feather in her cap.

Another human, successfully rehabilitated.

"Please tell me you didn't do it because you felt sorry for us." I was aware the expression on my face was probably ugly, and I stood slowly, still all too conscious of the fact she was still naked. It made it really hard to think.

"I did it because you deserve the chance, Jack, and I wanted to see you happy. You needed help; the responsibility was so heavy, and the foundation had the resources to give your dad the help he needed. Now he can be treated, the progression of his disease can be better managed, and you have an entire team to support you."

I shook my head as I stood there staring down at her. She'd done me a huge kindness, yet I felt utterly betrayed.

"So you and Tyler cooked this up together? Poor old Jack can't hack it, right? He's got nothing and his life's a mess, so we should help patch things up and see if he can get out of his rut, whatever that takes. Even if you had to sleep with me to get me out of that rut. I was a pity fuck." My chest ached. I had been so sure what I'd felt from her last night was genuine affection, tenderness, maybe even love.

In the cold light of day, it looked a whole hell of a lot more like pity.

"Jack, no." She threw the blankets back and moved with alarming speed to wrap her arms around my middle. I tried to step back, but I didn't move quickly enough and she plastered her body to mine, hugging me with ferocious strength.

I couldn't think when she touched me, the warmth of her skin like the hit of a drug I desperately craved. She'd made me this way one small touch at a time—made me dependent upon her.

Made me need her.

This.

Whatever it was she was doing to me whenever her skin touched mine.

"I have to go," I said woodenly, trying to unwrap her arms from around my ribs. She was surprisingly strong and persistent, her forehead rubbing against my chest when she violently shook her head no.

"I'm serious, Daphne," I said, feeling my own resolve weakening. "Let me go." I said it firmly, even though it was the last thing I wanted her to do. I wanted her to refuse; to hang on tighter and beg me to stay, because no one had ever begged me to stay.

She dropped her arms to her sides, her head folded down to her chest and I watched her shoulders rise and fall several times before she looked up at me. I expected tears, but her eyes were dry, full of disappointment and sadness.

"Okay Jack," she said softly. "You can have it your way."

She turned slowly, opening her closet door and reaching inside to snag another huge sweatshirt. She slipped it over her head and pulled her hair from under the collar, quickly slipping into a pair of joggers. "I'll go make your excuses to my parents."

Then she left the room without a backward glance, her shoulders sagging.

I couldn't face Jonas again, so I took the chickenshit way out and let myself quietly out the front door. There was an expensive new AMG parked right next to my truck and I sighed when I saw it.

Mrs. Masters had known from the second they pulled into the driveway that her daughter was slumming it with me, the other name in what was probably a pretty thick file in some corporate office.

Jonas had looked at me the way any overprotective father would, and I swallowed hard as I turned over the engine of my truck.

If I were Jonas, it wouldn't have mattered that Daphne was a grown, successful woman, because she'd *still* be my baby girl. I'd have a background check run on any man she mentioned and I'd have a damn good gun collection and a crack aim, in case the need arose to employ either.

The look Daphne had given me haunted me as I drove home. I had watched the hope die in her eyes, and I wondered how many times she'd been let down before, left to handle things on her own.

That I had snapped at her, completely irrational in the face of what had been her silent kindness and generosity, probably hadn't been a huge surprise. But after going to her when I needed her, and her welcoming me without question or reservation, being patient with me as I held myself back from her ... Shit. I pounded the flat of my palm against the steering wheel as I drove.

I just couldn't get out of my own way.

I wasn't entirely sure when this had happened: when the woman I'd prayed would come back to me night after night finally became the last thing I wanted. And in her place a tiny little raven-haired spitfire had begun to take up larger and larger spaces in my thoughts.

I sat outside on the steps of my house for a while, in the frigid December air, until the cold leaked through my coat and my skin started to feel numb.

I was tired of being so suspicious. It was exhausting. I was tired of pushing everyone away, and I was lonely. I was tired of the empty bed, the quiet house, solitary meals, a dead-end job and what was proving to be a largely joyless existence.

That was it, I thought: It was time to drive to the shelter and get a dog.

Tyler hadn't let me spend a single Christmas alone since Natasha left, and he showed up the next day, Christmas Eve, with baby Violet. He pulled her from her carseat and handed her over to me immediately as he unlaced his boots and shrugged out of his jacket, explaining that Generis needed to wrap gifts, so she'd kicked them out.

Not so secretly, he joked, he was hoping she'd take a relaxing bubble bath and have most of a bottle of wine before he came home, so the two of them could celebrate Christmas a little early.

I may have grimaced at the visual, but not because I was jealous of my friend. It was because the fresh memory of Daphne spread out before me was sweet and precious, painful, and it made more than just my heart ache.

"What's this?" Tyler's index finger drew a circle in the air near my face.

"My face," I huffed.

Damn yenta mind reader.

Violet squirmed in my arms, her chubby little fingers reaching up to smack my cheek like she didn't believe my bluster either.

"Mmmhmm," Tyler hummed skeptically, rooting through the enormous diaper bag he'd dropped from his shoulder when he walked through the door.

"You'd think I was taking the kid on walkabout through the Outback," he fussed as he pushed aside blankets and onesies, diapers and wipes, toys and books. "She could survive for two weeks in the bush on what that woman packs her for an afternoon away from home."

It made me smile in spite of myself. Generis was a good mother and though Tyler drove me batshit crazy, he was obviously a great dad, devoted to his little girl in a way that warmed my cold little heart to see.

I followed Tyler into my kitchen while he warmed some formula for Violet, who'd only just begun to look like she might entertain the idea of fussing. Currently she was too busy staring up at me with her big brown eyes, tugging on the collar of my shirt whenever she could stretch her fingers up to it.

Tyler handed me the bottle when it was full of warmed formula and we went back out to the living room, me carrying his baby and him carrying a beer. He set it on the small coffee table while I settled into one of the chairs, and I heard him rustling through the diaper bag again.

"G would kill me if I forgot this," he said quietly, moving toward the Christmas tree and placing two small, wrapped packages beneath it. The action stabbed my heart all over again. These were my friends, but I felt like I was a charity case to them, too. They were the extent of my Christmas each year, the only other people in the world who made sure I had at least one gift to open on Christmas morning.

I swallowed hard. "You didn't have to do that."

"Wasn't me." Tyler grinned. "If it was up to me, I'd have gotten you another blow-up doll. But ... what do I know? Maybe you'll get a Christmas miracle this year. Maybe a real, live girl." His eyebrows wiggled suggestively and his grin grew wider, shit-eating. "I know of a certain real, live, non-blow-up girl who's told Santa's elves that all she wants for Christmas is Jack." His eyes twinkled and mine narrowed, saying nothing as Violet slurped noisily at her bottle.

She was in for one hell of a burp later.

"Midget," I snarked. "I can see how she thought you were an elf."

He leaned back, giving me a smug look. I wasn't sure I'd ever seen Tyler get truly angry or ruffled; never anything but goofy and smiling.

"Says the Abominable Snow Beast, or whatever you are, jackass." He gestured lazily toward me before taking another sip of his beer.

I had nothing more to say, and I sat feeding Violet with an ache in my chest that spread down my arms and into my hands. Everything *hurt* today, a hurt from the inside, something deeper than my muscles, joints or nerves.

Maybe it was a heart attack.

"Mama sees it too, Jack," he said softly, and I snorted. The man was in so deep. He hadn't even married Generis yet, and already he was calling Catalina "Mama."

"Why do you keep fighting it, man?"

His bottle was empty and he stood, taking it with him to the kitchen. I was silent as he did, staring down at Violet, trying desperately to fight the burning sensation gathering behind my eyes.

"Oh, shit." Tyler was standing in the doorway, watching me, and I didn't know how long he'd been there. "You *stopped* fighting it."

I looked up at him finally, aware I couldn't hide the misery in my expression. The man could read my every thought even before I processed it.

I looked around me, at all the decorations Daphne had so lovingly put up for me. I could imagine her still there, in front of the tree, stringing lights with that soft pink sweater slipping down her shoulder and the very thought made me swallow so hard, Violet looked up at the noise my throat made.

"I went over there last night."

Tyler raised an eyebrow. "And?"

"And." My look was so significant, the realization flashed across his face.

"Oh."

"Yeah. Oh."

"And?" he led again, looking hopeful.

"And nothing. I'm not telling you. But when I went downstairs to get coffee this morning, her parents were there and her ma knew exactly who I was."

"That was a bad thing?"

"She asked me how Pop was doing."

Tyler's face pinched a little, because he knew exactly where I was going with this. "Shit, Jack." He breathed a heavy sigh, lowering himself onto the sofa. "And knowing you, you got all bent out of shape after making up some crazy story in your head about why her family was involved, because God forbid you should trust *anyone*, or let anyone in. Or..." He feigned a gasp. "*Help you with a single damned thing.*"

Fucking Tyler.

I pressed Violet against my chest and gently covered her other ear with my hand before hissing at Tyler. "It makes me a damn charity case."

"Oh, get off it." His beer bottle slammed down onto the coffee table and Violet's eyes flew open. "Everything that woman has done—*everything*—has been because she cares for you, you overgrown asshole."

I covered Violet's ear again and shot him a warning look. The *language* this man used in front of his own daughter.

"Has it ever occurred to you that she *chose* you?" he asked, his eyes wide, his nostrils flaring.

Holy shit, was Tyler actually angry?

"All you do is push her away and hurt her, when all she's ever done has been to show you someone cared. Even when she told me she didn't want to break up our group; that you didn't like her and she was afraid she made you uncomfortable, she kept showing up. Because I *begged* her, Jack.

"I see the way you look at her. I see the way she makes you light up when you think no one is looking. And I haven't seen you look at a woman that way *ever*. Not even Tash."

Violet's little eyes had drifted shut. She squirmed a little and I shifted to adjust her in my arms.

All I could do was shake my head at Tyler.

"Oh, poor Jack," he sneered, getting himself as worked up as I'd ever seen. "His stupid little airhead wife left him and he just can't get past the woman who was *so second-rate*. So instead, he shuts people out.

"Have you ever thought of this from her perspective? Watching her husband cheat on her for *years*? She's been his second and third choice since the *beginning* and she put up with it because she never thought she deserved anything better."

He was on such a roll, I was pretty sure he wasn't ever going to stop yelling at me.

"Do you know how hard it's been for her to gain any sort of confidence? After all these years with that douchebag, why do you think she's *finally* ready to leave him?"

I sat quietly, Violet sleeping uneasily in my arms, and when I shifted her a loud burp ripped through the room.

She slept on.

Put that way, it did make me look like an asshole. I hadn't had to watch Tash cheat on me time and again, over the course of decades.

I hadn't sat alone at Christmas with our child, explaining despite my own broken heart that we were alone because there was something more "important" that needed to be done; that someone else was more important than us.

I hadn't been abandoned while young, pregnant and terrified, left to raise a child on my own.

Sitting back in my chair, I felt defeated. Again, I'd pushed too hard. I'd punished her, body and soul, for what Natasha had done to me. I'd hurt her, hoping to feel some kind of vindication, and she'd taken it and given me more of herself. She'd given me tenderness when I hadn't earned or deserved it. She'd taken me into her body and her heart and let me see her at her most vulnerable—the most beautiful moments I'd ever been given by another human.

She gave me what I'd needed to see, making sure I saw her come undone because of me.

Because she wanted *me.*

Tyler took Violet from me a little later, over his angry outburst, and I ordered in some pizza. I had a refrigerator full of food from Catalina, but I didn't have the mental fortitude to even heat something up.

"Fix it, man." Tyler's face was as serious as I'd ever seen it.

"What do you mean, fix it?"

Playing dumb with him had never gotten me anywhere. When would I learn?

"Don't be the one who walked out on her, simple as that."

"I don't think I'm ready for..."

Tyler cut me off. "Look around you, Jack."

I did, slowly, taking in the beauty and care she'd brought to my house, all over again.

"You see it? You see the life she breathed into your sad existence? Yeah? K. Now ... imagine her in it. Every day. Waking up to her ... and coming home to her." He looked at me significantly, lowering his head as he did to make sure I got the benefit of his full glare. Then he tucked Violet into her car seat, hoisted her diaper bag and, after slapping me on the back, he was gone.

It was growing late, the light turning grey as day faded into evening and as I sat contemplating, there was a soft knock at the door. It made hope flare violently in my heart.

Maybe she's come for me.

I hurried to the door, a smile on my face, ready to admit I had been a complete ass.

Daphne had to know she was my Christmas wish.

My every wish.

She was what I'd been wishing for since all those months ago, the night she grabbed my shotgun and obliterated that stupid target. She'd all but obliterated my ability to resist her.

A blast of frigid air whooshed in as I pulled the door open and I paused, the smile dying on my lips when my brain finally cataloged the blonde hair and icy blue eyes.

"Baby." Natasha's voice was warm and seductive when she leaned up to press her cold lips to mine. "Merry Christmas."

11

Daphne

Mama seemed to know I needed some time to process my thoughts and she remained quiet as I drank my third cup of coffee, mindlessly shoving toast into my mouth without checking to be sure it was buttered. I just needed something in my stomach. Something that would stabilize the freefalling, terrifying queasiness happening there as my brain spun around and around.

I couldn't understand his reaction to something I hadn't even considered a secret—it was just something I hadn't felt I needed to tell him, since I hadn't been fishing for thanks. I didn't care for it.

It was Tyler who had opened my eyes to the need, and to Jack. How could I not do everything in my power to help the man who twisted up my insides every time I looked at him?

"Eat." Mama pressed a plate of pasta into my hands and I looked up at the clock from where I sat on the sofa, surprised to find it was already time for lunch. "You're burnin' up all kinds of calories over here with that smoke pourin' out of those ears," she teased, and Daddy looked up from the sports section of the fat paper he held in his hands, taking in my disheveled appearance without more than a small smile.

The day faded into an early evening and Daddy graduated from the living room to the small office on the ground floor. I could hear the TV in there, knowing he was conducting "market research," as he called it, while I sat sipping another cup of the tea Mama had pressed into my hands.

How had this happened? How had I let this man worm his way inside my head and my heart when the last thing I needed was a complication? I could have stayed away, but I made the decision every time to search him out. To find him and push him just a little, hoping for a sign that he needed from me what I needed from him: affection, tenderness, a refuge in his arms where I could hide from the world, taking the sanctuary I'd never before had in the shelter of his big body. I'd fallen in love with him, and it hurt. The huge, angry, miserable beast had turned me inside out.

Jerk.

I sat there for a long time, trying to piece together where I'd gone so terribly wrong.

Mama was watching me like a hawk, patiently, but warily. "I hate to see you like this, baby," she finally said gently, and I was genuinely impressed she'd manage to keep her thoughts to herself for the entire day. "All twisted up over this man. Don't you try tellin' me it's anything else." She held up a hand to shush the protest I wasn't quite ready to offer. "I'm not a fool, baby girl, and I can tell you right now that I know that look. It's the look your sweet daddy had on his face when I told him he had a choice to make.

"Life gives us hard decisions sometimes, and I think you've learned that the hard way more than once." She moved closer to run a hand through my tangled hair. "I was doin' everything I could to get him past the slump."

I looked up in surprise. Mama had *never* talked about what she went through when Daddy's career had ended and he'd spiraled into depression and alcoholism.

"I thought I'd die sometimes, it hurt so much." Her eyes filled with tears. "I was watchin' the man I loved more than anything in life—except you of course, Sweet Pea—" she pinched my cheek. "I was watchin' him die a little more every day, and that was his *choice*. It just made me so goldarn angry!"

Whoa, that was a heavy curse for her.

She sighed deeply, running a finger delicately beneath one eye to repair the damage any stray tears might have done. She was never anything but perfectly put together, emotional moments being no exception.

"I know what you've been through with Hunter, sweetheart." There was that hand again, to shush me. "You were far stronger than I'd ever have been. When I discovered your father was cheatin' on me, I packed you right up and we left. There was no way I was puttin' up with an unfaithful man and lettin' my daughter grow up thinkin' that was some kind of acceptable behavior."

My eyes were wide. She had *never* talked about my birth father, and for most of my life I'd assumed it was because he left us.

"Looks like I didn't leave him soon enough, because here you are, livin' out the very life I escaped." She looked sorrowful and I shook my head, trying to get her to let me interject.

"Sweetheart, it's time. The world will think no less of you—Daddy and I will think no less of you—for going your own way."

Oh, so Mama thought I'd needed permission?

No, not at all. What I had lacked for decades was the self-confidence to think I deserved better. It was a pattern I knew and though I hated it, even the most detestable pattern can be a trap if you crave familiarity and routine.

"This Thompson boy..." Mama switched tack so quickly, I heard the whiplash in my skull. "He may not be able to give you what you need, Sweet Pea." She reached for my hair again, something she did in tense situations.

"You know your daddy did a little digging on him before we released funding for his father's treatment program." She raised her eyebrows at me, maybe expecting I would be surprised. "He's had a rough past, with that time spent in Syria and his much younger wife leaving him. It's a real blow to a man's ego." She went quiet for a moment. Then, "They lost their baby, you know."

My eyes whipped up to her face and she nodded sadly. "Sweet little thing. Not more than a few months old. Crib death, according to the records."

A chill washed over my skin like an incoming tide as I thought of the video with him holding Violet.

He'd been a father.

"My guess would be that the marriage was already in trouble." Her voice was gentle, the way a person speaks to a feral cat when trying to coax it out from hiding. "But it seems that brought on the end: She blamed him. He blamed himself. You know how those things go."

My heart ached and I leaned into Mama's side as she put her arm around me. No more words were necessary; she knew I didn't want to hear anything more, and she sat quietly with me as I breathed slowly and just *felt*.

Mama made a thick, comforting chili and spicy cornbread for dinner and the three of us ate together on the sofa—they ate while I picked—watching a Christmas movie together.

Daddy cleared the dishes, rinsing while Mama stacked them into the dishwasher and I half-listened to their playful flirting. All these years later, and still Daddy found her the most irresistible woman he'd ever met.

I wanted that.

When Daddy dropped back down onto the sofa beside me, it was with a tall glass of soda.

Mama, not to be outdone, threw herself down next to me with a very large travel cup in each hand and I raised an eyebrow at her as she handed me one, sniffing cautiously and stifling the sharp cough that threatened. I took a cautious sip and winced. "Thanks, Mama. Great ... tea."

She snorted.

"For the love, woman." Daddy leaned around me to fix Mama with a glare. "I can handle watchin' you drink from a proper wine glass now and then. There's no need to treat me like a fool. I can smell the stuff, you know. I can look at it without sufferin' a relapse."

I chuckled, taking another sip of the wine Mama thought she was so cleverly disguising. I loved that she'd spent all these years trying to protect Daddy.

She leaned forward and squeezed his big face in her small hand, kissing his cheek while I leaned back and tried not to gag. They were adorable, it was true, but oftentimes it was disgusting.

Blair had declared me "entirely too depressing" and had decamped to Georgetown to spend the rest of Christmas with her father and "The Incubator," as she'd jokingly taken to calling Cassandra. I was glad she found it funny, at least, because I found it thoroughly sad.

Lucky for Carrick, Daddy had been letting him out all day, playing fetch, giving him food and water. Because clearly I couldn't be counted on to so much as move from the sofa.

I couldn't shake the memory of the look on Jack's face when he'd accused me of charity.

I fell asleep after tossing for hours, dreaming terrible dreams of Jack and a baby lying cold in her crib.

12

Jack

I'd lasted all of five minutes with Natasha before telling her I had somewhere else to be.

I invited her to take whatever she needed from the cupboards. She could do her laundry in my house.

There were sheets and blankets in the linen closet.

As far as I was concerned, she didn't live here any longer and if she needed a place to stay overnight, she was damn well going to sleep in the garage I'd worked so hard to convert for her.

"Don't you want to know why I'm here?" she teased me, running her fingers up the back of my neck and into my hair when I turned to pull a heavy blanket out of the linen closet for her.

"Don't care," was my caveman answer and though I didn't see her eyebrows rise, I felt it happen. Clearly she'd been expecting the welcome of the Prodigal Son, all party favors and confetti and shit, and this was hardly meeting with her expectations.

"Jack, baby." Her voice was low, but I recognized whining when I heard it. "Don't be like this. Aren't you happy to see me?"

"What the hell do you want, Natasha?" My voice was louder than I'd wanted, not shouting, but my irritation was pretty damn clear. "Because the last memory I have of you is being told that I was a mistake and watching your back as you walked out that door. You left *me*. You don't get any further input, now that I've withdrawn my response and signed the paperwork. I don't care if you've changed your mind, because you waited too damn long. This. Is. Over."

She sighed heavily, like I was being overly dramatic, which was something I never was. She was really good at manipulating people and emotions and situations, though, so at least there was one thing about her that had never changed.

"We can talk about it tomorrow when you've had some sleep," she said gently, like I was just a little too fragile to know what I really wanted.

"There's nothing to discuss," I said firmly, shoving the blankets at her. "The garage is just as you left it and I'll leave the back door unlocked if you need anything, but I have somewhere to be." And with that I grabbed my heavy coat and stomped out of the house.

At first I considered crashing with Tyler and Generis, but he'd let it slip a few times that Violet's birth had been difficult, the healing slow, and Generis hadn't exactly been eager to reintroduce sex to the relationship equation. He'd probably kill me if I showed up on his doorstep just as he'd convinced Generis to give it a go.

I drove into Baltimore, turning my truck through the familiar streets, carefully pulling a parallel and hopping out of the cab with nothing but my keys, wallet and phone. I hadn't exactly thought far ahead enough to pack a bag, I'd been so eager to get away from Natasha.

I knew Natasha well enough to know how she worked: She wove her fingers into your thoughts, twisting and manipulating and confusing. Before you knew what had happened, she'd convince you she was right and you were wrong. She was a dangerous snake.

Unlocking Pop's front door, I let myself in, thankful the boiler seemed to be working just fine, as the house was comfortably warm. I hadn't been back to his house at night since we'd completed the work and I walked the small space, snapping on the lights to admire the fresh paint and carpet.

My childhood bedroom had fresh paint and new carpeting, just like the rest of the small house. The full size bed was made with cozy flannel sheets, which was a nice touch.

I tossed my jacket on the desk before walking back through the house to turn out the lights and get a drink of water from the kitchen.

Chances weren't good Pop would come back here, certainly not without some kind of supervision. He was going to need steady care going forward. Someone who made sure he got his meds and regular meals. Someone to keep him on a schedule and get him to regular appointments. And I just knew it was going to be a struggle.

I checked my phone for the seven hundredth time that day, like I expected Daphne to call or text me after I'd ripped her apart that morning. I couldn't expect her to understand that while I did all the pushing, I was pretty sure I needed her to come after me. To know I was *worth it*, and I knew that made me a selfish bastard, because her wounds ran just as deep.

Tossing my phone across the bed, frustrated, I pushed down my pants and flipped off the light, crawling under the heavy duvet, shivering a little, and my brain went straight for Daphne. I couldn't help but imagine opening the door to the room to find her already there, in my bed, the smell of her sweet skin and hair pulling me across the room and into her arms.

I would slide in behind her and pull her little body tight to mine, my face in the curve of her shoulder, kissing and nibbling while she giggled sleepily and pulled my hand under her pajama shirt to the soft curve of her breasts.

Shit.

I groaned. That was all it took to get me hard and now I was stuck, alone in my childhood bed, with no Daphne to be found.

I didn't have the energy to manage the situation on my own, so I rolled over and tried instead to drift into an uncomfortable sleep.

Damn woman chased me into my dreams.

Christmas morning dawned icy cold and bright. I took my time driving back to my place, half surprised to find Tash wasn't in the house yet, and built a fire in the living room fireplace before making waffles for breakfast. This was about as fancy as I ever got.

I wasn't feeling particularly jolly, and I knew exactly why. It had occurred to me that after lunch I should drive back to Daphne's place to make my apologies and maybe she could find it in her heart to forgive me for being an asshole. Again.

Tash drifted into the house a few moments later, wrapped up in leggings and a soft sweater that left her shoulders bare. It seemed an odd choice for a seventeen-degree day, but I suspected she still thought she had a shot in hell at seducing me.

She'd changed tack entirely overnight, suddenly being sweet and demure. Using weird words like "Please," and "Thank you," and shooting me adoring glances that made me extremely uncomfortable.

We ate a very awkward, stilted breakfast at the small table and while I cleaned up she said she was going to find "A Christmas Story" on TV, since it was her family's Christmas tradition. I could hear her cursing softly as she tried to figure out the remote and I stacked dishes into the dishwasher, wondering if it was too early to show up at Daphne's house.

I was at a loss as to what to do with myself after breakfast. Surely Daphne was busy, celebrating Christmas with her family, and since there were all of two presents under my tree, I did my best to ignore them until later.

Instead, I went outside to split more wood for the fire. I didn't need it, considering I'd been splitting wood for weeks, every time the frustration of Daphne had become too much—which was to say I had split enough wood to last me several seasons. But I had to get out of the house and away from Tash; away from her strange behavior and the way she watched me.

She was still sitting on the sofa, wrapped in a blanket and watching a Christmas movie when I stomped into the house. She'd clearly made herself right at home and she looked up with a smile as I slammed the door behind me. "The heat in the garage is acting up again ... and there are some cookies in the kitchen if you'd like."

I wanted to tell her to leave. To ask her what the hell it was that she was doing, looking settled and comfortable in *my* home. But my thoughts were scattered, and I needed more coffee, so I headed into the kitchen to make coffee, toast and eggs. Second breakfast and all that.

There were cookies out on the counter and the room smelled like warm vanilla, like they'd been freshly baked. I looked around suspiciously for packaging and found none, leading me to believe Natasha had made them from scratch. That was a sure sign of the apocalypse, and I stood there staring at the evil little fuckers as she moved into the kitchen behind me, splashing more coffee into her cup.

"Why are you here?" I asked finally, spinning around to lean against the counter and cross my arms over my chest.

"Because I made a mistake," she said quietly, setting her cup down on the counter and mirroring my pose, and I couldn't help the sharp laugh that I barked out.

"Which one?" I asked. "Treating me like garbage? Leaving? Living in a van in Argentina with that deadbeat kid you were fucking? Vinnie, was it?"

"All of it," she said, not meeting my eyes and I looked her up and down suspiciously.

"You'll have to forgive me if I don't trust or believe you," I said bitterly. "I learned a long time ago that you have ulterior motives, so I suspect you're here not because you missed me, but because you need something."

She lifted huge, tear-filled eyes to me then, something that might have worked a few years earlier, but I recognized all of her ploys. She'd cried wolf far too many times and I knew the signs. I shook my head at her again. I'd been through too much with her already. "Whatever it is, Tash, you made your choice. I've signed the papers and I want to put this behind me. You can go home to your parents and do whatever you need to do to get your shit together, but you are not my responsibility anymore."

"You don't want me anymore?" She looked incredulous. That was Tash, though. She'd always had a high opinion of herself, and for a time I *had* found her irresistible, which fed that monster. Now that I could resist her, she couldn't believe it.

"Nope." I shook my head at her. "What I do want is you, packed and out. I'll put you on a bus or drive you to your parents' if you have nowhere else to go, but this?" I gestured between the two of us. "This was over before you left."

Funny how I'd just realized it now.

She swallowed hard. "Can I stay a couple days while I figure things out?"

"Fine." I sighed. "I'll take a look at the heat, but you're still staying in the garage."

I left her in the kitchen, taking a cup of coffee with me as I let myself out of the house and into the garage.

As I'd suspected, the heat worked just fine, which led me to believe that if I'd stayed in my own bed the night before I'd have awakened this morning to find her wrapped around me, naked.

I was relieved to find the thought genuinely repulsive.

It was late morning when the sound of Tash's voice, indistinct and low, drifted back into the kitchen and I thought at first she was on the phone.

My stupid heart slammed into my chest when I heard Daphne's voice and I moved closer to the doorway to hear what was being said between the two women. I peeked around the cased opening, able to see Tash from behind but not Daphne, since she still stood outside the front door.

Tash held one arm along the door, the other wrapped around her front and when I heard a soft cry from Daphne I moved toward Natasha, alarmed by the sound.

"What's going on?" I asked sharply and Tash turned quickly, her expression startled.

"Nothing, baby," she answered innocently and my eyes narrowed before I caught sight of Daphne standing on the front porch, pale, her eyes glittering.

"I don't know what you think you're doing," I started, and Tash bulldozed right over me.

"This sweet little thing brought you Christmas presents." She pointed a disdainful toe at a small collection of boxes sitting next to the door, and the way she looked at Daphne made her disgust very clear.

This was the Tash I knew.

"Judging by the rings on her hand, Jack ... well, there should have been coal in your stocking this year." She smirked.

Daphne held up a hand, dashing fingers beneath one eye and sucking in a shaky breath while I tried to formulate some kind of intelligent response to the things Natasha was spewing in a hateful tone.

"Merry Christmas, Jack," Daphne said softly as my mouth opened and closed and no words came out. "I hope you finally got your wish."

There was so much hurt in her voice that I felt the pinch in my chest, and I watched a tear break the dam, hurtling down her cheek before she turned and hurried out of the porch, across the snowy lawn. I knew she was dashing at her face with her hands, her movements sharp and jerky as she stumbled toward the curb.

Daphne climbed quickly up into her truck and I watched Natasha's lip curl in disgust as the truck roared to life.

Tash was a woman who had never appreciated the *truly* finer things in life, like noisy vehicles or a cold beer, or an afternoon at the range.

"What did you say to her?" I demanded, grabbing my phone to dial Daphne, not surprised when it went straight to voicemail.

Natasha looked up at me innocently. "I told her the truth, baby: I'm your wife. I came home to work things out between the two of us and I hoped she could wish us the best, because we were finally going to be a family." She rested a hand on her belly and a sick, sour understanding started curdling in my gut.

"So you hurried home to me, because I'm the safe choice." My stomach rolled and pitched like I was going to be sick. "I have health insurance and a job and a roof over my head, so you thought you'd show up and throw yourself at me." I couldn't even fathom that she might actually be pregnant, trying to pin another man's child on me.

This was ludicrous.

This was *so* Natasha.

I handed her my phone. "You have a phone call to make. Your pick. Whoever can drop everything on Christmas day to come pick you up, that's who you're calling. Because by the time I get home, I expect you to be gone."

Natasha's face went slack with shock. She'd spent an entire lifetime manipulating people and it was inconceivable to her that she might not get what she wanted.

I pulled my jacket out of the narrow closet while she dialed, swallowing hard, and I shoved my arms through the sleeves while she had a stilted, awkward conversation with someone I assumed was one of her parents. It didn't matter which, in my opinion. They were both assholes and it should have been my warning years earlier when they asked her, right in front of me, if I wasn't a little old for her.

She dropped the phone back into my waiting palm, her face downcast. For the first time ever, she'd lost that superior look she always wore. Instead, she looked worried and it was a relief to me, to realize that while she was still beautiful, *I* no longer found her beautiful.

"Great manners, by the way," I said as I laced up my other boot and straightened, zipping my jacket before opening the door. "That was Daphne Preston." I waited for the penny to drop, but she just looked confused.

"You were just a total bitch to the woman who designed your wedding dress."

Her jaw dropping was the last—very satisfying—thing I saw as I walked out the door.

Jonas was out in the backyard with Carrick when I finally pulled into the driveway. I could hear them around the back of the house and I followed the sound. I needed to apologize to his daughter, but first I needed to explain myself to the man I knew probably wanted to have me "disappeared."

"Expected you here yesterday," he called across the frozen lawn and Carrick abandoned his slimy ball to dart across the lawn, throwing himself against my thighs. I braced, but he still nearly knocked me over, the monster. Not a mean bone in his body.

Hands shoved into my pockets, I had a very, very hard time meeting the man's eyes and it shouldn't have been hard, because we were the same height. I knew it was because of the weight pulling down on my spirit.

"You scared of my daughter, Thompson?" The man barked at me, his expression more vicious than anything Carrick could throw my way.

I nodded slowly and watched the corners of his mouth turn up.

"Expected as much. When one of these women puts her mind to gettin' in here," he slammed a fist against his huge chest, "pretty good chance the little lady's gonna get her way. No amount of struggle gonna keep her out. No sir, not with my girls." He stepped back, launching another ball for Carrick, who took off like a shot despite his size.

"Don't say I didn't warn you." He cracked a small grin in my direction.

"Might be too late for a warning," I mumbled, and his grin grew bigger.

"That's my girl," he said fondly, the smile stretching and creasing his eyes. "No use in fightin' it, son. My Daphne's like a deadly tide: patient, persistent, slow risin', creepin' in on you, fillin' up the whole place 'til all you can see is her."

Yeah, that pretty well described the way the woman had infiltrated my every thought.

I shuffled a little, kicking at the snow.

"Don't hurt none that she's pretty as her mama."

No, that she was beautiful certainly didn't hurt my feelings, but the word didn't seem sufficient, because there was so much more to her than just the attractive outside. The thing that had intrigued me about her from the start, the fact that she surprised me—kept me constantly on my toes.

"She's something, all right," I mumbled and Carrick dropped the slobbery ball at my feet, looking up expectantly. If a dog could grin, he was doing it.

"You gonna man up?" he asked, fixing me with one steely blue eye as he leaned over to pat the dog's head. "Useless husband of hers been draggin' her through the mud for years. Definition of a fuck-up if I ever saw one. She don't need more of that." He shook his head, more to himself than anyone else.

It was so cold out, the tips of my fingers were starting to go numb. If this was Jonas's interrogation tactic, it was brilliant, because though I'd been the one to seek him out, I knew he'd keep me out there until he got the answer he wanted.

"I don't have much to offer, sir," I said, swallowing hard and feeling like I was all of fifteen years old, telling the father of the woman I loved that I wanted to provide for his daughter, though all I could offer was the salary from a part-time job at a fast food restaurant.

His face softened. "Daphne don't ask for much," he said, turning to face me full-on. "Never has. Girl's always made her own way and kept her head about her. Smart, hard-working, and soft-hearted. Got you stuck in that big heart of hers, I expect." One bushy eyebrow raised. "Hell of a shot though, so I suggest you mind your Ps and Qs. Probably don't wanna be on her bad side."

I couldn't stop the smile that spread across my face. He had me there, and he knew it.

"Yes, sir."

He nodded shortly. Whatever had passed between us, it seemed he thought it sufficient for the time being. With a sharp whistle he summoned the dog, and Carrick and I followed behind him, trailing into the house.

My heart hammered as I shut the door behind me. Just one little woman to face in this house, and she was damn well my undoing.

Christa's eyes missed nothing. "Didn't expect you back so soon, sweetheart." She had cleaned up after breakfast and was nursing another cup of coffee as she swiped through pages on her e-reader, her bag at her feet and her coat draped over the back of her chair.

I raised an eyebrow, because I had graduated to "sweetheart."

"I know this wasn't the plan," she said slowly, and I stood in the middle of the room, an uncomfortable No Man's Land, eyeing the coffee pot, the redeemer in every awkward social situation. And this was one of them; I was praying for something to distract the parents while I waited uncomfortably for Daphne to appear.

"I was thinking since we're already this far north, maybe Jonas and me will head up to Daphne's place in the city for a couple days. Do my baby some good to get away for a minute; year's been hard on him. Now that he's gotten through the season he's gonna be a grumpy old bear just bangin' around the house, lookin' for somethin' to do." She smiled, but it was a little tight.

According to ESPN, there had been pressure on Jonas to retire the past couple seasons, but he'd always insisted he had another good season left in him.

Christa fixed me with an appraising look. "Expected you'd be here to talk to her daddy—about time you showed up, too. And speakin' of men and talkin'," she started right back up and I splashed some coffee into a cup, my temples threatening to throb as I watched Jonas saunter casually into the living room, away from the weighted conversation I knew I was about to have with his wife.

"Hunter called this mornin' to wish us a Merry Christmas." The corners of her mouth turned down ever so slightly, the only indication she wasn't Hunter's biggest fan. "Said that since Daphne decided she's done with him, he'll grant her wish early. He's talked to the PR team and says he'll file." Her eyebrows moved ever so slightly. "Subtext, in my opinion? He noodled a live one this time. She's probably got him by the JV team, if you know what I mean."

I couldn't help the face I pulled. That was the last thing I wanted to envision, but hearing it from Daphne's mother's lips was enough to turn my stomach. "Huh." I was still staring holes into the counter. "Doesn't seem like him, to be magnanimous like that."

"Oh, he's not." She huffed loudly. "I'm sure it will cost her, probably in more than one way. But she's well and truly done with him and I think he knows it."

There was a noise. "You love my sweet girl, Jack?" Christa was right up in my face. "You gonna take care of her? Treat her right, like that trash *should* have been treatin' her all this time?"

I kind of liked this woman, the original version of my Daphne, fierce and loyal and maybe just a touch crazy.

"I do, Mrs. Masters," I confessed. "But I haven't told her yet, so I don't feel like it's right for me to say the words to anyone else first."

"Good boy." She tucked her e-reader into her bag, looking resolute. "You need to tell that to my sweet daughter. The girl's been driving herself bananas over you for months, I'll have you know. And the only thing I want for her is to see her happy. You must know that."

I did.

Nodding, I kissed the back of her hand, releasing her before Jonas rounded the corner with Daphne under his arm. She seemed so small next to him, deflated, and the light was gone from her eyes.

I had done this.

13

Daphne

"Sweet Pea." It was Daddy, wrapping an arm around me and I looked up, up, up to his craggy face. He was still so handsome, such a *man*, I could see what Mama saw in him. "Your mama tells me that she's dragging my sorry backside to New York, when I've just gotten here to spend some time with my best girl."

Mama's glance was positively withering. "Jonas Emerson Masters," she hissed loudly. "This is not the time to be a cock blocker!"

I choked. Loudly. And Mama had the good sense to go completely purple at the words that had just left her very polite mouth.

Daddy choked too, for a similar reason I was sure, and he looked down at me like he couldn't believe I was no longer six. He set his jaw hard, his head turning slightly, and that was when I felt Jack's presence in the room. Jack was the only one who hadn't snorted, but over Daddy's shoulder I could see the small smile pulling at his lips.

"Come visit us on your way back through?" I asked, a million unspoken things passing between Daddy and me, and a sweet smile crossed his face.

"Wouldn't miss it for the world, sweetheart. Gotta sit down and have a talk about my roster for next year. Got some thoughts on this Harrington fella, comin' out of South Carolina."

"Got some thoughts on that too," I grinned back. "Good ones."

He nodded shortly and held out a hand to my mother. "Well then, kids," he announced, nodding quickly at Jack, "we'll get outta your hair. See you in a couple days."

Their departure was so sudden, the house felt empty when they grabbed their coats and shut the door behind them.

I had a feeling Mama had packed the car while I'd been driving to Jack's, hardly eager to stick around for more awkward breakfast conversations. She'd been watching me moon around the house, hovering, and had apparently decided that a good dose of Jack was what ailed me: The sickness and the cure.

Jack didn't say anything, just stood frozen in place while the silence wrapped itself around us.

"Hunter's girlfriend is making him file," I whispered finally, and he nodded slowly.

"I kicked Natasha out." He fidgeted with a belt loop. "She showed up at my door and that's when I came to you. If she *is* pregnant, the kid's not mine. I haven't touched her in years, and I don't want to anymore. I don't want her at all."

"What do you want then, Jack?" I wasn't trying to play coy. After the push-pull-push of how he reacted to me, I needed him to be the one to take the first step.

He moved slowly, keeping his eyes locked with mine as he moved toward me and when he stood only inches away, he dropped to his knees. Wrapped his arms around my middle and pressed his face to my stomach.

"I want to stop fighting it." His words were muffled by my sweater. "Stop letting you haunt me. See you in my days, because without you I can't sleep at night." He lifted his eyes to me then and I could see in the shadows beneath them that he'd been sleeping just as poorly as I had the last few nights.

"I don't know if I'm staying, Jack." I swallowed hard, digging my fingers into his hair and his eyes went hard.

"You're staying, Daphne, because I'm not letting you go. You'll live in my house with me and sleep in my bed and be *mine*." His arms tightened.

Who was this man?

"My pop will come home and we'll sell his house; get him an assisted living apartment nearby so he feels independent but he's safe, and if you don't like my place, we'll sell that too. We'll find something bigger and better. Whatever you want. Wherever it takes us."

What was happening? I looked around me for a second and he mistook my silence for reticence, fear suddenly in his eyes. He swallowed hard, his expression vulnerable, and I understood we'd turned a corner—*he* had turned a corner, because he had just opened his heart to me.

"What I want," I said slowly, finally meeting his eyes, "is to be where you are. You might have to go a little easier on me at first, though." I patted the top of my head and grinned, and he grinned back. "Uh ... except..." I pulled a face. "I'm not a very good cook."

His smile got bigger. "Seems Catalina might be looking for a new position, and I live a hell of a lot closer to baby Violet than you do."

My eyes brightened. "Sold. Let me grab a few things and you get the dog."

"You're coming with me right now?" He looked delighted, but shocked.

I leaned in then, feathering soft kisses from the collar of his shirt to his jaw and his breathing became harsh and erratic. "Okay, yes..." He sighed. "Right now." He smacked my butt. "Get a move on, woman. We have better things to be doing."

Carrick could hardly believe his good fortune when I took off his collar for the invisible fence and let him out the front door. It took next to no convincing to get him to jump into the backseat of my truck, and I followed Jack home with a small smile on my lips. There were a lot of things that needed resolution yet, but the idea of spending a few quiet days with him was too strong a pull for me to resist.

When we pulled up to the house Jack pulled into his driveway and I parked on the street, noticing the second slot in his driveway was taken up by an expensive, sleek black sedan. I didn't recognize the tiny logo, leading me to believe it was something foreign and probably out of reach for most people.

The grin on Jack's face was wicked when I let Carrick out of the back seat and he called the dog to him, leading him up the steps and opening the front door.

There was a wail of dismay from inside the house as the dog disappeared into it, and an older woman with expensive blonde hair came flying down the front steps with a look of terror on her face. "You keep that beast away from me," she gasped to Jack, and he shrugged nonchalantly.

"I invited the dog into my home; I didn't invite you."

"You have some nerve." The woman drew herself up imperiously, and even in her heels she was still eight inches shorter than Jack. "Throwing your wife out into the street; relying upon the compassion of relatives to see to things that are your responsibility."

The briefest flash of anger crossed Jack's face and he gave the woman a tight smile. "Natasha stopped being my responsibility two years ago, when she moved to Argentina to live in a van with a professional bum."

The woman looked like she smelled something bad.

"Your daughter showed up on my doorstep a few days ago with the idea in her head that she was going to jump right back into my bed." Now he was the one who looked like something smelled.

Natasha appeared, and it didn't escape my notice that she couldn't meet my eyes. Instead, she gave Jack a wide berth, moving past him to open the passenger door of the expensive car and she tossed in a small bag before climbing in herself.

"My guess is that things went tits-up with her teenage boyfriend," Jack sneered, one hand rubbing at his chin. "Chances are good your daughter got herself knocked up and thought she'd come back to pin it on me."

Something in the woman's face crumpled and she huffed at Jack before marching across the frozen expanse of lawn to get into her car.

I pulled my bag from the truck and crossed the lawn slowly to stand next to Jack, where he stood deep in thought as he watched the car back out of the driveway and roar down the street.

Carrick was draped over the sofa when Jack shut the door behind us, and I pointed sternly to the floor. He grumbled at me, oozing slowly off the cushions and collapsing instead on the rug in front of the fireplace, and Jack chuckled.

He took the bag from me and walked it up the stairs as I followed, unsure of what to do with myself. I'd never had an adult sleepover, not ever, and I wasn't sure how these things were supposed to go.

He set my bag in the small chair in the corner and turned to face me, shoving his hands into his back pockets with a strange expression on his face. "I am probably not going to be a very good host," he said with a tight smile and I knew it meant because he was used to doing his own thing. I might be a hiccup.

Finally slipping off my shoes, I took off my coat and hung it on the back of the bedroom door. In the light of day his room was still a warm, cozy little cocoon and his eyes followed mine when I gave the bed a lingering glance.

"Maybe we could sort of ease into this together," I suggested in a small voice. "We're both so used to doing our own thing, it'll take a while to smooth out the rough edges."

Like he was reading my thoughts, he kicked off his boots and tossed his jacket onto the chair, on top of my bag, before pulling back the blankets on the bed. "Care to join me?" He crawled right in with an evil grin on his face, and I threw myself across the space to crawl in next to him.

"You're wearing too many clothes," I whined, curling my fingers into the soft flannel of his shirt and he trailed warm fingers down the side of my neck before leaning over me, pushing me back into the pillows as he kissed my neck.

A girl could get used to this.

There was something slower, gentler, and less fearful happening in him, I suspected, his hands careful when they slipped beneath my shirt to smooth across my skin. I knew he was being gentle for my sake.

"What does 'too much' mean, Jack?"

It slipped out, the thought that had been a sharp splinter in my brain the last few days and it was enough to make him freeze, his breath warm against my neck as he stilled.

"She said I was too rough with her."

"Were you?"

"Not at first."

Something uncomfortable started to tingle in my throat.

"After the baby..." His voice trailed off and when I felt him swallow hard I lifted a hand to his cheek, smoothing my fingers over his face.

"I know," I whispered, a quiet encouragement for him to continue.

"That was when she started sleeping in the garage conversion almost all the time, and I was ... desperate for my wife." His voice caught and I shifted so I could pull him closer. "We had nothing left. We'd lost the baby and she blamed me. She stopped touching me or looking at me ... speaking to me.

"The handful of times she came to me in the middle of the night. I wasn't as gentle as I should have been. I was angry and hurting and what we did was more about fighting without words than it was about loving each other."

I heard him drag in several deep, painful breaths. "At that point I would have done anything to get her back. I was in love with a woman who didn't want to breathe the same air as me, and she would taunt me. Tell me I was weak and pathetic, a washout, and she needed a real man who could meet her needs."

I turned my head so I could see his face, but his eyes were closed as he relived the painful memories. I leaned up then, to softly kiss each eyelid, and there was an expression on his face of hurt and shame.

"*That* time ... it was really angry and rough, and she just kept goading me, telling me I wasn't capable of pleasing her ... and when we were done she got dressed and drove herself to the hospital. She claimed what we'd done hadn't been consensual and there was enough ... bruising ... to give her story credibility."

He paused for a long time, dropping his forehead to my chest for a moment. "That was just before Christmas. She filed a report, threatened to press charges, then she packed up her stuff and pawned all her jewelry. Left me a note to expect a divorce filing. She said we were incompatible in all the ways that mattered and that over time I had become violent and uncaring. I didn't meet her needs or see to her happiness."

I sighed softly. "Feeling abandoned leads us to do desperate things," I said finally and I felt his head move in a slow nod.

I leaned up then, rolling him gently onto his back and crawling over him. We were going to take things slower this time, I decided, and our clothes stayed on for the next hour while we kissed and ground our bodies together like desperate teenagers.

When he finally peeled my clothes off and worshiped my body with hands and lips and tongue, I shook with my desire for him. He brought me skillfully to the edge over and over, backing off at the last moment only to start all over again.

Finally his clothing came off as well and when he crawled back into the bed he flipped me quickly, so that he covered me from behind. He was gentler that time, leaving me unbound, and I didn't crack my head into the headboard, but I didn't have the connection with him that I needed.

"Jack," I whispered finally and he stilled, his chest heaving with the exertion of his breaths.

Carefully separating our bodies, I rolled under him and reached for his hips. He had no choice but to look at me now, and I wondered if being face-to-face and breath-to-breath was too intimate for him. Turning me away from him had been a way to disconnect.

I watched his expression tighten and then go flat, and when I reached up to touch his face, he leaned slowly into my touch as if it woke him from a terrible dream.

We moved together slowly and it was as if he couldn't focus, little grunts of frustration leaving him from time to time as he worked over me.

Leaning up to him, I put one hand at his hip to still him, while the other hand cupped his face. I kissed him then, long and deep, something with tenderness and promise and when he began to move again he was gazing down at my face with focus. Watching my expressions intently, and as I gave myself over to the things he made me feel, I whispered to him that he was everything I needed.

That I wanted to lie in the circle of his arms every night.

That I wanted to wake him in the middle of the night to make love, slowly and quietly sometimes, and other times frantically and loudly.

That I wanted him to come home to me every day and crawl in next to me every night.

Then the things I was saying stopped making sense, because I had no coherent thought. It was only sounds, soft sighs and moans and when I cried out for him I felt him let go too, his expression one of soul-deep relief.

We were after one another for hours, giggling and teasing and touching gently, then panting and sweating and moaning, and when I woke in his arms to a room growing dark, I could hear Carrick snoring at the foot of the bed. I nestled back in, pressing a kiss to Jack's chest as I cuddled closer. He stirred as I did, making a contented sleepy noise in the back of his throat and I lifted one knee to tuck and nudge between his legs, winding myself up in him.

I closed my eyes again, to drift off for a few more moments. He would be awake soon, if what I felt stirring was any indication. And when he woke, I knew what I was in for.

14

Jack

Daphne and I spent the next few weeks creating a new routine and each time she offered to pack up and go home, to leave me in peace for a while, I didn't want to let her leave. Coming home to her every day filled me with a peace I hadn't known for a very long time and the first thing I did each day, after walking through the door, was to gather her up in my arms and just let the relief wash over me.

She stayed.

Carrick was terrorizing the neighbors and Daphne mentioned, at the risk of being presumptuous she said, that she'd have an invisible fence installed around my property if I didn't mind.

The dog was my best new buddy. From the time I got home to the time I went to bed, he was at my side or in my lap, resting his head on my knee or leaning into my leg. He'd have slept in the bed and I probably would have let him, but Daphne wouldn't hear of it, so he curled up on the floor next to me and if I got up during the night I had to be careful not to step on him.

Daphne wasn't kidding when she told me she was stepping back from her business, and most days I came home to find her with papers and a laptop spread out on the dining room table, sticky notes everywhere and a smile on her face.

Jonas and Christa had been through on their way back to Alabama and we'd sat in my small dining room with takeout and discussed what Daphne could do to help with Jonas's foundation.

I recruited the boys to help out one weekend and since Daphne had hardly moved into her enormous mansion, it took the group of us less than a weekend to pack up the house and put boxes into storage. She listed almost all of the furniture for sale, had a few things shipped to Hunter, and the *For Sale* shingle was in the front yard before the last pickup truck pulled out of the driveway.

In hindsight, I can say maybe we moved a little too fast. I received my finalized divorce papers only a few weeks later, but Daphne's husband still hadn't filed. For some reason that made me nervous and uncomfortable, like I was somehow sneaking around with her behind his back. Anyone with sense would know that wasn't true, but I couldn't get past it and I started to let it nag at me.

"Relax, baby," she said to me one night as she stirred some sauce on the stove. I had gone down to the basement to work out when I got home from work and when I followed my nose up to the kitchen she told me Catalina had cooked down some sauce and she was going to make pasta bolognese.

There was something so comforting about her presence in my house. It always smelled warm and welcoming, since Daphne liked to eat as much as I did, and she fussed over me and spoiled me like I was her kid.

I grabbed her by the hips and pulled her back against me to drop a kiss in her hair before leaning over her shoulder to take an appreciative sniff. "I'll bet there's cologne that smells like that in Italy," I said with a grin into the side of her head and she snorted, leaning back against my shoulder and bringing one hand up to wrap around my neck.

"Any word from Hunter?" I tried to ask nonchalantly, and I felt her sigh. Lately I'd been finding creative ways to ask her every day, though I knew as well as she did that my answer would come as a process server at the front door.

"I gave Cassandra my new address today," she said quietly, and I froze.

"You called the child?"

"You seem eager to have my marriage concluded, Jack. I thought the best way to expedite the process was to give the necessary information to the woman who hates me most."

That was kind of smart, I had to hand it to her. But as the week wore on and each day was as uneventful as the last, I started to get nervous again.

When it was time to pick up Pop from the facility, Daphne packed sandwiches and thermoses of hot coffee and we put the dog in the back of her truck to make the trip to Long Island.

She grinned over her shoulder at me as I drove, Carrick's head resting on the console between us, his eyebrows shifting back and forth from Daphne to me. "So..." she led with a slow drawl. "You're a convert?"

So busted. I loved her truck, her dog, these new routines with her...

I gave her my grumpiest look and she burst into laughter. I couldn't hide anything from her; she could see right through me.

Pop lit right up when he saw Daphne. He hadn't forgotten about her or a single moment that he'd spent with her, and I was relieved to find that he looked healthy, having put on a little more weight and the tremors were less noticeable.

Daphne helped him carefully into the truck and fussed over him like he was a small child, which delighted him to no end as he let her do it.

Daphne dove into the cooler as we drove away from the facility and pushed sandwiches and a smoothie at Pop. She had been learning some basics from Catalina, worried about Pop's nutrition once he came home.

Carrick abandoned me for Pop, crawling right up on the seat and plopping his head into Pop's lap, where he stayed for the entire ride home.

Daphne had made a few changes to the little guest room, adding comfortable touches with soft, cozy linens and a few pretty pictures. She'd hung curtains too, to hide the stark, cheap plastic blinds I'd hung over the window.

Catalina had been to my place that afternoon and she left wrapped dishes in the oven for us, along with a sweet note for Daphne, telling her to "Take good care of my Jackie."

Daphne sat us both down at the dining table to eat and while I cleaned up the dishes after, she took Pop upstairs to learn about his medications and to wait around while he showered and got ready for bed. He didn't seem disoriented or uncomfortable, which made me feel a little better, but Daphne had firsthand experience with the progression and she'd gently warned me about signs to watch for and things to expect.

I was offered a position with the Capitol Police late that spring, after an old buddy of mine recommended me for the spot, and I cleared all the necessary checks and interviewed. I wasn't excited about the considerably increased commute time, but the salary didn't hurt my feelings and Daphne was a real big fan of my new uniform. Honestly, I didn't see a lot of difference, but it turned out she had a thing for guys in uniform ... and I used that every chance I got.

Pop got a little worse as spring bled into summer and Daphne and I discussed installing a stair lift, since the house was old and the stairs were steep, and Pop's balance was getting more and more unsteady.

Daphne's house sold that summer and Blair spent the summer in Georgetown, living with her father and her new baby brother, and she commuted into Annapolis Junction each day to work for the employer she'd had the summer before. Daphne went to the city a couple times to meet up with her, but more often Blair came to us and when she stayed over she'd sleep on the living room sofa.

Carrick had completely given up on the rest of us, the traitor. He was Pop's shadow, always at his side, watching him carefully as if he knew he needed to guard and protect someone who was no longer capable of doing it for himself.

To his credit, Pop stayed off the booze. Either rehab worked or he forgot about the stuff, and Daphne got so good at mixing up what she called "mocktails" that maybe he didn't miss it at all.

I came home from work late one day in the middle of July. It was hotter than hell out, the air swampy with humidity. It had been a long, difficult day. There had been a rally in the city and some of the attendees had gotten a little out of hand, which led to a heightened state of security in all the government buildings and I didn't go off-shift until almost nine, which was hours past my typical clock-out.

My eyes drooped as I drove home and I arrived to find the house dark and quiet. It was unlikely they'd both gone to bed early, but not impossible, so I let myself in and Carrick was immediately at my side, whining softly. That put me on edge and I snapped on the light, rushing through the house calling for Daphne and Pop.

There was a scrap of paper on the dining room table, a hasty scrawl in Daphne's handwriting: *Call me. Taking Dad to the hospital.*

I couldn't fucking breathe and without even thinking to give Carrick a pat, I turned and rushed out of the house, throwing myself right back into my truck before I realized I didn't know which hospital she was talking about.

A pin popped up on my phone and I tapped it, grateful to see Daphne had sent me the address. I made the short drive in half the time it should have taken, hurriedly parking and rushing into reception in full uniform. The desk attendant looked up and I felt her eyes sweep over me appreciatively, her lips pursing in a way I found almost offensive.

"Thompson," I barked at her. "He was brought in earlier."

She took her sweet-ass time clicking through the records on her computer and finally said, "Yes, he was brought in by ambulance about two hours ago."

I didn't wait for her to continue. I took off toward the ER, slipping through the doors behind an orderly who didn't seem eager to question whether I belonged once he got an eyeful of my badge and security tags.

"Jack." It was Daphne's sweet, soft voice, full of relief and I rushed toward her, where she sat in a curtained cubicle at Pop's bedside. "He'll be okay." She sighed into my shirt when I crushed her against me and I finally let the hot panic crawl all the way up my throat and start to sting my sinuses and eyes.

"What happened?" I tried to keep my voice down. Pop's eyes were closed and it looked like he was sleeping, a nasty bruise on the side of his head and a row of stitches closing up one cheek.

"He decided to sneak upstairs for a shower while I was making dinner." She sniffled a little. "I put him on the sofa in front of a movie, but he's been a little ... unsettled ... nit-picky ... argumentative ... all day. And he wanted a shower, which I told him we'd handle after dinner."

"And he fell," I finished for her flatly, scrubbing the palm of one hand over my face. I didn't for a second think Natalie had neglected him and I was angry with myself for not being home, because I should have been. I'd been seeing to shower time.

"I'm so sorry." Her eyes filled with tears as she looked up at me and I wrapped my arms tighter, leaning down to kiss her lips.

"Do you really think I'm angry with you?"

"He was on my watch. I should have made him sit in the kitchen with me—I know better. I know better than most people."

"Daphne." I leaned back a little to look down into her eyes and I grabbed her chin in my hand. "You were *seven* when your Gramps lived with you."

Her eyes dropped and I could see the shame in her beautiful features. "I still should have known."

A throat was cleared somewhere behind me and a small woman wearing glasses and a cardigan the color of potato skins was scowling up at me. "Mr. Thompson?"

My eyes flicked to the badge pinned to her sweater.

Oh hell, here we go: Someone sent a social worker because they think Pop's being abused.

Daphne worked her magic with the sour little woman, answering questions in her sweet voice and dashing at her eyes while I sat next to Pop, glowering at the woman.

When I say Daphne worked her magic, I mean that inside of fifteen minutes the woman was consoling *her*, in a voice far gentler and kinder than she'd used when she walked into our little cubby.

"I swear it," Daphne was saying when my attention snapped back. "This is not going to happen again because I won't let it. We're going to find a place where he's safe. I have the means and the resources and I will not let this happen again."

That was when I knew.

I sat quietly, absorbing the feelings in the moment. Daphne loved my Pop. She spent her days caring for him, feeding him, making sure he was clean and clothed and getting his medications. She took him for walks and made him tea, told him jokes and read to him. And still, she threw herself into working with Jonas's foundation.

I needed to lock this woman down.

The doctor insisted Pop be kept overnight, worried he had a mild concussion from falling and smacking his head on the shower surround.

"I'll stay with him," Daphne said gently, her eyes still swimming. "You have work tomorrow, baby. Everything is probably still on the stove if Carrick didn't eat it. Go home and sleep and feed our boy."

The love and gratitude I felt for the woman was overwhelming. I slipped out of the chair and sank to my knees in front of her, wrapping my arms around her.

"I'm taking the day tomorrow," I told her softly. "I'll stay here with him and if they release him tomorrow, I'll bring him home."

I could tell she still hadn't forgiven herself.

"Babe, we knew this was coming. And you're right, we'll figure something out. I'll put gates in and set up his bedroom in the dining room for now and we'll look for another place with bedrooms on the ground floor. This was not your fault."

"I'm scared, Jack."

Yeah, me too.

"Go home and rest, Daph. Let Carrick sleep in the bed so you have someone to cuddle with. I'll be home tomorrow with Pop and we'll figure this out."

Daphne kissed me, something sweet and simple, just a soft press of her lips to mine, and I sighed contentedly into her hair as I pulled her close.

"Babe?" Daphne made a soft noise against my neck. "I'm bringing Pop home tomorrow ... and then I'm paying a visit to Hunter."

15

Daphne

It didn't take a rocket scientist to figure out what Jack meant when he said he was going to pay Hunter a visit, and although I was exhausted I didn't sleep well that night. It was the first night in months that I went to bed without Jack beside me, and although Carrick was a very willing cuddle buddy, he smelled and he farted in his sleep, and when he dreamed of chasing rabbits he started kicking me in the back.

Hunter still hadn't filed and though I should have stuck to my word and filed during the spring recess, I'd been so busy with the foundation and caring for Jack's dad that I'd let it slide.

Hunter's son had been born some time earlier and rather than feel bitter or angry or resentful, all I could feel was a sense of calm and relief. Because I had never felt loved like the way Jack made me feel loved. I felt *adored.* Worshiped. Like I was the sun in his heavens, and when he came home from work each day he still swept me into his arms and leaned down to kiss me long and slow.

Still incinerated my underwear every damn time.

Oh yeah, that ... he was a bad influence. I hadn't yet graduated to the mother of all curse words, and I probably never would, but I let a few of the little ones fly from time to time. It always made his Pop giggle like a little kid, and the goofball always gave me a thumbs-up from wherever he was sitting. Apparently he enjoyed seeing the progress Jack was making when it came to corrupting me.

I was up early the next morning. Something ached inside, something deep and fierce, and I was sure it was because Jack was miles from me, sleeping on a hard little sofa while he waited for his Pop to wake up.

After feeding Carrick again and cooking a quick breakfast, I wrapped up some breakfast sandwiches for Jack and Pop, then pulled together a change of clothes and toiletries for Jack—just in case.

The coffee was all wrong. I sniffed the canister—I'd only ground the beans days before—totally rancid. I threw it in the trash.

Dumping the cup I'd just brewed in the sink, I leaned over it as my stomach rolled at the smell and my eyes snapped open.

I had been pregnant eight times in my life. *Eight.* And I knew all the signs.

Please God, no, we're not ready.

Rushing upstairs, I almost didn't make it to the bathroom before I tossed all of my breakfast into the toilet.

I'm too old.

I would be forty in four months.

You can't tell Jack. You can't give him false hope.

That was the problem, too: I didn't know that he wanted children any longer, and our focus lately had been on anything but kids. I couldn't have him worrying about this, and the last thing I wanted was another dove tattoo.

I wiped my mouth and rinsed with mouthwash. I didn't need to take a pregnancy test to know what this was, though my eyes filled at the thought, because I'd always had a hard time getting—and staying—pregnant, and we hadn't exactly been cautious, but ... *timing*. Didn't it figure?

Pop was awake when I walked into his room just a little later that morning, and the sweet smile on Jack's face was enough to stab at my heart. He was all rumpled in his slept-in uniform, his hair as crazy as it could get with his short cut ... and I couldn't help myself. I hurried across the space between us to press my lips against his, and when his hands drifted to my butt and I heard Pop snort, I broke the seal of our mouths and stepped back.

"So, they were in early..." Jack rubbed at his eyes. "He's going for a scan in about ten minutes and then, if results are good, they just might spring him."

"'Bout time," Pop complained. "What's a man have to do to get a meal in here?"

My eyes went wide and I grabbed the tote I'd dropped on the floor when Jack distracted me. I handed them both the breakfast sandwiches and Jack moaned when he bit into his in a way that made me wish we were at home, in our own room.

The nausea hit me like a freight train when the smell of the sandwiches permeated the room, eggs and turkey bacon and cheese, and I closed my eyes and took a deep breath. Jack noticed immediately, because he was hawk-eyed, especially when it came to me. "Babe, you all right?"

I nodded slowly and tried to come up with something that was off-putting but not a total lie. "Yes, I'll be fine. I didn't sleep well last night."

He grinned up at me sweetly and gestured with one hand to the sofa that was really barely even a loveseat.

"Carrick's terrible at snuggling," I told him and I heard another snort from Pop.

Jack was watching me intently, silently, and he patted the seat next to him. I wanted to sink down into it but I feared the proximity to his sandwich might activate a projectile vomit response.

He sighed contentedly and balled up the paper I'd wrapped it in, reaching into the bag for the coffee and he patted the seat again as he unscrewed the cap. I sank onto the cushion slowly, eyeing the coffee, relieved to find the smell didn't bother me at the moment and he lifted one hand to rub my back.

After Pop's scan and visits from four different doctors, the day crawled into the afternoon and Pop was finally released.

Without a word, Jack started hauling things from the dining room out to the garage and I started taking apart the bed in Pop's room.

I wasn't entirely sure how this was going to work, even short-term, but Jack assured me there was a full and functional bathroom in the converted garage space, and only one step to manage between the house and the garage, so for the time it would have to do.

By that evening we had a makeshift bedroom set up for Pop in the dining room and I arranged things in order to give him a little privacy, since one had to pass through the dining room to get to the kitchen.

Carrick relocated willingly and easily, curling up on the rug I'd rolled out over the dining room floor. I was still concerned about leaving Pop downstairs while we slept upstairs, and Jack took the knobs off the stove before we went up for the night.

I could feel Jack's concern. He showered quickly and crawled into bed, chewing on his lip while I scrolled through property listings on my tablet. It took him a while to realize what I was doing and he shook his head at me slowly. "I don't know how to make this work, Daph. I've got a lot tied up in this house and a full renovation to add on a downstairs bed and bath is way out of budget."

Jack knew I had a successful career, but I'd never told him of the trust fund money that had been ballooning in my investment accounts over the years, or just how much money I'd made from the sale of the enormous airport hangar of a house.

I leaned into his shoulder, clicking on a property only fifteen minutes outside of D.C. "Closer to work," I said softly. "Decent yard. Walkable neighborhood. Twice the size of this house, one level, four bedrooms with full baths."

Jack's eyes popped when he saw the price, and I patted his thigh before scrolling through the photos. "Nice," I commented, and he grunted, but I knew he'd already written it off as a fantasy.

"Would it make life easier?" I asked, and he shrugged.

"Not if I have to get a second job to pay for it."

He switched off his bedside lamp and scooted down under the covers while I clicked the link to contact the realtor and with a little smile on my face, I set the tablet on the bedside stand and turned out the light, rolling up behind Jack to cuddle him.

"Pillow smells like Carrick," he fussed, quickly flipping the pillow over and I chuckled against his back.

Tomorrow I would take Pop house shopping with me.

What Jack didn't know wouldn't hurt him.

Pop and I went to see three houses the next day, leaving shortly after I fed Jack breakfast and he drove off to work.

It was getting harder to take Pop anywhere, not knowing if it would be a good day or a bad one, and his tremors seemed a little worse than usual that morning. That complicated breakfast a bit, and I helped him change his shirt before we left.

It ended up being the second house that I liked the best of all three, and when the realtor told me she expected it to be snapped up quickly I didn't hesitate to tell her I wanted to put in an offer.

Pop wandered happily around the nicely landscaped, fenced yard and I was relieved to find no pools or hot tubs, and one of the main floor bedrooms had a zero-entry shower. It was perfect for him, and the fact the house was a single story meant fewer surprises: no steep stairs, no scary transitions from one half-level to the next, and I knew I could install a top-of-the-line security system to keep Pop safe from himself.

I signed the paperwork on an offer and *then* I called Jack. I knew he was going to be upset—angry, even—because he had to be the man and I was overstepping my bounds when he should be the one providing and blah, blah, blah.

Jack had never asked me how much money I had, because he didn't care.

Jack had refused to let me pay for any of the bills associated with living in his house, though I had an obscene number of zeroes in my bank and investing accounts, and Daddy insisted I draw a salary from my work with the foundation.

If Jack had been a member of the primate world, he'd have been a Silverback gorilla: huge, imposing, protective, and aggressive.

I loved my Silverback, though if I was hard-pressed to admit it, I wasn't so sure I'd told him that.

There were nights he curled around me and woke with a shudder, folding himself protectively over my body and I knew that in his mind, he'd awakened in a foxhole somewhere in an unforgiving desert.

Those were the nights he let me take the lead, needing the connection with me to soothe him.

The nights he didn't want to play games or use toys.

The nights he needed me to crawl over him and love him with soft words and kisses, gentle touches and reassurances. The man had been starved for tenderness, and slowly I was filling up the hole in his heart.

I loved every facet of Jack, but it was the side that needed me so desperately that I delighted in. It was something I'd never had before, and to be the sun in someone's world was an incredible feeling, even if he didn't tell me with so many words. I just knew. I could see it in the way he looked at me.

Pop and I had spent the last several weeks looking at houses and I texted Jack a few minutes before I knew he'd be off work and asked him to meet us at the home, sending him the address. He didn't respond, but less than half an hour later his truck pulled into the driveway, and I watched him crawl out of it with a concerned expression on his face.

Pop was ready to go. We'd had a busy day of it and he hadn't gotten his usual nap, and to say he was fading faster than a toddler with low blood sugar was generous. He was snappish and irritable, and I dug around in my bag for some of the snacks I always kept on hand. I opened a bag of crackers for him and he sat on the porch swing, throwing them into his mouth while Jack took cautious steps up the walk.

"What are you doing?" he asked as he drew near, where I stood waiting for him on the second step, putting me at his height.

"Buying a house." I grinned back, leaning across the inches to kiss him just before his eyebrows furrowed together.

"You know we can't afford this, Daph." His voice was soft and low, like he was afraid to let Pop overhear him.

That was when the dam broke and all the words came pouring out.

"We *can* afford it, baby, because I can afford it. I have investments and savings and family money and I want to do this. It's close to your work and it's perfect for Pop and there's so much room, we can have pets and kids and..." Oops. I hadn't quite meant to take it that far just yet.

"We're a little old for the kids part," he said with a smile and the bottom fell out of my stomach. We *were* a little old for the kids part, but if I was granted a miracle, Jack would be a father in less than seven months.

To distract him, I grabbed his hand and pulled him toward the house, where the realtor waited quietly just inside the door. I pushed him into the gracious entryway before returning to the large veranda to fetch Pop. I had a chocolate-covered protein bar in my bag that I knew would come in handy in about thirty seconds.

Jack walked from one room to the next with an indecipherable expression on his face and when we stepped out into the back yard, Pop became animated, leading him across the yard to the small outbuilding the prior owner had used as a workshop.

The house was beautiful. It was newly renovated, with soaring ceilings and large windows. It was tucked back into an old, well-established neighborhood and the lots were large.

"What's the listing price?" Jack looked upset.

"Doesn't matter," I said softly. "I've already made an offer."

Jack didn't say anything, but I saw his nostrils flare and his face went hard. As I'd suspected, he was angry.

"Stubborn shit," Pop murmured from where he stood near the back door. I couldn't tell if he was talking about Jack, or about me. It could have gone either way.

Pop insisted on riding back home with Jack and it took both of us to help him up into the truck. It was harder to get him into Jack's truck, since mine at least had running boards.

Jack didn't look any happier almost an hour later, when we both pulled into the driveway of his house. I could sense a fight brewing and I wasn't sure I understood why.

Catalina had been in that afternoon and thoughtfully left dinner warming in the oven. What I would do without her, sometimes I didn't know, and I wondered to myself if I could convince her to move in with us once we closed on the house.

Jack took Pop up to shower and get ready for bed while I set the small table we'd shoved into a corner of the kitchen, and moved the serving dishes to the counters. I could hear low voices upstairs, the words indistinct but Jack was clearly being dressed down by Pop and his answers were short and plainly frustrated.

Pop offered a prayer over our meal that night and after cleaning up the kitchen I led him from his spot in front of the TV, back into the dining room and tucked him into his bed.

"Stubborn shit," he muttered again as I pulled the blankets up and around his shoulders and I giggled, because now I knew he meant Jack.

"He is," I agreed softly, "but I love him anyway."

"Good." Pop rolled carefully and patted the side of the bed so Carrick would come settle on the rug. "Ain't had much of that in his life and makes it hard on people who try to give it to him." He reached up to pat my cheek. "Thank you, Daphne."

My eyes misted over a little. Jack was a chip off the old block. Just like his son, Pop didn't express himself well and the words "thank you" were hard for him.

I kissed Pop's cheek, turned out the light, and took myself upstairs to get ready for bed.

"I'm sorry." Jack's voice was so quiet when I crawled into bed behind him, that I almost didn't hear him. I closed the gap between us, to tuck up behind him and kiss his shoulder, but I had nothing to say.

"Tash's family had money—has money," he said quietly, and this was the first time he had ever initiated a discussion about his ex. "She used to joke that I was her rebellion, but she learned real fast that she didn't like living without nice things. By then, though, her family cut her off so to spite them, and me, she took up with the kid. Probably drives her crazy she had to crawl back to them."

I hoped that wasn't regret I was hearing in his voice.

"Well, that's being an adult," I said finally. "We make decisions and we have to live with them and any consequences."

Jack breathed deeply and I knew there was more he wasn't saying, and I had a feeling it wasn't about Natasha.

He didn't have any nightmares that night, but he didn't reach for me either and since I was an overanalyzing people pleaser, I stayed awake long after his breaths became deep and rhythmic, and I worried I'd pushed too hard.

It was four nights later—four long nights Jack slept facing away from me, careful not to let our bodies touch. I came into consciousness slowly, like swimming up from the deep, dark depths, breaking the surface into a moonless night and I rolled slowly, trying to understand what had awakened me.

Jack stirred next to me. He was an even heavier sleeper than I was, and with a start I sat straight up in bed, because it was Carrick and he was howling, something he almost never did.

Without thinking to shake Jack, I threw the blankets back and groped blindly through the darkness to find my way out into the hallway and down the stairs. I could hear Jack thundering after me as I went, and I rushed into the dining room to find Carrick frantically nudging and licking Pop, who lay completely still in his bed.

I was on my knees next to Carrick when the overhead light snapped on and when I reached out a hand to touch Pop, his skin was cool. Every thought skidded to a halt and my gasp echoed in the room, a sound that caused Jack to drop next to me and put a hand on his father. I jumped up as he did, my eyes searching the room for a phone. Jack still had a house phone and just now I couldn't remember where it was, but I needed to call an ambulance.

Reaching around the doorframe into the kitchen, my hand slapped against the cordless phone in the wall dock and my fingers shook as I pressed the few buttons I needed to summon emergency services.

Carrick sat quietly now on the rug, staring expectantly at Jack while he gathered up his father in his arms and when I turned to see him sitting with Pop crushed into a hug, his mouth was open in a silent scream.

That was the sound I'd heard: It was his heart shattering.

16

Jack

There was nothing the medics could do to save Pop. They came barreling in through the door with a board held between them and they checked for pulse, respiration and skin tone. One shook his head and the other lifted the radio strapped to his shoulder to notify dispatch.

I'd moved to the side and stood pressed against a wall while a deputy asked questions and jotted down notes, then photos were taken. Daphne had put Carrick in the basement, and he set up an ungodly howling from just behind the door.

A phone call was made to his doctor—Daphne handled it for me, since I couldn't speak—and what might have been minutes or hours later, the medical examiner arrived and made the official pronouncement.

The entire time there was just a constant prayer loop in my head: *Please let him be okay. He has to be okay. I'm not ready.*

Daphne worked quietly in the background, making several quiet phone calls and speaking in a hushed voice to all the strangers suddenly in my home.

The medics brought in a collapsible gurney and loaded Pop onto it, explaining quietly to Daphne that an autopsy would be conducted and she could contact a funeral home to make arrangements, as his body would be available shortly for burial.

When Tyler walked through the door it was four in the morning, and over the next half hour Agnello and Marston showed up too. All three of them sat in my living room in silence with me, and Daphne brought out cups and a pot of coffee.

The guys waited for me to be the first one to talk. When I did, the sun was starting to come up and Daphne had returned to the room with plates of bacon, eggs and toast, and I definitely heard Tyler call her an angel. I couldn't even be mad; everything hurt too much.

I told a couple stories about Pop, some of the funnier moments we'd shared in the last couple months and the guys chuckled while Daphne hovered in the doorway, listening with a sweet, sympathetic expression on her face.

Tyler was the first one to stand and I knew he had to be to work in less than an hour. I'd missed working with him every day, the obnoxious loudmouth, and I stood quickly to pull him into a tight hug and clap him on the back.

He might have teared up when I did it.

Marston and Agnello weren't far behind him. Marston was working with a private security company now, driving one of those crazy-looking recon trucks you see every now and then in the DMV, with a full-on satellite dish strapped to the top.

Agnello had been tight-lipped about the job he'd taken at the beginning of the year, and I teased him that I'd like to see a little more of his spook ass when he had the time.

Not so much as a flinch from him, and I grinned. Good call, CIA. Real solid call.

And then the house was empty except for Daphne and me, Carrick slumped into a morose heap next to Pop's bed.

Daphne let me fall apart. She pulled me to the sofa with her and held me, with my head in her lap, until her legs fell asleep. I had so much guilt and regret, I didn't have the emotional bandwidth to express it or get it all out and she ran gentle fingers through my hair and dropped kisses on the side of my face as she waited with me.

When Daphne rose and I heard her quiet voice in the kitchen, I knew she'd made the phone call to my supervisor and when she reappeared in the room she whispered softly to me that I'd been instructed to take the rest of the week.

The days blurred together after that, while we waited on the official cause, and I tried to decide whether it had been a severe mercy or a cruel twist of fate. I'd just gotten him back. I'd just begun to get to know him as a whole and uncompromised person, and he was all I'd had left.

There was that. That was the hardest thing to swallow: I was all alone.

Daphne gave me something to help me sleep and while I slept for long stretches of time, she quietly pulled things together, finding Pop's friends and organizing a funeral, picking out the casket and the flowers, finding photos of him—don't ask me how she managed that—and when she guided my useless ass into the small church that Friday morning, I looked around in astonishment at all the things I hadn't even thought to do.

The service and the internment were small, only twenty people or so, and my brothers came in what was a show of support that meant the world to me. They helped Daphne at the meal afterward, set up, clean up and everything in between, and when Generis placed baby Violet in my arms I sank down onto the sofa to cuddle her. Catalina drifted past to drop a kiss on the top of my head. For the first time ever, she was silent rather than effusive, and I knew it was because she knew I couldn't handle it.

Catalina and Daphne worked in the kitchen together after everyone left and I could hear quiet sounds in the dining room. I knew Tyler and Generis were returning the space to its former purpose so I wouldn't have to, and I focused entirely on little Violet so I wouldn't have to give it a second thought.

The official report was that it had been a stroke. Pop had been put on a medication patch rather than pills a few months earlier, since it had gotten harder and harder to get him to swallow pills. And though he'd been monitored at his regular visits, it seemed that years of hard drinking, no exercise, and a shitty diet had hardened his arteries to something brittle and unforgiving. When the patch elevated his blood pressure—which his primary care doctor assured me was rare—a clot caused a logjam in his brain.

He didn't suffer, the doc said. It was massive and fatal and he went in his sleep, and while that gave me some comfort, it also fueled my guilt. Because it was my job to take care of him, yet I hadn't even thought to question the safety of switching him to the patch.

Daphne and I spent a quiet weekend at home. We didn't go out at all, and she didn't complain when I came downstairs each morning and collapsed onto the sofa. In fact, she'd make coffee and breakfast and then come sit with me, letting me be a caveman if I needed to be, and letting me talk when the mood struck.

In the early afternoons she'd get up again, knowing I'd used up all my mental bandwidth, and turn on SportsCenter or AMC. Then she'd put together a simple lunch and come back to the sofa to cuddle with me.

"Tash would have never done this," I said on Sunday afternoon as Daphne sat wrapped around me, our lunch plates on the coffee table. I'd been lying on my back with Daph lying on top of me, her head on my chest while we watched an old western. I felt her freeze when I said it, like she thought it was something condescending or unflattering.

"She wouldn't have stepped in and handled things like you did," I said quietly, realizing I was the idiot who hadn't even pretended to thank her yet, even when thanks weren't even close to sufficient. "She would've made me handle this on my own, because she hated Pop. She wouldn't have fed me or let me be such a total ass." I swallowed hard. It went without saying that Tash wouldn't have wrapped herself around me for days, leeching out some of my sadness with her tenderness, the way Daphne had.

My girl took me upstairs that night and made me sit in the bathtub while she washed me like a little kid. And then she took a page from my book and tied me to the bed so that I was helpless, and she took her sweet time teasing and coaxing and loving me with her hands and mouth and body, until I couldn't see straight and my mind was blessedly blank.

Finally, complete putty in her hands, I sank back into the pillows, exhausted, but the most complete I'd felt in days. She'd erased all thought and worry from my brain for hours and there wasn't a single bone in my body that didn't feel like liquid.

Throwing her leg over mine, she snuggled into my chest and yawned sleepily.

"I love you, Daphne," I said quietly—quietly enough that I didn't think she'd heard me, but I felt the movement of her face on my chest when her lips spread into a smile.

"More than anything, Jack."

What was my problem?

It seemed like I'd maybe skipped a couple of the necessary stages of grieving, because I jumped almost immediately to anger.

I took it out on the people at work.

I took it out on Daphne.

I took it out on Tyler every time he came to visit or wanted to meet up for dinner.

I managed not to take it out on Carrick, because I couldn't take it that far, but it hurt me to see him sometimes. He still wandered the house looking for Pop and from the look in his eyes, I knew he was sad without fully understanding why.

Daphne stopped talking about the new house and I knew she lost her earnest money on it. I felt guilty about that, because it was a lot of money. But it didn't seem to phase her, and I decided not to point out that almost anywhere else in the U.S. it was enough to buy a whole damn house, because I was pretty sure she knew that.

Almost immediately after the funeral, she stopped pushing. Her gentle arguments that it was closer to my work and gave me more space to spread out and work on projects ceased. For a time she'd even spoken hopefully about fostering a couple kids.

I wasn't there for any of it. I didn't want to think about moving or new routines, new hobbies, or even bringing kids into our home. I was busy being selfish and angry and mean to everyone who'd let me be mean to them.

Something had been different about Daphne for weeks. There was something softer about her, a woman who was already sweet and gentle and kind. It was something else: a patience. A serenity. Something in her eyes that looked hopeful. I didn't know what it was, but I didn't feel terribly hopeful, so I didn't fucking like it. It felt like a secret she wouldn't share.

It was nearing the end of October and Daphne's birthday was just around the corner when something happened that nearly altered our lives forever. It didn't need to go that way, but every now and then I fell back into the pattern of being a complete asshole.

The days had just begun to grow cooler and they were growing rapidly darker. Daphne had dragged out fall decorations and blankets and had taken to wearing heavy sweaters during the chilly morning and evening hours.

Catalina had called to discuss birthday plans, since she knew I was shit at planning, and we decided to have the guys over with G and the baby for a small surprise party at the house.

Blair had announced she'd be in the city that weekend, visiting her father and infant brother and though I knew it hurt Daphne on so many levels, she'd smiled bravely when Blair called to tell her and the two of them decided to have a Saturday brunch in Georgetown.

Daphne's actual birthday wasn't for another three days, but I needed the element of surprise, so while she was out with Blair we put up some balloons and Catalina brought in pans of food and a cake she'd prepared. After everything the woman had done for me, it seemed appropriate that I do something that demonstrated my appreciation. Besides, I'd been a real bear and she'd been nothing but patient and loving.

There was a noise outside that I knew meant Daphne was home and everyone hid, ready to pop out and surprise her when she walked through the door.

We waited ... and waited ... and waited. And finally I decided to go find her.

Stepping out the front door, I almost tripped over Daphne, who was sitting with her back leaned up against the jamb, a copy of a local paper in her hands that was just distinguished enough to be called tabloid. The paper was folded and her hands were smeared with black ink, like she'd been twisting the sheets in her hands.

Squatting down in front of her, I lifted her chin with my finger and noticed she'd been crying. "Hey," I said gently, dropping down onto my butt and pulling her into my lap, "what's this about?"

Daphne shook her head against my shoulder and I didn't know what that meant, so I took the paper from her and, with one hand, spread it out on the floor. There was a picture of us at the market the weekend before. It was actually a really good picture of us, Daphne backed up against the cart handle while I crowded in for a kiss.

Congressman's Wife Pregnant with Lover's Baby!

I skimmed the few paragraphs announcing Daphne had left Congressman Preston for a member of the Capitol Police and was expecting her first child with me. I chuckled into her hair. "Boy, they're really getting desperate. When is this hypothetical child supposed to materialize?"

Daphne was quiet for a moment and the smile fell right off my lips.

"Daph?"

She looked up at me slowly, and her eyes were swimming with guilt.

"Daphne." My voice came out sharper than I'd have liked. "Is there something you need to tell me?"

"If I don't talk about it or recognize it or even hope for it, the baby will be okay," she said softly and I felt all the blood drain from my face.

"When?" I croaked, leaning back.

"The middle of March," she said softly, and I quickly did the math in my head.

"That means you're nearly four months along?" I asked, shocked, and she nodded miserably, unwilling to meet my eyes.

"I can't add another dove, Jack." I almost couldn't hear her. "I just ... can't."

I sucked in a big breath. I felt like she'd slapped me across the face, everything so clear and sharp that it almost stung.

"I don't know what to say." I shook my head, shocked, and more than a little freaked out. I loved Daphne, I had no problem admitting that to myself, but we'd never talked about kids–joked about it maybe once, and the awful realization hit me that maybe that was her plan all along. After seven lost babies, maybe I was the missing ingredient and she wanted just one more shot.

"I didn't do this on purpose, Jack."

I was already on my feet, adrenaline coursing through me so quickly that my heartbeat was hammering in my ears. I'd forgotten all about the people inside the house and when I opened the door, "Surprise!" came pouring out.

Sigh.

Daphne looked up, startled, and I held out a hand to haul her to her feet. There was confetti all over the living room and Violet had been startled awake by the noise, her face puckering up for a good wail.

Daphne went for Violet like she was magnetized. She scooped her right out of Tyler's arms and cooed down into her little face, completely oblivious to everyone else in the room.

Everyone else was staring at me and I wondered just how much they'd overheard. One by one, each of them moved to squeeze Daphne and wish her a happy birthday, and Tyler sidled up to me with the smallest grin pulling at his mouth. "Good news, man. Violet could use an honorary cousin, you know."

Shit, they'd heard it all.

I looked into the kitchen, where Catalina was fussing over Daphne and Violet, and Violet squirmed until her head rested on Daphne's shoulder, against her neck. She shoved a fist into her mouth and drooled and chewed contentedly as Daphne scooped up treats to offer her.

Violet was growing like a weed, no thanks to Tyler's genetics. She was walking and babbling and into everything, and it was a credit to Daphne that the little girl was content to be held in her arms.

Agnello had brought a woman with him—someone he introduced as "his girl," and Generis's eyes had gone wide with mischief. She commandeered the woman immediately and they spoke in hushed tones while Catalina shoved food into everyone's hands and pushed them to "Eat, eat!"

My brain spun as I watched Daphne with Violet, and I couldn't help but tell myself that she was—would be—a good mother. Violet was drawn to her and soothed by her presence and her touch, her little head resting on Daphne's shoulder, her eyes wide open as she quietly observed the room while chewing on her fist.

I kind of knew how she felt. Daphne had that soothing effect on me, too, which clearly made me no better than a toddler.

There were a few small gifts for Daphne and she exclaimed over each, letting Violet take each from her hands to inspect thoroughly and Tyler grinned at them. "My kid likes you better than she likes me," he complained, and Generis called to him, "That's because you don't have these." She cupped her breasts with both hands and lifted and all the men in the room laughed while Catalina shook her head.

Daphne got ready for bed earlier than usual that night and I sat for a while in the living room, trying to sort and piece things together. Daphne and I had never talked about how far along she'd been when she lost any of the prior pregnancies, but something told me this was as far as she'd ever gotten and she was living every day in fear of the signs she knew so well.

She was rolled over on her side, facing the wall when I finally slid in behind her and I could feel an intense sadness rolling off of her. I didn't know what to say or do, and I was still so knocked sideways that I couldn't risk touching her and losing my train of thought. So rather than pull her close and comfort her; whisper in her ear that I loved her, cradling her tiny belly and telling her how quickly the idea could grow on me, I made a frustrated noise and turned to face the opposite wall.

With any luck, I'd have a better handle on this tomorrow.

17

Daphne

Jack came home late every night the rest of that week. I knew a couple of times he'd called an emergency meeting with the Boys Club, because Tyler always called me on his drive home. I tried to be understanding, because I knew Jack was trying to wrap his head around this, but I couldn't help but think with each passing day that he was viewing this as a burden and not a blessing.

Each night he came home and took off his boots, stripped off his uniform and showered while I wrapped up the dinner I knew he wouldn't eat.

Each morning I felt the cracks in my heart split a little further when I realized he'd slept facing away from me the entire night, the man who'd never been able to hold me close enough in his sleep.

Jack quietly packed a bag that Friday night and I watched as warm clothes went into it and he loaded up one of the gun bags. Tyler had called earlier in the afternoon to clue me in, thank God, or I'd have lost my mind watching him pack. So I remained silent but observant and he kept looking to me, waiting for me to ask the questions as he packed up for a hunting trip to Pennsylvania.

There was no clearer way to tell me that I was not his first priority. He hadn't bothered to share plans with me and while I'd never have stopped him, it hurt that he'd turned off his emotions and affection. He was a roommate now. No more sweeping me into his arms when he got home at night. No more sneaking up behind me and spinning me around for a kiss. It felt like punishment, taking away the thing that had filled me with such peace and joy. The dopamine loss was like coming down off heroin, wondering if I was going to die.

I knew he would leave early and I was up at four to make him sandwiches and a thermos of coffee. He took the items from me with a guilty expression, and without a single word or even a kiss on the cheek he hoisted his bags to his shoulder and walked out to the truck. He didn't even bother to come back into the house—he drove away.

For the first time all week, I sat down and sobbed. I let it all out, my arms wrapped around my belly as I thought of how much my life had changed in just over a year. It had all been positive until he found out, and it wasn't like I could have hidden it much longer, but the last time I'd miscarried I'd been at sixteen weeks. I'd wanted to wait just a little longer, to pass that point, before I felt I could safely tell him that we were maybe, probably, just possibly out of the danger zone.

The problem was that he found out first.

I cried until my eyes burned and my head ached, and finally I pulled myself off the bottom stair step with a numb backside and stumbled into the kitchen for a glass of water. I was still suffering morning sickness, weeks beyond the point I'd ever suffered from it before, so I popped a few pieces of bread into the toaster and ate the toast dry.

Later that morning I called Daddy. We talked every couple days, a scheduled meeting at ten on Mondays and Thursdays to discuss any necessary foundation issues, and though we'd always take a couple minutes to catch up, those weren't really Father-Daughter phone calls.

"Sweet Pea." His voice was groggy and rough, and I knew I'd awakened him from a mid-morning nap in his favorite chair in the newly redecorated den.

I dissolved into a fresh fit of tears, which was exactly what I'd sworn I wouldn't do, and finally I let everything spill out. I told him about the baby, about Pop, about the house I'd almost purchased, and that the last thing Jack seemed to be was pleased.

There was a noise in the background, the telltale clink of ice in a glass, and Mama's voice sounded far away. "Darling, what the man needs is a little distance." Of course Daddy had me on speaker. "He's been blindsided, darlin', and you well know the man does not handle change, or surprise, or ... well, much of anything, all that well."

I wasn't sure whether there was a solution buried in Mama's ramblings.

"Why don't you come for a visit, Pea?" It was Daddy again. "Give the man a little space. Can speak from experience that nothin' makes a man rethink his choices like realizin' his woman's up and left."

That seemed severe.

"You mean leave without telling him?" I asked, not so sure I was getting great quality parental advice.

"That's up to you, Sugar," Mama said and I could hear her refilling her glass of iced tea. "You do what you think needs to be done to motivate him, but a stubborn man like that is goin' to need a real hard shove."

I hated it when Mama was right.

Perhaps I should have extended Tyler a similar courtesy and relayed my plans.

Maybe I should have told Catalina what I was doing.

I probably should have left a note for Jack.

Instead, I packed up the things I had at his place—not a lot, mostly just clothes and a few books—and I loaded them into the back of my truck. I locked up the Tonneau cover tight, expecting to drive through the rain forecast for the next several days.

Jack would be home by Sunday night, I knew from Tyler, and Carrick was perfectly capable of letting himself out into the yard through the huge doggy door, in order to do his business. So I sent a text to Generis to ask if she'd mind checking in on the dog this evening, and again early afternoon tomorrow. Then I filled up his food and water bowls and patted his head. "I shouldn't be gone long, boy. I'd take you with me, but I think Jack needs you right now." Even though it would break my heart to leave behind the dog who was like a child to me, my loyal protector. He'd begun sleeping by my side of the bed, having realized something was happening with my body that he decided to watch over.

I contemplated writing a note for Jack, but I didn't know what to say. Instead, I tidied up a little, fixed a few sandwiches for my own trip and then removed the house key from my ring and left it sitting on the dining room table, in plain sight. It was as clear an indication as I could give him that I wouldn't be back until he invited me.

The drive to southern Alabama would take me just under sixteen hours if I didn't stop at all, which was completely unrealistic with pregnancy bladder, and I chose the route that cut across Tennessee in order to bypass Washington, D.C. and Atlanta.

I didn't drive all day—I couldn't. I drove for ten hours that Saturday, stopping late to get a hotel, and I didn't bother with getting up at the crack of dawn.

By the time I rolled up Mama and Daddy's long private drive, it was well into the afternoon and my stomach was roaring since I hadn't wanted to stop for lunch.

I left everything in the truck and let myself into the house, Mama's tiny little King Charles, Daisy, bouncing at my feet and demanding I pick her up. I carried her into the kitchen with me, where Mama stood next to her housekeeper as the two of them dished food onto plates.

"Just when I expected you," Mama said with a smile and I saw Nettie surreptitiously pull another plate out of the cupboard.

"That my girl?" A voice boomed from Daddy's study, and I couldn't help the smile that stretched across my face. I could count on him for all the hugs I needed.

Hurrying to hug Mama and Nettie, I walked down the hallway toward Daddy's study just in time to hear his chair creak as he pushed to his feet.

"Pea." He held out his arms, and I fought the sharp sting behind my eyes as I walked into his grizzly bear hug. He was a man who did everything with his whole heart and you never wondered where you stood, something I had always loved about him.

"Let me look at you." He waited several beats before stepping back and critically surveying me from head to toe. "Look good, Sweet Pea. Just need to put a little more meat on you. Got just the fix for that."

Daddy loved his beach shack seafood and I knew he'd drag me down to the huts on the shore the first chance he got, but the very idea made my stomach roll dangerously.

"Just been a little busy lately," I said. "There was so much going on with Pop, and then all the legal mess of backing out of buying the house ... and Jack's been fussing that Hunter hasn't filed, but I really didn't have the time to do it for him."

Daddy's face fell. "You think Hunter has something to do with this?" He made a swirling motion and I sobered immediately. I hadn't thought of it that way.

"You think he's afraid I'll run back to Hunter? That's not even a possibility."

"Why you suppose the man ain't filed yet?" he asked, and he picked up a coffee cup I suspected contained a little something Mama didn't need to know about. Daddy's fortification had always been bourbon, and though he rarely drank, I knew it was because he was carefully keeping himself on the wagon.

"My guess, darlin', is the man's been thinkin' on marryin' you, and he needs you to display a little more enthusiasm. Now you got his baby in there," he gestured toward my belly, "he's gotta be real worried about lockin' you down with all those loose ends you got."

I laughed, because that was completely ridiculous. Not only had I never given Jack a reason to suspect I wasn't serious about us, but he hadn't mentioned Hunter in a very long time.

"That last one probably did a real number on him," Daddy said quietly and my eyes snapped to his. What did he know about Natasha?

"Girl tried to hit us up for money earlier this year. Said you got in between her and her husband and if someone didn't pay up, she'd sell the story. Seems she was just smart enough not to go after you directly. Probably figured we'd pay to hush her up."

I wondered if the tabloid piece had been instigated by Natasha.

"I hope you didn't."

Daddy grinned. If he had one thing, it was a flesh-eating lawyer with a love for a good fight, and I could only imagine how Natasha must have smarted as she slunk away with her tail between her legs.

"Few more things came out when I had my guy look into her. Seems she might have been pregnant when she left your Jack that first time, but ain't no record of birth anywhere she been the last couple years."

Something sick rolled inside my gut as I thought of what that meant. A child conceived in hate, disposed of like trash.

"Did she come home pregnant?" I asked, and Daddy shook his head. "If she did, she kept it real quiet and took care of that, too. More likely her mama did."

I finally turned and made my way toward the small couch set near the window.

Daddy let me sit quietly for a time, and when I looked up he had a plate of food right in my face. My stomach roared and I patted my belly.

"Demanding little thing," Daddy said with a wink. "Just like his momma."

I looked up at him in surprise. It was too early to tell, and he grinned at me. "Coach's intuition," he teased. "Got a future quarterback in there."

Mama didn't pester me at all that afternoon, and I knew she was just full to bursting with questions. But instead of following me around the house like Daisy, she guided me toward the guest wing of the house where there were several spacious bedrooms.

After a short nap I felt a bit more myself, and I glanced at my phone. I hadn't expected to hear from Jack all weekend, and I was sure he wouldn't be home until quite late that night, but I started to wonder for the first time if I'd taken it just a little too far.

I was surprised and a little hurt—okay, a lot—to wake in the morning and realize Jack hadn't texted or tried to call, not that I'd have known what to say to him if or when he did. I told myself I'd just take a few more days and get my head on straight; try to make a plan for the future ... figure out what I wanted to do with the unsettled parts of life. Because I suspected, with a bolt of terror, that Jack wouldn't be inviting me back.

During the week I went into the foundation's physical office Daddy kept in Spanish Fort. He'd grown up in the town and liked to head back whenever he could. He loved our tiny southern town, and he chartered a small plane a few days every week, since he and Mama refused to move to Tuscaloosa and "lose their souls" in a university town. It worked well enough, though I knew Daddy had started to shift more and more responsibility to some of his assistant coaches. He was seventy-one and though the game kept him young, I knew there were things he and Mama still wanted to do, and a college football season often got in the way of those things.

I was the only remote employee for Daddy's foundation, so meeting the other two full time employees face-to-face was long since overdue. They were both new. Daddy cleaned house when I told him I wanted to help, and he joked I'd saved him the dead weight of five salaries when he jettisoned all five underperformers and Mama acted as HR director, interviewing and hiring two new employees. Both were young, both female, one just out of college the previous spring and the other having returned home after a few years of non-profit work in Chicago.

The three of us worked together well, and when I walked into the office unannounced, both squealed and jumped from their seats, rushing over to hug me. Both their eyes went wide when they realized what was happening under my shirt and I nodded slowly. I'd made the mistake *just once* of asking an obviously pregnant woman when she was due and she'd laughed it off and told me she was just overweight. The mortification had been swift and unforgiving.

Working with them on-site for a few days that week helped me to keep my mind off Jack, at least temporarily, and when a full week had passed without word, I texted Tyler.

Tyler was mad at me.

Daph, I didn't tell you what Jack was up to so you could leave him. I was just trying to give you peace of mind.

I thought about my response for a while, because I wasn't sure Jack had told Tyler I was pregnant, but I decided to go for it.

Jack needs to decide what he wants from me, Tyler. Apparently that didn't include kids, and when I upset the status quo he stopped talking to me.

The dots bounced for a long, long time. They'd stop, start up again, stop again. And then all that popped up was **He's wrecked.**

There was no elaboration or forthcoming explanation and I sighed as I set my phone aside.

He's wrecked. Yeah, I know how that feels.

I curled a hand under the little belly that had begun to show and thought about Daddy's pronouncement that there was a little quarterback in there. He might not be all that far off, with Jack's height and build, and I let myself drift into a fantasy world where I could envision our son or daughter, dark and handsome or breathtakingly beautiful. Because I had no doubt our child would be gorgeous—look at Jack.

The days stretched into weeks and I cried myself to sleep every single night. I thought sometimes I'd die of loneliness and heartbreak. It was like half of my heart had been ripped out and I couldn't get it back, and though I'd been destroyed before, it had been *nothing* like this. I had never felt for Hunter even half of what I felt for Jack, and that scared me. Because I knew I'd lost him, and that I'd never find something like that again.

On the bright side, I made a new friend, and she was a fearsome force of nature. Natalie had redone a couple rooms in Mama and Daddy's house, and when it came up that she needed something understated, elegant and breathtaking for my sort-of-ex-cousin's upcoming events, Mama offered my services and Natalie came over to the house for fittings.

I loved her right away. She was quiet and sweet, but the woman had a will of steel. She reminded me a lot of myself, and for the first time I felt I'd found a kindred spirit, a match that was not an "opposite attraction."

Thomas, who'd been married to my cousin Lydia for a very long time, was starting life over with Natalie. She would keep him interested for the rest of his days, though I suspected that had to do much more with her heart than the dresses. But for his part, he was clearly smitten with her and if photos of the events proved anything, it was that I hadn't lost my touch. Natalie looked amazing.

I wanted someone to look at me like that: like Thomas looked at Natalie during the moments she was in his arms. Like she was a goddess, and the love he'd never had before. It was both encouraging and completely dispiriting, because the man who *had* looked at me like that was no longer speaking to me.

Christmas loomed, and I managed to keep myself largely upright without tears during the day, but as my belly grew, so did my distance from Jack. I hadn't heard from him in weeks—almost months now—and Tyler also had gone radio silent. I suspected it was a show of loyalty to his old friend, but it hurt a little because it meant that he was completely behind Jack, not me, and I could have used a friend.

Blair and I talked at least once a week. She'd come to spend a week of her Christmas break with me and her grandparents, and I finally had to make peace with the fact I was going to be a single mom—again. Not like I could hide it from her anyway, and her jaw scraped the floor when I rounded the corner and she caught sight of my belly.

Everything was enough to make me burst into tears these days, and when I saw her face the waterworks fired right up. She immediately apologized and rushed over to hug me, her eyes searching mine as her hand rested over her new half-sibling.

I expected recriminations and "How could you do this to me?" but instead I got "I never saw this coming, Mama ... with Jack?" I nodded, sniffling mightily to keep from getting snot all over my daughter, and a beautiful grin stretched over her face. "Good," she said softly, pulling me back in for another hug. "He loves you in the ways Daddy never could."

That was it. The dam burst. I leaned into her shoulder and tried not to sob, but some of the sorrow escaped anyway.

To her credit, she said nothing, just squeezed me and whispered, "I'm sleeping in your room tonight and you're going to tell me all about it."

One could say Blair and I had grown up together, and our relationship was open, honest and realistic. That I'd managed to keep a secret of this magnitude from her for so long had taken considerable effort and practiced denial.

We stayed up late that night, snuggled up in my big bed while we whispered back and forth about plans for the future, about the new boy she'd begun seeing, and I wisely kept my mouth shut when it came to badmouthing Jake. Nonetheless, I was relieved. Jake came from money and still hadn't identified his ambition in life. Since Blair knew exactly what she wanted, and she was working hard to get it, I'd been fearful Jake would be a deadweight. His father was a high-powered attorney in D.C. and it seemed likely he would push his son into a similar political track—something I wouldn't have wished on my daughter for anything.

I woke bright and early on Christmas morning to the little one kicking me in the bladder, bright, sharp jabs that had me awake in no time and rushing across the room, fearful I wouldn't make it.

"Mama?" I could hear Blair's sleepy voice through the door as I washed my hands and when I opened the heavy door I could hear sound carrying from somewhere else in the house. It was big and deep and booming, a sound I almost never heard: Daddy was yelling at someone.

Blair shot out of bed, her eyes big. "It has to be him," she said, shoving her feet into slippers and rushing over to comb her fingers through my wild hair. "Quick, Mama. Mouthwash, lipstick, a robe—chop, chop." She snapped her fingers in my face and I whirled back around to swish mouthwash, apply a colored balm and run a brush through my hair while she fished a suitable robe out of my closet, since my sleep shorts bordered on obscene.

Blair and I rushed down the long hallway and down the stairs, toward Daddy's voice. It carried all the way from his office and Blair rear-ended me when I stopped short in the doorway.

It wasn't Jack.

Blair made a sound of surprise and pushed me forward, and I stumbled into the room.

"Tyler."

Daddy's face was beet red and Tyler's face, to his credit, was still a healthy olive shade. I half-suspected that beneath all that melanin, he was deathly white in the face of Daddy's fury.

Tyler's eyes dropped immediately to my stomach and his face fell. "Daph, I didn't know what else to do..."

Daddy looked like he was about to have a stroke and I held up a hand. "Daddy, this is Tyler. He's Jack's closest friend."

There was a sound from Daddy that suggested it might have been a snort, and I looked at him quickly.

"Your man can't even bother to come apologize to you proper, Pea? He has to send on some representative to do the grovelin' for him?"

"Jack doesn't know I'm here." Tyler looked guilty. "G and her ma sent me—they're worried about Jack. He's not doing so good, Daph."

Like I was. I snorted, gesturing at my rounding belly and for the first time in a week a small laugh worked its way out.

Tyler looked warily at Daddy. "Sir, if I might have your permission, I'd like to speak with your daughter for a moment—alone."

I couldn't see Blair, since she stood behind me, but I could feel her eyes go wide and heard her suck in her breath. She was surely communicating with her grandfather through telepathy, as he nodded shortly while looking over my shoulder and moved toward the door. I moved to let him pass.

"Nothing funny, son," Daddy warned, shaking one meaty finger at Tyler, and behind Tyler's confident smile I thought his teeth were chattering.

"Yessir, sir." He coughed nervously.

I sat in one of the chairs across from Daddy's desk and Tyler sat next to me, turning his body so he could look me in the eyes.

"You gotta come home," he blurted. "We got home from the trip and you were gone, and he lost it, Daph. He holed up in the house for weeks and wouldn't come out. He wasn't eating or sleeping, and he looks like shit all the time."

"Tyler, why hasn't he tried to call me?"

Tyler swallowed hard. "Tash broke him, Daph. When she left he swore he'd never be with another woman again—not like this. He had a few here and there..." He made a winding motion with one hand and I wrinkled my nose without meaning to do it.

"He swore he'd never get all tied up with another woman because it meant she could leave him, and you and I both know Jack doesn't handle being left very well. Look at how you had to nurse him along after his Pop..." his voice trailed off and he looked guilty.

"I've been left too, Tyler," I said softly and his shoulders folded forward in a shrug.

"He'll never admit to it, Daph, not out loud, but you got all the way in. You found that one crack in his heart and you crawled right in and sealed it up behind you and now he doesn't even want to get you out. It's eating him alive."

"Whatever," I clucked, and the baby kicked me sharply, like he couldn't believe what he was hearing.

Tyler reached across the short distance in a silent plea for me to take his hand, and when I held mine out, he squeezed my fingers almost painfully. "He's lost both of you, or he thinks he has, and he thinks there's nothing he can do to fix it."

"He's told you that?"

"Not in so many words."

I stood slowly. "Thank you for coming, Tyler."

I wanted desperately to run from the room and hide so I could sob. The pregnancy hormones had given my emotions an exponent and these days I cried over everything, including vacuum cleaner commercials.

"Daphne," Tyler said quietly and I turned to look at him again. "This is a rescue mission."

I watched his Adam's apple bob.

"If I don't come back with you, I'm scared what'll happen to Jack."

"Tyler, I have been gone for two months: eight weeks. Every single night I have stared at my phone, waiting for him to call or text. He made it very clear he was not ready to take this step with me and he slept with his back to me the entire week before he left for his hunting trip."

Tyler shook his head slowly. "Yeah, he's an emotional Neanderthal. I drive him crazy with my jokes and cheerfulness. But he's a good man, Daph. You know that. You know how much he loves you."

"No, Tyler." I shook my head sadly. "No, I don't—not anymore."

Tyler pushed himself slowly out of his chair and came over to wrap his arms around me in a tight hug. He was only a few inches taller than me.

"You deserve to be happy." He put a hand gently on my belly. "But so does my friend, and I see the way you two are with each other. You don't think anyone notices, but it's like you use up all the air in the room when you're both in it. You're his magnet, Daph. He can't resist your pull. So just ... follow the pull back home, okay? Before this little guy shows up?" He was pleading.

I shrugged noncommittally. After being thrown over by Hunter, I wasn't eager to be doing any chasing.

Tyler sighed and squeezed me once more before moving past me and out of the room, and I heard Mama speaking to him in low tones, trying to get him to stay on for breakfast, then lunch, then to spend the night before heading home.

"Must be real bad if the man showed up on Christmas mornin'," Mama mused as she watched Tyler crawl up into a truck parked in the driveway. "Got to be somethin' big if a man leaves his family durin' this time of year."

I narrowed my eyes at her, sensing an impending guilt trip. Mama dealt in guilt trips like they were currency, sweet as pie the whole time, so that you wondered if you were making it all up. She didn't just manipulate you without you knowing it, she pulled a full-on gaslight.

Daddy's face still hadn't returned to its normal color and Blair was on the sofa beside him, cuddled under his arm while he groused about men who weren't man enough to take care of their own business.

Daddy was upset with Jack, I knew, but he'd spared me his opinion of the man while he waited for said man to make the right decision. That he would make the right decision eventually, Mama was sure, but Daddy was a much harder sell since he was anything but a diehard romantic.

The rest of the day, I burst into tears at the slightest provocation and Daddy's face grew tighter each time. He cranked his jaw down hard, to bite down on the words I knew wanted to spill out, and after we opened gifts and had breakfast, Mama sent me back upstairs for a nap. It was no secret she was sending me up so she could conduct a top-secret family meeting, minus the pivotal family member in question.

I curled up in the bed and eventually fell asleep, dreaming of Jack and Carrick and a sweet little black-haired boy toddling through the backyard of a house I'd never before seen in my life.

18

Jack

When I got home from Pennsylvania and Carrick rushed out the door as I unlocked it, I felt the sweetest sense of relief to be home. The weekend away, bitching it out with Tyler, had helped me to better wrap my head around the things I felt had blindsided me.

This year had been a lot: Daphne, moving her in with me, selling her house and talking about buying another, caring for Pop, and then finding out she was pregnant had really thrown me for a loop. It had brought up old fears of unfaithfulness and being found lacking, and the fact she still hadn't filed for divorce from Hunter scared me half to death.

Was I being unreasonable? Probably. But I didn't have the best track record when it came to women.

Come to think of it, Daphne's track record obviously wasn't great either.

When I could finally convince Carrick to come in from the yard, I dropped my bags inside the door and breathed in the familiar, comforting smell of home. The lights were on and it smelled like Catalina's cooking and Daphne's shampoo, and I knew the reason I'd slept like shit all weekend was because my body had been missing the usual closeness with hers. I'd already petulantly slept with my back to her for the entire last week, and finally I was ready to admit I'd been a miserable little bitch.

Finding her key on the table was like being kicked in the chest by a mule. It was sharp and painful, shocking enough that I felt my heart stop for several beats and the breath whooshed right out of my lungs. I'd clutched at my throat, a tightening, clawing feeling telling me I wouldn't be able to draw another breath and I threw myself down into one of the chairs while Carrick nuzzled into my side and whined.

If Carrick could speak, I knew what he'd say: "You really muffed this one up, buddy. No fixing this."

Her truck hadn't been in the driveway, I finally realized. I'd been in such a hurry to rush into the house, throw my things down and pull her into my arms that I hadn't even noticed the hulking black beast was gone.

To say I was a miserable son of a bitch over the next couple months would be pretty generous. I called in for two weeks straight and it was a miracle I didn't get fired, and for those two weeks I turned into a caveman.

I didn't shower.

I barely ate.

I slept in the same sheets the whole time, trying to draw every last molecule of her scent from the fabric before I had to give it up and admit she was gone.

I'd have done old Pop proud though, because my beer consumption for those two weeks was obscene. The guys who picked up my recycling every Tuesday morning probably shook their heads at each other when they noticed the majority of the bin was filled with empty bottles, and when I discovered I could order alcohol delivered to my door, it was game on.

I stared at my phone day and night, waiting for her to call or text me. Waited for her terms, her demands, her angry words or tears or pleas. Anything, just so long as it meant she was still willing to talk to me.

It was Generis who showed up two long weeks later and refused to go away until I let her into the house.

"Hold this," Generis instructed, shoving a squirmy Violet at me and I took the toddler from her arms. Violet looked up at me and grinned, a row of tiny, perfect white teeth coming in and it made my heart clench painfully.

Cuddling the little girl close, I followed Generis into my own living room and watched her wrinkle up her nose as she took in the few takeout containers on the coffee table, the rest of the glass topped real estate taken up by empty bottles.

"This is disgusting, Jack."

SportsCenter played on in the background, and Violet looked up at me and pronounced me "Dack," before smacking my cheek with her tiny palm. She seemed to realize something then, and her little face crinkled up in disgust as Generis started to laugh hysterically.

"That's right, baby. Uncle Jack is stinky!" Generis waved a dramatic hand in front of her face and Violet's face twisted up further. I was fairly certain some of the muscles would suffer paralysis if she kept it up, and Violent nodded slowly at me.

"Dink."

Well, apparently there was one woman who could get me to shower, and I was pretty sure she still wet the bed at night.

"Gimme." Generis held out her arms and I handed Violet back, the sudden emptiness of my arms an intense and aching loss.

Generis pointed up the stairs and I trudged up slowly, putting myself through a shower while dishes clattered downstairs and a vacuum ran, the noises intermixed with sprinkles of Spanish I knew were some of G's more creative curses.

I took a long time in the bathroom. I showered and hacked at the beard that had shown up in the past couple weeks, and when I came back downstairs Violet's little face twisted into a grimace before she started to cry.

"Vivi," G cooed at her daughter. "It's Uncle Jack, but now he's nice and clean. See?" She crossed the room and leaned over in my direction, still solidly a foot and-a-half from me when she inhaled loudly. "Mmm," she said to Violet, holding out her hand so the little girl would toddle over. "Nice."

I'd better smell nice, damn it. I'd used soap and shampoo and even put on deodorant, each step feeling like a monumental task as I tried to rejoin the land of the living.

Scooping Violet back up, I held her close against my chest while she eyed me suspiciously. "Dack," she said again, like she was trying to convince herself, and finally she folded into me and rested her sweet little face right up against the curve of my neck.

I damn near fell apart, and Generis watched it all happen in real time. She didn't say anything, but the woman was uncannily psychic. She had always been able to read my thoughts just by watching my expressions, just like Tyler.

"Mama sent some food for you, since I wouldn't let her come with me," she said gently, and I looked around for the first time to realize while I'd been scraping layers of filth off myself, Generis had cleaned my house.

"There are chicken taquitos in the oven, because she says you eat like an overgrown child and she knows you love them." She went quiet for a moment and drew in a deep breath. I'd never seen this look on her face before, something that I thought might be worry.

"We all love you, Jack, and we want to see you happy. But you ... you make yourself unhappy because you're so stubborn. You don't *let* people love you because you're afraid you'll owe them something."

There must have been a curious expression on my face, because I'd never thought of it that way before.

"Yeah, don't bother saying it," she said with an eye roll. "I already know I'm right."

The two of them stayed a little longer and I fed tiny pieces of taquito to Violet, who opened her mouth like a little bird and then swooped in to chomp them from my fingertips.

"Careful," Generis warned me. "She'll get you. Why do you think I had to stop breastfeeding so early?"

I made a face. I loved G, but I didn't want to think about her tits. That was Tyler's territory and his worry.

"Bet you miss having her here," Generis said nonchalantly, dropping a bite of cheesy, chicken-filled goodness into her mouth and I knew without looking up that I was being baited.

"Must be cold and lonely in that big bed of yours."

My nostrils flared.

"Bet Daph was all soft and warm and smelled really nice, and now it's just you and a smelly, fluffy dog who farts in his sleep."

She had no idea how well she'd pegged the current situation. I'd taken to letting Carrick sleep in the bed the last couple nights because I'd been desperate to feel like someone was beside me.

"This isn't good, Jack." She gestured broadly to my entire person. "I don't like seeing you like this. You're suffering. And if you look like this, I can only imagine what *she* is going through."

That was it. I had to lean my forehead into my hand, so I could cover my eyes. Thinking about Daphne made dangerous things happen to my tear ducts. Until she'd left, I hadn't known I *could* cry. Not like this. All I'd ever done before was bluster and rage and throw things, but this time it was deeper and heavier and scarier, and the stupidest things had me swiping at my face.

"She left me, G," I said quietly without looking up.

"She felt like you left her first," she said softly. "You checked out when she needed you, and you need to remember that she's been left before too. I know all about her and Hunter, and the crap he pulled when she got pregnant with Blair. And you can shake your head at me and tell me no and say that I'm wrong, but she had to feel like you were doing the same thing."

I sat up straight, finally viewing it through her eyes and realizing that was probably exactly what had happened.

"We'll leave you to think about it," she said gently, pushing back from the table and holding out her arms for her daughter. Violet fussed at her, but she went, and I knew naptime would happen in the car.

"Get yourself together and get back on routine," she said gently as she stuffed things into the overflowing diaper bag. "But think about this hard, Jack, because you need to make a decision and you don't have a big window."

I wondered what she knew that I didn't.

I kissed baby Violet goodbye—covered her in kisses, really, because I couldn't stay away from that kid. She had my heart wrapped around those sticky little fingers of hers.

Then I kissed G on the cheek and thanked her for trying to save me from myself, and when I shut the door behind them all the joy they'd brought with them was gone again, possibly shoved back into that ridiculous diaper bag.

Carrick sat watching me while I sank down onto the sofa. I patted the cushion beside me and he willingly sprang up and threw himself down beside me, resting his big head on my leg and looking up at me with soulful eyes and wiggling eyebrows. I knew Daphne had to miss him and I wondered if she'd left him just so I had something to come home to.

I let the dog sleep in the bed again that night, and I had to crack a window because God knew what that dog was eating when I had my back turned. I already knew he preferred toilet water to the bowl of fresh water I kept out for him, and I suspected he pinched food from the trash, but I supposed we all had our bad habits.

The next morning I got out of bed and showered, put on the uniform that didn't fit as well these days, and I made a sad attempt at breakfast before taking Carrick outside and throwing a ball for him while I sipped at my coffee. The yard wasn't big and he could cover it in just a few big bounds, but he happily brought back the tennis ball every time and I threw it until my fingers began to go numb and I coaxed him back inside.

The two of us developed a sort of routine: I came home from work and took him out to use the yard and chase the ball around, then we scrounged through the fridge or the freezer and ate whatever was easiest—he usually ate more of my meal than I did.

Some nights I worked out, having lost my sense of routine when Daphne left, and when I was done I'd sit on the sofa for a while and watch an old movie or, more often than not, just stare at the wall.

The two of us were usually in bed by ten, since my days still started quite early, and most nights I fell asleep with the dog literally breathing down my neck.

Rinse and repeat for five work days every week, and by the time Saturday rolled around I'd pick up a few groceries and go visit Pop's spot at the cemetery. Sometimes I brought Carrick with me, though I knew other folks didn't like it much, but it was so much colder than usual that winter and I was usually the only fool out there.

The winter finally thawed into a tenuous spring. It seemed like winter wasn't eager to release its icy grasp on the DMV, and already the public schools had used up all their allotted weather-related days.

Finally February rolled around and still I was just taking it day by day. Daphne wasn't coming back, I knew that much by now, and the thought was still as sharp and painful as it had been the first night I realized she'd gone.

My phone buzzed in my pocket just as I was leaving the building, headed out to grab a quick lunch that I'd bring back and eat in the breakroom. It was the same number that had been texting me for weeks, and my finger hovered over the delete button. But something stopped me this time, and I clicked on it with some trepidation. Instantly the screen was taken up by a photo, a shot of a woman with long, dark hair standing on the beach, facing the ocean so that only her back was visible and my heart seized, because I would recognize that woman anywhere.

Who is this? I typed quickly, and immediately the little dots began to bounce.

You know who this is, sweetheart.

It sure as hell wasn't Jonas. I had a good feeling he wanted to rip my nuts off and feed them to me right now, and if I took a minute to put myself in his shoes, I'd have to agree that seemed the proper course of action.

Please resend everything.

I had been deleting Christa's texts for months, since the first one came through around Christmas, and my phone buzzed again and again as photo after photo of my favorite woman in the world flashed across the screen.

Lunch forgotten, I sank down onto the edge of the reflecting pool and greedily devoured photo after photo of Daphne. Christa had been sending one every three days or so since Christmas, always a picture when Daphne hadn't known it was being taken.

It took my breath away to stare at the beautiful woman who'd become even more beautiful as our child grew inside of her, and as the photos and text updates continued to flood in from Daphne's mother, I put my head down on my arms and tried to get my shit together.

I wiped my eyes before lifting them skyward, and in my heart I said a prayer that I wasn't too late.

19

Daphne

Mama's phone had been buzzing all afternoon and it was starting to drive me a little batty.

"What is going on over there?" I finally snapped, and Mama's eyes flicked up to mine quickly. Guiltily. Oh, she could try to hide it, but I knew it when I saw it. Mama was a planner and a schemer, and she'd always been, and she was Up. To. Something.

I'd been working from home the last few days, Braxton-Hicks contractions making me uncomfortable, and today I had a heating pad on my back for the dull ache that had settled between my hips. I was miserable and fat and pregnant as a whale, and I was darn good and ready to bite someone.

The baby was due in four weeks, and the doctor had expressed some concern about how quickly he was growing. Mama, who hadn't missed a single appointment, had chuckled and made a reference to "You should see the baby's father," before she caught herself and looked guiltily at me. I had forbade her from talking about Jack, because I couldn't trust myself to keep from bursting into tears, even all these months later.

"Yeah," I'd snorted bitterly as the tech moved the wand over my belly and a little face came into view. "Damn Neanderthal."

"Daphne!" Mama looked horrified. "Language, Sweet Pea!"

Mama hadn't taken to my new cursing habit with much enthusiasm.

I'd been working myself a little too hard lately. Natalie and Thomas had gotten engaged a few nights before, and I'd stupidly insisted on making her wedding dress. She was pregnant too, and Thomas insisted they would be married within the month, which didn't leave me a lot of time.

I wasted no time at all. I'd taken the last few days to design Natalie's dress and have her over to take measurements. I'd already cut the fabric and started piecing it together, and Mama made leading comments late every night when she passed by my workspace as she headed to her bedroom—on the completely opposite side of the house. "Don't overdo it, Sweet Pea. You need your rest."

When Thomas had dropped to his knees and proposed to Natalie in the middle of a chaotic scene, his hands on her belly and his eyes all shiny with emotion, I'd felt a swift, terrible stab of jealousy.

I tried to rewrite my memory of Jack's reaction. I tried to swap it out with what I'd witnessed between Thomas and Natalie, something tender and beautiful and deeply emotional.

But I couldn't. I kept coming back to the hard expression on his face and the way his eyes went flat when he accused me of keeping something from him.

I sniffed and smeared a hand under my eye as I tried to focus on the delicate row of stitching. I really had to stop doing that, I thought, realizing I held a pin in that hand.

I'd nearly stabbed myself in the eye.

Natalie's dress was simple and elegant. She didn't want fancy or fluffy, dripping in crystals or rhinestones or sequins. I knew it was because she didn't want the dress at all—she wanted the man, and she didn't care if she had to wear a potato sack to marry him.

Leaning a little closer to the machine, I winced as the baby jabbed me in the ribs and when I looked down at my stomach, it was doing The Wave.

"What is going on in there, little one?" I asked, wincing, feeling like I was being stretched out from the inside. There were little heels pressing into my side and tiny fists hammering organs I couldn't name, and I wondered what I'd done to piss him or her off.

"Gonna need two more days, baby," I said quietly. I'd been working on Natalie's dress nonstop, fearful that the baby would decide my timeline was not his or her own, and that if I didn't go into labor early I would be induced. The baby was already nineteen inches long and over eight pounds, already much larger than Blair had been when she was born, and that was when she was full-term. It made me nervous, wondering if I'd be able to get the kid out by the time the due date actually rolled around. I had a feeling we wouldn't be waiting all that much longer.

I winced again, the dull ache in my back throbbing down into my pelvis and I flicked the heating pad on again.

Natalie was back the next day for a quick fitting, and I knew she wouldn't grow much over the course of the next few weeks, though the dress would hug every curve and stretch just enough to grant forgiveness for a few extra pounds. She would look incredible in it too, her curves only accentuated by her pregnancy glow, and I knew most of that glow was due to being in love and being almost violently loved in return. Thomas was fiercely protective of her, the woman who'd quietly, patiently, gently coaxed him back into humanity.

Finally I stood and walked out the ache, the insistent waves of dull pain radiating through my pelvis and starting to reach around to the front of my stomach. I was familiar with this. I had always been slow to go into labor, the process taking days for me rather than hours, and that fact had been cruel with each painful, drawn out miscarriage.

Carefully hanging the dress, I sighed in relief that Natalie had chosen a simple design and there were just a few finishing touches to put on it, in addition to completing the hem the next day, once I had Natalie on the step and I could pin it to the proper length.

I slept fitfully that night, the ache waking me time and again, and I rubbed my belly and whispered soft things to the baby. It was more to soothe myself than anything else, and eventually the little one calmed, stopped the gymnastics and the pain receded enough that I fell back into a troubled sleep. I dreamed again of a dark-haired child toddling through the yard while

Jack played fetch with Carrick. It was a beautiful dream, the colors muted like a photograph that had begun to break down over time, and when I woke in the morning my clear mental snapshot of the loving smile on Jack's face was gone.

Waking that next morning, I was sore and stiff and achy, and I stretched out slowly. Every joint and tendon felt like it might pop, and the skin of my belly was stretched so tight I feared I might rip if I sneezed.

Oh, but to take a truly deep breath again...

The baby had dropped the week before, said the doctor, who had felt my belly but hadn't bothered with another sonogram.

Judging by last night's acrobatics, I wasn't so sure. The party going on in my lower body felt an awful lot like a little one turning him or herself completely around to assume the position.

Mama's face was tight when I shuffled into the kitchen for breakfast, and Daddy beamed at me from where he sat at the island.

"Didn't you have a flight this morning?" I asked, because his season was over but there were still things to handle a few days each week.

"Got one of the kids handling it." He smirked, taking another chug of his coffee.

I wondered if it drove his forty-something assistant coaches bananas when he called them "kids."

Mama's fingers were flying over the screen of her phone when I looked up, and something in her expression caused me to narrow my eyes at her. Mama looked mad, and she *never* looked mad.

"Everything okay, Mama?" I asked sweetly, helping myself to orange juice and a large helping of eggs and the fluffy pancakes the housekeeper had prepared not an hour before.

"Right as rain, Sweet Pea," she answered cheerfully, but from the slight crease between her eyebrows—the one that happened when she was really fighting against her Botox—told me things were not, in fact, right at all.

I wasn't able to eat much, what with the real estate my stomach usually occupied being taken up by the small human I'd affectionately nicknamed The Tiny Terror. The kid didn't like to let me eat, sleep in peace, and lately had been kicking me in the bladder at the most inopportune moments. I had actually wet myself a little two weeks before, in the foundation's office, when I hadn't been able to end a call to a facility quite quickly enough.

That had been fun.

Natalie showed up half an hour later and I'd just finished breakfast, so I quickly rinsed my dishes and Mama shooed me out of the kitchen as she continued to type furiously.

I could have *sworn* I heard her take a photo, but when my eyes snapped to her she was one hundred percent focused on the screen, her fingers still tapping away.

Something was going on here.

Natalie and I moved toward the large room I used for a workspace, and her hand drifted quickly to my stomach when I winced. "Your tummy is tight," she said softly, and I nodded. We both knew what that meant, though I wasn't ready for what was coming. I'd told myself I had several more weeks, but in all likelihood I had until this evening.

"Daphne, this is ridiculous. You need to go to the hospital. You can't be fitting me for a wedding dress today, sweet girl."

Her face was so kind and understanding, I knew the woman would absolutely forgive me if I left her high and dry and she had to get married in a sports bra and yoga pants.

Natalie had become a real friend, and the last thing I was going to do was leave her stranded, so I shushed her and hurried her into her dress, and while she stood on the step and spun slowly at my instruction, I carefully pinned up the hem. (I say carefully because my belly was like uneven ballast: If I leaned too far forward, there was no doubt I'd topple.)

While she watched, I carefully stitched the flowing hem, then added the few simple, tiny embellishments that completed the piece.

"This is your best work," Natalie breathed, and I grinned at her despite myself. There was no way it was my best work. I hadn't actually made a piece on my own in so long, the last time I'd touched a sewing machine was when I'd made the two dresses she took to California. But, like getting back on a bicycle, there were some things that just had a muscle memory to them.

I winced as a pain shot through my back and Natalie's expression went from concern to panic. "Daphne, that was a big one. Are you okay?"

"It was nothing," I panted. "It passed immediately; I'll be fine."

My water hadn't broken, so the last thing I was, was concerned.

"Sweet Pea," Mama's voice preceded her. "I brought you girls some tea—figured you could use some after a tryin' mornin' finishin' up all this fittin' business." She moved into the room with two mugs and set them on my large table. Her phone buzzed and she pulled it from the pocket of her full skirt with a huff. "Oh, that ornery man," she fussed, and when I looked up at her, she quickly ironed out the expression on her face. "I'm so sorry, darlin'. I've been havin' problems with one of the landscapers this mornin'. You know, the ones we hired to put in that new hedge down by the beachfront."

I knew of no such plans, or contracts, or landscapers, and when she set her phone on the table and hurried over to exclaim over Natalie's dress, I flipped the phone so that it was face-up. Mama had been acting shifty all morning.

Mama was an easy read. Her passcode was a combination of my birthday and her wedding date to Daddy, and immediately the messaging program opened. There were words and photos—photos of me—and words in response from Jack.

She's so beautiful.

I miss her so much.

I love her, Christa, but they deserve better.

My eyes were burning and I scrolled further down, to find the most recent interactions.

No, I can't come. She won't want me there.

The words followed a picture of me standing in the kitchen at breakfast, the sun streaming through the windows at my side and illuminating my belly through the thin nightgown I wore.

Mama's message to him was **It'll be any minute now. She won't admit to it, but she's already in labor.**

I threw the phone down onto the table with a clatter and both Mama and Natalie spun to face me.

"Why?" I cried, slapping my hand down next to her phone.

My mother had been in contact with the man I loved for months, and she hadn't said a word to me. She hadn't relayed a single thing that might have fed me a drop of hope during the long, dark, lonely nights when I cried until I was spent.

"Why what, Pea?" Mama asked, and by the way her mouth twitched I knew she was nervous. Mama had always had a tell when she was caught out.

"This!" I held up the phone in my fist and shook it. "You've been sending him pictures of me!"

Natalie's face went pale and her mouth dropped open just a little, just before a violent cramp folded me in half in my chair.

"Oooh," I moaned as I felt a wet rush. "I've ruined the chair."

"No worryin' about a silly chair." Mama forced a laugh, clearly relieved to be let off the hook. "Let's get you cleaned up real quick and Daddy can get us to the hospital."

Mama and Natalie both helped me from the chair and I saw Natalie's eyes go wide.

"What is it?" I asked, and Mama shushed and clucked at me. "It's nothin', Pea. Let's just ... let's just go *now*, shall we? You know, be on the safe side of things." There was no hiding the worry in her expression.

"Jonas!" Mama called down the hallway and I thought her voice sounded shrill and worried. "Sweetheart, we need to take our baby girl to the hospital. Seems this little one's plannin' on makin' an early appearance."

I heard Daddy's heavy, hurried footsteps and from the immediate jingling of keys I knew he'd had them in his pocket the whole morning.

"Time to do this thing, Pea," he bellowed down the hallway and I'd taken only a few steps when I was slammed by a tsunami of pain. Something hot started running down the insides of my thighs and it left me dizzy, disoriented, and my knees started to buckle.

"Jonas!" Mama screamed, and I heard Daddy's feet pounding across the marble floor.

The last thing I remembered thinking was, *He doesn't have pennies in his loafers.*

20

Jack

Christa had been blowing me up all morning, telling me that Daphne hadn't been feeling well, and a mother's intuition told her the baby was coming soon.

Carrick had been pacing since he'd gotten up, like he sensed a shift in the force, and I joined him as he paced. We walked the short distance from kitchen to dining room to living room, then from living room to dining room to kitchen, and I refilled my coffee three times as we wore a groove into the flooring.

I was terribly worried about Daphne. I'd witnessed only one birth, when Natasha gave birth to our sweet little baby girl, and when that precious baby died only a few months later, our marriage went the same way.

It didn't take a therapist to tell me I feared the same outcome. By removing myself from the equation, I'd told myself, the outcome might be different. Daphne could raise a happy, healthy baby, free of the curse I dragged around with me. I ruined everything I touched.

Congress was in a State Work period, and my schedule was relaxed for the next several weeks. Staffing was still necessary, but I'd indicated to my supervisor that if he could shift me down the list, I'd be grateful, as it was possible I'd have some family responsibilities to tend to.

I just wasn't sure exactly how I was going to do that.

When Christa's text came through that Daphne might be in labor, I was frantic. I packed a bag, having already told myself I wasn't going anywhere, and then I took Carrick outside to throw the ball.

I was too wound up and accidentally threw the ball over the fence, and the dog leveled me with a glare that said *you asshole* just as plainly as if he'd said it out loud.

It was early March and unseasonably warm, the smell of thawing, warming dirt in the air and Carrick quickly busied himself with digging a hole in the corner of the yard that I couldn't be bothered to investigate. I was too busy, watching the screen of my phone, waiting for something—anything—totally at Christa's mercy.

Carrick was solidly eighteen inches deep in the yard when the next text came through and I gasped as I read Christa's words: **Daphne's hemorrhaging. We're rushing her to the hospital and Jonas will be in touch to relay your flight information.**

There was no arguing with the woman, and I almost wondered if she'd engineered the situation to get her own way. She was a force of nature—the original one—and I wondered if her daughter had observed her mother's hurricane force and had opted instead for slower, smoother, more insidious tactics.

My phone rang moments later and I didn't even bother looking at the number before I answered. Jonas barked frantic instructions into my ear and I could hear Christa in the background, murmuring something. I thought to myself that Jonas sounded more stressed than if he were down twenty points in the fourth quarter.

"I'll be there," I assured him quickly, and I texted Tyler to make sure he could handle Carrick while I rushed to Alabama. Then I winced, quickly texting my supervisor to tell him my pregnant girlfriend was in trouble and I didn't have great news yet.

To my surprise, he texted me back immediately: **Family is everything, Thompson. Congratulations. Now go, and let me know when you know they're okay.**

Tyler called me thirty seconds later. "I got Carrick," he said quietly, and I knew he was just as freaked out as I was. "Go get her, Jack. Bring her back. Bring her back with the baby—I'm giving you *one* job, jackass."

I grinned in spite of myself. I loved the guy.

"Thanks, man. You're..." My voice died off when I couldn't say the words.

"Yeah," he chuckled. He knew. "I know it. Now go."

He hung up on me.

I grabbed Carrick's face and gave him a big old kiss right on the top of his wiry-haired head. Swear to you he smiled up at me, like he couldn't understand what had taken me so long.

Grabbing the bag I'd thrown down the stairs, I snatched my wallet, keys, and sunglasses off the side table and ran out of the house without locking the door.

Hopping into my truck, I gunned the engine and drove like a bat out of hell to get to BWI, parking my truck in long-term parking since I had absolutely no idea how long I'd be gone.

I just knew I had to get to her.

There was no question I'd waited too long, because I was stubborn and scared and stupid. I'd known that for a while, but hadn't been willing to accept any of the blame.

Don't ask me how he did it, but a golf cart pulled up behind my truck as I was parking and the guy driving barked at me, "Jack Thompson?"

I looked around for a second, like an idiot, before realizing that was me. "Uh, yeah."

He gestured toward the empty row behind him and I hopped on, plopping my bag next to me.

"Hang onto that." He hooked a thumb toward my bag before stomping the accelerator to the floor, and I thought only that I'd never known a golf cart could move so quickly. We zipped through traffic and across lanes that were unquestionably pedestrian, traveling in a wide arc until we paused before a large gate and after a few interactions between my driver and the man standing guard, the gate began to roll back slowly and we moved forward into what I understood was not the commercial strip.

"Godspeed." He held up a fist like I was supposed to bump it, and I did, but it took me a second.

"Follow me, sir." The flight attendant was a very pretty blonde, tall and willowy, and her smile was welcoming. "I'll just need to check you in quickly and confirm a few things."

I'd never flown anything other than commercial before, and that had only been twice: to and from the honeymoon in Barbados that Natasha had insisted upon. To be fair, I hadn't hated it. The destination was lovely, but considering how infrequently we left our room, we could have just stayed home.

I tried to push away the bitter memory as I boarded the plane. That had been the last time Natasha had shown any *real* interest in me. She'd soured pretty quickly once we got home. I guess I lost my unicorn glitter or something.

My leg didn't stop bouncing the entire trip, and by the time we landed in Mobile the flight attendant had offered me coffee, tea, water, whiskey, and several pills from her own stash of Xanax. I hadn't accepted any, and whether or not that was stupid I would determine shortly.

There was a town car waiting when I stepped off the plane, a man leaning up against the wheel well on the passenger side. "Billings, sir."

I detected a southern drawl, but I said nothing about it. Instead, "Thank you, Billings. Have the Masters relayed any information?"

My phone had been woefully silent.

"Afraid not, sir. Only that Mr. Jonas's daughter was in a real bad way. Understand that's why you're headed there."

Damn straight. Now I just needed someone to tell me what the hell was going on.

We drove in silence, my driver clearly more at ease than I was, and my leg bounced again as we rushed toward what I assumed was the hospital.

"Jack, darling!"

I winced when I heard Christa's voice, because I wasn't ready for her.

"Oh sweetheart, I'm so glad you're here..."

That was when I realized the woman was close to tears.

"It took hours and was real close."

A chill rushed through me, convincing me that I was entirely too late. I had pushed too hard and waited too long, and now I was going to lose everything because I'd been stupid and stubborn and slow.

"Jack."

I looked up into Jonas's steely blue eyes, and for a second my heart stopped. I saw the worry and grief and anger in the man's expression and I knew immediately that he'd seen more sorrow than I'd ever witnessed. He had me beat, and hard.

"Our girl's not doin' so well," he said softly, so softly that Christa didn't seem to hear it.

I couldn't help my reaction, even if it gave me up. I sank to my knees, hands over my eyes.

I have been such a fool.

"Jack." Jonas's voice was urgent. "Need you to come with me, son."

I pushed back up to my feet and followed him blindly, terrified and angry with myself. All these months, it had been about me. I hadn't given real thought to what she was going through, just that she had chosen to leave me.

"Don't suppose I need to tell you that she's filed for divorce?" He turned suddenly as we walked down a long hallway, and I absolutely tripped over my own feet.

"Wh-what?"

Yeah, that was all I had.

"Stupid boy ... you ain't been ready for this?" He whirled around suddenly. "This was you, son—all you. When my Sweet Pea came home and told us she was havin' your baby, both my wife and me were ... well, we were struck stupid. We been here before, you understand."

I knew a few things about this.

"I'm so sorry, Mr. Masters. It's just that..."

"Ain't no 'just,' boy. None at all. You love my sweet girl or you don't, simple as that. The rest works itself out."

"I do."

I couldn't stop the words. They flew from my heart, right out of my mouth, because I knew at that moment that Daphne was the only one who had saved me, and I had been my own worst enemy.

Nothing new.

"She's in ICU. Hemorrhaged real bad while havin' the baby." His voice caught in his throat, and for a second I recognized how much he loved his adopted daughter.

"Can I see her?" My voice was almost a whisper, and I knew it was the right answer when he held out a giant paw. I took it, a little scared. I'd never held another man's hand before, but in this situation it seemed kind of important.

"Family only," he said, in a voice that told me everything I needed to know: I hadn't yet proven myself *family*.

"I will be," I said quietly as we stood outside of the doors leading to the unit that held the woman I loved. "If she'll forgive me for being a total dumbass, I will be the father she wants for our baby, and if she'll let me be her husband, well..." I faltered, my stupid throat threatening to close over.

"Good boy," Jonas said, in a voice that sounded an awful lot like a bark. "She been all kinds'a miserable without you, but ain't no one called her on it, 'cuz that's her thing to figure out an' not ours."

The moment broke and Jonas dropped my hand, gesturing I should proceed into the unit even as the glass doors slid open.

"She doin' better?" Jonas asked a nurse as we passed onto the floor, and the girl sized me up quickly before answering him, "Yes, sir. She's stabilized—took a lot of blood, but she's awake now, I believe."

Suddenly, I realized I didn't know whether our child had survived, and I turned to Jonas quickly: "Tell me."

"Yup." He knew the question I couldn't ask and his craggy old face was wreathed in smiles. "Gonna be a quarterback, I tell you what."

A son.

"Jonas, I'm..."

"I know, boy. Pea's told me about it and I'm sorry. But this time..." He chuckled. "This time there were some quality genetics—that Hunter was a real mutt on a good day. I blame him for my girl's troubles. Nature's way of tellin' that man he shouldn't be reproducin'." He made a disgusted face. "Only good thing he ever done was knock my girl up with my granddaughter."

Now I was both *son* and *boy*, and I couldn't decide whether either term was meant to be endearing.

No one questioned the man as he led me toward the room the nurse had left only a moment before, and I knew it was killing him to stand just outside the door. "One at a time, as I understand it," he said quietly and he nodded at me shortly. "Gotta go get her Mama; you take first shift." He gestured that I should go in.

Daphne was hooked up to all kinds of machines that beeped and purred and spit out all kinds of numbers on a screen near the bed. There was an IV in her arm, taped down tight, and I was relieved to see the bag hanging from the tree was dripping clear fluid into her and not the blood I'd expected to see.

She looked so small and fragile in the hospital bed, and I scrubbed a hand over my face as I approached the bed. It looked like she was sleeping, and I could only imagine she was exhausted after the battle she'd just been through.

Carefully lowering myself to my knees, I leaned onto the side of her bed and took her hand, pressing a gentle kiss to the back. There was no point in stopping up my tear ducts anymore, I figured, and I put my face down into the thin blanket and just let it out.

I missed all of it. I should have been here.

"Jack," she whispered, her voice tiny and her hand slipped from mine to slide into my hair. I wanted to crawl in next to her and gather her up in my arms, but she winced when I shifted and leaned my weight into the bed. "Ow. Tarnation, that smarts."

I couldn't help the grin that chased away the moisture in my eyes. There was my girl, silly, nonsensical expressions and all.

There was a noise behind me and I looked over my shoulder to see Christa and Jonas hovering at the door, one of his big arms holding his wife to his side as she dabbed at her eyes with a delicate little hankie.

"I'll give you a minute with your mama," I whispered to Daphne and she opened her eyes fully, gesturing I should bend down. When I did she grabbed my face with both hands and planted a solid one right on my lips.

"You owe me, Thompson," she whispered up to me, a little smile on her face as I straightened.

Yeah, I sure as hell did owe her, but I had no idea how to make good.

"Take a trip to the nursery, son?" Jonas's voice was uncharacteristically gentle, and Christa was already shouldering me out of the way in an attempt to get to her daughter.

Jonas was a huge celebrity in these parts, and our progress was halted again and again as people stopped him to congratulate him on "another great season," or to have him sign anything they could get their hands on.

It took us almost half an hour to get to the nursery and my patience had long since been used up. Jonas knew it, too, and I could tell he thought it was hilarious. Payback, probably.

"That handsome little fella, right there." He thumped one huge index finger against the plate glass and I stared down at the little bundle wrapped tightly in a blanket with blue and pink teddy bears, a small blue hat that looked like gauze on his head.

"Nurse," Jonas bellowed over my shoulder and he held up his opposite wrist, tapping at a band I hadn't noticed before. "Gonna need one of these for our boy, here. This is the daddy."

That was what made it real, the D-word, and I must have looked panicked because Jonas chuckled and put an arm around me. "Toughest job you'll ever have," he said gently, gesturing toward the baby who lay quietly in his tiny bassinet. "You just do what you can and hope it's enough, and no matter what, you love 'em. You love 'em hard."

That made me feel a little guilty, because my steadfast love track record wasn't looking all that great. There were some serious gaps.

A nurse moved up beside me, looking skeptical, and when she demanded to see some ID I whipped out my wallet so she could check my license against a tablet she held in her hand. I knew this was somewhere beyond her standard procedure and I wondered if this was due to Jonas's influence.

I looked down at the band as the woman tapped notes into her tablet, and I caught my breath. *Baby Boy Thompson.*

"She ain't named 'im yet." Jonas was grinning at me. "Said she was thinkin' on Tyler."

I snorted so hard, my sinuses burned. The fuck she would. The old man had to be messing with me.

"Hell if she will," I muttered, and Jonas chuckled beside me.

"Wouldn't push her if I were you, son. Been testin' what that woman's made of long enough, now."

"I'm sorry," I whispered, dropping my eyes in shame just as a nurse moved toward my son's bassinet and began wheeling him out of the nursery.

"Know a few things about why you reacted the way you did," Jonas said in a much gentler voice than I'd expected, and the door swung open.

"They'll be moving her in a few minutes," the nurse said softly to Jonas. "You two can visit with him for a minute and then I'll take all three of you up to her new room."

Jonas pointed me toward a chair near the nurses' station, and when I sat the nurse gently lifted the baby and placed him in my arms. He squirmed and fussed in his tightly wrapped blanket, making tiny little kitten noises and a little tongue poked out from between tiny lips.

"Just don't let it happen again." Jonas's voice was firm and I had to blink back the moisture in my eyes before looking up into the man's face. "You got a family now, boy. You got to step up and be the man they both need. Take care of 'em, and not just by puttin' food on the table." He nodded shortly and patted a hand over his heart, as if satisfied that we'd concluded our Come to Jesus moment.

I couldn't stop looking at the little boy in my arms. He fit so perfectly, nestled right up against my chest, and I gently brushed back his hat to see a head full of Daphne's thick black hair. No doubt about it, the kid was going to be gorgeous if he ended up looking anything like his mother.

"Nine pounds, twelve ounces," the nurse said quietly and I looked up to see her shaking her head in dismay. "Wouldn't have believed all that baby could come out of such a tiny woman if I hadn't seen it for myself."

I winced as I thought of what that meant for Daphne. She had to be in some serious pain after pushing out a kid nearly half her size.

Jonas plopped down beside me and started up some ridiculous commentary on how the boy would be tall and strong and talented, and he expected football ran in my little man's veins just as it did his.

Half an hour later the nurse tucked the baby back into the bassinet and we followed her as she wheeled him carefully through the hallways until we arrived in a much brighter, more cheerful room.

"Look who's here!" Christa chirped, a huge smile on her pretty face. "My stars, all three of our handsome men."

Daphne smiled weakly from the bed and I knew she was used to Christa's theatrics. That was the one thing she hadn't gotten from her mother: drama.

The nurse handed the baby to Daphne and Christa bustled Jonas right out of the room, followed shortly by the nurse as Daphne lowered her gown and nestled the baby to her breast. My eyes went wide as she did and she gave me a sleepy smirk. "Don't be jealous of your son, Thompson."

I couldn't stand not touching her for a single second longer, and I pulled the chair up right next to the bed and watched the baby figure things out, my hand resting lightly on Daphne's thigh. For now it would have to be enough.

Nurses and a doctor drifted in and out over the course of the day and Jonas brought up some food for everyone, then held the baby as Daphne tried to eat. She was still tired and weak, and despite her protests she finally gave up trying and let me feed her.

Christa watched me with a knowing smile on her face, watching me hover over the two of them and fuss over Daphne. I knew I had a long way to go to prove myself to her parents, but right now I couldn't even be bothered worrying about that because first I needed to prove myself to her.

The light in the room indicated it was getting late, and Jonas had dozed off in a chair in the corner, occasionally waking himself with a snore that would slip out every time his head dropped to his chest.

"Time for me to get my old man home," Christa said with an affectionate glance at the grizzly bear sleeping in the corner. "You stayin', Jackie?"

Jackie.

I couldn't help the grin that stretched across my face, and in a display that was rare for me I leaned over and scooped the woman up into a bone-crushing hug. She didn't squeak or squeal or protest, just leaned right into me and hugged me back with surprising ferocity. "I knew," she whispered into my ear and it could have meant so many things, but I chose to believe it meant she knew I'd make good.

"Thank you," I whispered back, and my words meant more than one thing as well, but I was especially thankful for her persistence in trying to give me small, frequent pieces of Daphne.

I slept on a little cot next to Daphne that night, and the baby stayed with us in the room making little piglet noises when he ate and contented kitten snuffles while he slept. The cot was narrow and uncomfortable and we were awakened several times during the night as nurses checked on Daphne, but each time we fell back asleep with her hand in mine and finally, after months of being unable to breathe without her, I slept peacefully.

21

Epilogue

Daphne, one year later...

I stretched out contentedly on the lawn chair in the warm sunshine, a smile on my face as I closed my eyes. Carrick was yapping excitedly and Jameson was squealing as Jack swooped him around the yard in a game of Airplane.

It had taken a long time to heal after Jameson's traumatic birth. By the time Daddy rolled up to the emergency room, I'd been unconscious for a while according to Mama, and Jameson was in trouble by the time they hooked up the fetal monitor.

To hear Mama tell it, I'd transitioned in a matter of moments and Jameson showed up like a tsunami, ready to get the heck out. Problem was, at that point I wasn't conscious and couldn't push, so my sweet boy came out with the help of forceps. You can imagine what that did to me and how many stitches went into places that had never seen the sunshine, in an attempt to piece me back together.

It had taken a very, very long time before I invited Jack back into my bed, and to his credit he'd been patient with me. Loving. He often got up for Jameson's nighttime feedings so I could sleep and whenever I'd drift past him during the day he'd sweep me up into a gentle hug, never letting go until I relaxed into his chest.

I might have been convinced to resume activities sooner, but it took me a very long time to heal, and for months even walking was extraordinarily painful.

Without a word, Jack sold his home in Maryland and turned in his notice and a week after I'd bid him a tearful goodbye, he was back in Mama and Daddy's driveway with a moving truck and Carrick.

When Carrick came barreling into the nursery, it took me a second to understand what was happening. I pushed myself out of the glider and set the sleeping baby in his crib, shuffling down the hallway. Jack came flying around the corner with a smile on his face that absolutely melted my heart, and I burst into tears right there and collapsed into his arms. The thought of being without him again for long stretches of time had hurt terribly, and when he'd left it had been with a straight face and the promise that once I felt well enough to travel with the baby, I'd return to Maryland.

My divorce was quickly finalized and Hunter didn't want a fuss, since he didn't need any more negative publicity, and the very day I received the final notice, Jack got down on one knee and asked me to marry him. He claimed he didn't want to wait a second longer, and when my jaw dropped in dismay I saw the fear flash through his eyes. I leaned down to him immediately and took his face in my hands, kissing him like I meant it, because I really did, and when I could breathe again I said yes.

Come on, I was going to tell this guy no? I wasn't that stupid. I knew exactly what I had, and I wasn't about to let go.

All three of us lived with Mama and Daddy while Jack and I went house shopping in the area. He said he wanted me to be close to family, because Alabama and its people were in my blood and he wanted our son growing up in a place that told his family's history.

In the end, we purchased a piece of land and had a house built. It was the house from my dream; I recognized it the instant I saw the plans, and we'd planned to have the wedding in the backyard.

Jack took a job with an old Army buddy, Scott, who'd started his own security company in New York. It paid very well and he had a lot more free time, since he had the freedom to choose the contracted jobs. It did mean he was sometimes away from us for a few days or weeks at a time, but he was the happiest I'd ever seen him. Sometimes he even *smiled.*

"Someone looks like she's enjoying a nap in the sunshine."

A dark shadow loomed over me and I looked up to see two smiling faces. Jack looked down at me with our sweet boy in his arms, and I couldn't help but think just how much Jameson looked like his father. He was going to break some hearts.

"What time does our girl get in?" Jack asked casually, holding out a hand to help me up and I glanced quickly at the face of my phone.

"She'll be a few hours yet, I think," I said. Blair was flying in this evening for many happy reasons: to see our new house for the first time, to celebrate our wedding, and she would spend a week with us, helping me unpack and decorate, and she couldn't wait to spoil baby Jameson.

Tyler, Generis and baby Violet—who wasn't such a baby anymore—were coming in tomorrow and staying with us for the wedding that was happening in four days' time. We also expected Natalie and Thomas, Ava and Lincoln, and our house would be full to bursting in no time.

A wedding for her only daughter meant Mama was in her element and though I'd wanted small, her version of small meant there were three hundred people ready to crowd into my back yard.

No pressure or anything.

The last time Jack had talked to Tyler, Tyler hinted they had big news to share, and I suspected Violet was about to become a big sister.

"A few hours?" Jack's eyes gleamed and his tongue peeked out to touch his top lip. "You know, I think I've worn this little man out," he said, wiggling his eyebrows at me. "I'm going to put him down for a nap, then what do you say I wear *you* out?"

I grinned at him and slowly shook my head, like I couldn't believe him. I couldn't get enough of the man and though we'd had to slow things down in the boudoir, as Mama would say, Jack had been patient, gentle and inventive while my body slowly returned to normal. The rough, angry man I'd taken into my bed was calmer, but no less creative.

I had never known a love like Jack, and I'd never known a lover like Jack. I was blessed among women, I knew, and only once I'd mused aloud that our lives had been forever altered by just one silly little wrong turn.

Jack had shivered when I said it, and I knew just what was running through his head. "Thank God," he said softly, pulling me close and wrapping his body around mine, and I knew he was envisioning what life would be without Jameson, Blair and me.

"Life without the three of you wasn't worth living," he'd murmured into my hair and I mused over the change I'd seen in him in just a few short years. The quiet, closed off, angry man was warm, smiling, affectionate and kind. Love had flowed into all the cracks and broken places in his heart and sealed it right up, healing him from the inside out, teaching him patience and trust and tenderness.

Jack put the baby down in his crib and softly shut the door, turning to me with a glint in his eye. I loved it when he looked at me like that, like I was the present he couldn't wait to unwrap, and I bolted down the hallway with a giggle. He always caught me, and he did again, scooping me up to set me gently on our bed as he crawled over me, pressing gentle kisses to my face and throat, my breasts and stomach, and I lifted my hips for him when he tugged off my leggings.

Jack's favorite thing was to drive me to the edge of reason with his hands and mouth and watch me fall apart, and when my body relaxed he crawled back up, waiting for me to wrap my legs around his body. When I did we came together slowly, savoring the closeness and intimacy of a moment neither of us felt like rushing.

"I love you, Daphne," he said, looking down at me seriously and I grinned back up at him and the sweet emotion I saw in his eyes.

"You'd better," I whispered. "Because in just a few days you're stuck with me forever."

He grinned. "Is that supposed to be a punishment?"

I shook my head. No, it was nothing but a reward for both of us.

"I was stuck with you the minute Tyler decided to invite you to that stupid gun range." He chuckled softly. "He would not quit."

"Tyler was our fairy godmother," I agreed, my hands drifting to his hips and sliding down to his backside. Things were beginning to grow rather urgent and I needed to hurry him up.

"I love you more, Jack," I sighed, the pleasant pressure starting to build and sizzle along my nerve endings, and the maddening man slowed even more.

"Promise me you'll tell me every day for the rest of our lives."

"Deal," I agreed quickly. "But under one condition."

He looked down at me with a slight wrinkle in his forehead and I clenched the muscles deep inside, gripping him tightly. He grinned down at me before picking up the pace.

Message received.

"This," he said gently, and I completely lost the darn plot. I looked up at him, and something about the way he was looking down at me made my heart skip a beat. "This is what I've never had with anyone else, Daph. I feel safe with you." He looked a little embarrassed and I leaned up to kiss him. He accepted it and then leaned his forehead against mine. "You're my family. You and Jameson and Blair are *my family*, and I will do everything in my power to keep you safe and happy and healthy, and I will love all of you with every piece of my heart."

My eyes got a little watery and I slapped his chest playfully. "Stop distracting me, you sweet talker. That sounded an awful lot like you were practicing your vows."

"Pffft, I got vows way better than that, baby."

There was no freight train or fireworks that time, only a gentle, rolling calm that finally blanketed both of us and left us sighing together.

He rolled to lie beside me, pulling me against his chest and I sighed contentedly as his heart tapped gently against my shoulder. This feeling was new and welcome, flooding every dark corner with what I suspected might be peace.

There was a sound from the corner of the room and Jack groaned. "What does that dog *eat*?"

I giggled and pulled the blanket up over my nose, snuggling deeper into Jack. Farting dog and all, these were the silly, sweet, *real* moments I would remember all my life: The life I would share with the man who loved me in his perfectly imperfect way. He was everything I needed.

The End.

You haven't met Scott and Mia yet, as Scott only just got his honorable mention in the epilogue. If you want a peek at their story, keep turning!

22

Sneak Peek of Unforgiven - Mia

Dad shook his head as he closed the door behind him, and he eased himself down onto the porch step beside me. It wasn't an easy task. He wasn't as young as he once was, and years of my mother's cooking meant gravity was a formidable foe.

Snowflakes drifted down and I was shivering, so he wrapped an arm tightly around me and after a deep sigh, said "I don't suppose it's any surprise that you come from a very long line of volatile women."

"You must mean damaged," I said bitterly, and he remained silent for a moment. There was no point to be argued, so we sat together and watched the snow drift down, making the sound only falling snow can make as it blanketed the yard and the dozens of cars parked all the way down the winding drive.

"She gets it from her ma," he finally said. "She had a temper and a mouth and it was all your ma ever knew. And when Nonna started with the grappa ... Dio mio." He crossed himself and lifted his eyes to the heavens. "It was over."

"Nonni Gigi wasn't much better," I offered quietly, and Dad's snort sounded like a hiccup.

"Gigi was absolutely no better," he agreed, and I wondered if he missed his long-dead mother. He never talked about her.

"But at least she never learned English, so when she went off on a tirade in public, most people didn't understand her."

"Too bad Mom knows English," I sighed. "I understand every word from her mouth with perfect clarity."

"Maybe even some of the ones she doesn't say," He commented, and he swung his leg to knock the side of my knee with his.

Someone opened the door to peek outside, and a sonic boom erupted from the house. My enormous Italian family had been shocked into silence moments earlier—no small feat—when Mom lit into me for my second divorce. My mother clearly didn't remember the bitter fights or how frighteningly thin I'd been when I'd begun to feel my marriage was dissolving.

"He was the best thing that ever happened to you," she'd railed at me, clearly not taking in the total disbelief written all over my face. She had to be drunk, because we were no longer talking about David. Now that I was divorcing my second husband, she wanted to throw me back into the arms of the first.

Mom knew a few of the sordid details about the second split, but now that I was home and desperately poor while my divorce languished through a term of due process, she took every chance to remind me I was a failure. Two scrapped marriages with no children to show for either, and not a half-decent job to keep body and soul together.

My life, the perpetual dumpster fire.

All the heat had leaked from my body, and my teeth began to chatter despite the warmth emanating from the solid wall that was Dad. He was nearly as wide as he was tall, I realized not for the first time as he hoisted himself up with a wince. His knees were bothering him again, but he wasn't about to lose weight or consult with a doctor about replacement surgery.

I struggled to my feet after him and slapped the circulation back into my numb backside. I wasn't eager to go back into the house, but I was losing feeling in my fingers and toes.

My mother's eyes glittered, unblinking, as I slipped back into the house behind Dad. She looked like a snake, tracking her prey with unmoving eyes, waiting to strike when the moment was right. She was biding her time in the kingdom of her kitchen, surveying her domain and holding court amongst the relatives while I hid in the hallway.

Mom only allowed herself to drink with the family or on holidays, and since we were Italian there were a number of those observed in our household.

When my mother drank, the wine loosened her caustic tongue. It was already quite loose by most standards, but fueling it with alcohol made her mean. The little self control she may have had went right out the window and inside thoughts turned into real, spoken words that spilled in long, uncontrollable streams from her mouth. By the time she was three glasses in, family members could expect themselves to be treated to a frank assessment of their weight, haircut, outfit, or commentary regarding their poor life choices and the consequences they'd brought upon themselves.

As a result, the family at large had agreed years earlier to allow her to host only when the rest of the aunts were too desperately busy to handle duties themselves. She was on slightly better behavior when she was a guest.

When I rolled into the driveway in my little Subaru the month before, Mom took one look at my packed-to-the-gills car and bit down on bitter, vitriolic opinions. She couldn't understand why I'd felt unsafe in my own home, afraid of the man I'd married, and as we went through the divorce process he'd refused to move out. He had the means, since he maintained his small apartment in Manhattan, but he was impossibly stubborn.

Mom called each of the aunts two days later, announcing that this year's Feast of the Seven Fishes would take place at her home. She believed in providing plenty of warning, and she'd follow up weekly to make sure no one disappointed her by not showing up.

"No, don't bring anything," I heard her tell each of my aunts. "I have Mia to help me prepare everything. She won't have a job anyway. Dio sa quando..."

I heard every word rattling through the quiet house, and I reminded myself that my mother had never been one to spare my feelings. I slipped back up the stairs toward my old bedroom, I kept to the edges of the carpet, careful not to disturb the fanned vacuum pattern in the hallway. There would be hell to pay if I did.

Lucky for me, Zio Fortunato claimed he needed someone to run his little bakery in town and since I'd spent six summers running the place for him when I was a kid, I was a shoo-in. Honestly, I wasn't sure he needed me there at all, but my mother had probably made a phone call and activated her famed guilt trip on her brother-in-law.

Working at the bakery meant I was able to bring home stacks of cookies, cakes, pies and pastries, all carefully wrapped in paper, for the family feast. There was no sense in throwing things away that were only a day or two old, and I didn't tell my mother I was bringing home the day old's, or there'd have been hell to pay. Into the freezer they went–another abomination in her eyes–and when they came out no one would be the wiser. (Except for every member of my entire family. They could sniff out the age of a pastry with a single glance.)

"You make these?" Angelo called from across the room as he scooped up another pignoli and dropped it into his mouth. I nodded and he kissed his fingertips in my direction before turning his attention to the brightly colored seven-layer cookies. Past experience had taught me he could polish off an entire tray by himself, something he'd perfected in our teenage years and if the way his shirt stretched across his stomach was any indication, I was pretty sure he'd maintained the practice for the past few decades.

I'd called Angelo Mostro Biscotto, or Cookie Monster, since he was four, and it seemed like he was in no hurry to relinquish the title to any of his four equally-capable sons.

"We've been here for two generations and still we haven't learned any manners." Giulia's voice was low in my left ear and I whirled quickly. I hadn't realized she was standing behind me, because I hadn't seen her come in. I threw my arms around her, the cousin who'd been closer than my own sisters for as long as I could remember.

"I haven't seen you yet tonight. In fact, when did I last see you?"

"I just got here—don't tell Nancy, or I'll get a lecture about being rude. And it's been a really long time, I think. Maybe..." She screwed up her beautiful, fine-boned face for a second. "Wow, yeah ... it was when you brought that scumbag home to introduce him to the family. I knew he was a useless sack of shit even then." She smirked, because she was showing great restraint in her choice of words. She had a reputation for her ability to weave together curses that would make sailors wince, and in five different languages. She was beautiful and brilliant, with a quick and cutting sense of humor.

"There are a few more colorful things we could call him," she agreed, "but that one might be the most succinctly accurate. You know: boiling it down to just a handful of words. You never told me what happened, anyway." She kept her voice low.

"You don't have the time and I'm not sure I have the inclination." I shrugged lightly, hoping she would understand that I wasn't ready to spill my guts. I was still processing the horrible details myself.

"I can't get anything out of the family," she sighed, "which means you haven't said a thing, because you know how well our family keeps secrets. Especially the scandalous ones–and ask me just how I came to learn that."

"Some of the details are just too ... I haven't really pieced things together yet. There were a lot of little things to begin with, and over time they added up and multiplied and little things I could overlook or ignore turned into big, scary, dangerous things. I didn't assess the situation for what it was until it was far too late."

"Too late." There was a deep furrow between Giulia's eyebrows as she hitched one upward. "Too late, as in the bastard was beating you?"

I sucked in a deep breath before pursing my lips. "That was at first. Eventually he learned to do the things that don't leave marks."

"Oh, hell no." Mia mashed her lips together in an angry grimace. The storm that passed over her face was frightening to behold. "He doesn't do right by you in the end, you let me know. I know a couple guys."

Those couple guys were probably cousins of ours, and I couldn't hide my grin. In families like ours, everyone "knew a guy" or two. They weren't always cousins, but sometimes brothers or uncles.

I tried to envision David: small, trim, blond, Presbyterian, against tall, bulky, swarthy, Orthodox Angelo. David would try to win with words, knowing if things turned physical he would lose horribly. Choked out by Mostro Biscotto, and what an ignominious end. I let the laughter roll out as it played out in my mind's eye, and I could feel the gorgon stare of my mother.

How dare I enjoy myself.

"Jimmy!" someone hollered from the other side of the house, and I felt my chest tighten. There was only one Jimmy in the family these days: Dad.

Unless ... oh, by all of the apostles ... if Nancy invited him I would absolutely die and come back to haunt her. She would definitely do something like that on purpose.

Suddenly Mom couldn't meet my eyes, and her face broke into a wide grin as she maneuvered her small frame around, through, and under the cluster of family members clogging up the arteries of her gracious, beautiful home. She moved through the throng of noisy relatives, heading in the direction of the commotion coming from the den, where a door opened into the three-stall garage.

Jimmy had *always* used the garage door.

"Mimi." Warm lips rested on my ear and I startled again. When would these people stop sneaking up on me? "You look great." James spun me and held my arms away from my sides, admiring me in the way he'd always done. "How do I keep getting older but you just stay young and beautiful?"

I snorted and rolled my eyes. The man must have his beer goggles on, because I was working on a wicked case of crow's feet and had packed on twenty pounds in the past year from stress eating. There were also wiry silver strands creeping into my dark hair, and I hadn't had the time or the energy to magic them away with a box of color.

Oh, never mind. That was why he hadn't noticed: He was staring at my boobs. They'd always been one of my best features, but the added weight had padded my hips, butt and chest even more.

You were built like a taxi cab with all the doors open, ran through my head. One of the kinder things his mother had ever said about me.

"You've been telling yourself some lies." My voice came out a little harder than I'd meant it to sound. "I think you were the last person I expected to see tonight, James."

"No," Giulia called from a few steps away, where she leaned against the wall, nibbling a pignoli and holding a glass of Pinot in her other hand. "That would have been David."

There was a strange expression on Jimmy's face, and I realized he was still just as astonishingly handsome as he'd been in high school—more maybe, as age was adding a certain dignity to his features. Hopefully he wasn't as dumb as he'd been in high school, I thought, self-consciously running a hand down my front to make sure I didn't need to fasten another button. Jimmy's gaze already threatened to burn a hole through my sweater.

"Giulia." Jimmy grinned, and he leaned back to reach a hand out toward her. It made her smile, and she stepped forward to give him a hug.

"Long time no see, Meathead." She smacked his cheek heartily, then swiftly wiped away the red lipstick she'd left behind.

None of my family had gotten over losing James.

"Hey, not my fault someone moved to Italy for years and then was too big and fancy to move back to her hometown. Miss High and Mighty, living in your fancy Tribeca loft."

My eyebrows raised just slightly. How did James know any of that?

"Jimmy!" Mom's voice was falsely bright as she sailed down the hallway and wrapped her pink-and-white talons around his muscular upper arm. She was pulling him forcibly away, into the vast sea of hair gel, gold jewelry and barely-contained cleavage. "Tell me," she cooed, "how is Little Jimmy these days?"

There was a violent snort from behind me and I wondered if Giulia had a pine nut rattling around in her sinus. "Holy shit," she giggled into a clenched fist, attempting to suppress her mirth. "Did Nancy just ask your ex about the state of his dick?"

Leave it to Giulia. I grinned, remembering the days when Jimmy had indeed named his impressive body part that very thing.

"No, sorry to say." I clapped her on the back. "He has a kid now—Nathan. I'm surprised I know that and you don't." I raised my eyebrows at her significantly. "Your ma didn't pass along that little tidbit? Angie Basso's got him making child support payments that would make the Vatican treasury envious."

"You mean that tramp from high school? Like a year younger than us?" Giulia was incredulous.

"The same. Hasn't changed a bit since high school, either. Still sporting the big hair, big tits ... still definitely a Mensa member."

"First I'm hearing about that." Giulia snorted. "I always thought that girl was a little slow."

I grinned again. "Relax, I was being sarcastic. That girl couldn't find her way out of the guys' locker room with signage."

Giulia grinned. "A person has to be able to read to do that."

"Well, she figured out how to read *something*," I responded, "because she managed to get herself knocked up by someone who had a little money."

Giulia rolled her gaze in James's direction, where he stood in a thick haze of cashmere and Fracas as all the aunts fussed over him. "A little bit?" She snapped her eyes back to me. "You forget his family owns the largest fuel distribution service in the Tri-State?"

"They also own every lawyer in the northeast," I reminded her, and she clucked her tongue.

"Yeah, I didn't forget that part. That was unfair—wasn't like you had a whole lot to begin with."

"Lesson learned." I made a fist and a knocking gesture against my skull. "I guess they thought I deserved it and to hear his mother tell it, I practically had a full-time job as a dominatrix. She was convinced I was a tramp since day one, and she walked in on us that one time..." My cheeks flamed red as I remembered the horrified look on the woman's face when she walked into our bedroom to find me on my knees in front of my husband. "She taught both her boys that anything other than the missionary position is an affront to God."

"I'm pretty sure Jimmy had zero complaints about your sex life, and I can personally guarantee that Daniel knew about a hell of a lot more than the missionary position." She grinned. "If Jimmy had complaints then, it doesn't look like he's holding a grudge these days."

It was well past midnight before the last guest left, and I helped to clean in silence, collecting wine glasses from table tops, the mantle pieces of both fireplaces, countertops, windowsills–there was even one on the back of the toilet in the half-bath. I wrinkled my nose when I found it, setting down the other glasses in my hands in order to give the bathroom a good fogging with Lysol.

I could hear Nancy in the kitchen, dishes clattering as she stacked both dishwashers full of plates.

There was the soft whzzz of plastic wrap sliding off the roll as she wrapped up leftovers to walk out to the fridge and freezer in the garage.

The robot vacuum had already been emptied twice and it trundled through the house, bouncing noisily off millwork, sputtering and gagging on crumbs, dust and long hair. It ground to a halt and began beeping noisily—probably sucked up someone's forgotten scarf, I thought as I set the glasses on the kitchen counter and wandered off in the direction of the beeping.

Fishing the vacuum out from under the sofa and flipping it over to assess the situation, I was surprised to find a bright gold tangle around the small beater bar. I dug a finger into it and as it unwound, a harder object kicked back and nicked my nail. I picked at it carefully, trying to pull it past a snag without snapping any of the delicate links.

"I'm not going to be the one to give it back to him," I announced to my mother as I dropped the necklace on the kitchen counter. It had been one of mine once, a long, long time ago, all of my nicer jewelry given to my first husband as part of our divorce settlement.

"It wouldn't have killed you to spend a little time with him tonight." Mom's tone had been mellowed by several glasses of wine, but the criticism was still razor-sharp.

"Ma!" My hands curled into tight fists without consulting with my brain. "I did not ask you to invite my ex-husband to the family Christmas party!"

"He may be *your* ex," she sniffed, "but he's always going to be a part of my family." Her face was stubbornly set. Resolute.

"You will always love him more than me." I couldn't help but say it through clenched teeth. "Not once did you stand up for me, or defend your own daughter. I lost *everything* to his family."

"Yes, maybe you did," she conceded as she rinsed out the sink. "But that was entirely due to some poor decisions made on your part. And now here we are, on the second verse of that very same song, about to watch you lose everything to David."

"I can't believe you." I turned quickly, needing to get away before I really let her have it, and I rushed up the stairs, desperate to throw furniture and slam doors. I wanted to throw my things into a suitcase and leave, but where would I go? I had nothing and no one and the feeling was one of helplessness, I thought as I closed the bedroom door with a great deal of restraint and sank onto the soft bed.

The stack of photos on the bedside stand caught my eye and I sighed heavily. I had pictures of my home, where other, normal people had pictures of their kids. The house was practically my child. I'd spent all my time and energy making it the perfection it was today, and I slid the first photo to the back of the stack as I stared wistfully at the tile I'd painstakingly laid on the master bathroom floor. I'd set all the tiles in the shower pan, on the bathroom floor, the backsplash and all the way up the shower walls. Then I'd tiled the niche and designed a mosaic on the wall running alongside the beautiful cast iron tub, the one I'd found on Craigslist and hauled home to refinish in my backyard during the last warm days of summer a few years before.

Flip.

A picture of my kitchen and the acres of marble I'd found in a stone cutter's discard pile, and the thick tiles of the backsplash. I'd collected those, a few boxes at a time, every time my favorite online retailer had a sale. The boxes had taken forever to arrive from Florence.

Flip.

The beautiful yard I'd spent countless months landscaping. Trip after trip to the nursery, up to my armpits in dirt and dust, sweat streaming into my eyes as I planted one bulb, one hedge, one tree after another.

The property went from overgrown and neglected to a sweet little haven filled with boxwood, lilacs, Japanese maples, irises—anything I could get my hands on that was beautiful and made me happy.

I landscaped quiet little hiding spots into the yard, hiding a bench in a ring of shrubs. Tucking chairs into alcoves created by plants and trees. Hanging a swing on the branch of a weeping willow with growth so long, the fronds reached the ground like the tentacles of an octopus, creating a beautiful cocoon of yellow-green leaves.

David had certainly appreciated all those sweet little hiding spots, I thought with a flare of anger.

I was exhausted. I dropped the photos back on the nightstand and turned over into my pillow. The day had been long and busy and the evening emotionally taxing, and I fell asleep in seconds, the lamp on, still completely dressed.

23

Scott

Blowing out a huge puff of air, I set the cell phone down face-up on my desk. I'd converted the small space over my garage to function as a personal office while I built up my business, and I leaned over to switch on the space heater next to the desk. I'd been through worse, but now that I had access to creature comforts, my days in the military long over, I took advantage of them when I could.

I'd just gotten a call from a buddy. We'd kept our conversation brief, relaying only the essentials. He'd been on the wrong end of an IED planted in an Afghani villager's home and daily patrol quickly turned into a rescue mission. He'd been patched up in the field and flown to a base in Germany for additional medical care, since he required a number of surgeries, but the bigger problem was that he'd failed his mental evaluation. The Army had just effectively told him "Thanks, but no thanks," that if he didn't want to take a desk job they were cutting him loose with an honorable discharge.

Honorable or not, this sucked for Brandon. He had never known anything but the life of a soldier, and now he had no choice but to learn how to be a civilian.

I made a couple phone calls on his behalf and scribbled his ETA on my calendar. Once he went through demobilization at the base, I would be there to pick him up and take him to my home, where he'd stay for a while to get his feet under him.

Brandon was a good guy. I'd brought him up myself, from the days he was a young soldier, giving him more and more responsibility, until it was time for me to call it, and he was appointed Commanding Officer in my place.

We were the men of the First Brigade Combat Team, a new and improved special troops battalion operating out of Fort Drum. The 10th Mountain Division was a tough bunch of motherfuckers, and we lorded it over soldiers from other units as often as we got the chance. No one was as tough as us, surviving record snowfalls and twelve-mile runs in twenty-below weather even before we shipped out to our own personal hell.

The problem with living in hell was that more often than you wanted, you brought it home with you. It showed up in flashbacks and nightmares, hair-trigger responses and too-short emotional tethers. It was almost always a predictable outcome, too, for the guys who couldn't deprogram: broken marriages, custody battles, drinking problems and often losing the battle with gainful employment.

My problems? Well, those were pre-Afghanistan. I mean, it wasn't like I was baking cupcakes and throwing tea parties in Kandahar. I saw shit there that would take me the rest of my life to unpack, but somehow that wasn't the stuff that woke me at night.

No, what woke me at night was Naomi. Or her ghost. Wrapping her icy fingers around my subconscious mind and whispering to me that it was all my fault. And if I woke myself from the horrible dreams, it was because I was yelling and sweating.

There were a few things I was going to need to tell Brandon before we were officially roomies. He didn't know the details about Naomi, or that I still had nightmares.

He also didn't know that I'd been involved in a custody battle with my ex-wife for my kids. It had been going on for some time, and between trying to really get my business off the ground and making appearances in court, I was exhausted.

Picking up the phone, I called another old buddy. Lincoln was a few years older than me and had taken me under his wing years earlier, during my first trip to Afghanistan, just after Naomi...

"Got a buddy coming in," I said when he picked up. He was a man of few words and would waste no time getting to the heart of the matter. Besides, he already knew it was me, the damn spook.

"And?" His voice was as rough as my own. My excuse was shrapnel to the voicebox, but his was fire. He'd never told me the whole story—all I knew was that it happened before he joined the Army.

"Might need to help him get settled in. Entire career with the First Brigade...good man. Hard worker, great leader, just a real decent guy. Hadn't exactly planned on his Army career ending this way..." I let it trail off, and Lincoln knew what I meant.

"Honorable discharge?" he asked, and I sighed.

"Yeah, you know how that goes."

"Sure do."

"Don't know what he wants to do when he gets out, because I don't think he planned for any sort of 'after.' You got any ideas?"

"Mmm, maybe." Lincoln lapsed into silence for a long moment. "Got a buddy with the FBI looking to fill a spot in the city's field office. If your guy has the necessary security clearances, he might be a shoo-in."

"It's Brandon," I said, and I heard a snort on the other end of the line. As far as Lincoln was concerned, that meant he was dying of hilarity.

"The hell didn't you say so?" he barked. "Boy's guaranteed to make the spot."

The boy in question was well into his forties, but I figured making that point would only irritate Lincoln, a man with zero tolerance for irritation. Even less than me, and that was really saying something.

"I'll put in a good word," he rasped. "He'll still need to interview when he gets in, and it goes without saying the necessary checks and clearances will be in place."

I made a sound of assent. I knew this meant it was as good as done, and I sighed with relief, knowing I'd done a good friend a solid.

"Thanks, man."

"No thanks necessary." He actually chuckled. "I like this one. He'll be good in the spot, and it won't take much to convince Hendrickson."

I didn't know Hendrickson well, but I was fairly certain the man was a political opportunist. I'd dealt with him in limited interactions in the past, and I wasn't his biggest fan...but maybe that was just me.

"Just need to see my friend settled," I said, and I knew Lincoln understood. We had deep connections, and my connections to Brandon would translate to his connections with my friend.

"Hear you, man," he responded slowly. "I'll do what I can–don't think he'll have a problem, though. Just let me know if I need to pull favors..."

No favors would be necessary, because Brandon was amazing. I mean, I couldn't tell that to anyone else, but the guy adapted quickly, easily, and fit into any situation.

Made me a little jealous.

"Thanks, man," was all I said. "Owe you one."

"Not even a thing," Lincoln responded. "Thanks for letting me know. Hendrickson'll shit himself when I tell him. Guy's got a real hard-on for ex-military." He paused for a second. "Hit me when you're free for dinner and drinks. Gotta do some catchin' up, my man."

He wasn't wrong. I'd been neglecting my relationships with friends and family while I tried to get my life in order.

"Sure thing," I responded. "I'll give you a call when I get back from Tel Aviv."

He grunted. "Another transportation job for State?"

I made a noncommittal noise in response, because Lincoln knew my biggest contract was with the State Department, providing security in a number of situations.

After talking to Lincoln, I called Giulia. We had a history that went back a handful of years, and imagine my surprise when it turned out she wasn't just a fancy-pants realtor. Apparently her day job, selling penthouses lining the park to folks with more money than sense wasn't thrilling enough for her, and she was also running a nice little side gig as a State Department operative. I'd never asked how she got into her secondary line of work, but I'd coordinated with her several times already.

"Good morning, darling," she purred, and it made me smile. Giulia was the modern version of Sophia Loren, all legs and curves and long, dark, glossy hair. She was way too much for me to handle, so I didn't even try.

"Hey, G." I leaned over to turn off the heater that had begun burning my legs. "You get the details for my next transport?"

She made a sound that could have indicated irritation or disbelief. "Please, Katsaros. You know I was lining things up even before you got the phone call."

"Don't put this one in your building," I joked, and that definitely elicited a sound of irritation. We'd pulled off a particularly sensitive relocation just over a year earlier. It had been last-minute and dangerous, and Giulia had scrambled to find a suitably safe place to stash the little drug lord we smuggled out of Colombia. He was of value to the government, for whatever reason, and it wasn't our job to question the reasoning.

The annoying little man had been tucked into the unit just below Giulia's in her secure Tribeca building and he'd been making her life a living hell ever since.

"The first chance I get to relocate that little shit," she huffed. "I just have to get the paperwork signed—I've already got a location in mind."

I had a feeling the location she had in mind was at the bottom of the Hudson, but I kept that suspicion to myself.

Getting off the phone with Giulia meant it was time to do the one thing I'd been putting off all morning: Contacting Gretchen about my schedule so we could arrange visits for the kids.

To say Gretchen and I had a contentious relationship was glossing over it. As far as she was concerned, I needed to go overseas and never return.

I sighed and logged into the program she and I used to communicate. It was something that had been suggested by our mediator, as a way to keep things as neutral as possible. Unfortunately, Gretchen's way of keeping things neutral was to be passive-aggressive, and I knew it would be hours or days before she responded. Quite probably I'd already be in Tel Aviv.

Sighing, I tossed my phone down on the desktop and leaned back in my chair, looking around. This...this was all I had to show for a lifetime of struggle. Something had to give.

Acknowledgements

To the men in the guard booth (and that super-hot cop who saved me from myself) at the NSA this past summer: thanks for not turning it into a strip search in a darkened room, boys, because Mama wasn't ready for that. (And thanks for the inspiration, because at least at first, the story wrote itself!)

Thanks to the people who wake up every morning and put on a uniform: police officer, military member, healthcare worker ... you've all answered a higher calling, for safety and country and care, and you keep showing up even when you're absolutely exhausted.

Thanks to my husband, who finally realized the only way the dishes were going to get done was if *he* did them, because let's be honest: When I disappear into my office to start writing, I might not reappear for hours. Things like laundry, vacuuming and dishes often get pushed aside with excuses of "I'll be right back, hang on—I need to edit fifteen more pages!"

And sleep, if you're out there, I miss you. Let's get to know each other again real soon, k?

About the Author

Erin's making good use of her degree in Journalism by making things up all day long. Born in the Midwest, she's a fan of big trucks, strong-minded men, grocery delivery services and happy endings.

Years after obtaining a degree she didn't use, she's returned to writing the kinds of stories she's been penning since she was ten years old: sweet stories of love lost, won, broken or regained. Her characters have seen some things and they tend to be a little older, a little broken, and just redeemable enough to get their shit together, usually after a few seriously stupid missteps. (Because life is hard, but the mistakes can put us on the path we're meant to travel, right?)

Erin's family relocates with some frequency, thanks to her husband's career. For now she lives with her very own Alpha male and two children in the Metro D.C. area.

Most days you'll find Erin trying to write in a cloud of Mastiff fur, a cat in her lap and the space heater set to "nuclear." (True story, it's a setting.)

You can find links for my socials, my e-commerce store, and my website at linktr.ee/erinfitzgeraldwrites. Find me there and let's be friends!

Other Works & Coming Soon

The Atholton Series

Forsaking All Others - (Seraphina & Mateo)

The Battle Back Home - (Aaron & Harlowe)

All The Days After - (Noah & Eve)

The Things I Can't Say - (Asher & Olivia)

When I Had Nothing - (Thomas & Natalie)

Men of the First Brigade

Unexpected - (Jack & Daphne)

Unforgiven - (Scott & Mia)

Unwelcome - (Brandon & Giulia)

Unstoppable - (Alex & Lauren)

Unrequited - (Lincoln & Ava)

Wolf Mountain Ranchers

www.ingramcontent.com/pod-product-compliance
Lightning Source LLC
Chambersburg PA
CBHW060026060826
49398CB00032B/297

* 9 7 8 1 9 5 8 8 0 2 2 8 1 *